UP TO NO GHOUL

HarperAlley is an imprint of HarperCollins Publishers.

Up to No Ghoul
Text copyright © 2022 by Cullen Bunn
Illustrations copyright © 2022 by Cat Farris

Library of Congress Control Number: 2021950886
ISBN 978-0-06-289613-1 — ISBN 978-0-06-289612-4 (pbk.)

The artist used Clip Studio Paint, ink, watercolor, and mixed
media paper to create the illustrations for this book.
Typography by Rick Farley
22 23 24 25 26 RTLO 10 9 8 7 6 5 4 3 2 1
First Edition

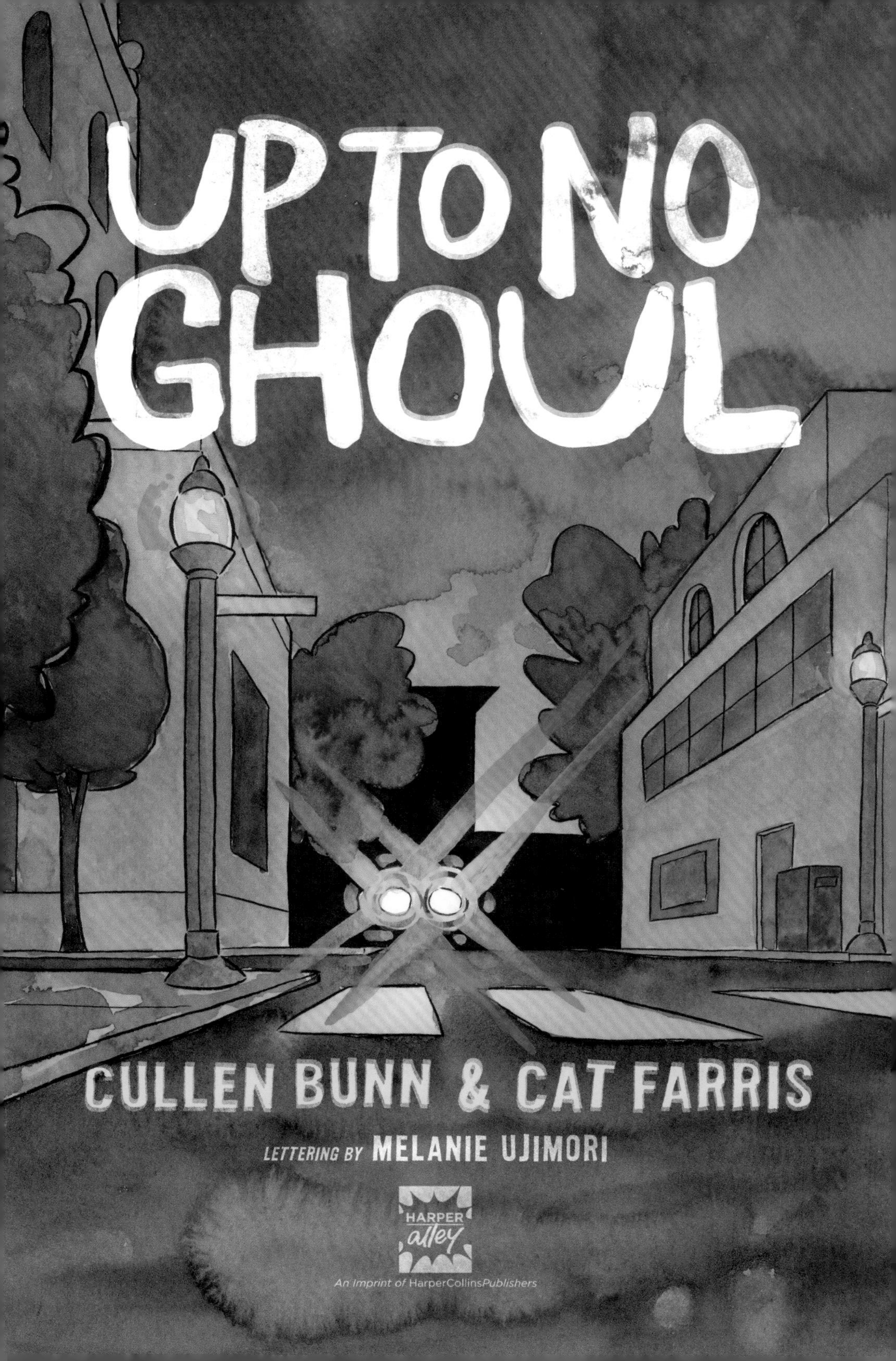

UP TO NO GHOUL

CULLEN BUNN & CAT FARRIS

LETTERING BY MELANIE UJIMORI

HARPER alley

An Imprint of HarperCollinsPublishers

For Anton, who might love ghouls even more than me.

—C.B.

For Jesse Hamm; thank you for being a friend.

—C.F.

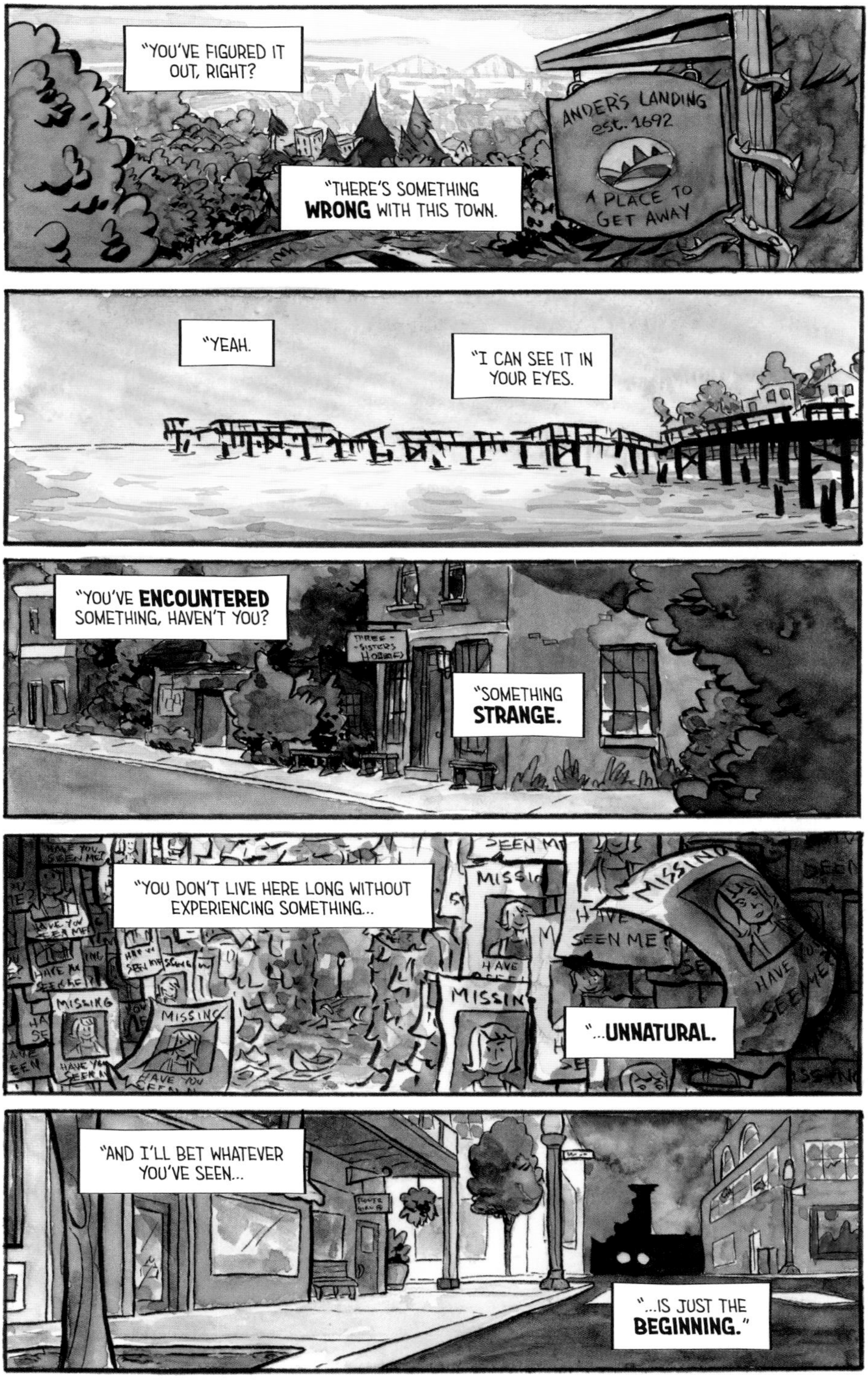
"YOU'VE FIGURED IT OUT, RIGHT?
ANDER'S LANDING
est. 1692
A PLACE TO GET AWAY
"THERE'S SOMETHING **WRONG** WITH THIS TOWN.
"YEAH.
"I CAN SEE IT IN YOUR EYES.
"YOU'VE **ENCOUNTERED** SOMETHING, HAVEN'T YOU?
"SOMETHING **STRANGE.**
"YOU DON'T LIVE HERE LONG WITHOUT EXPERIENCING SOMETHING...
"...**UNNATURAL.**
"AND I'LL BET WHATEVER YOU'VE SEEN...
"...IS JUST THE **BEGINNING.**"

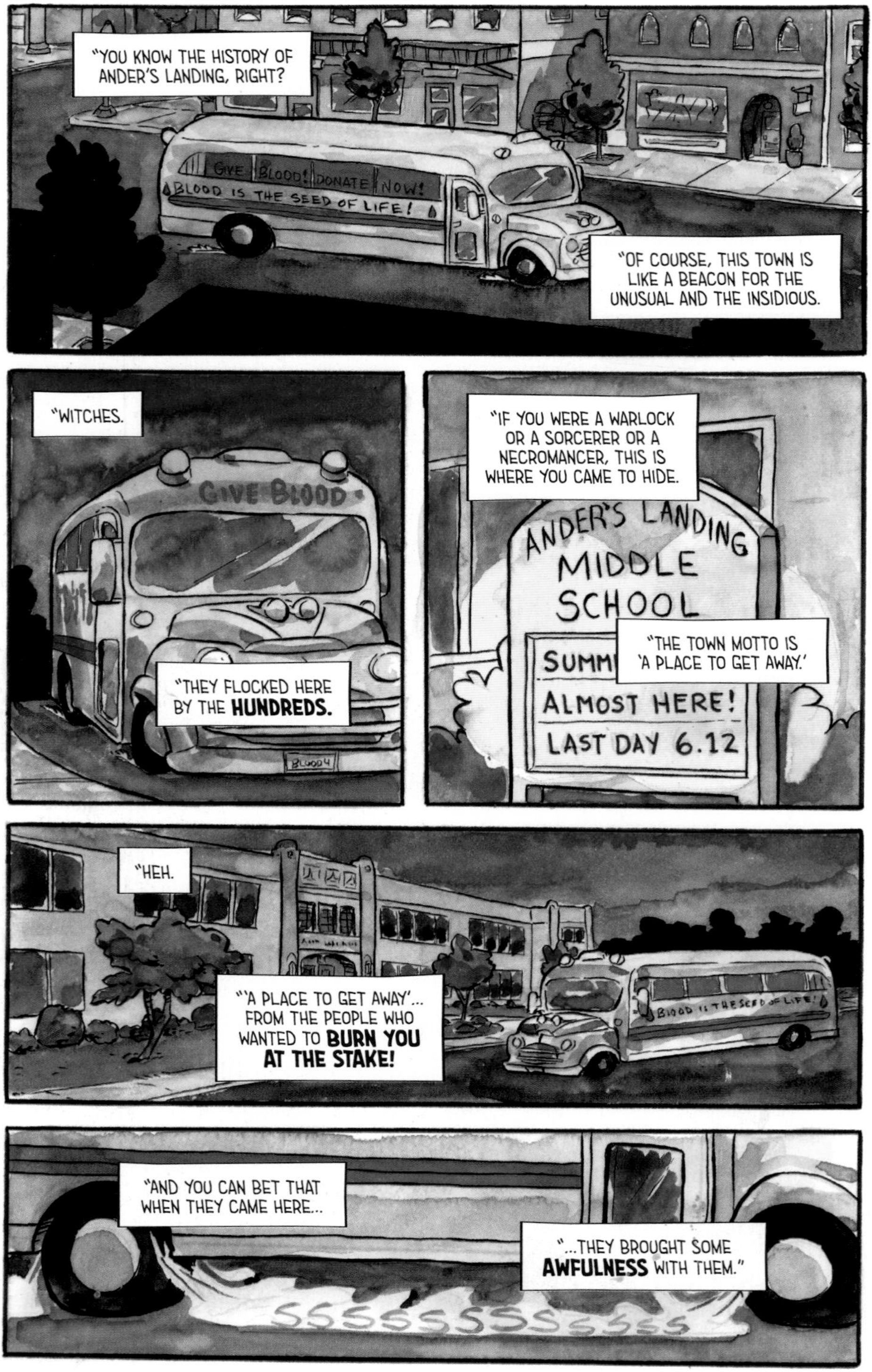
"YOU KNOW THE HISTORY OF ANDER'S LANDING, RIGHT?
GIVE BLOOD! DONATE NOW!
BLOOD IS THE SEED OF LIFE!
"OF COURSE, THIS TOWN IS LIKE A BEACON FOR THE UNUSUAL AND THE INSIDIOUS.
"WITCHES.
GIVE BLOOD
"THEY FLOCKED HERE BY THE **HUNDREDS.**
BLOOD4
"IF YOU WERE A WARLOCK OR A SORCERER OR A NECROMANCER, THIS IS WHERE YOU CAME TO HIDE.
ANDER'S LANDING MIDDLE SCHOOL
SUMM
ALMOST HERE!
LAST DAY 6.12
"THE TOWN MOTTO IS 'A PLACE TO GET AWAY.'
"HEH.
"'A PLACE TO GET AWAY'... FROM THE PEOPLE WHO WANTED TO **BURN YOU AT THE STAKE!**
BLOOD IS THE SEED OF LIFE!
"AND YOU CAN BET THAT WHEN THEY CAME HERE...
"...THEY BROUGHT SOME **AWFULNESS** WITH THEM."
SSSSSSSSSSSSSS

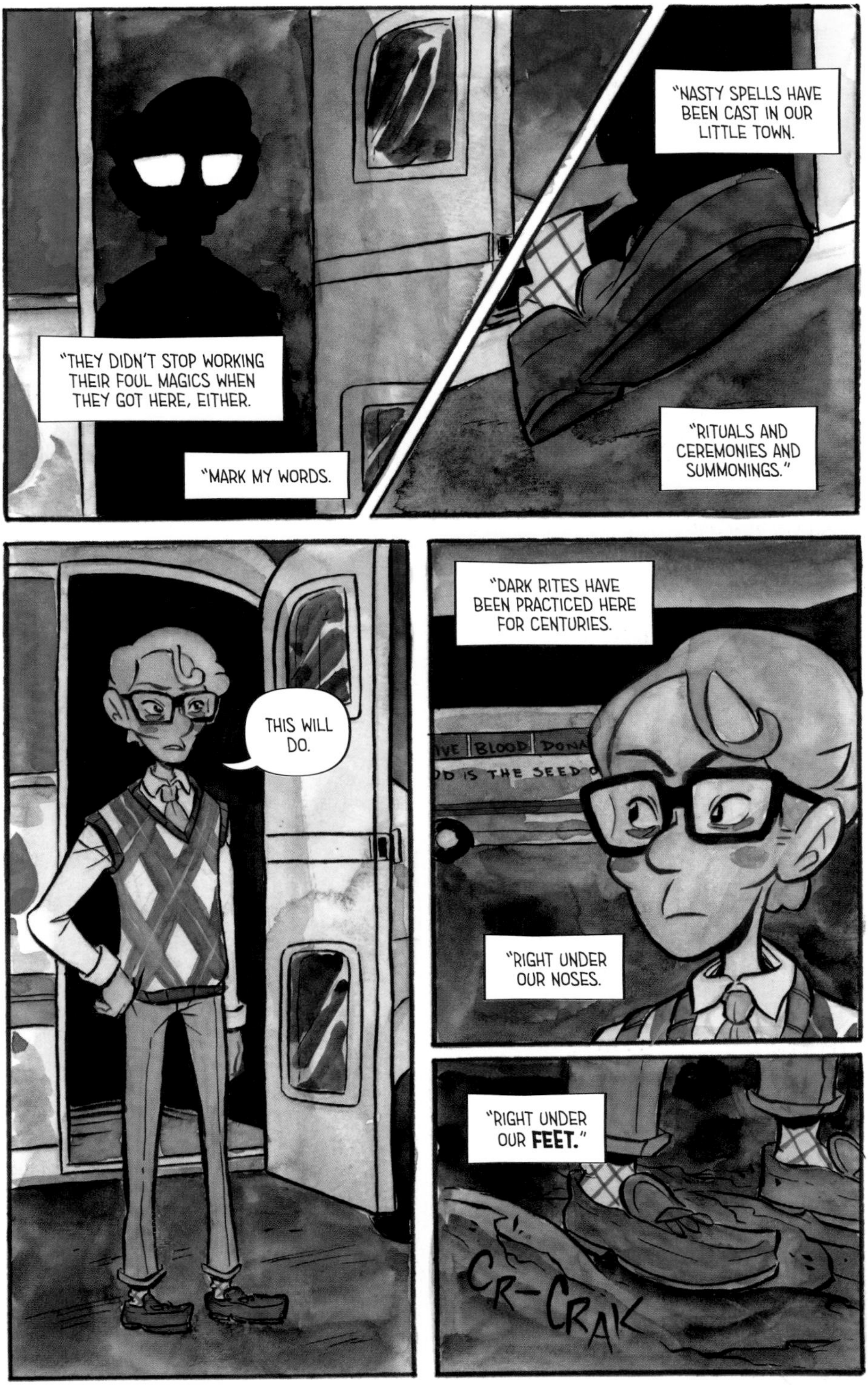
"THEY DIDN'T STOP WORKING THEIR FOUL MAGICS WHEN THEY GOT HERE, EITHER.
"MARK MY WORDS.
"NASTY SPELLS HAVE BEEN CAST IN OUR LITTLE TOWN.
"RITUALS AND CEREMONIES AND SUMMONINGS."
THIS WILL DO.
"DARK RITES HAVE BEEN PRACTICED HERE FOR CENTURIES.
"RIGHT UNDER OUR NOSES.
"RIGHT UNDER OUR **FEET.**"
CR-CRAK

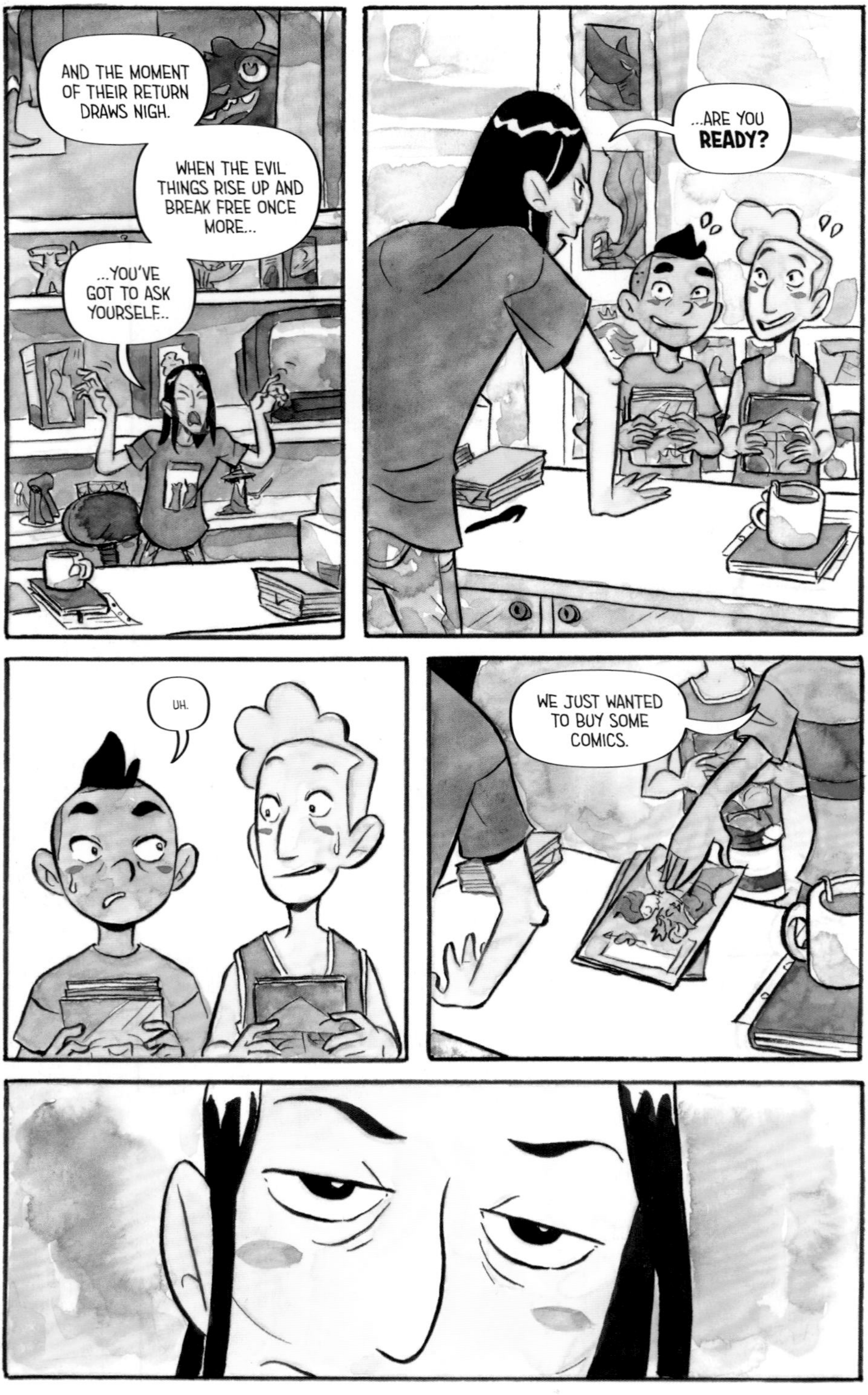
AND THE MOMENT OF THEIR RETURN DRAWS NIGH.
WHEN THE EVIL THINGS RISE UP AND BREAK FREE ONCE MORE...
...YOU'VE GOT TO ASK YOURSELF...
...ARE YOU **READY?**
UH.
WE JUST WANTED TO BUY SOME COMICS.

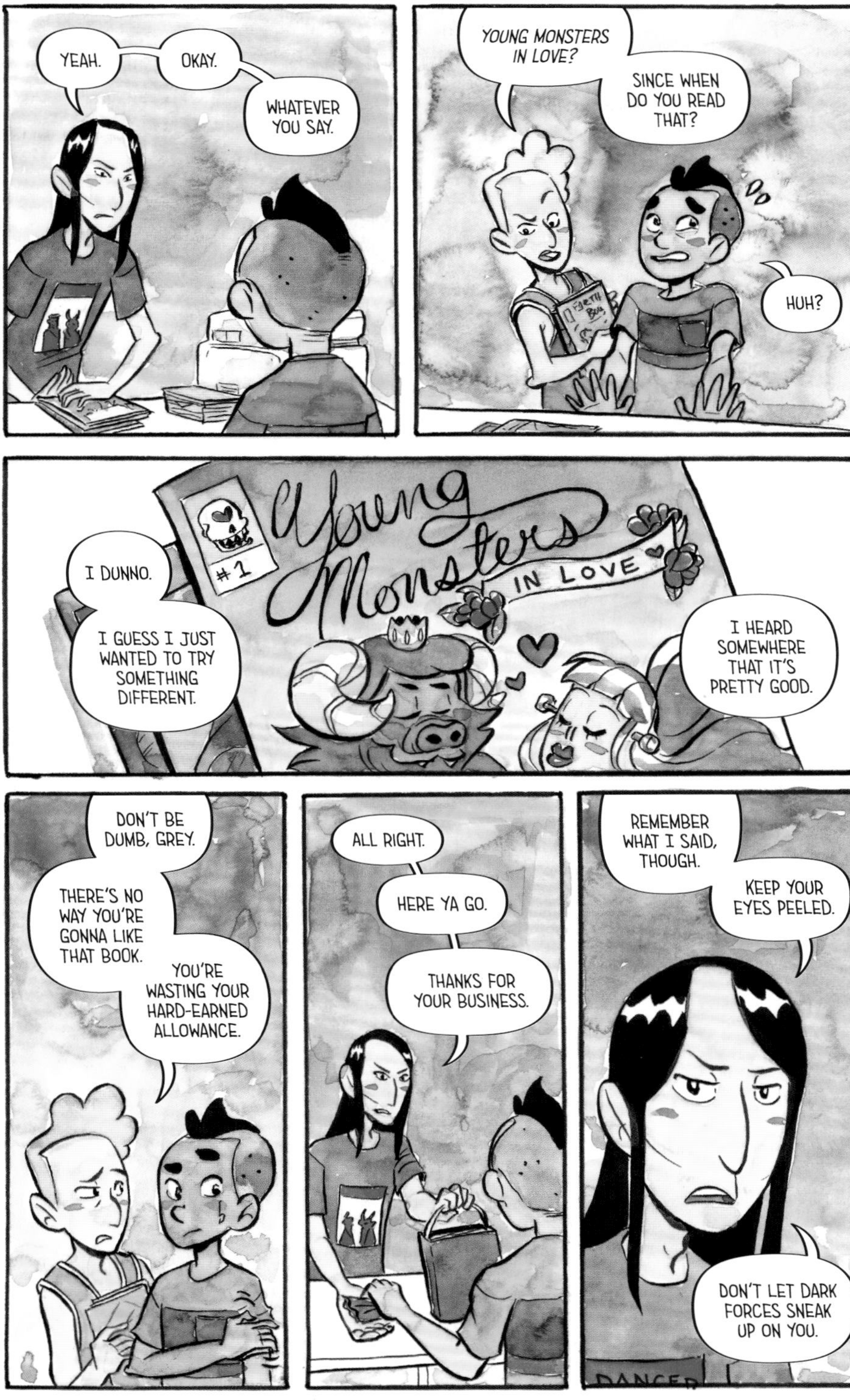
YEAH.
OKAY.
WHATEVER YOU SAY.
YOUNG MONSTERS IN LOVE?
SINCE WHEN DO YOU READ THAT?
HUH?
Young Monsters IN LOVE
#1
I DUNNO.
I GUESS I JUST WANTED TO TRY SOMETHING DIFFERENT.
I HEARD SOMEWHERE THAT IT'S PRETTY GOOD.
DON'T BE DUMB, GREY.
THERE'S NO WAY YOU'RE GONNA LIKE THAT BOOK.
YOU'RE WASTING YOUR HARD-EARNED ALLOWANCE.
ALL RIGHT.
HERE YA GO.
THANKS FOR YOUR BUSINESS.
REMEMBER WHAT I SAID, THOUGH.
KEEP YOUR EYES PEELED.
DON'T LET DARK FORCES SNEAK UP ON YOU.

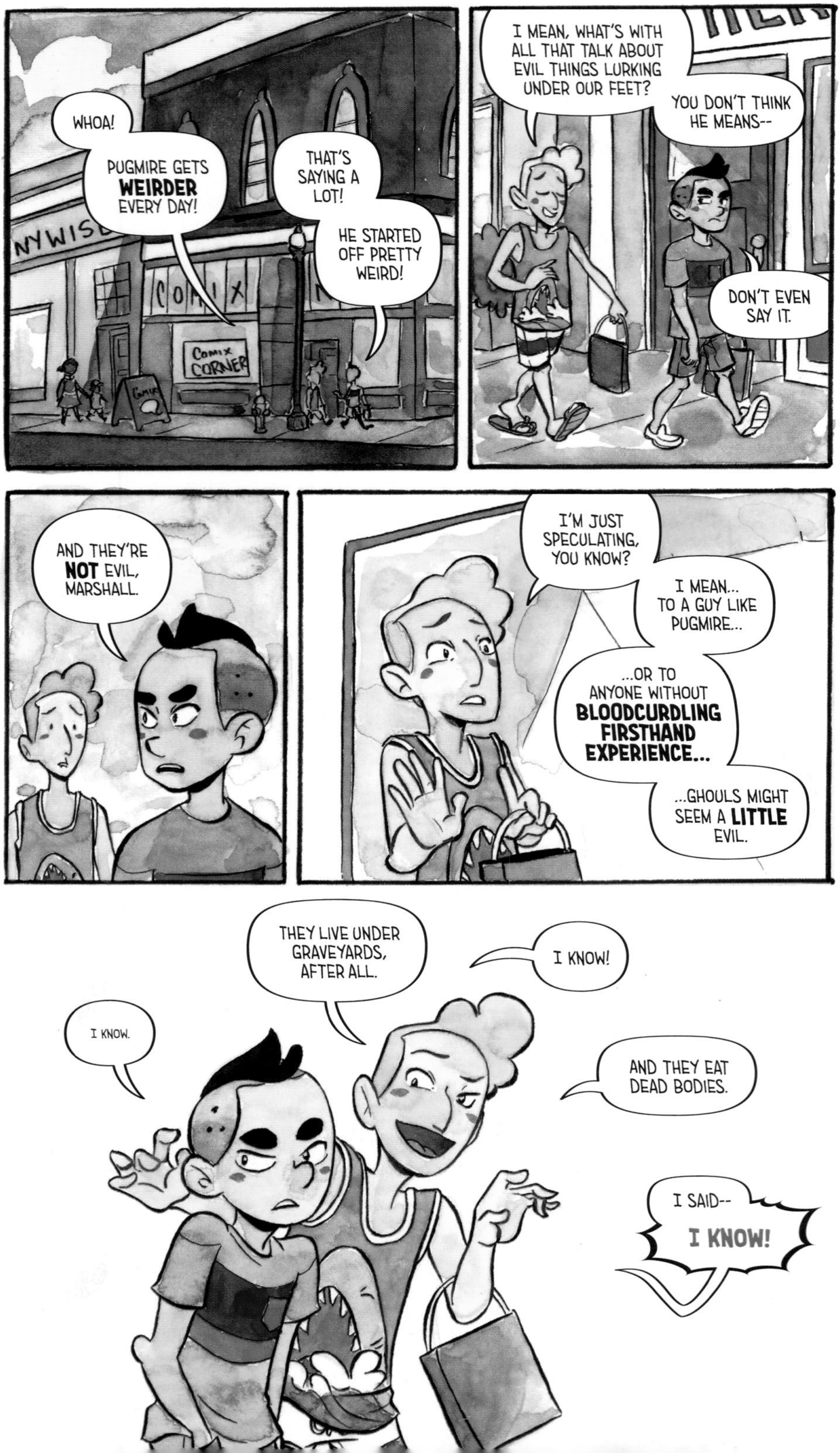
WHOA!
PUGMIRE GETS **WEIRDER** EVERY DAY!
THAT'S SAYING A LOT!
HE STARTED OFF PRETTY WEIRD!
NYWIS
COMIX
COMIX CORNER
I MEAN, WHAT'S WITH ALL THAT TALK ABOUT EVIL THINGS LURKING UNDER OUR FEET?
YOU DON'T THINK HE MEANS--
DON'T EVEN SAY IT.
AND THEY'RE **NOT** EVIL, MARSHALL.
I'M JUST SPECULATING, YOU KNOW?
I MEAN... TO A GUY LIKE PUGMIRE...
...OR TO ANYONE WITHOUT **BLOODCURDLING FIRSTHAND EXPERIENCE...**
...GHOULS MIGHT SEEM A **LITTLE** EVIL.
THEY LIVE UNDER GRAVEYARDS, AFTER ALL.
I KNOW!
I KNOW.
AND THEY EAT DEAD BODIES.
I SAID--
I KNOW!

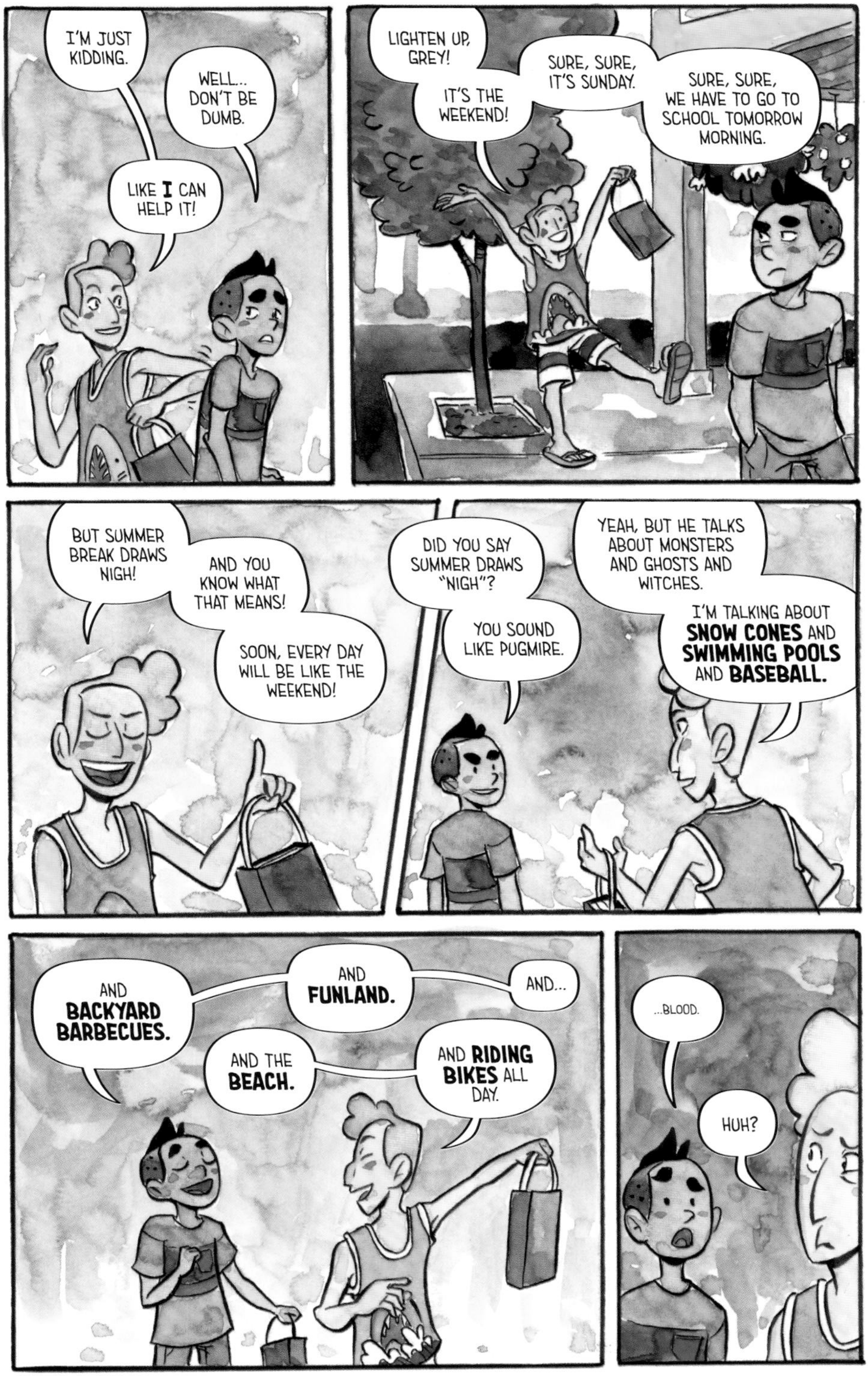
I'M JUST KIDDING.
WELL... DON'T BE DUMB.
LIKE I CAN HELP IT!
LIGHTEN UP, GREY!
IT'S THE WEEKEND!
SURE, SURE, IT'S SUNDAY.
SURE, SURE, WE HAVE TO GO TO SCHOOL TOMORROW MORNING.
BUT SUMMER BREAK DRAWS NIGH!
AND YOU KNOW WHAT THAT MEANS!
SOON, EVERY DAY WILL BE LIKE THE WEEKEND!
DID YOU SAY SUMMER DRAWS "NIGH"?
YOU SOUND LIKE PUGMIRE.
YEAH, BUT HE TALKS ABOUT MONSTERS AND GHOSTS AND WITCHES.
I'M TALKING ABOUT **SNOW CONES** AND **SWIMMING POOLS** AND **BASEBALL.**
AND **BACKYARD BARBECUES.**
AND **FUNLAND.**
AND...
AND THE **BEACH.**
AND **RIDING BIKES** ALL DAY.
...BLOOD.
HUH?

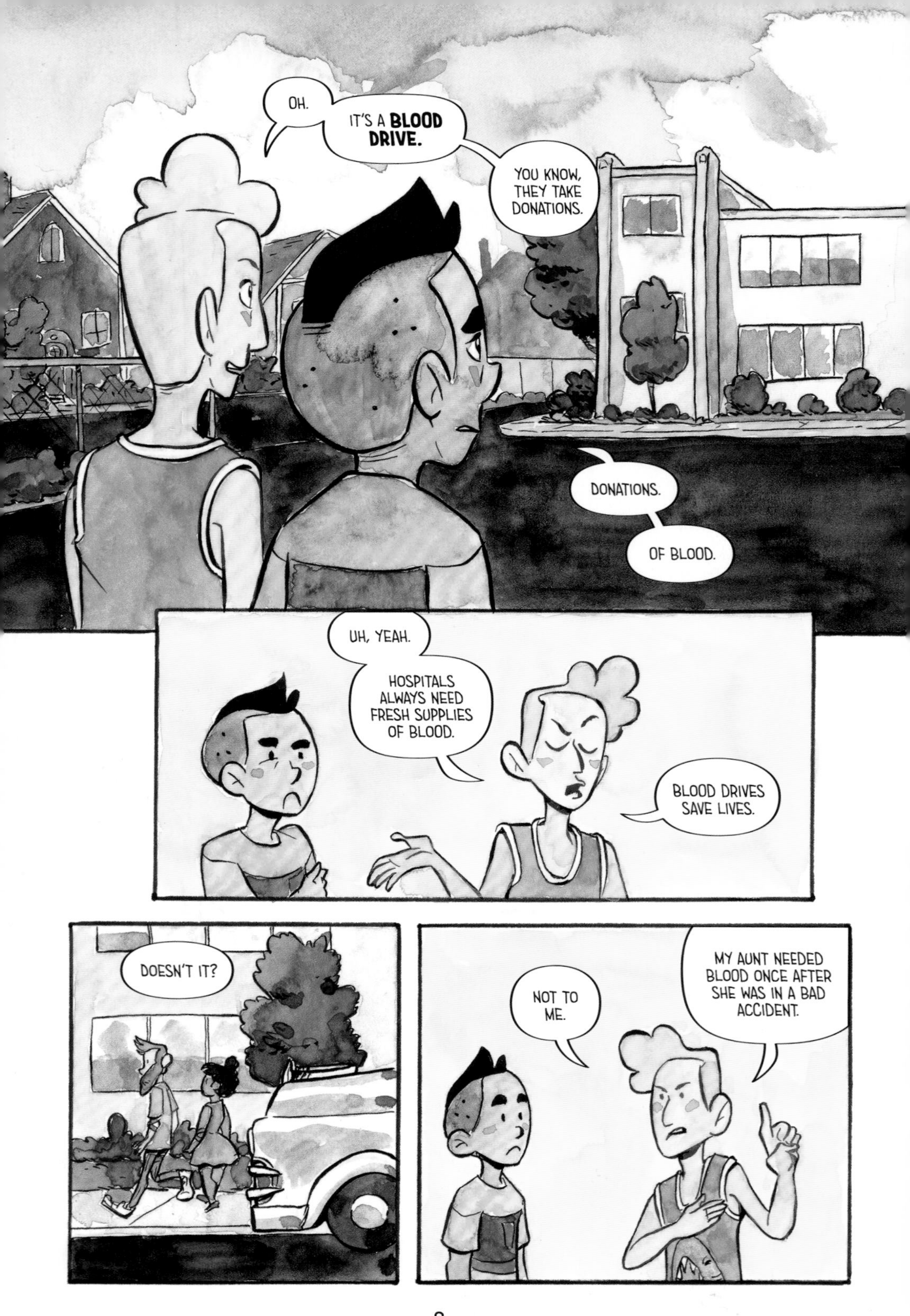
OH.
IT'S A **BLOOD DRIVE.**
YOU KNOW, THEY TAKE DONATIONS.
DONATIONS.
OF BLOOD.
UH, YEAH.
HOSPITALS ALWAYS NEED FRESH SUPPLIES OF BLOOD.
BLOOD DRIVES SAVE LIVES.
DOESN'T IT?
NOT TO ME.
MY AUNT NEEDED BLOOD ONCE AFTER SHE WAS IN A BAD ACCIDENT.

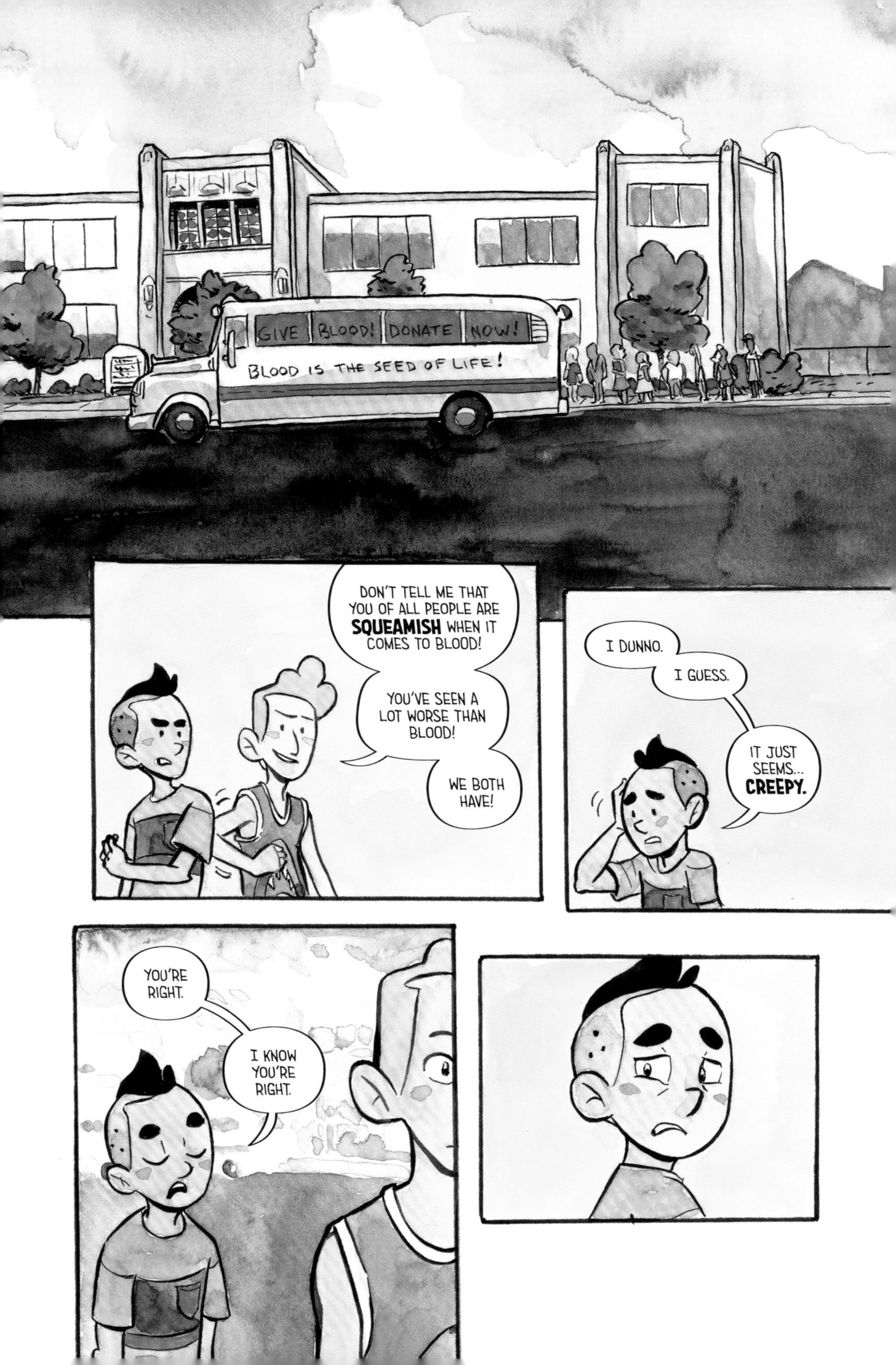
GIVE BLOOD! DONATE NOW!
BLOOD IS THE SEED OF LIFE!
DON'T TELL ME THAT YOU OF ALL PEOPLE ARE **SQUEAMISH** WHEN IT COMES TO BLOOD!
YOU'VE SEEN A LOT WORSE THAN BLOOD!
WE BOTH HAVE!
I DUNNO.
I GUESS.
IT JUST SEEMS... **CREEPY.**
YOU'RE RIGHT.
I KNOW YOU'RE RIGHT.

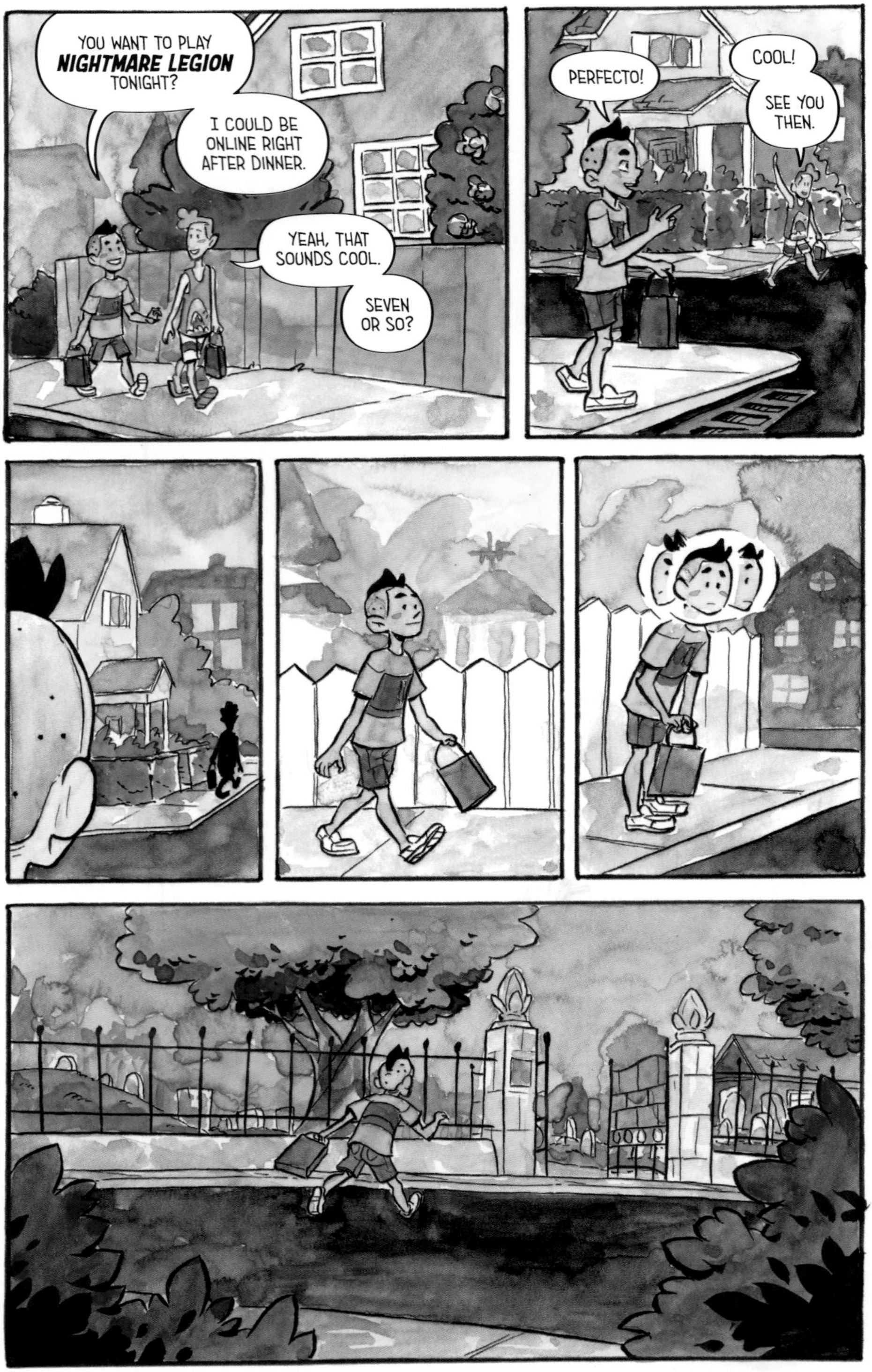
YOU WANT TO PLAY NIGHTMARE LEGION TONIGHT?
I COULD BE ONLINE RIGHT AFTER DINNER.
YEAH, THAT SOUNDS COOL.
SEVEN OR SO?
PERFECTO!
COOL!
SEE YOU THEN.

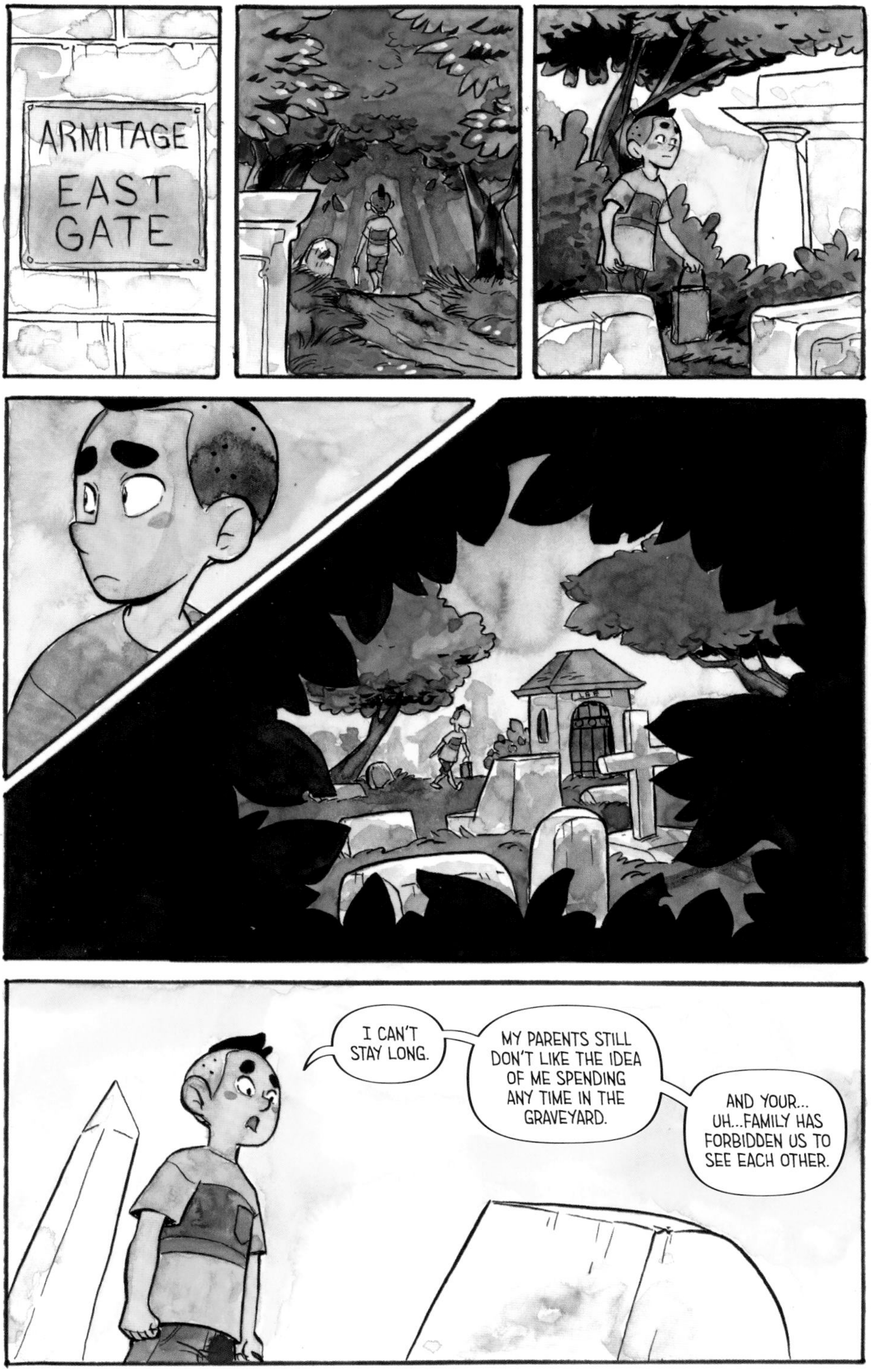
ARMITAGE
EAST GATE
I CAN'T STAY LONG.
MY PARENTS STILL DON'T LIKE THE IDEA OF ME SPENDING ANY TIME IN THE GRAVEYARD.
AND YOUR... UH...FAMILY HAS FORBIDDEN US TO SEE EACH OTHER.

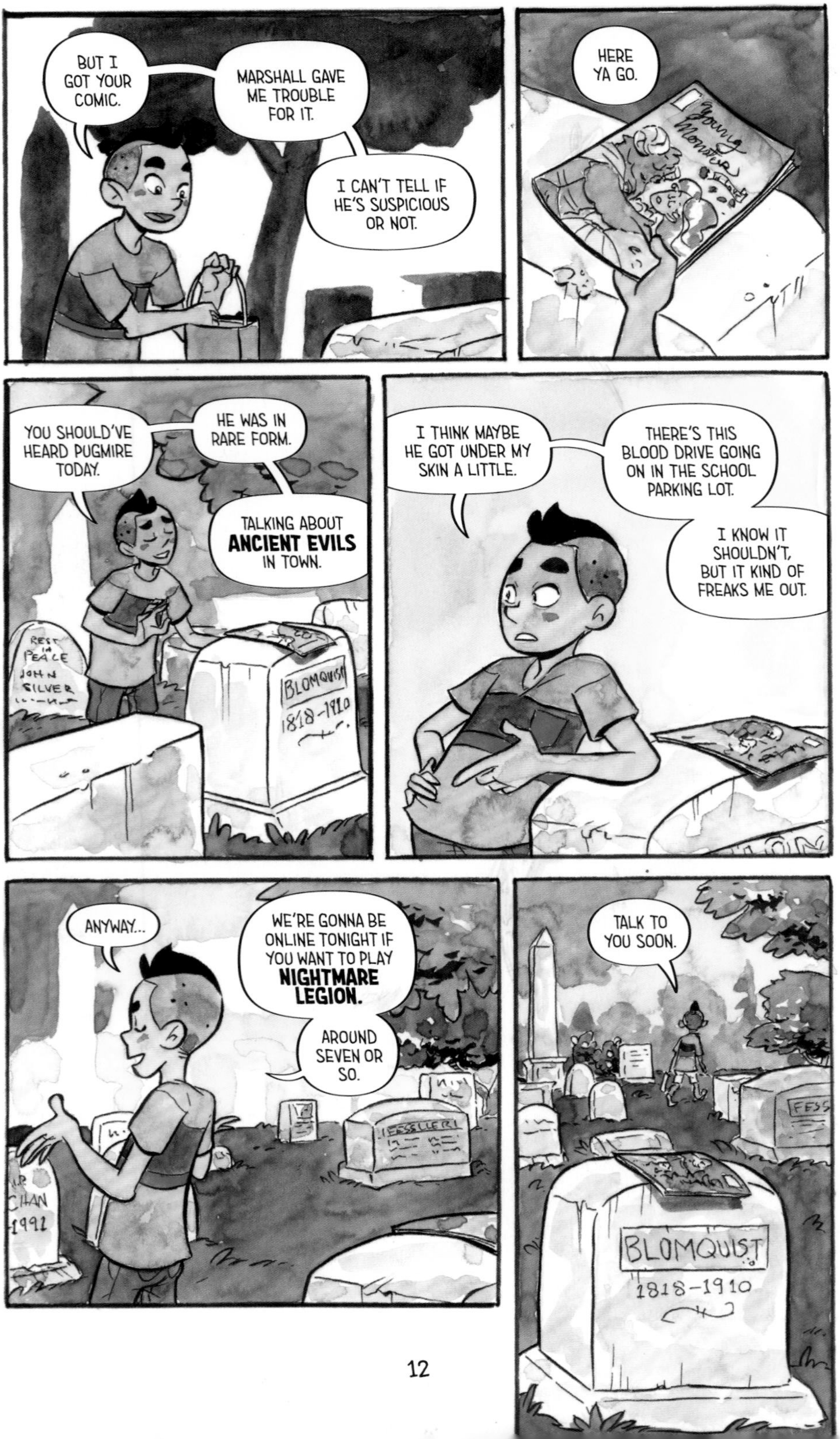
BUT I GOT YOUR COMIC.
MARSHALL GAVE ME TROUBLE FOR IT.
I CAN'T TELL IF HE'S SUSPICIOUS OR NOT.
HERE YA GO.
Young Monsters
YOU SHOULD'VE HEARD PUGMIRE TODAY.
HE WAS IN RARE FORM.
TALKING ABOUT **ANCIENT EVILS** IN TOWN.
REST IN PEACE JOHN SILVER
BLOMQUIST 1818–1910
I THINK MAYBE HE GOT UNDER MY SKIN A LITTLE.
THERE'S THIS BLOOD DRIVE GOING ON IN THE SCHOOL PARKING LOT.
I KNOW IT SHOULDN'T, BUT IT KIND OF FREAKS ME OUT.
ANYWAY...
WE'RE GONNA BE ONLINE TONIGHT IF YOU WANT TO PLAY **NIGHTMARE LEGION.**
AROUND SEVEN OR SO.
FESSLER
1991
TALK TO YOU SOON.
BLOMQUIST
1818–1910

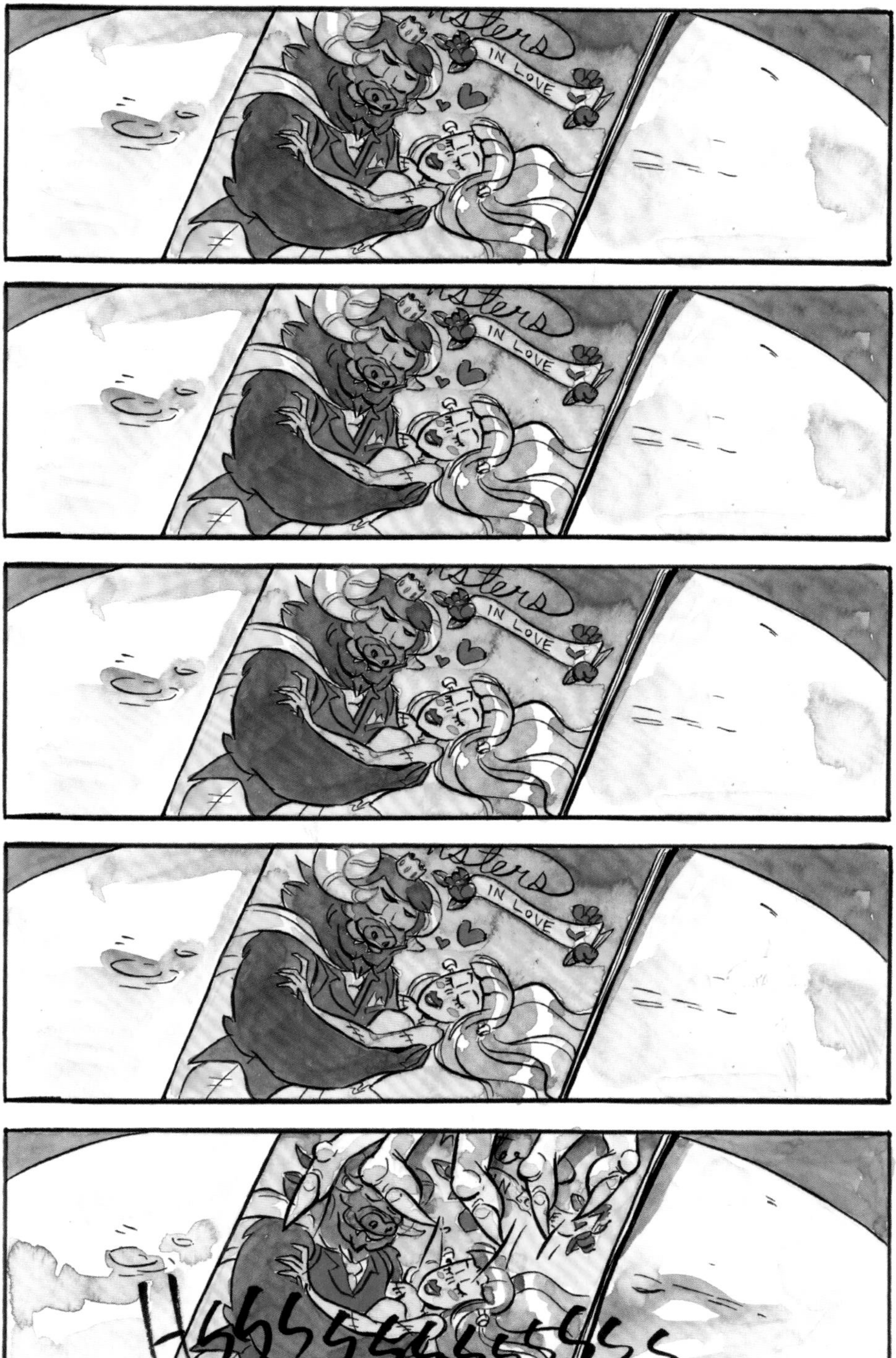
IN LOVE
IN LOVE
IN LOVE
IN LOVE
Hssssssssssss

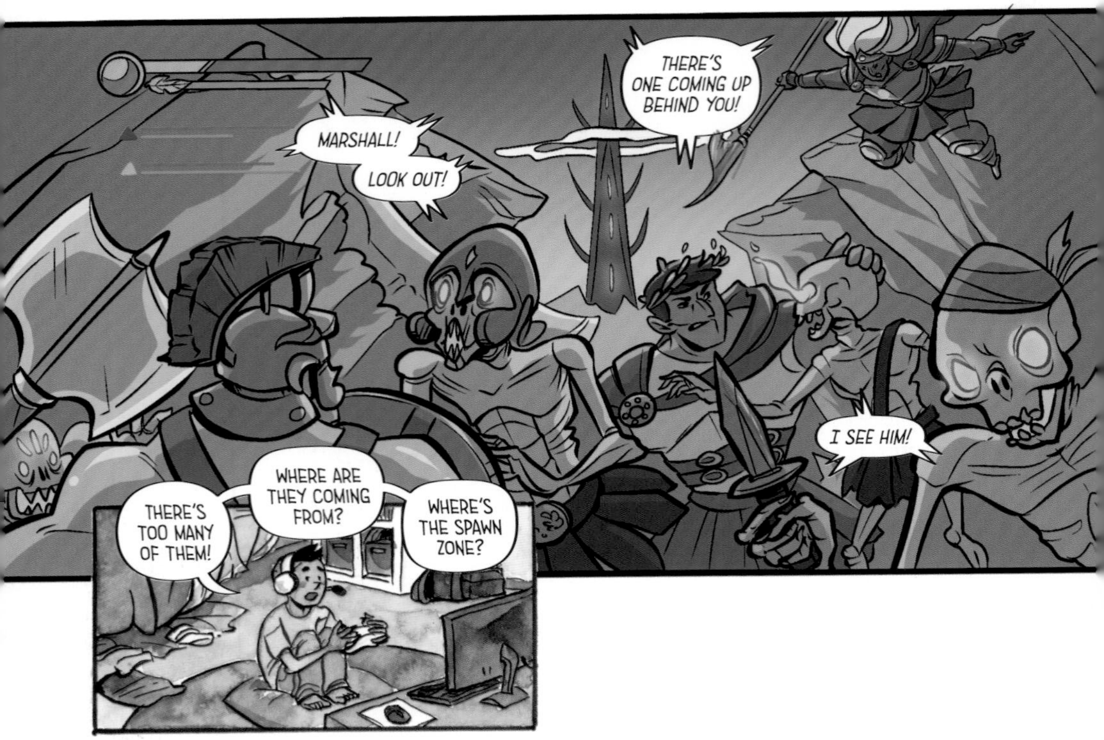
MARSHALL!
LOOK OUT!
THERE'S ONE COMING UP BEHIND YOU!
I SEE HIM!
THERE'S TOO MANY OF THEM!
WHERE ARE THEY COMING FROM?
WHERE'S THE SPAWN ZONE?

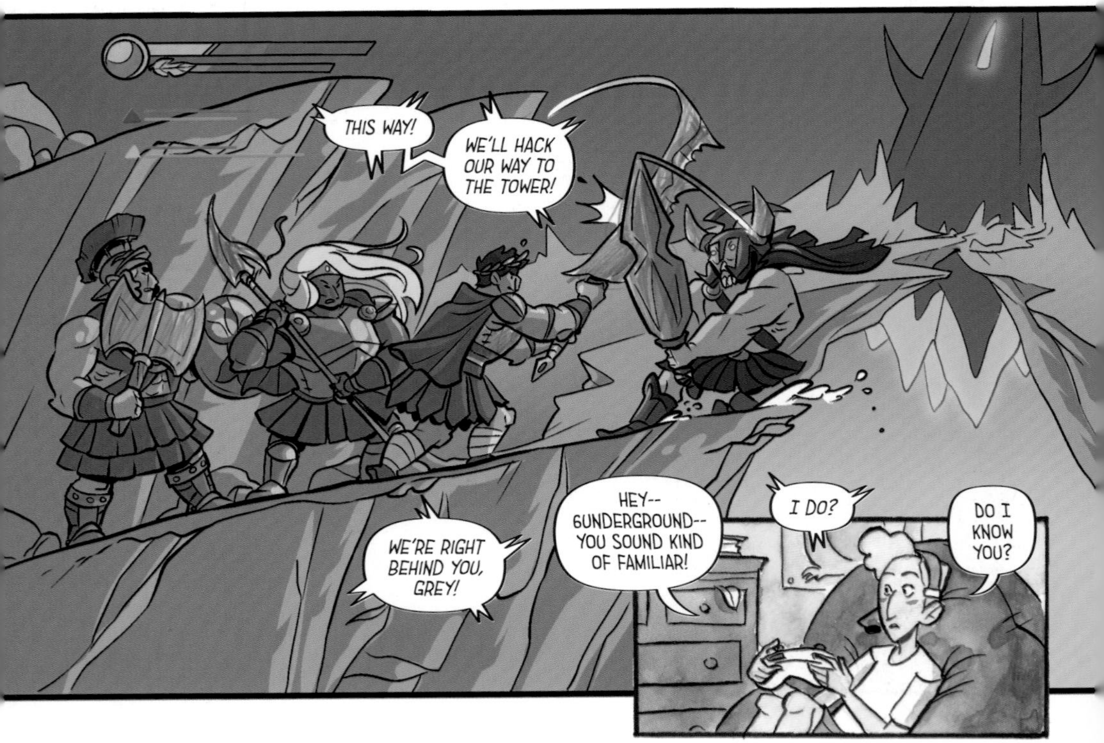
THIS WAY!
WE'LL HACK OUR WAY TO THE TOWER!
WE'RE RIGHT BEHIND YOU, GREY!
HEY-- 6UNDERGROUND-- YOU SOUND KIND OF FAMILIAR!
I DO?
DO I KNOW YOU?

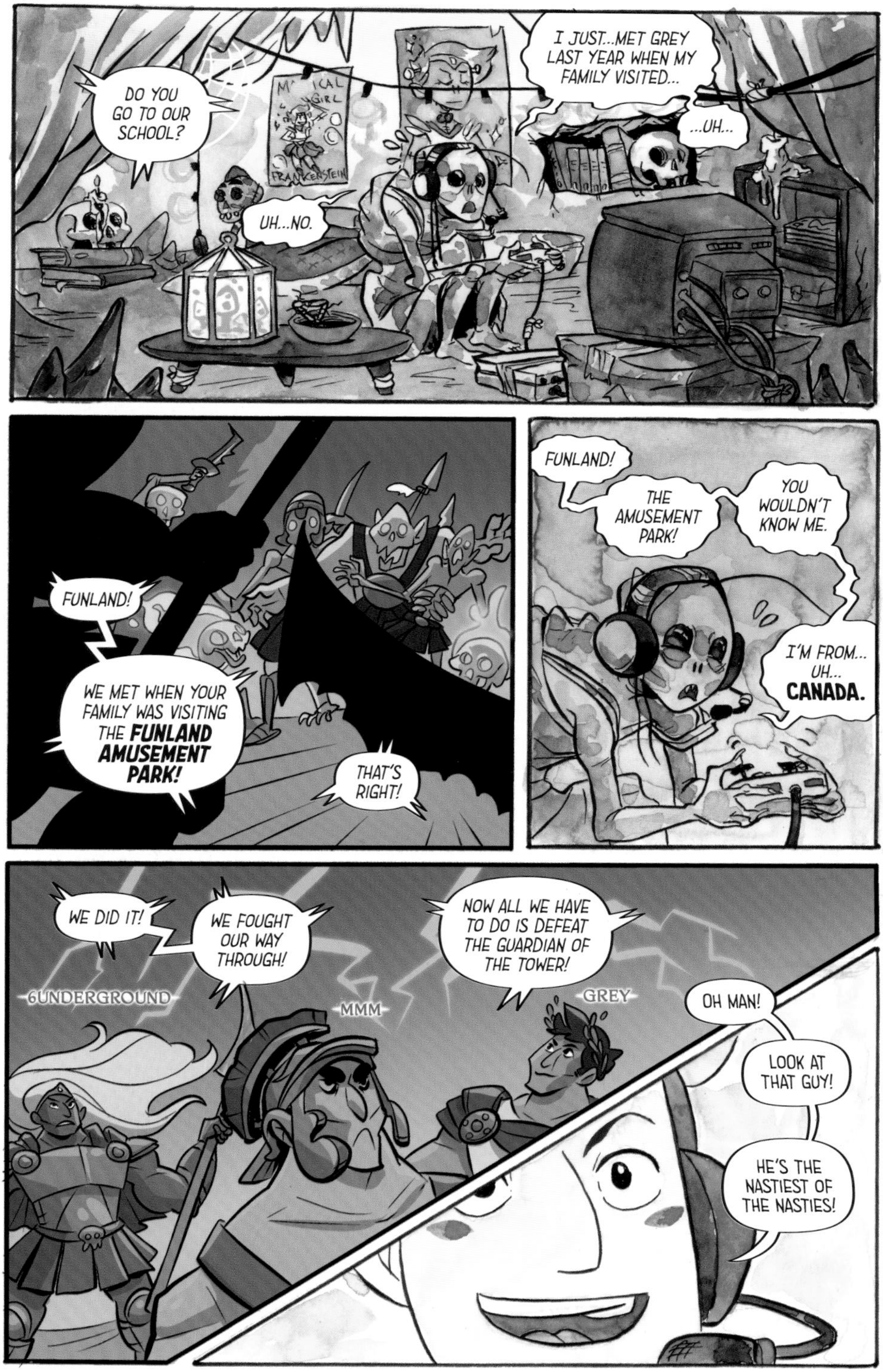
DO YOU GO TO OUR SCHOOL?
MAGICAL GIRL FRANKENSTEIN
UH...NO.
I JUST...MET GREY LAST YEAR WHEN MY FAMILY VISITED...
...UH...
FUNLAND!
WE MET WHEN YOUR FAMILY WAS VISITING THE **FUNLAND AMUSEMENT PARK!**
THAT'S RIGHT!
FUNLAND!
THE AMUSEMENT PARK!
YOU WOULDN'T KNOW ME.
I'M FROM... UH... **CANADA.**
WE DID IT!
WE FOUGHT OUR WAY THROUGH!
NOW ALL WE HAVE TO DO IS DEFEAT THE GUARDIAN OF THE TOWER!
6UNDERGROUND
MMM
GREY
OH MAN!
LOOK AT THAT GUY!
HE'S THE NASTIEST OF THE NASTIES!

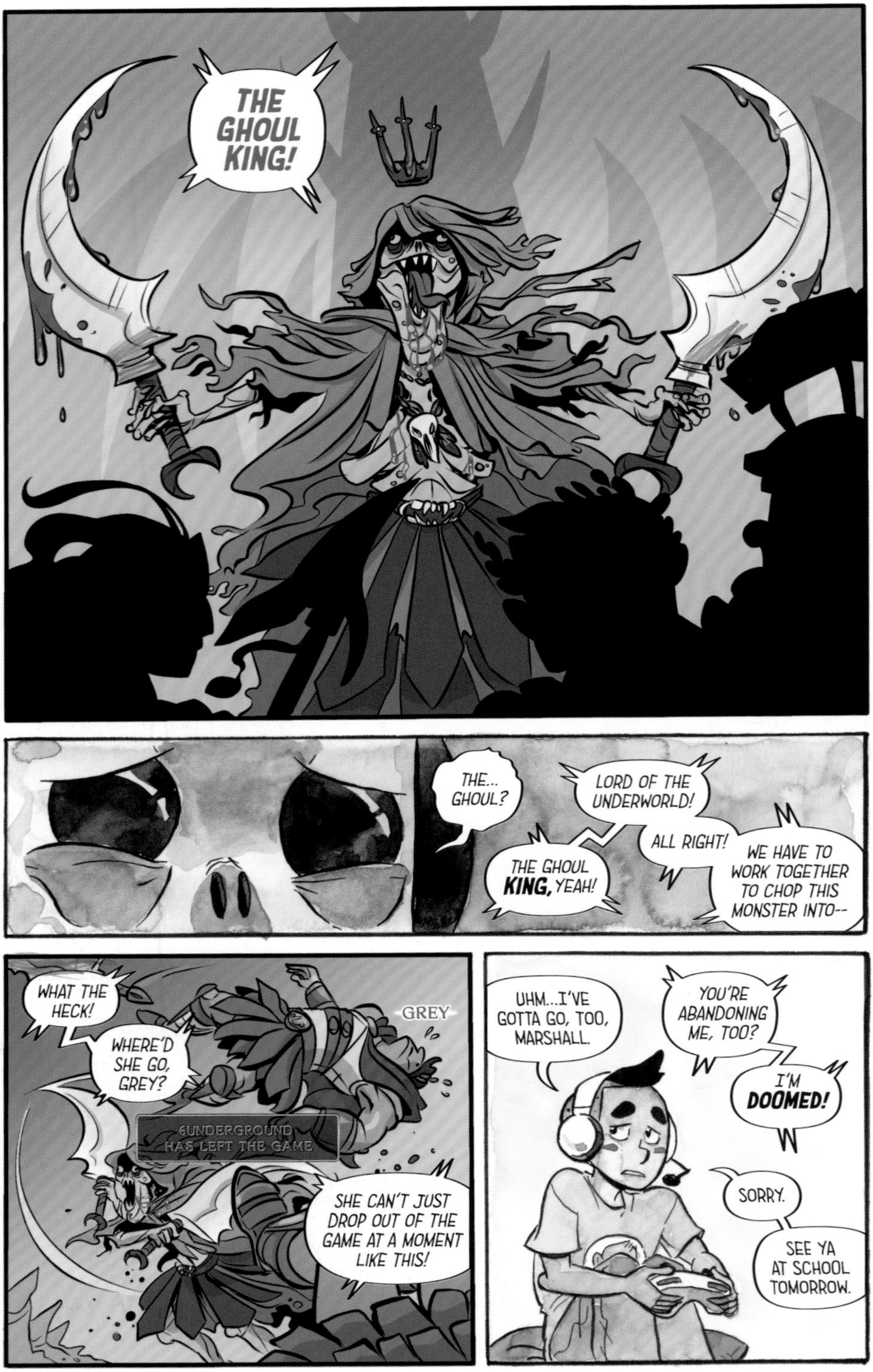
THE GHOUL KING!
THE... GHOUL?
LORD OF THE UNDERWORLD!
THE GHOUL KING, YEAH!
ALL RIGHT!
WE HAVE TO WORK TOGETHER TO CHOP THIS MONSTER INTO--
WHAT THE HECK!
GREY
WHERE'D SHE GO, GREY?
6UNDERGROUND HAS LEFT THE GAME
SHE CAN'T JUST DROP OUT OF THE GAME AT A MOMENT LIKE THIS!
UHM...I'VE GOTTA GO, TOO, MARSHALL.
YOU'RE ABANDONING ME, TOO?
I'M DOOMED!
SORRY.
SEE YA AT SCHOOL TOMORROW.

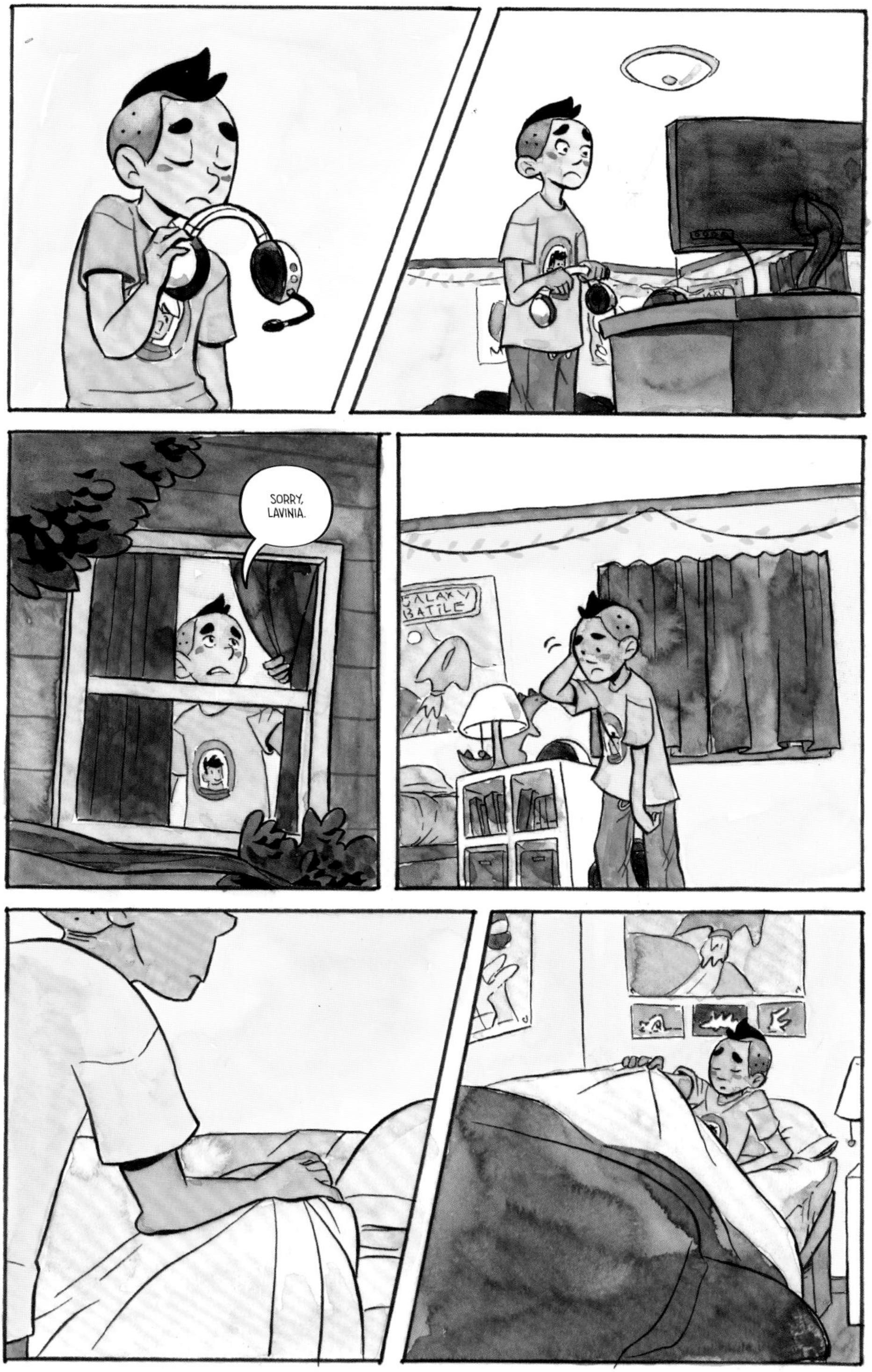
SORRY, LAVINIA.
GALAXY BATTLE

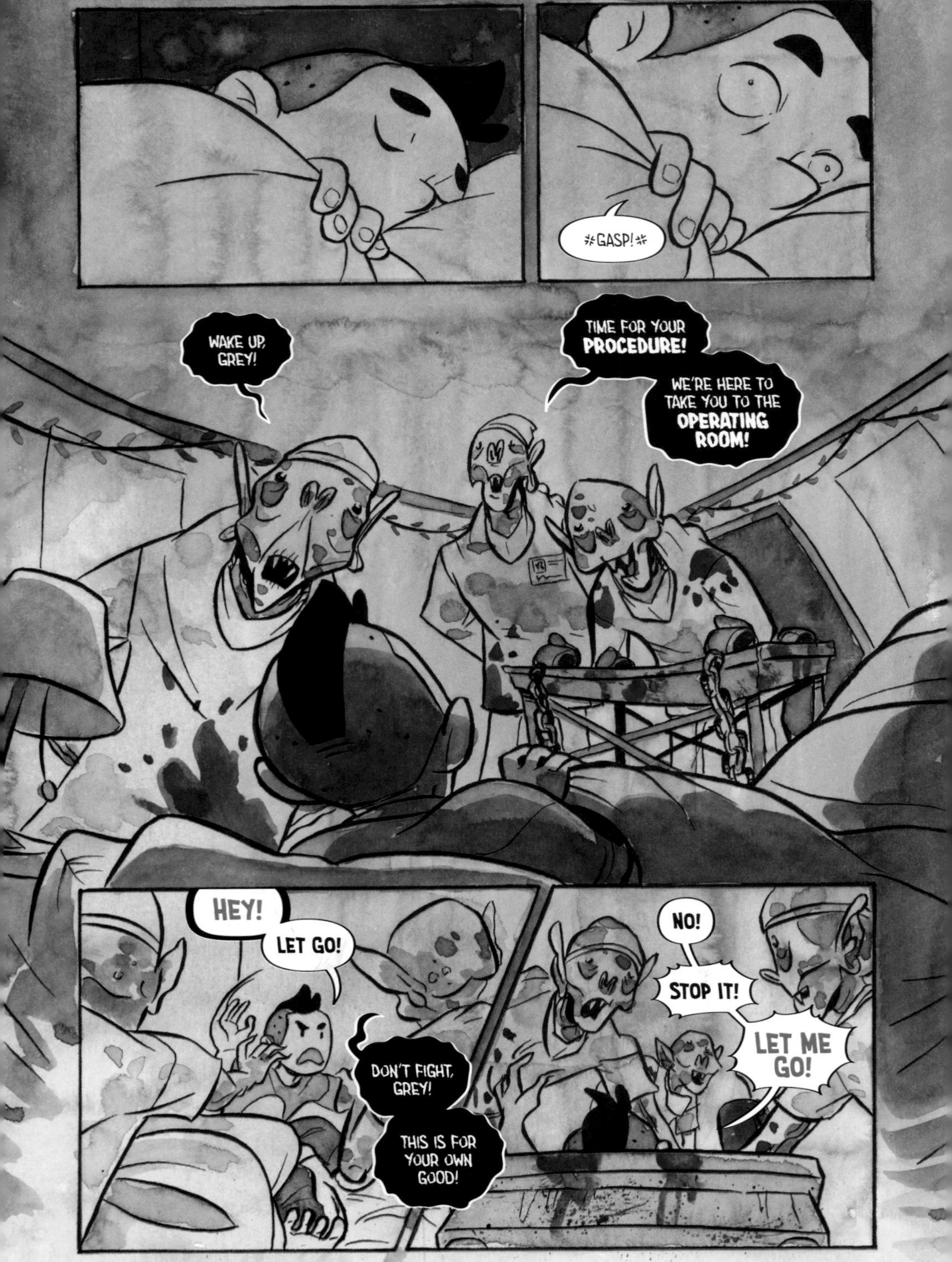
GASP!
WAKE UP, GREY!
TIME FOR YOUR PROCEDURE!
WE'RE HERE TO TAKE YOU TO THE OPERATING ROOM!
HEY!
LET GO!
DON'T FIGHT, GREY!
THIS IS FOR YOUR OWN GOOD!
NO!
STOP IT!
LET ME GO!

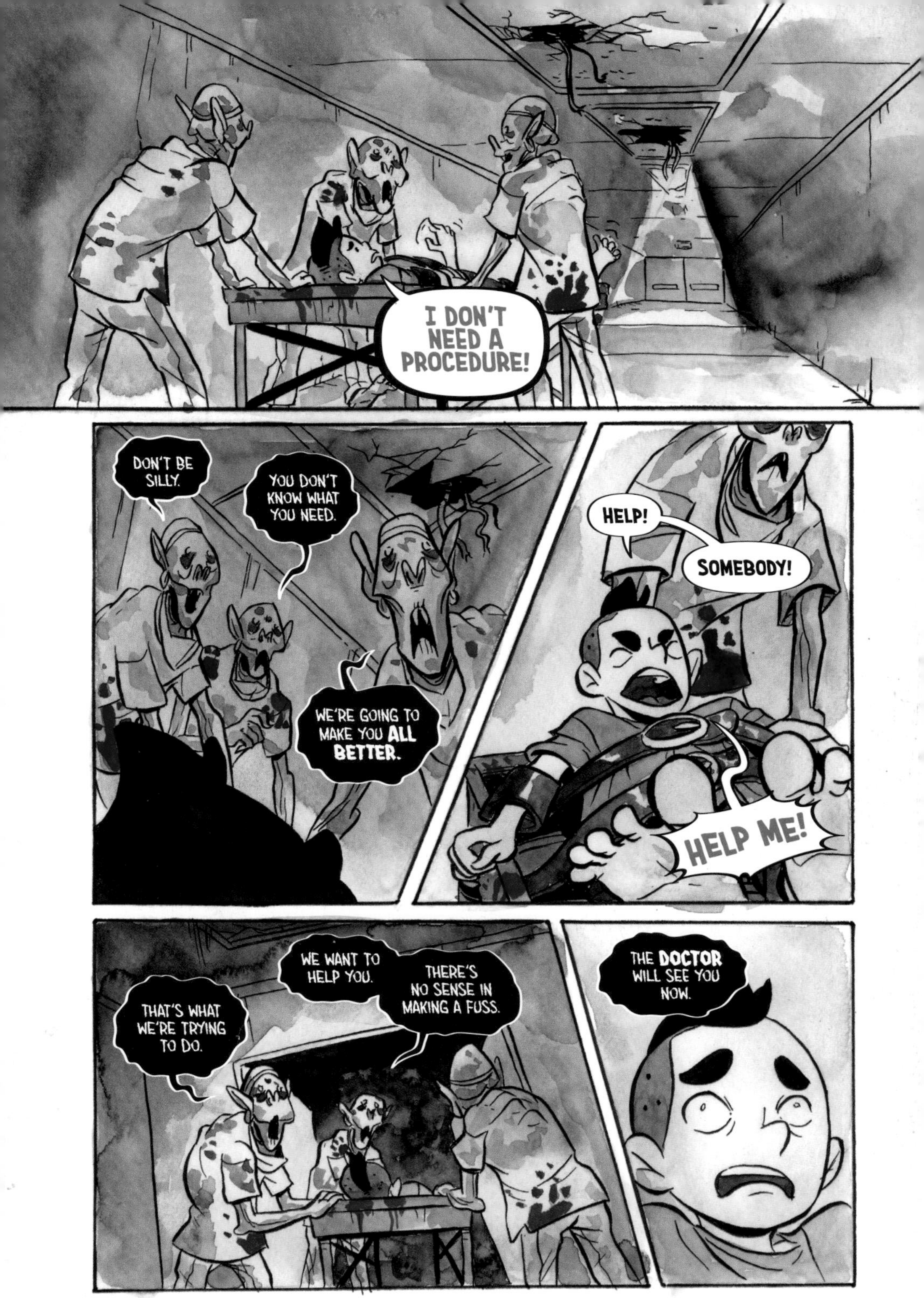
I DON'T NEED A PROCEDURE!
DON'T BE SILLY.
YOU DON'T KNOW WHAT YOU NEED.
WE'RE GOING TO MAKE YOU **ALL BETTER.**
HELP!
SOMEBODY!
HELP ME!
THAT'S WHAT WE'RE TRYING TO DO.
WE WANT TO HELP YOU.
THERE'S NO SENSE IN MAKING A FUSS.
THE **DOCTOR** WILL SEE YOU NOW.

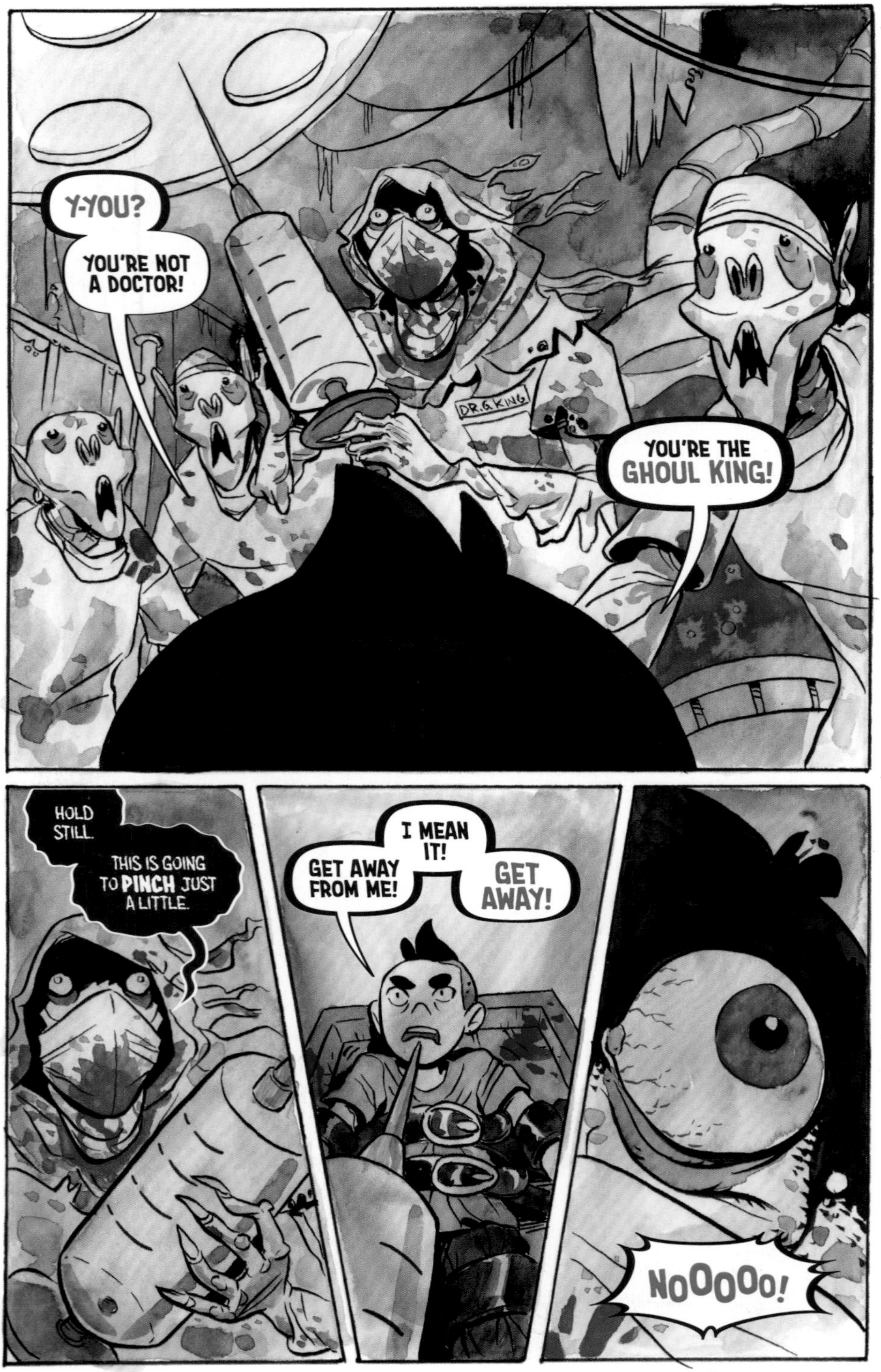
Y-YOU?
YOU'RE NOT A DOCTOR!
DR. G. KING
YOU'RE THE GHOUL KING!
HOLD STILL.
THIS IS GOING TO PINCH JUST A LITTLE.
GET AWAY FROM ME!
I MEAN IT!
GET AWAY!
NOOOOO!

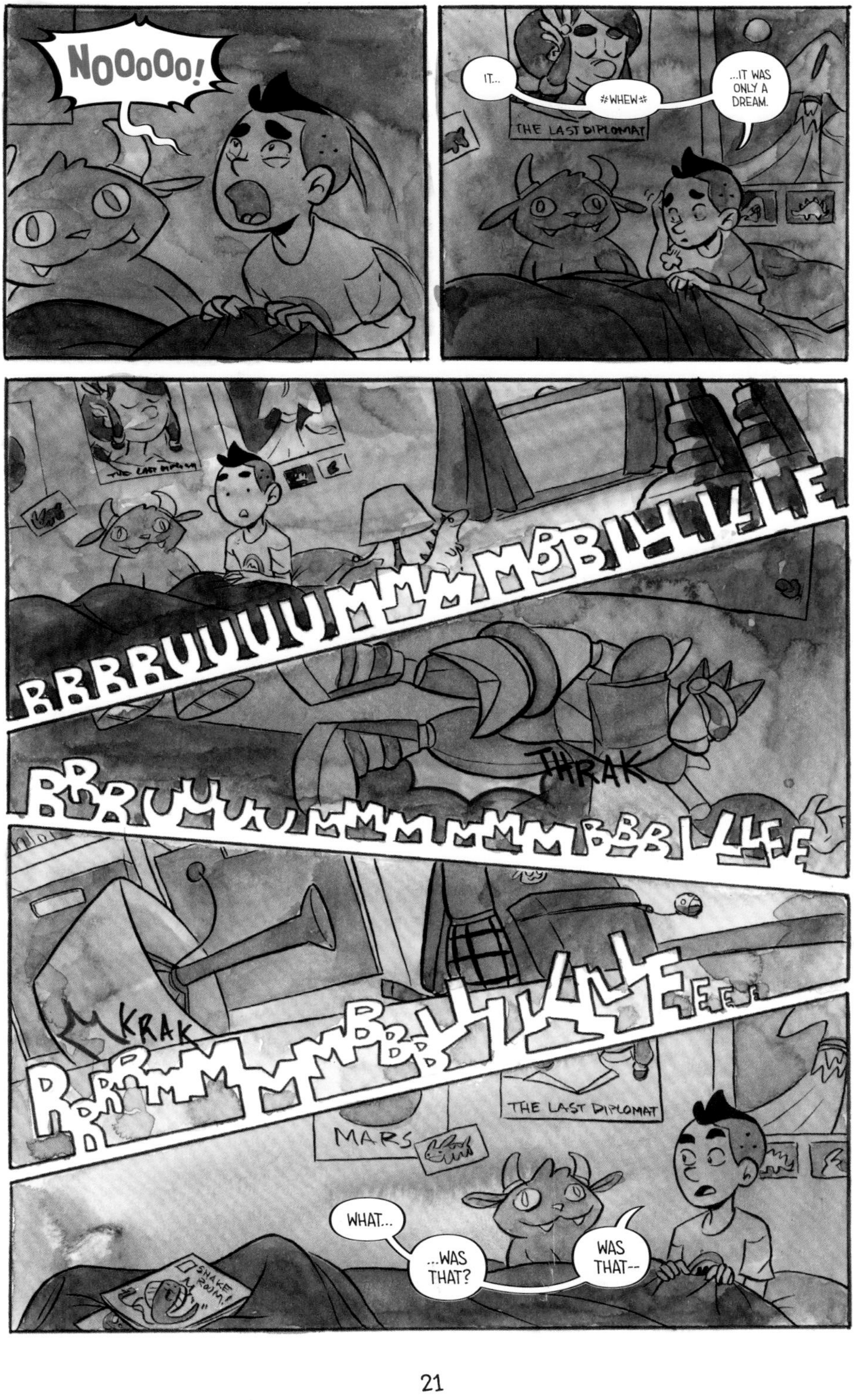
NOOOOO!
IT...
WHEW
...IT WAS ONLY A DREAM.
THE LAST DIPLOMAT
BRRRUUUUMMMMBBLLLLE
THRAK
BRRRUUUMMMMMMMMBBBLLLEE
KRAK
RRRRMMMMMBBBBLLLLLEEE
THE LAST DIPLOMAT
MARS
WHAT...
...WAS THAT?
WAS THAT--

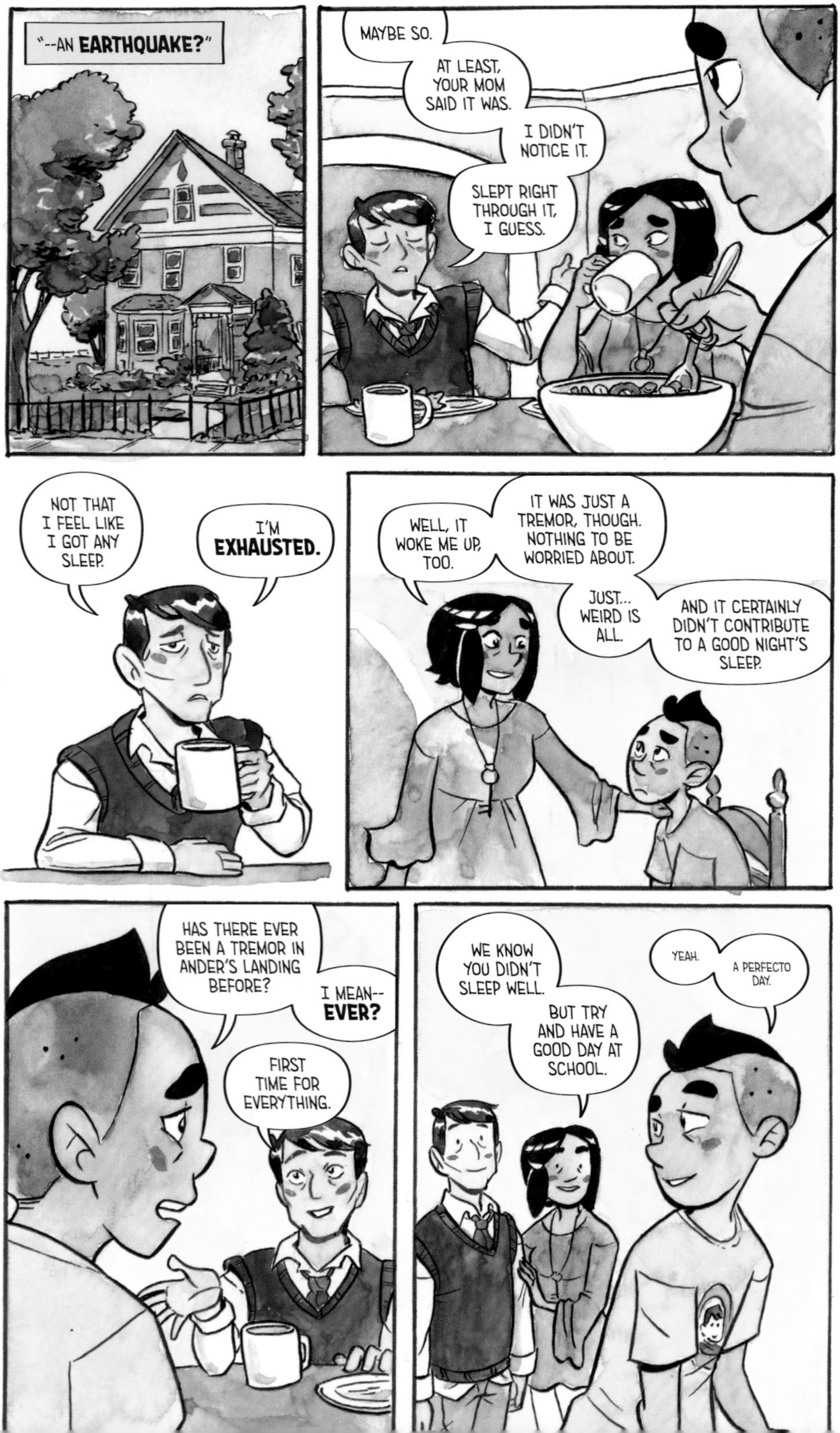
"--AN **EARTHQUAKE?**"
MAYBE SO.
AT LEAST, YOUR MOM SAID IT WAS.
I DIDN'T NOTICE IT.
SLEPT RIGHT THROUGH IT, I GUESS.
NOT THAT I FEEL LIKE I GOT ANY SLEEP.
I'M **EXHAUSTED.**
WELL, IT WOKE ME UP, TOO.
IT WAS JUST A TREMOR, THOUGH. NOTHING TO BE WORRIED ABOUT.
JUST... WEIRD IS ALL.
AND IT CERTAINLY DIDN'T CONTRIBUTE TO A GOOD NIGHT'S SLEEP.
HAS THERE EVER BEEN A TREMOR IN ANDER'S LANDING BEFORE?
I MEAN-- **EVER?**
FIRST TIME FOR EVERYTHING.
WE KNOW YOU DIDN'T SLEEP WELL.
BUT TRY AND HAVE A GOOD DAY AT SCHOOL.
YEAH.
A PERFECTO DAY.

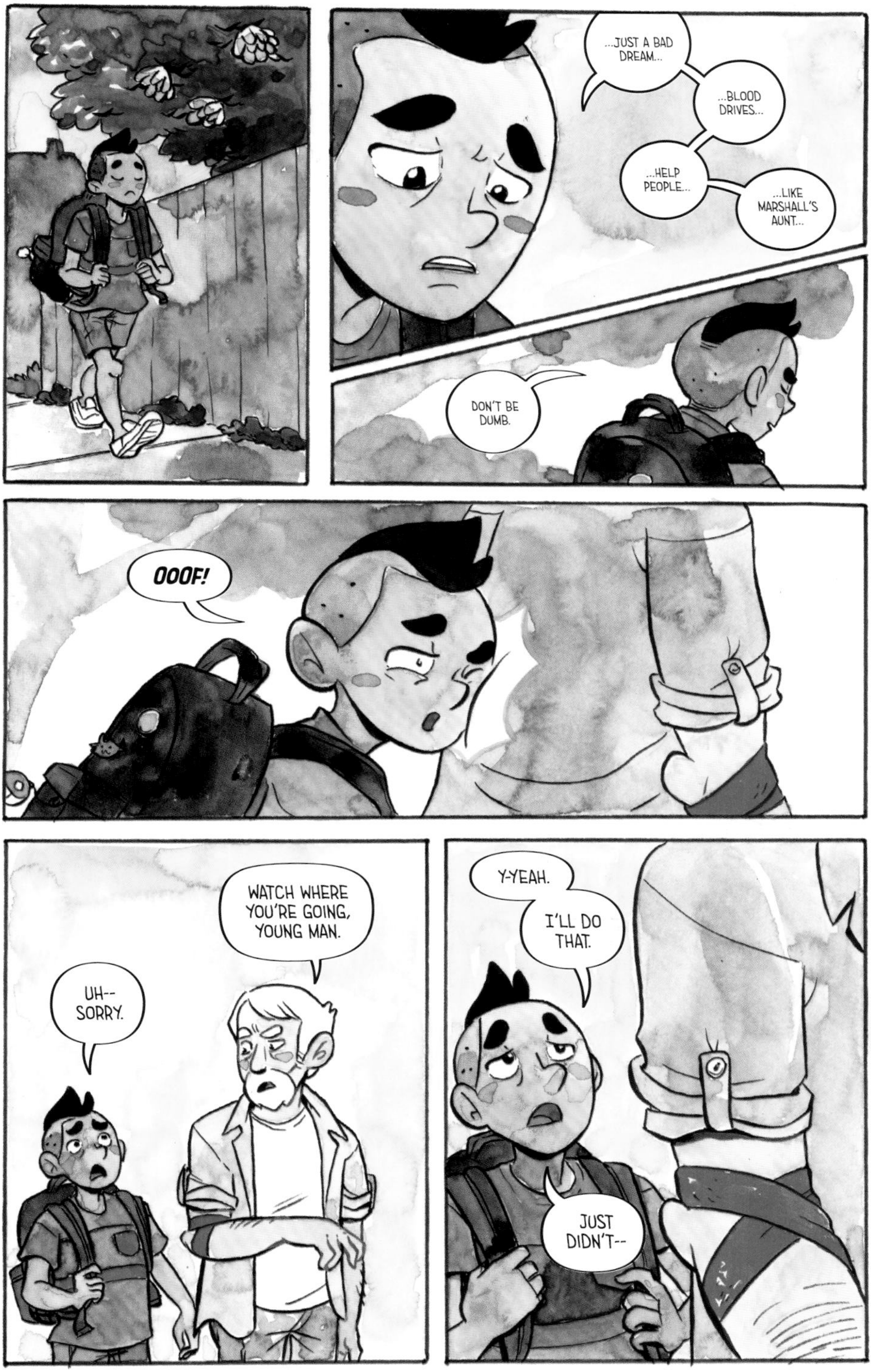
...JUST A BAD DREAM...
...BLOOD DRIVES...
...HELP PEOPLE...
...LIKE MARSHALL'S AUNT...
DON'T BE DUMB.
OOOF!
WATCH WHERE YOU'RE GOING, YOUNG MAN.
UH-- SORRY.
Y-YEAH.
I'LL DO THAT.
JUST DIDN'T--

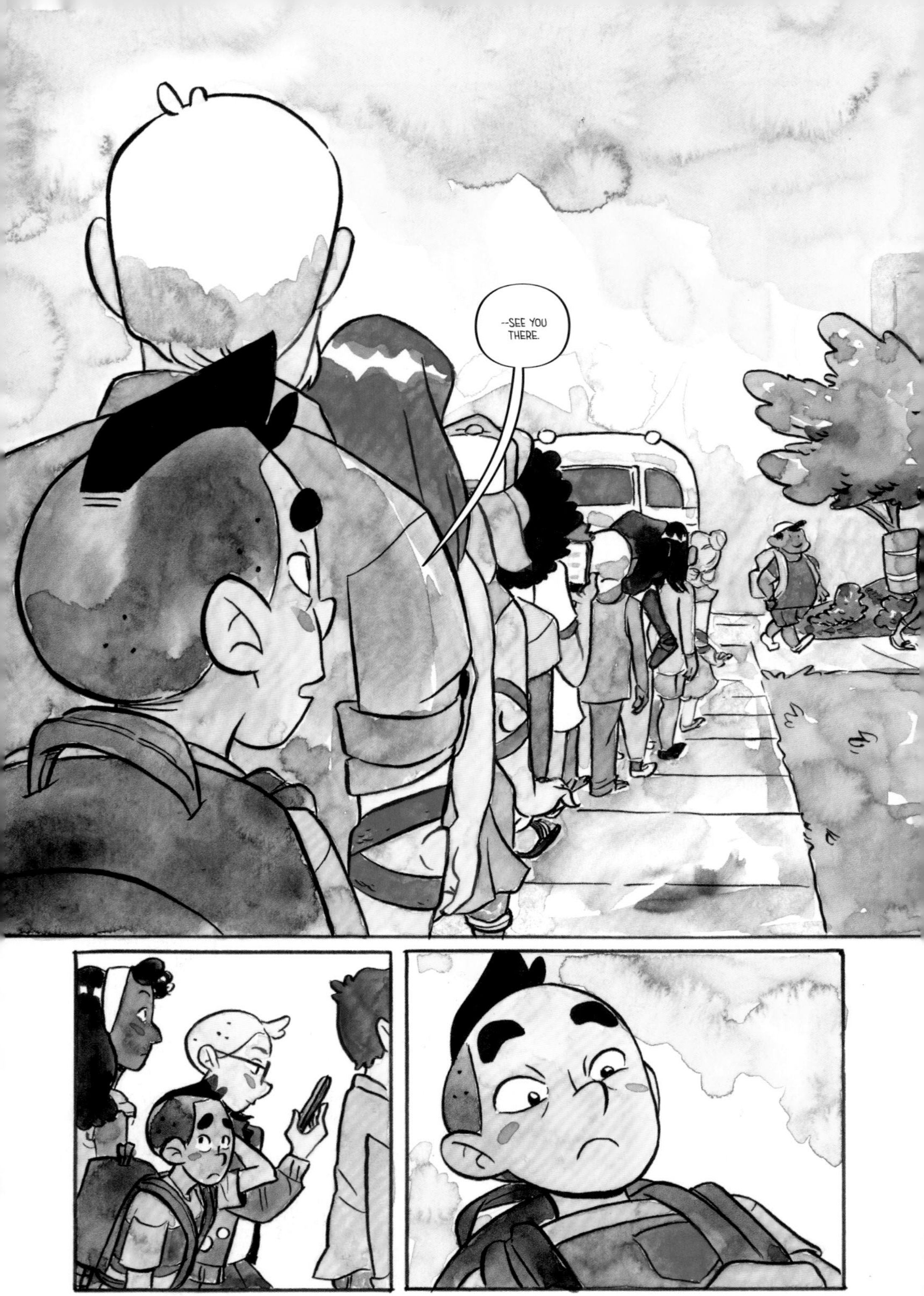
--SEE YOU
THERE.

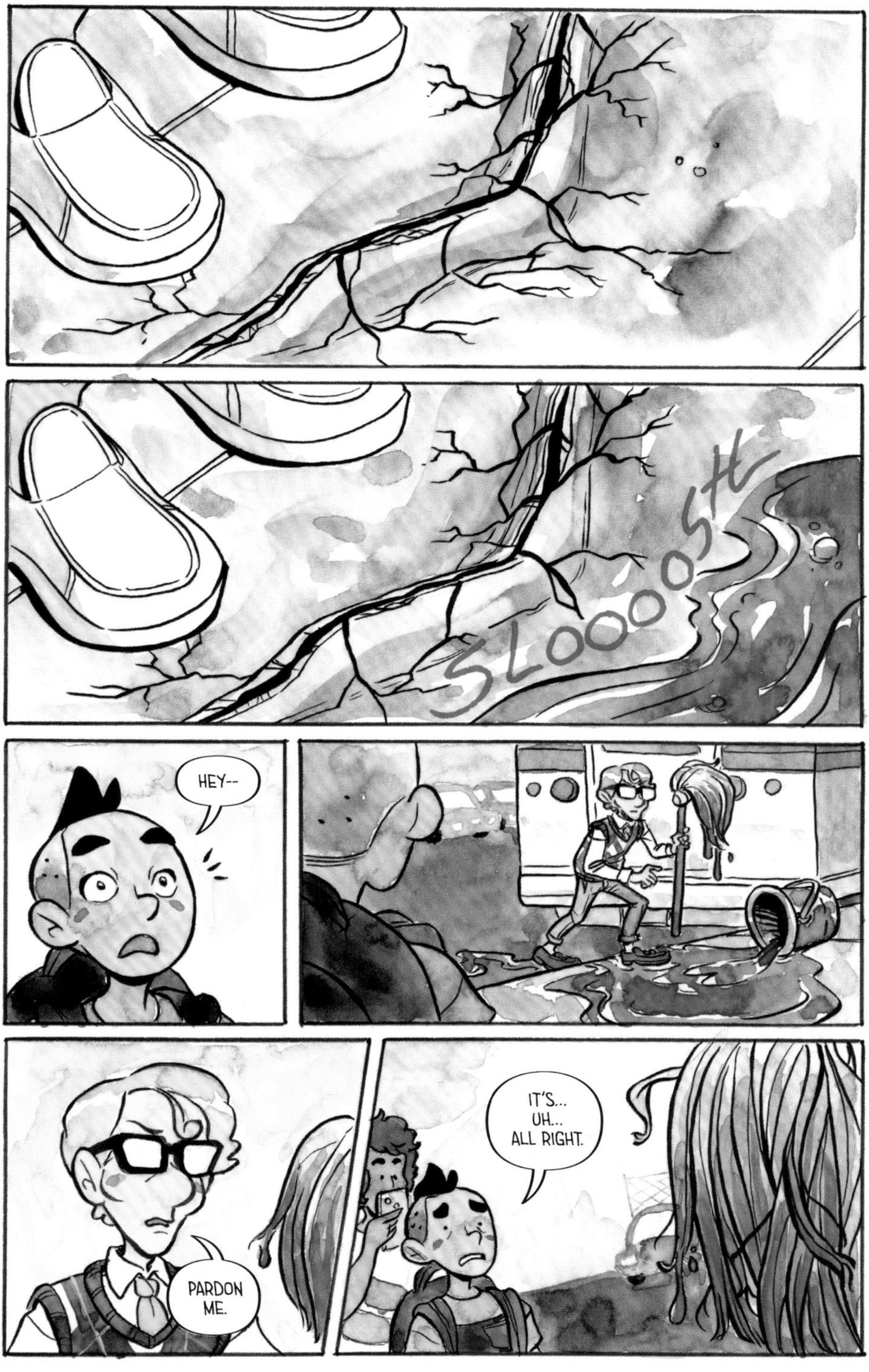
SLOOOOOSH
HEY--
PARDON ME.
IT'S... UH... ALL RIGHT.

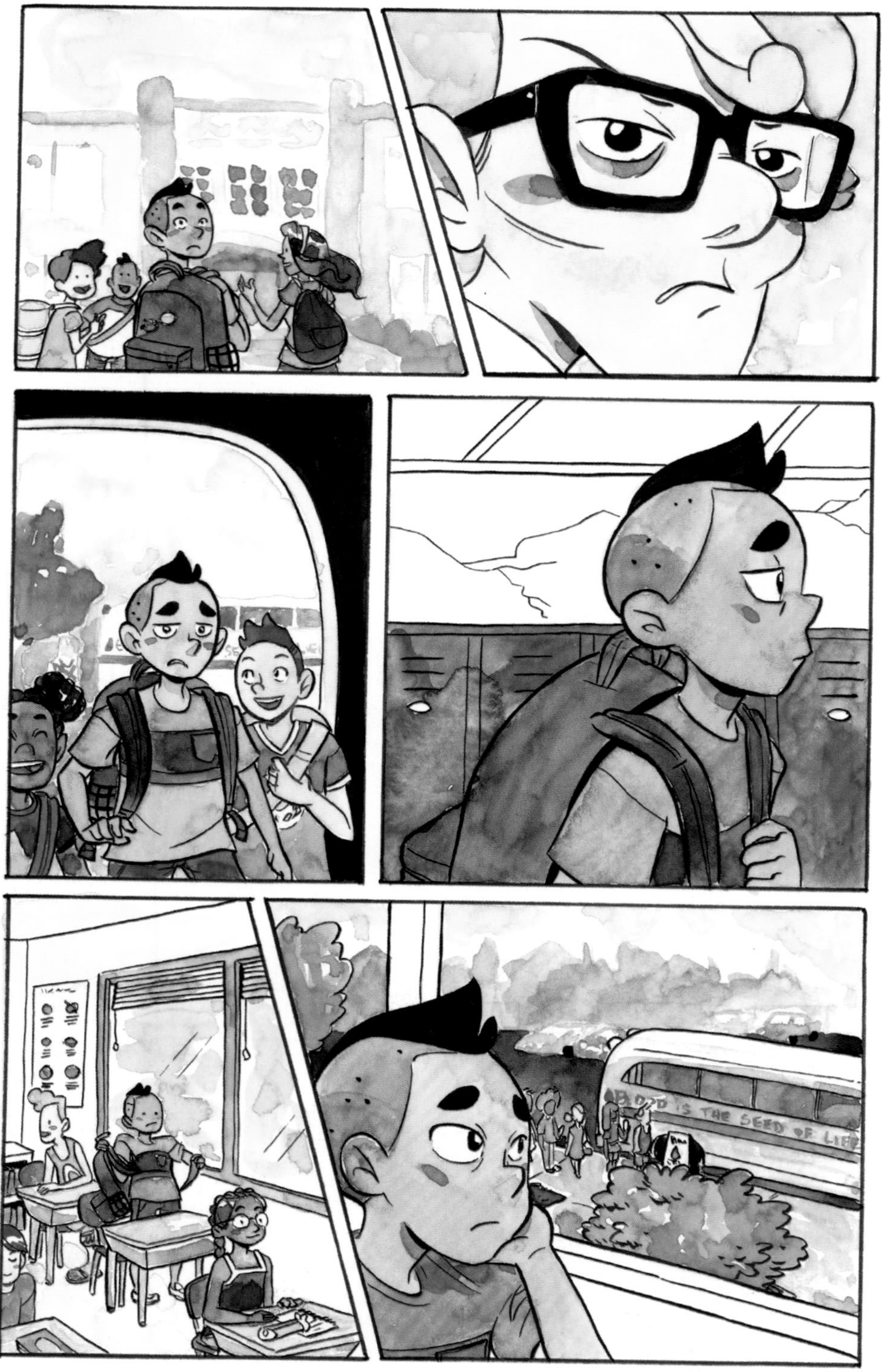

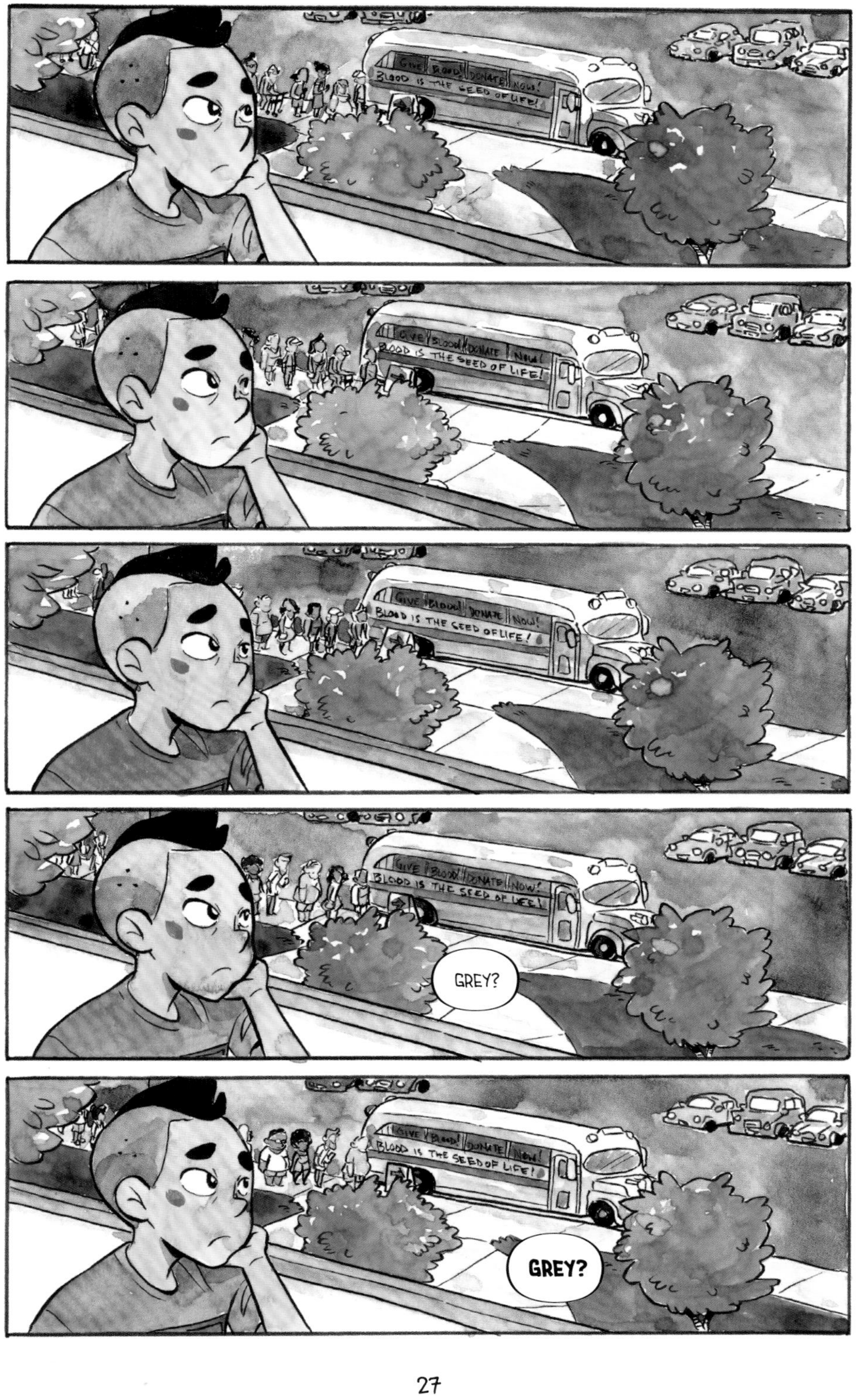
GIVE BLOOD! DONATE NOW!
BLOOD IS THE SEED OF LIFE!
GREY?
GREY?

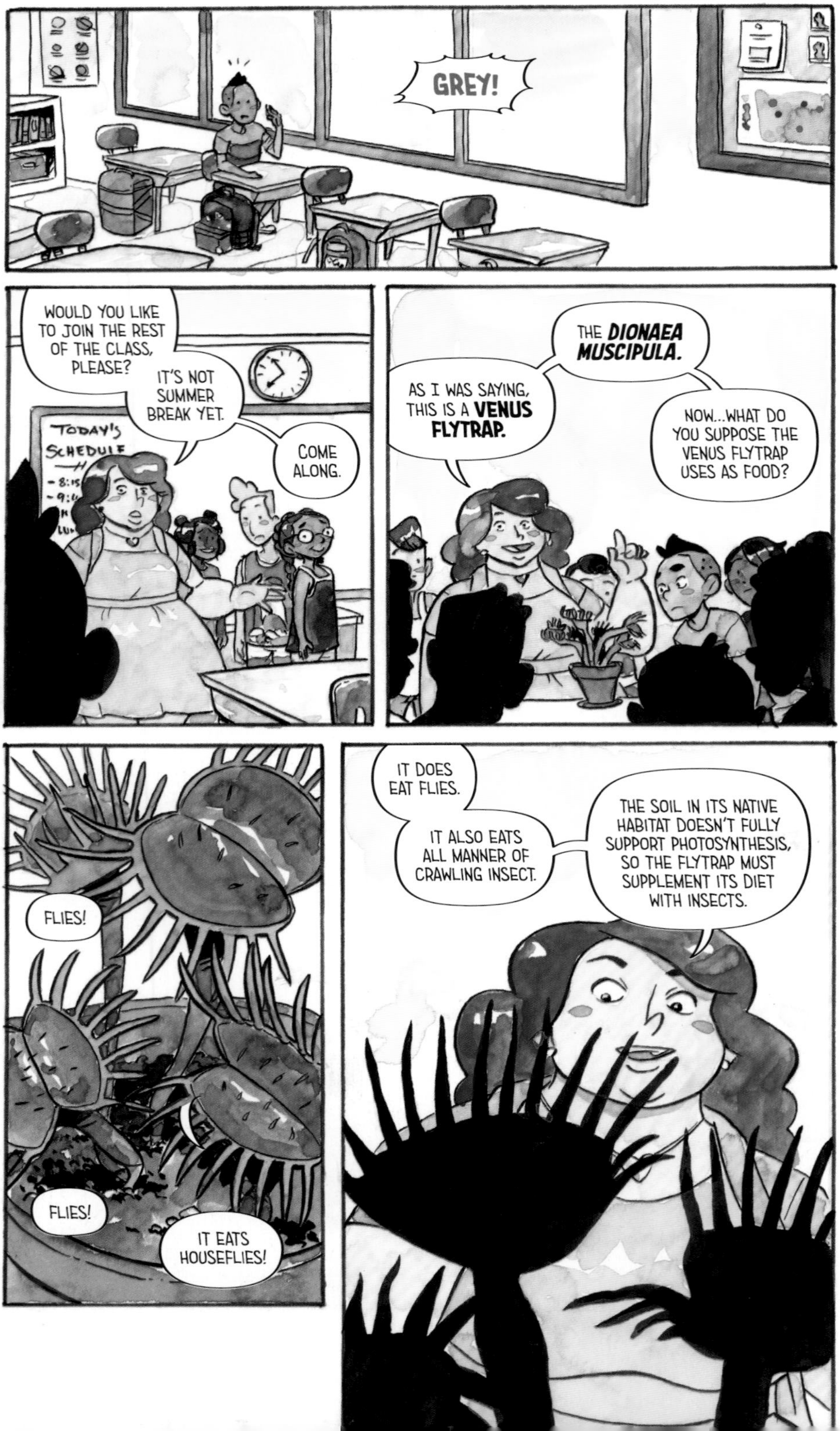
GREY!
WOULD YOU LIKE TO JOIN THE REST OF THE CLASS, PLEASE?
IT'S NOT SUMMER BREAK YET.
COME ALONG.
TODAY'S SCHEDULE
AS I WAS SAYING, THIS IS A **VENUS FLYTRAP.**
THE ***DIONAEA MUSCIPULA.***
NOW...WHAT DO YOU SUPPOSE THE VENUS FLYTRAP USES AS FOOD?
FLIES!
FLIES!
IT EATS HOUSEFLIES!
IT DOES EAT FLIES.
IT ALSO EATS ALL MANNER OF CRAWLING INSECT.
THE SOIL IN ITS NATIVE HABITAT DOESN'T FULLY SUPPORT PHOTOSYNTHESIS, SO THE FLYTRAP MUST SUPPLEMENT ITS DIET WITH INSECTS.

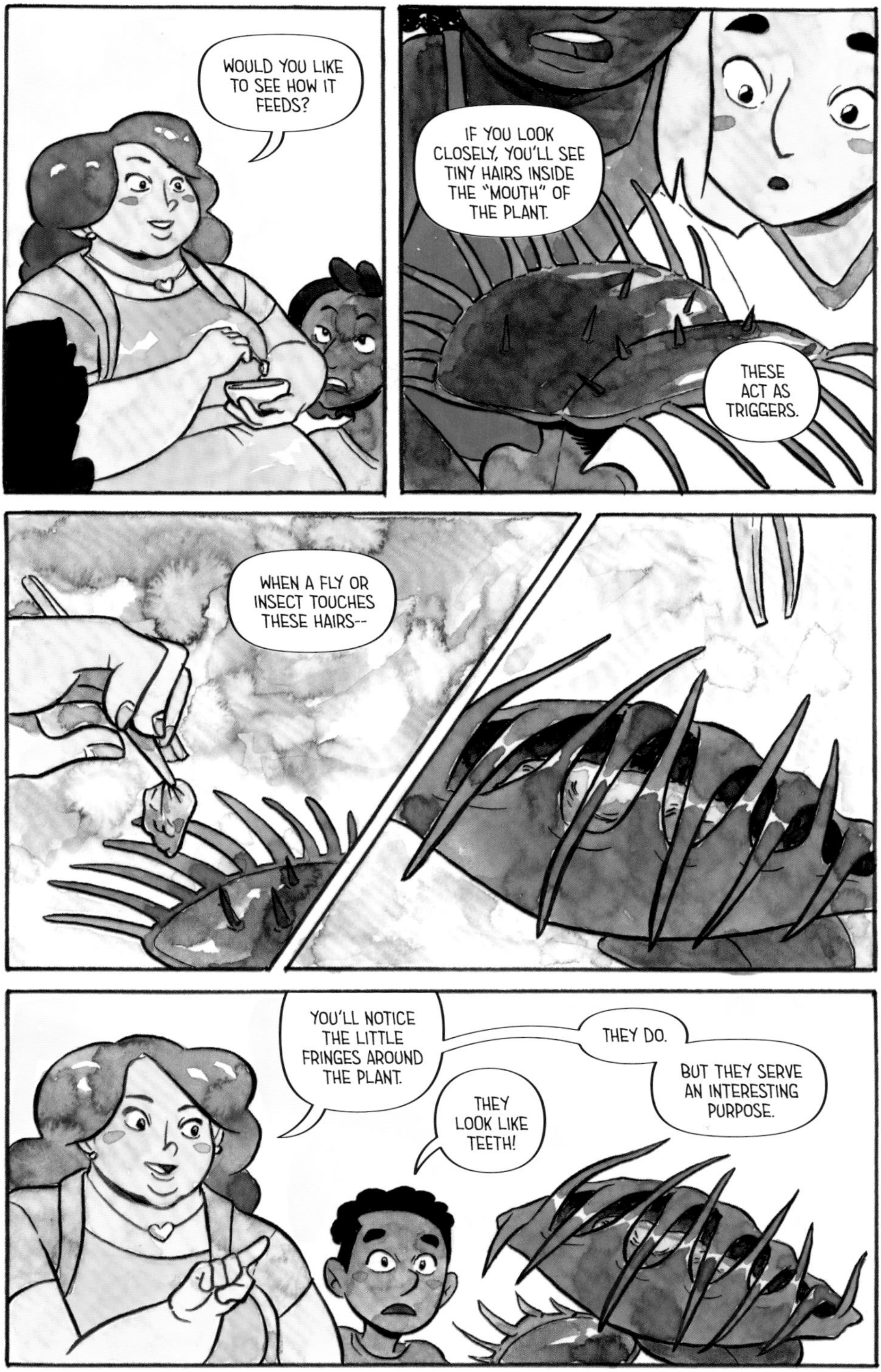
WOULD YOU LIKE TO SEE HOW IT FEEDS?
IF YOU LOOK CLOSELY, YOU'LL SEE TINY HAIRS INSIDE THE "MOUTH" OF THE PLANT.
THESE ACT AS TRIGGERS.
WHEN A FLY OR INSECT TOUCHES THESE HAIRS--
YOU'LL NOTICE THE LITTLE FRINGES AROUND THE PLANT.
THEY LOOK LIKE TEETH!
THEY DO.
BUT THEY SERVE AN INTERESTING PURPOSE.

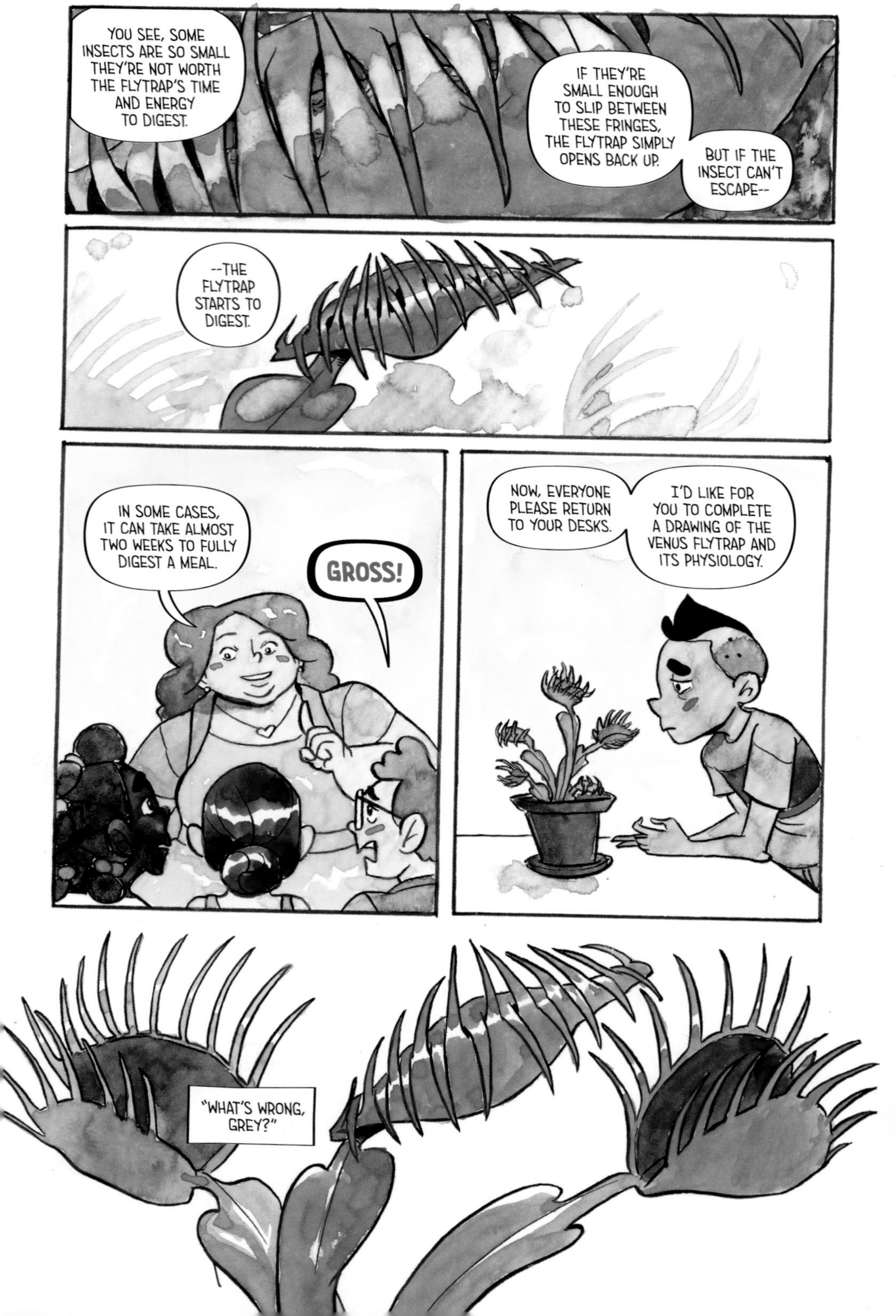
YOU SEE, SOME INSECTS ARE SO SMALL THEY'RE NOT WORTH THE FLYTRAP'S TIME AND ENERGY TO DIGEST.
IF THEY'RE SMALL ENOUGH TO SLIP BETWEEN THESE FRINGES, THE FLYTRAP SIMPLY OPENS BACK UP.
BUT IF THE INSECT CAN'T ESCAPE--
--THE FLYTRAP STARTS TO DIGEST.
IN SOME CASES, IT CAN TAKE ALMOST TWO WEEKS TO FULLY DIGEST A MEAL.
GROSS!
NOW, EVERYONE PLEASE RETURN TO YOUR DESKS.
I'D LIKE FOR YOU TO COMPLETE A DRAWING OF THE VENUS FLYTRAP AND ITS PHYSIOLOGY.
"WHAT'S WRONG, GREY?"

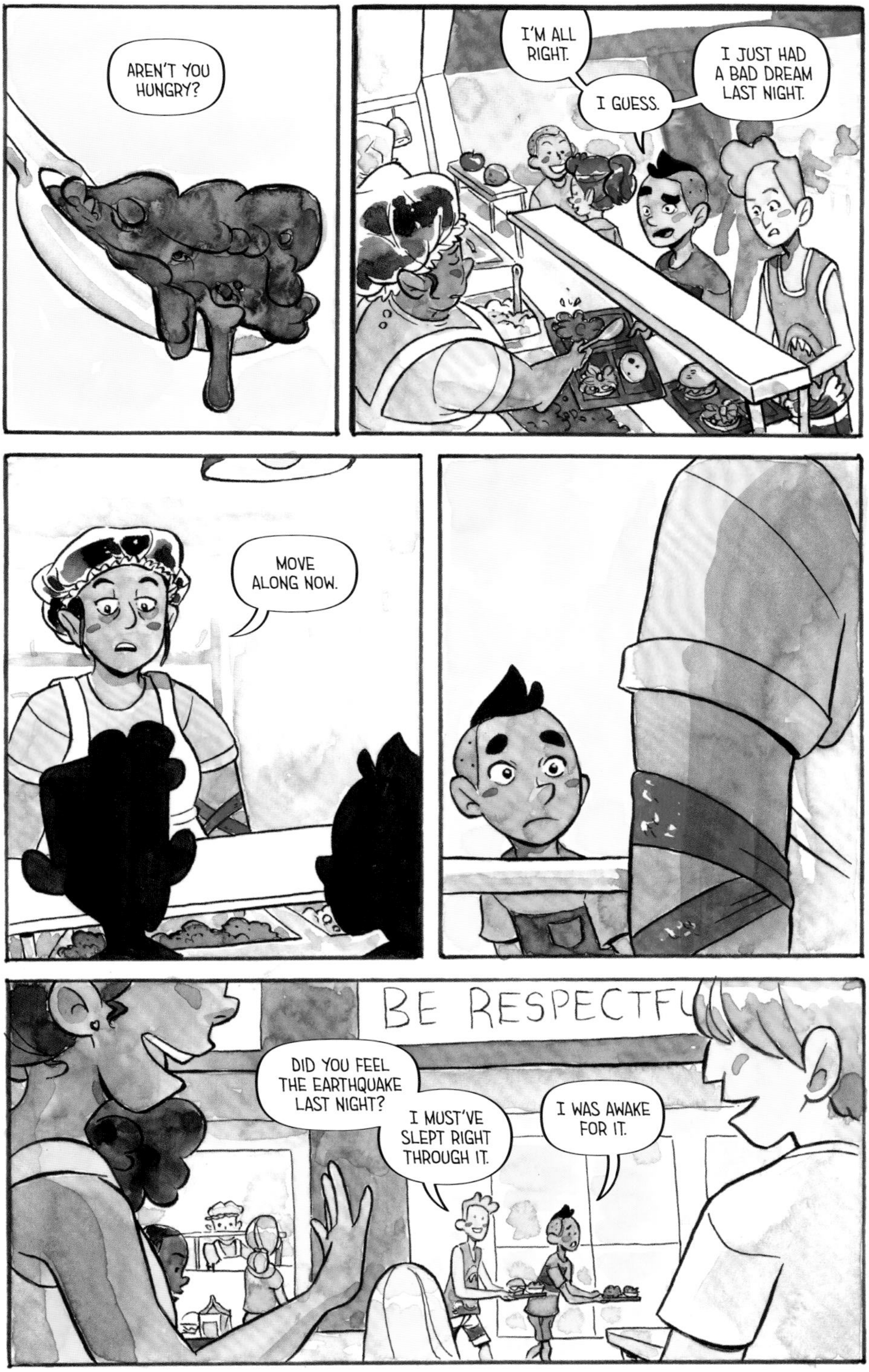
AREN'T YOU HUNGRY?
I'M ALL RIGHT.
I GUESS.
I JUST HAD A BAD DREAM LAST NIGHT.
MOVE ALONG NOW.
BE RESPECTF
DID YOU FEEL THE EARTHQUAKE LAST NIGHT?
I MUST'VE SLEPT RIGHT THROUGH IT.
I WAS AWAKE FOR IT.

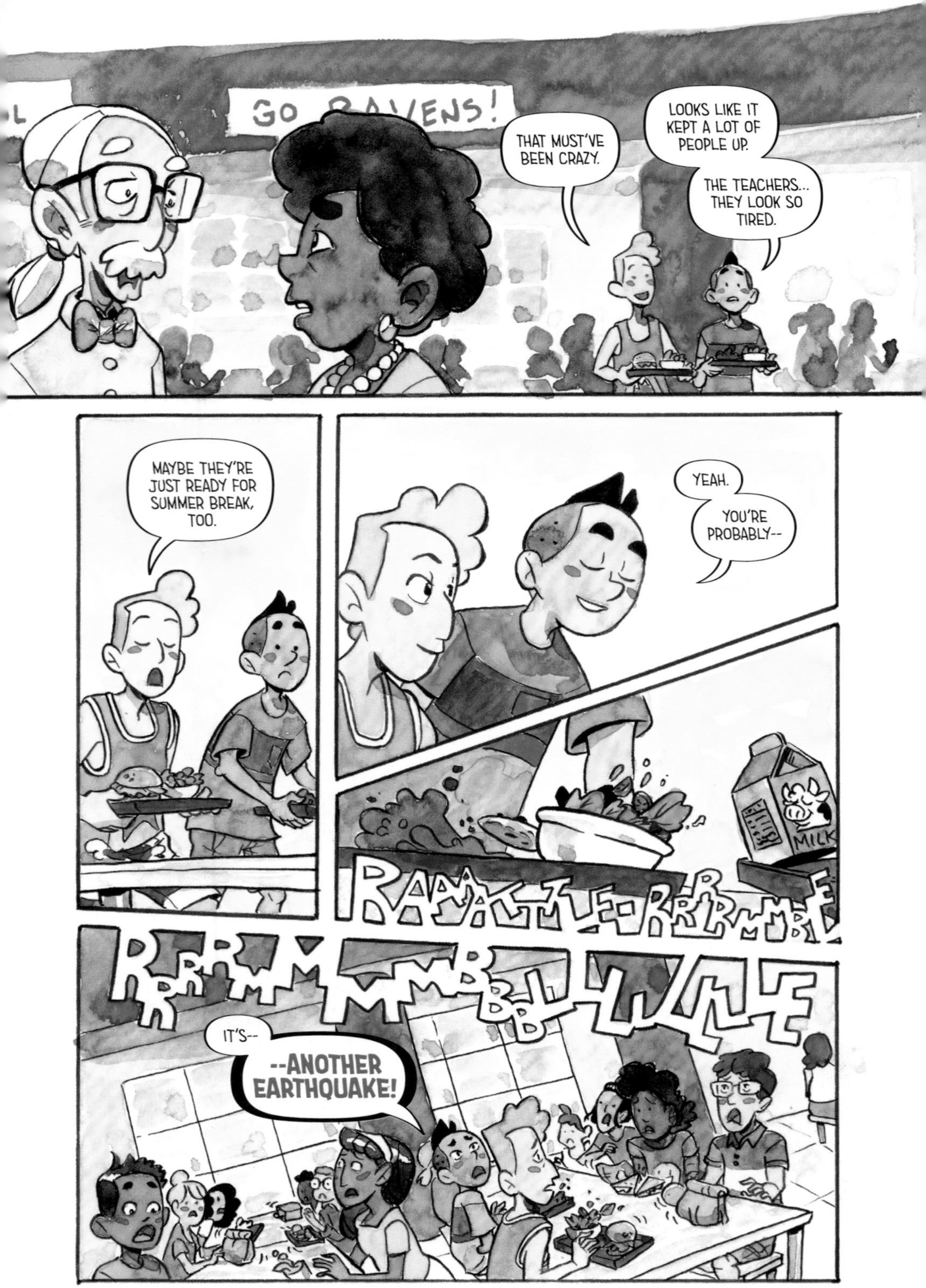

GO RAVENS!
THAT MUST'VE BEEN CRAZY.
LOOKS LIKE IT KEPT A LOT OF PEOPLE UP.
THE TEACHERS... THEY LOOK SO TIRED.
MAYBE THEY'RE JUST READY FOR SUMMER BREAK, TOO.
YEAH.
YOU'RE PROBABLY--
MILK
RATTLE-RRRUMBLE
RRRUMMMBBLLLLE
IT'S--
--ANOTHER EARTHQUAKE!

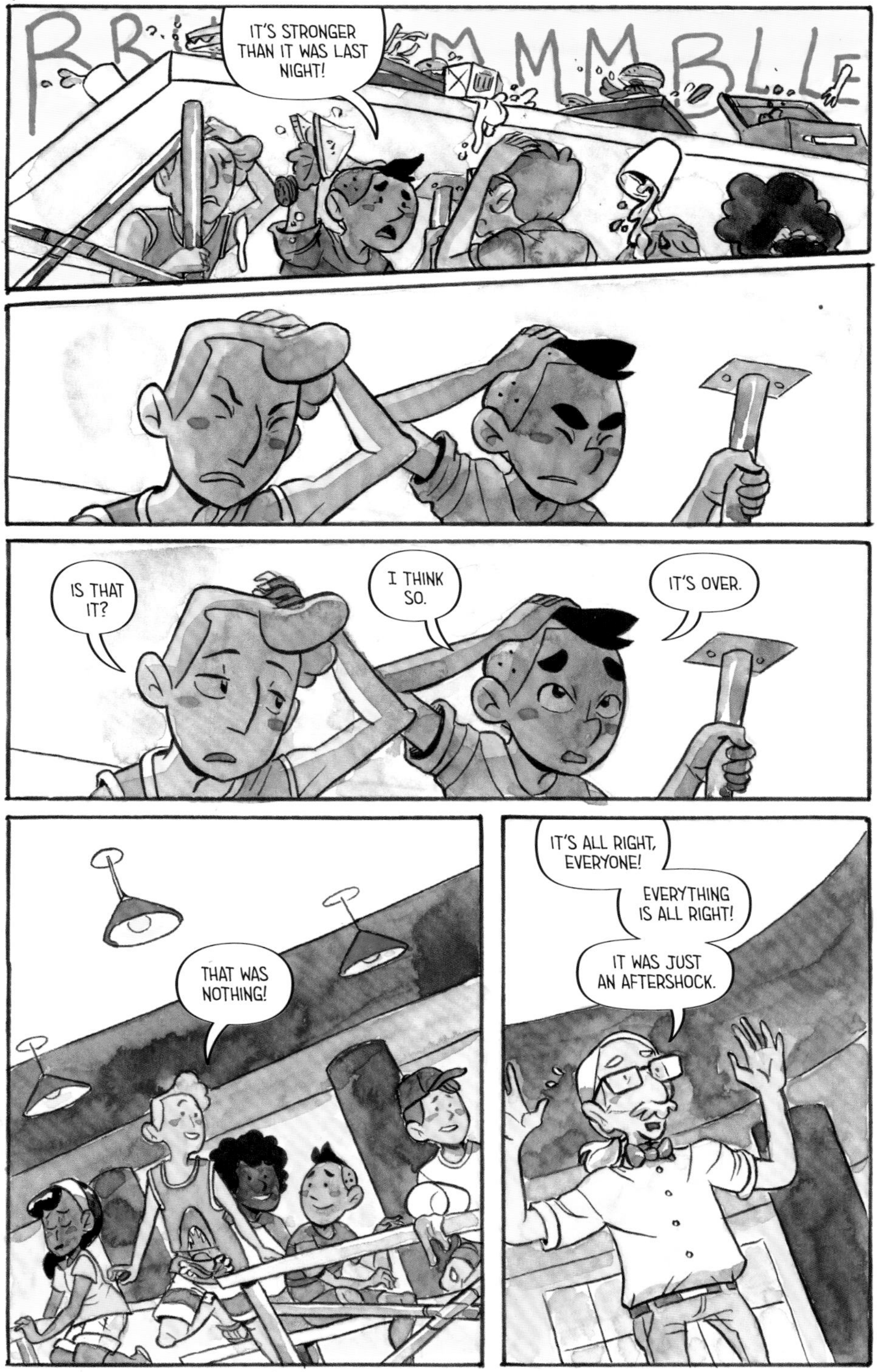
RR
MMMBLLE
IT'S STRONGER THAN IT WAS LAST NIGHT!
IS THAT IT?
I THINK SO.
IT'S OVER.
THAT WAS NOTHING!
IT'S ALL RIGHT, EVERYONE!
EVERYTHING IS ALL RIGHT!
IT WAS JUST AN AFTERSHOCK.

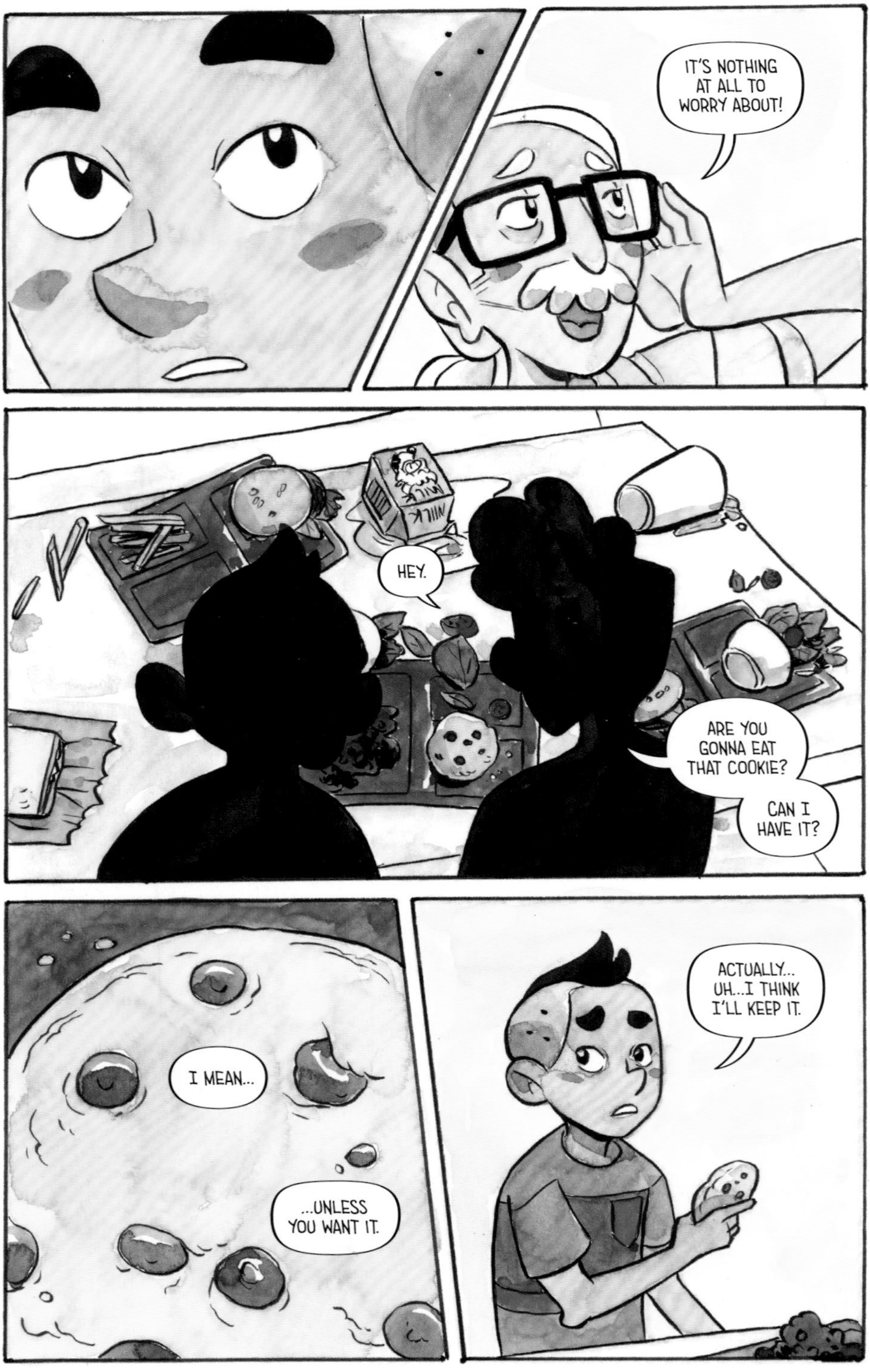
IT'S NOTHING AT ALL TO WORRY ABOUT!
HEY.
ARE YOU GONNA EAT THAT COOKIE?
CAN I HAVE IT?
I MEAN...
...UNLESS YOU WANT IT.
ACTUALLY... UH...I THINK I'LL KEEP IT.

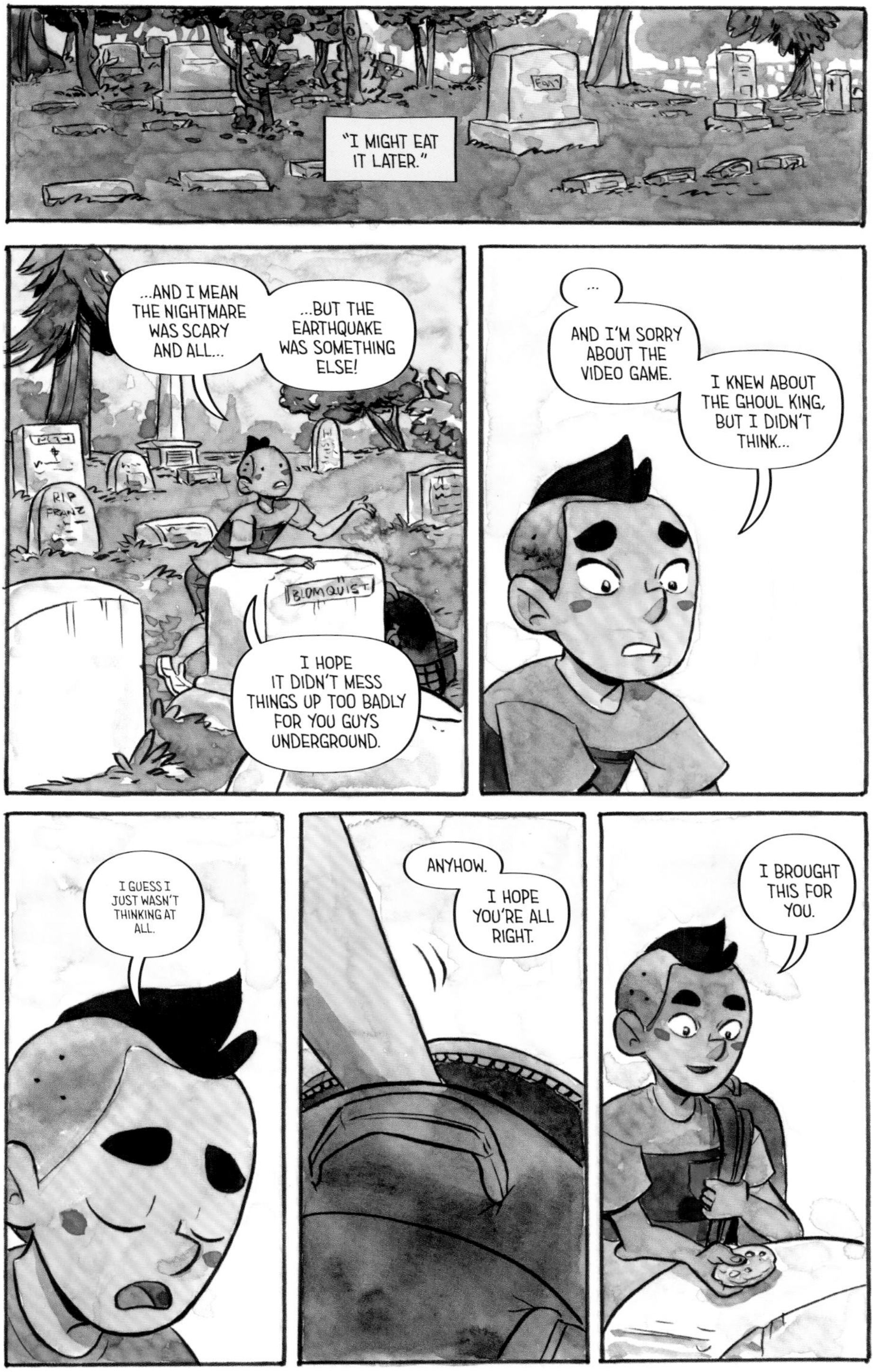
"I MIGHT EAT IT LATER."
...AND I MEAN THE NIGHTMARE WAS SCARY AND ALL...
...BUT THE EARTHQUAKE WAS SOMETHING ELSE!
RIP FRANZ
BLOMQUIST
I HOPE IT DIDN'T MESS THINGS UP TOO BADLY FOR YOU GUYS UNDERGROUND.
...
AND I'M SORRY ABOUT THE VIDEO GAME.
I KNEW ABOUT THE GHOUL KING, BUT I DIDN'T THINK...
I GUESS I JUST WASN'T THINKING AT ALL.
ANYHOW.
I HOPE YOU'RE ALL RIGHT.
I BROUGHT THIS FOR YOU.

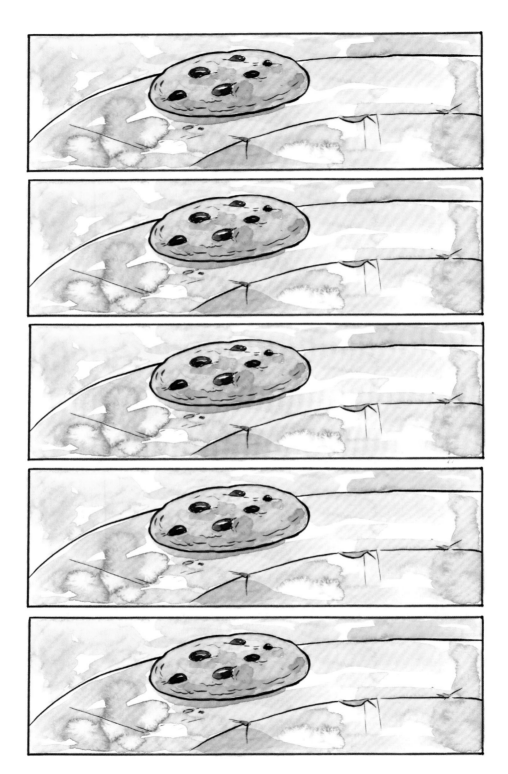

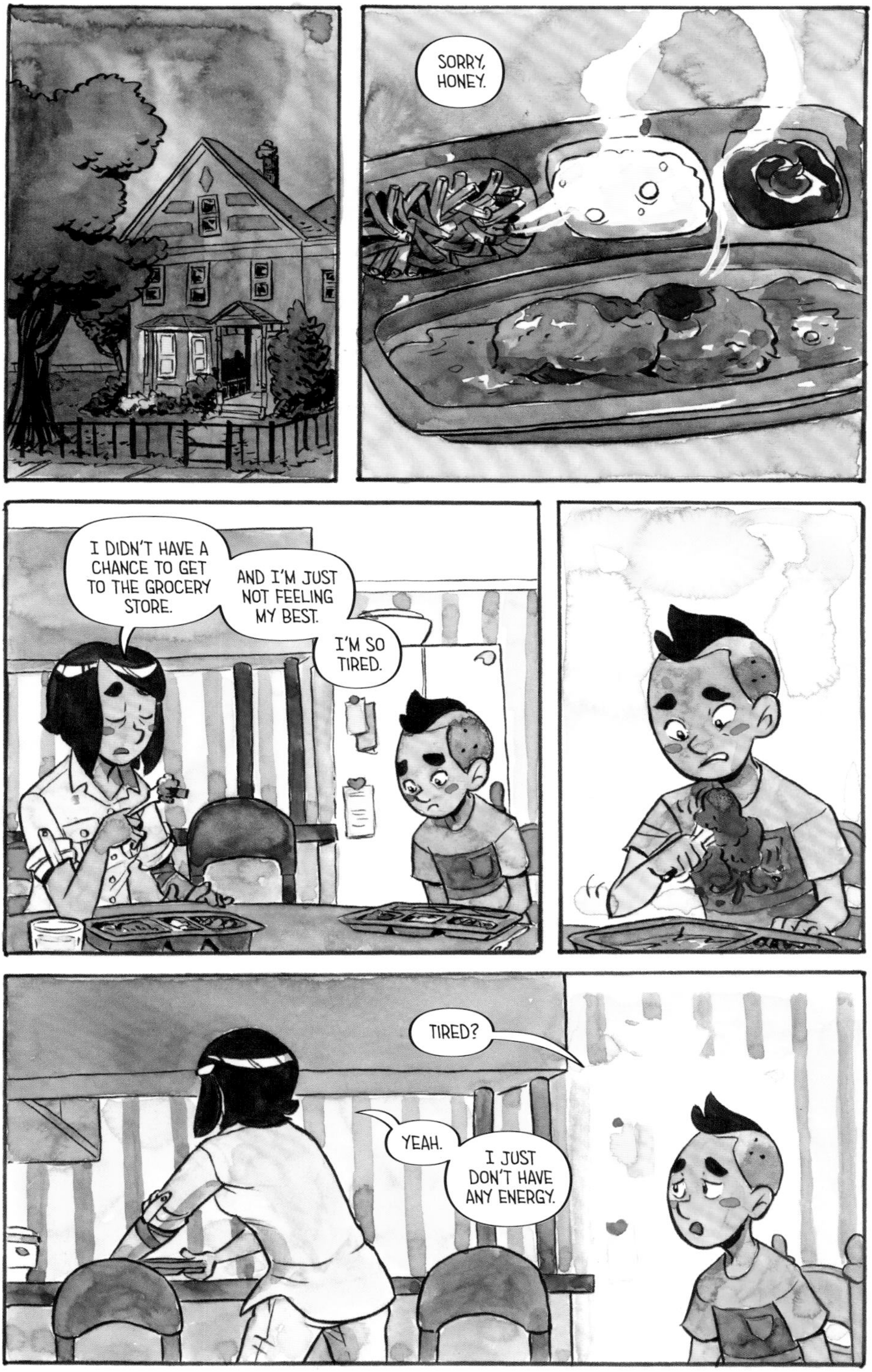
SORRY, HONEY.
I DIDN'T HAVE A CHANCE TO GET TO THE GROCERY STORE.
AND I'M JUST NOT FEELING MY BEST.
I'M SO TIRED.
TIRED?
YEAH.
I JUST DON'T HAVE ANY ENERGY.

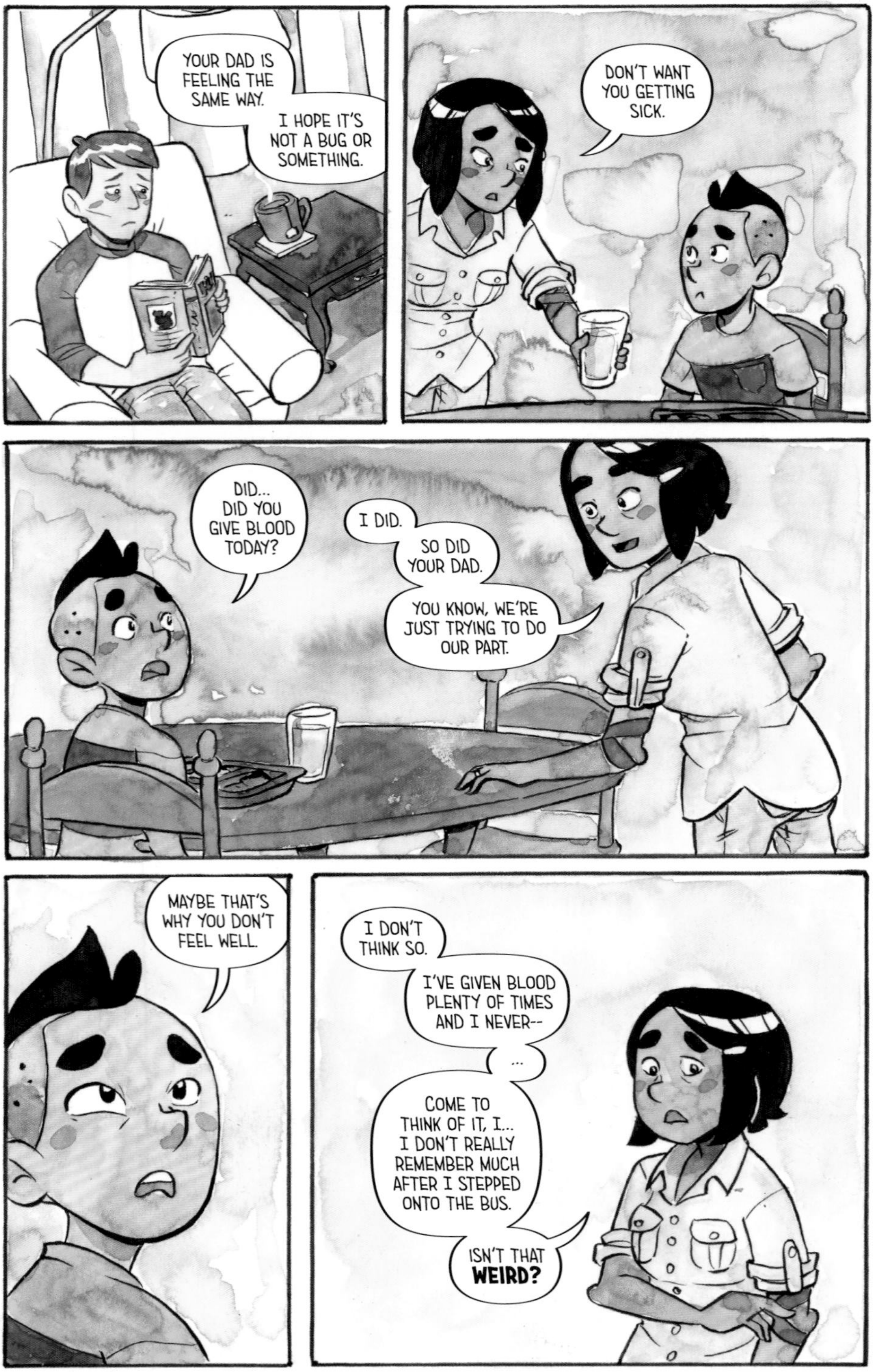
YOUR DAD IS FEELING THE SAME WAY.
I HOPE IT'S NOT A BUG OR SOMETHING.
DON'T WANT YOU GETTING SICK.
DID... DID YOU GIVE BLOOD TODAY?
I DID.
SO DID YOUR DAD.
YOU KNOW, WE'RE JUST TRYING TO DO OUR PART.
MAYBE THAT'S WHY YOU DON'T FEEL WELL.
I DON'T THINK SO.
I'VE GIVEN BLOOD PLENTY OF TIMES AND I NEVER--
...
COME TO THINK OF IT, I... I DON'T REALLY REMEMBER MUCH AFTER I STEPPED ONTO THE BUS.
ISN'T THAT **WEIRD?**

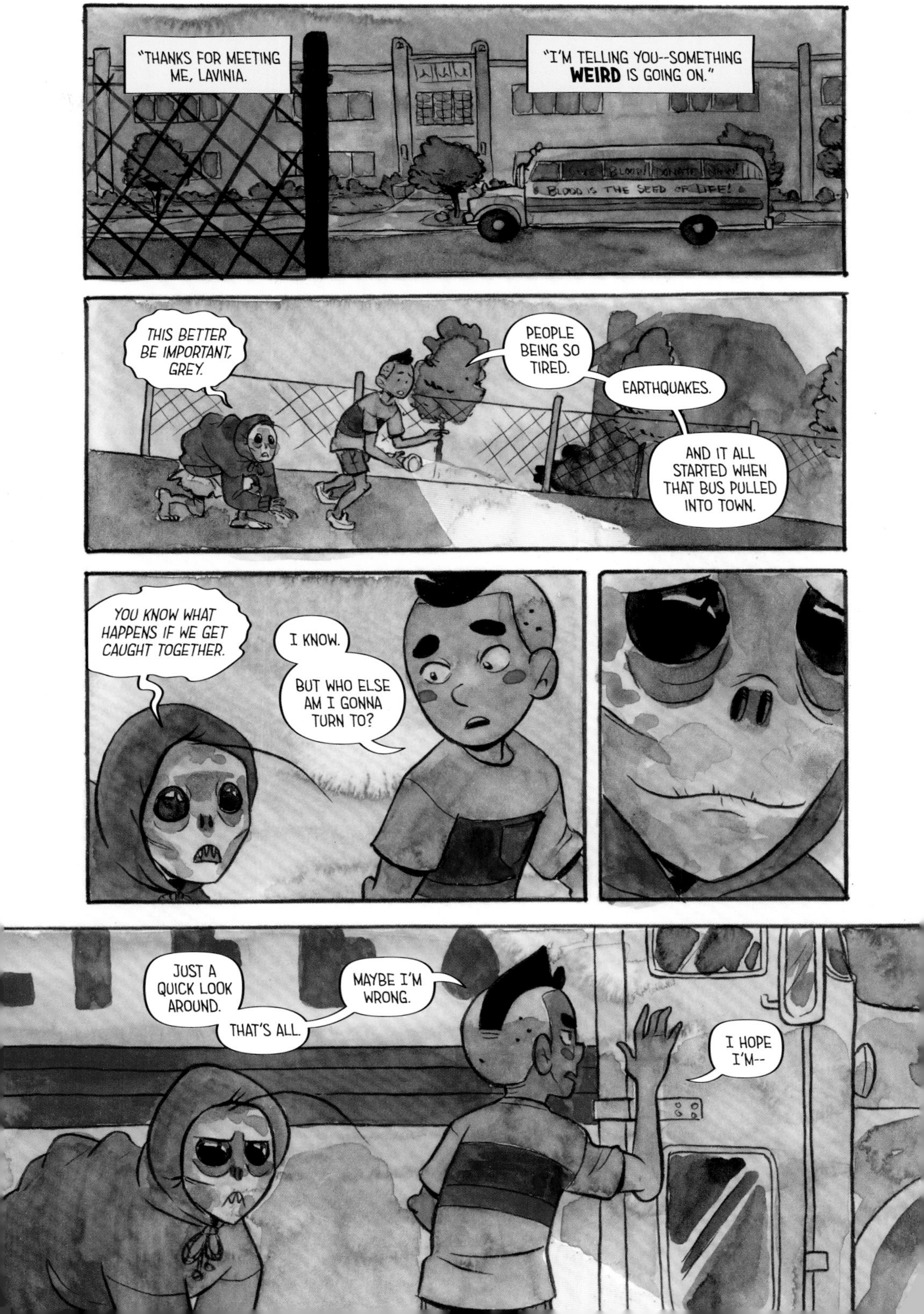
"THANKS FOR MEETING ME, LAVINIA.
"I'M TELLING YOU--SOMETHING **WEIRD** IS GOING ON."
SAVE BLOOD! DONATE NOW!
BLOOD IS THE SEED OF LIFE!
THIS BETTER BE IMPORTANT, GREY.
PEOPLE BEING SO TIRED.
EARTHQUAKES.
AND IT ALL STARTED WHEN THAT BUS PULLED INTO TOWN.
YOU KNOW WHAT HAPPENS IF WE GET CAUGHT TOGETHER.
I KNOW.
BUT WHO ELSE AM I GONNA TURN TO?
JUST A QUICK LOOK AROUND.
THAT'S ALL.
MAYBE I'M WRONG.
I HOPE I'M--

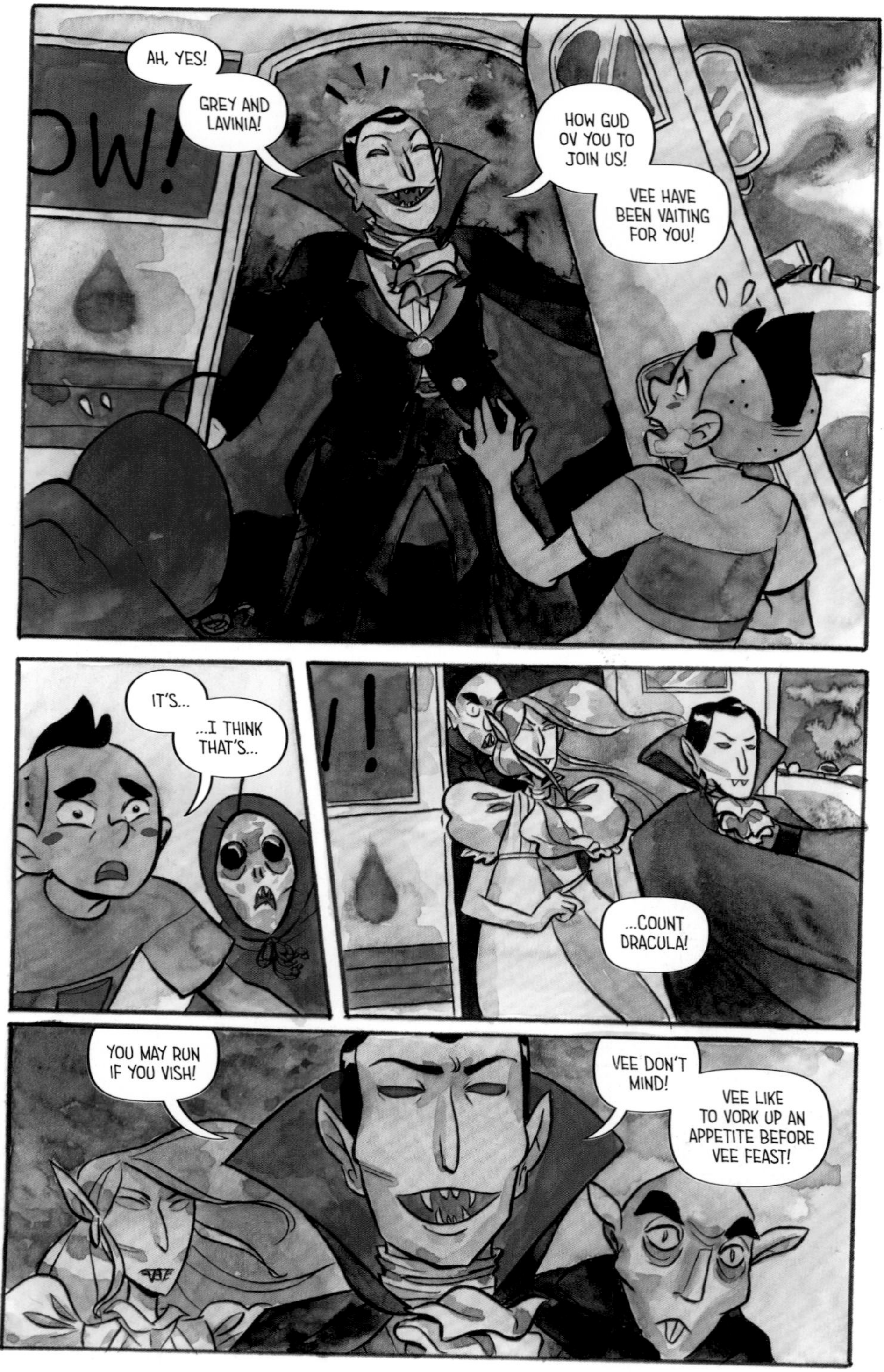
OW!
AH, YES!
GREY AND LAVINIA!
HOW GUD OV YOU TO JOIN US!
VEE HAVE BEEN VAITING FOR YOU!
IT'S...
...I THINK THAT'S...
!!
...COUNT DRACULA!
YOU MAY RUN IF YOU VISH!
VEE DON'T MIND!
VEE LIKE TO VORK UP AN APPETITE BEFORE VEE FEAST!

YAAAAAGGGGH!
LAVINIA!
WAIT!
DON'T LEAVE ME!

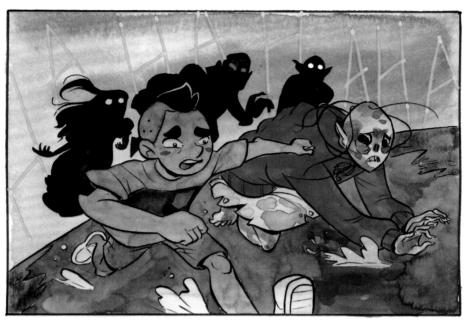

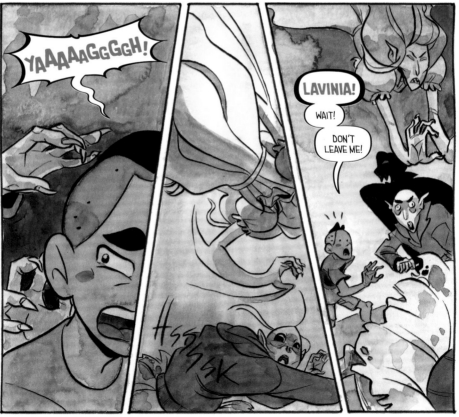

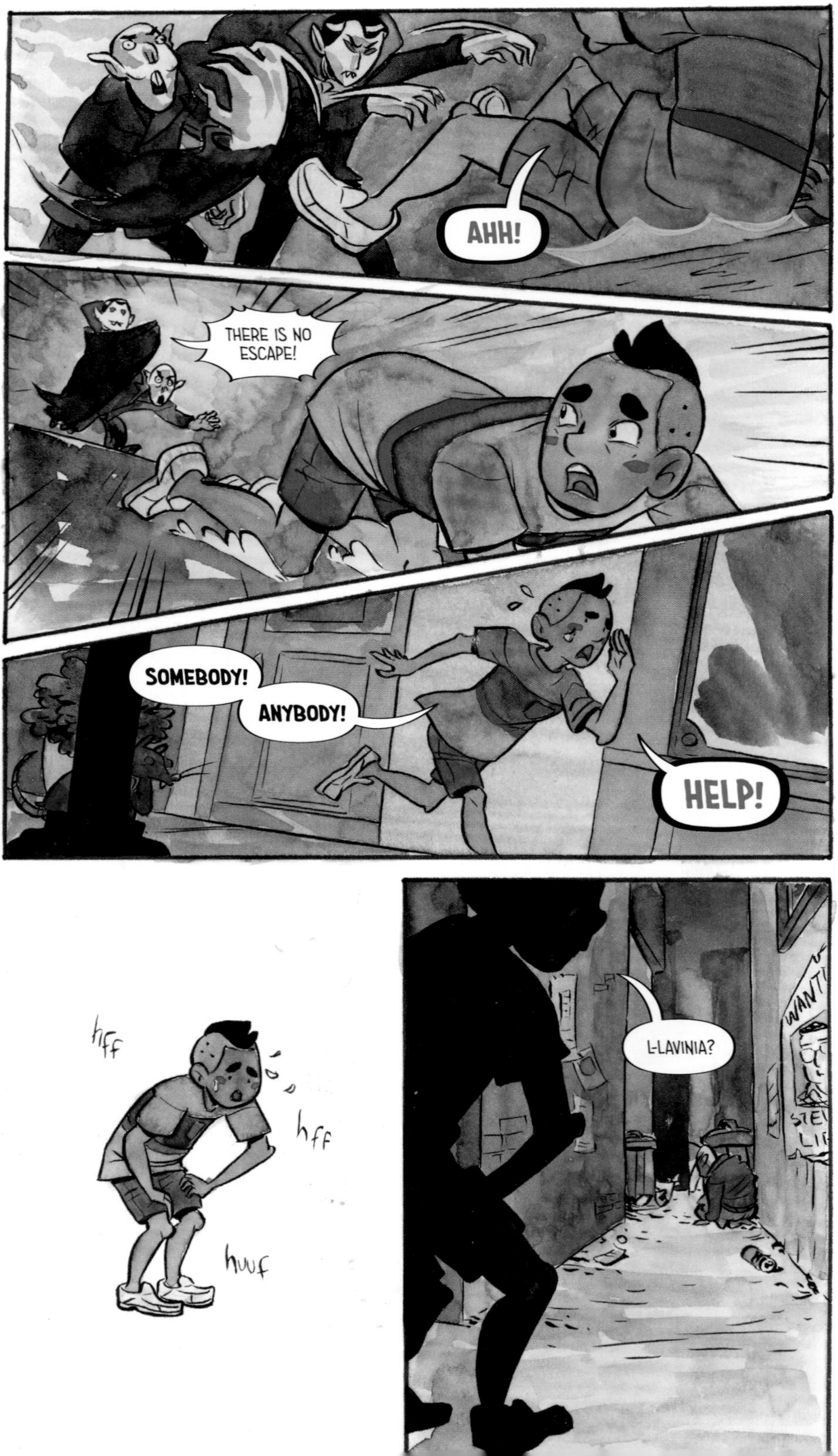
AHH!
THERE IS NO ESCAPE!
SOMEBODY!
ANYBODY!
HELP!
hff
hff
huuf
L-LAVINIA?

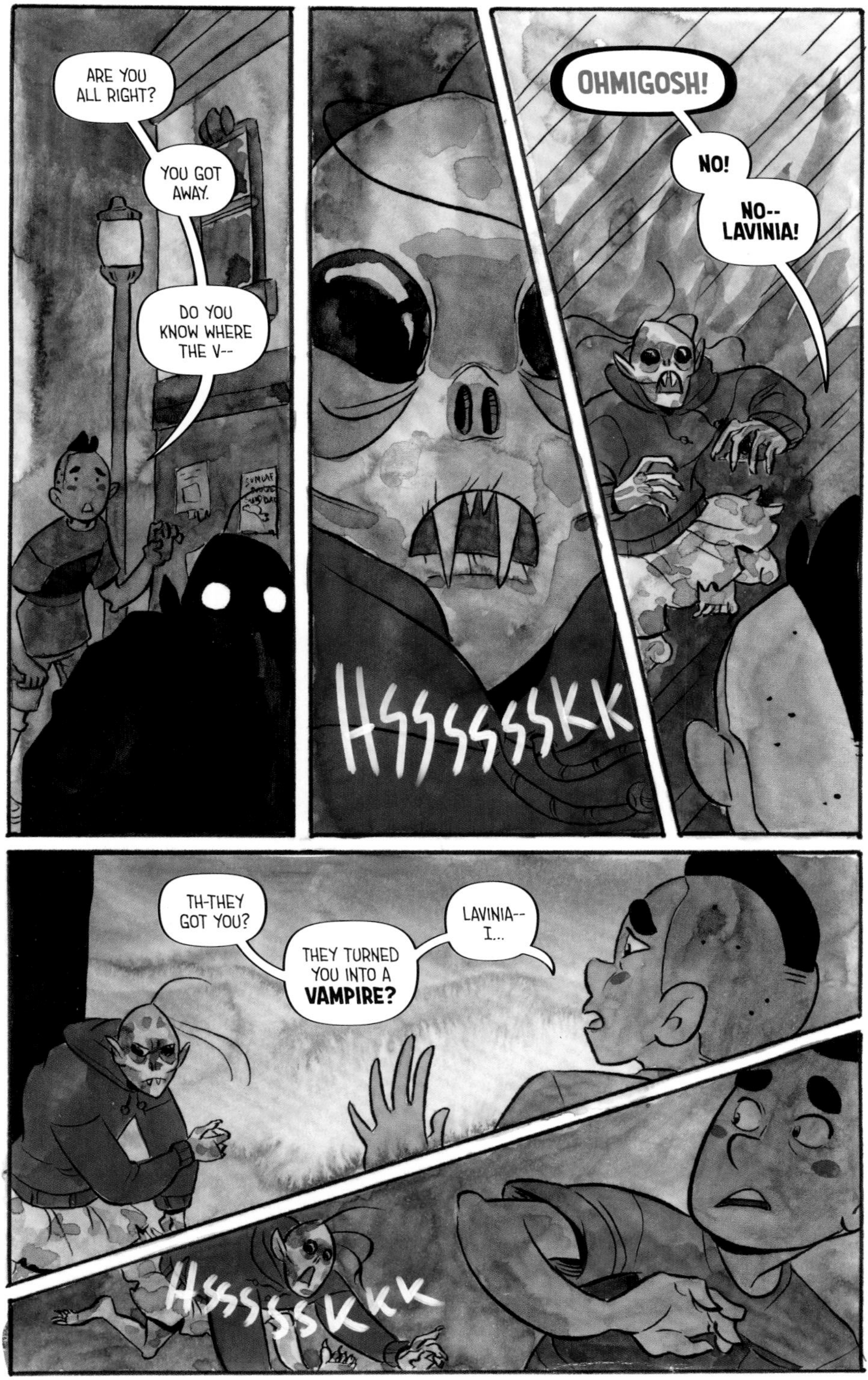
ARE YOU ALL RIGHT?
YOU GOT AWAY.
DO YOU KNOW WHERE THE V--
HSSSSSSSKK
OHMIGOSH!
NO!
NO-- LAVINIA!
TH-THEY GOT YOU?
THEY TURNED YOU INTO A **VAMPIRE?**
LAVINIA-- I...
HSSSSSKKK

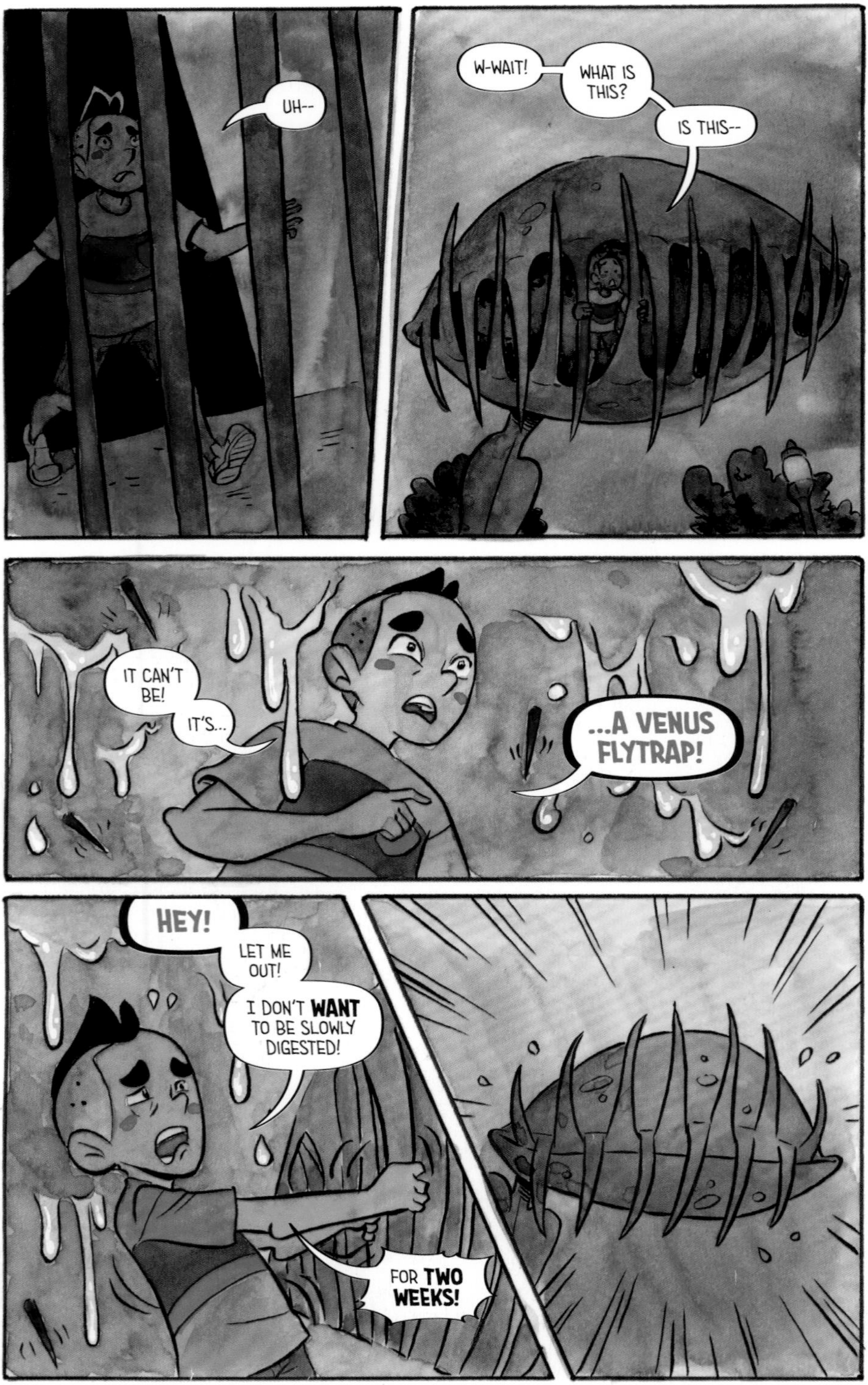
UH--
W-WAIT!
WHAT IS THIS?
IS THIS--
IT CAN'T BE!
IT'S...
...A VENUS FLYTRAP!
HEY!
LET ME OUT!
I DON'T **WANT** TO BE SLOWLY DIGESTED!
FOR **TWO WEEKS!**

NOT DIGESTED!
MARS
IT WAS JUST ANOTHER NIGHTMARE.

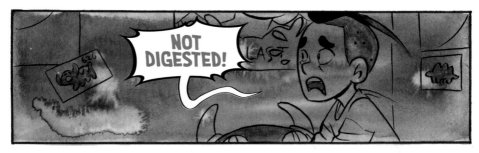

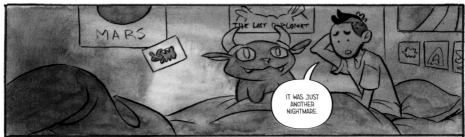

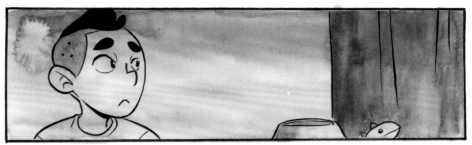

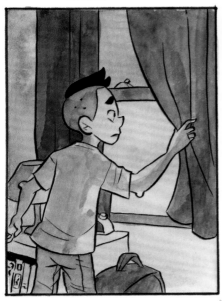

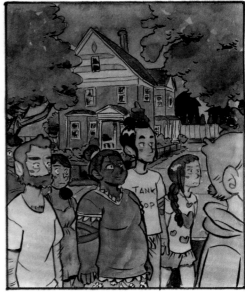

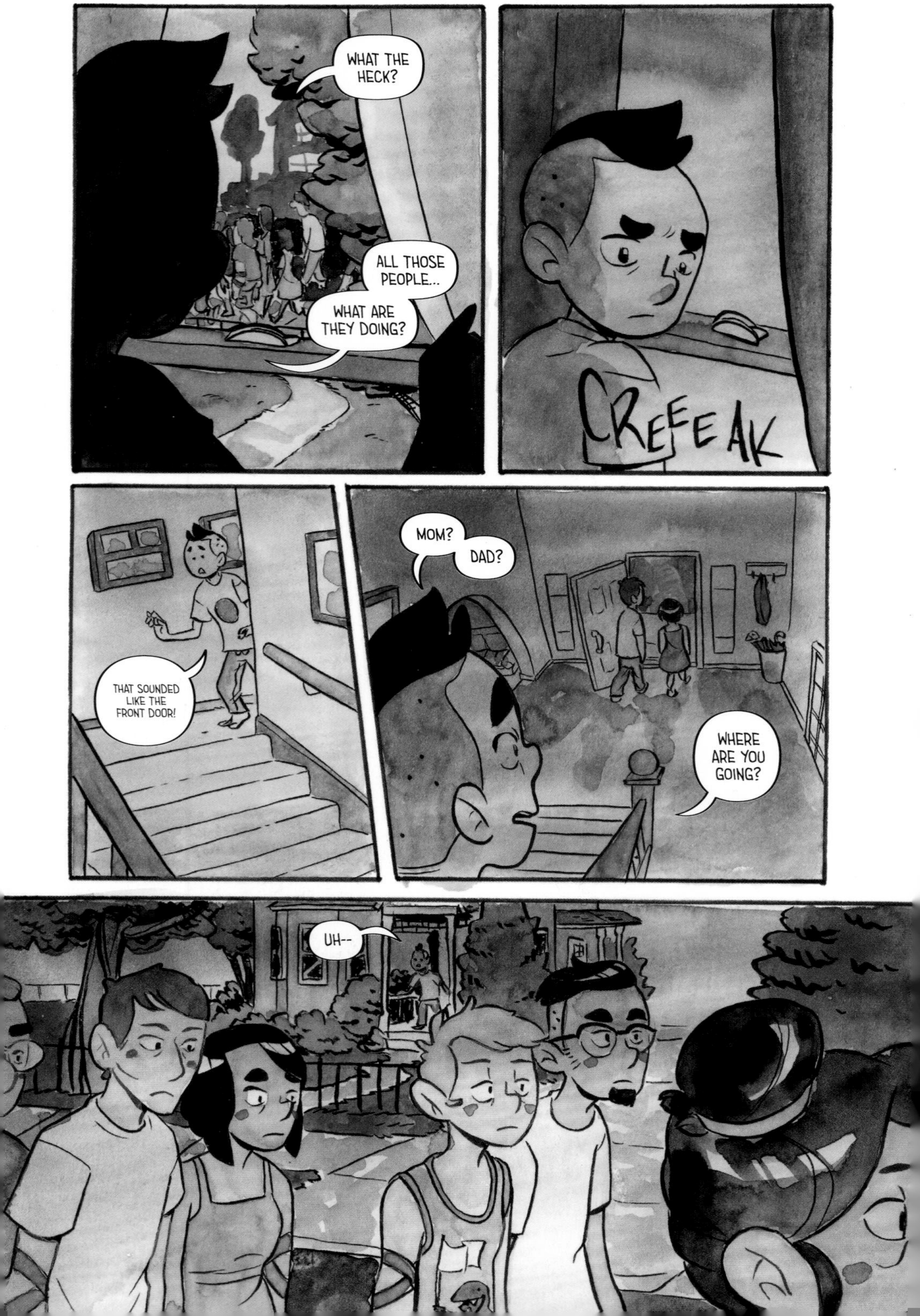
WHAT THE HECK?
ALL THOSE PEOPLE...
WHAT ARE THEY DOING?
CREEEAK
THAT SOUNDED LIKE THE FRONT DOOR!
MOM?
DAD?
WHERE ARE YOU GOING?
UH--

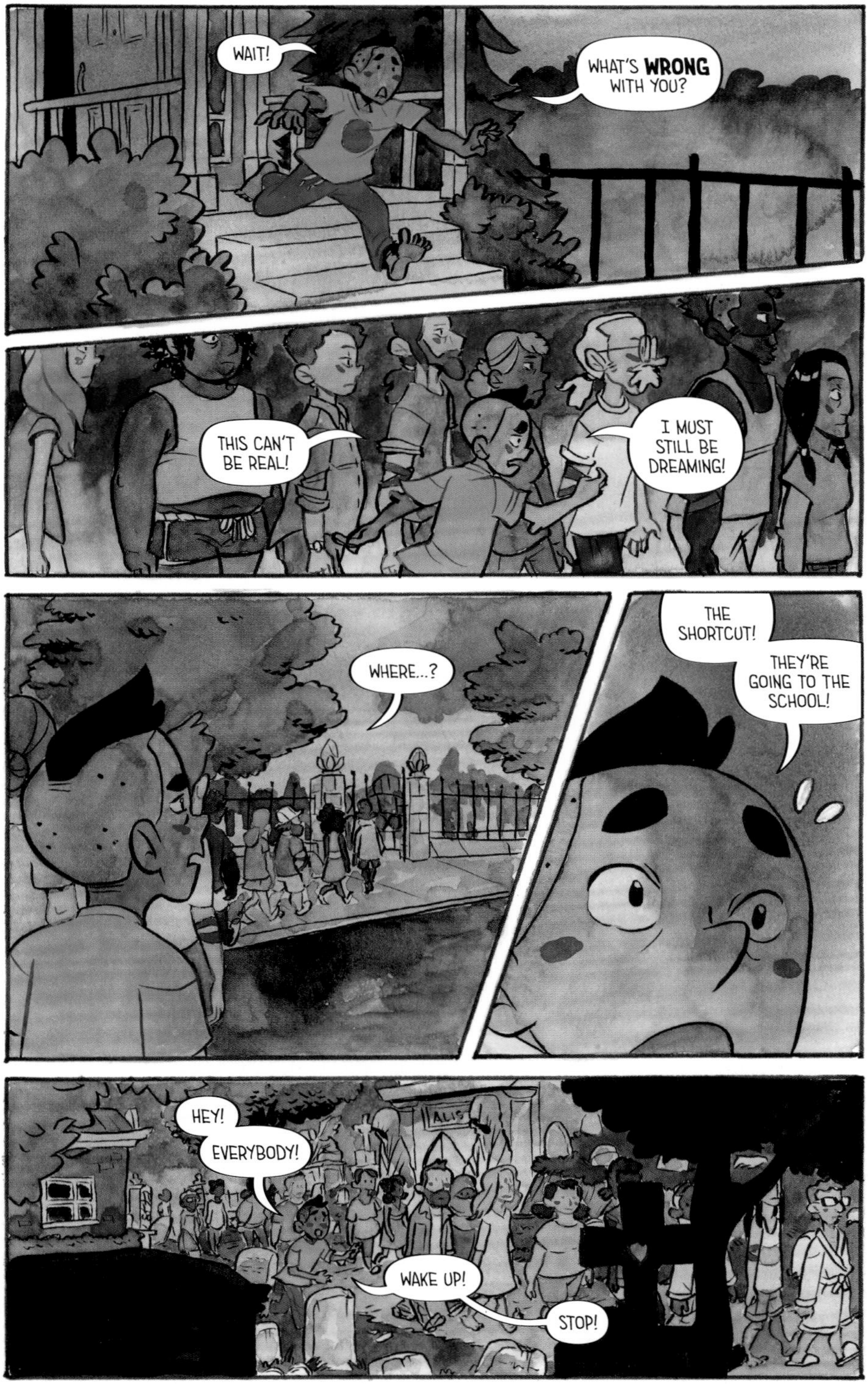
WAIT!
WHAT'S **WRONG** WITH YOU?
THIS CAN'T BE REAL!
I MUST STILL BE DREAMING!
WHERE...?
THE SHORTCUT!
THEY'RE GOING TO THE SCHOOL!
HEY!
EVERYBODY!
WAKE UP!
STOP!

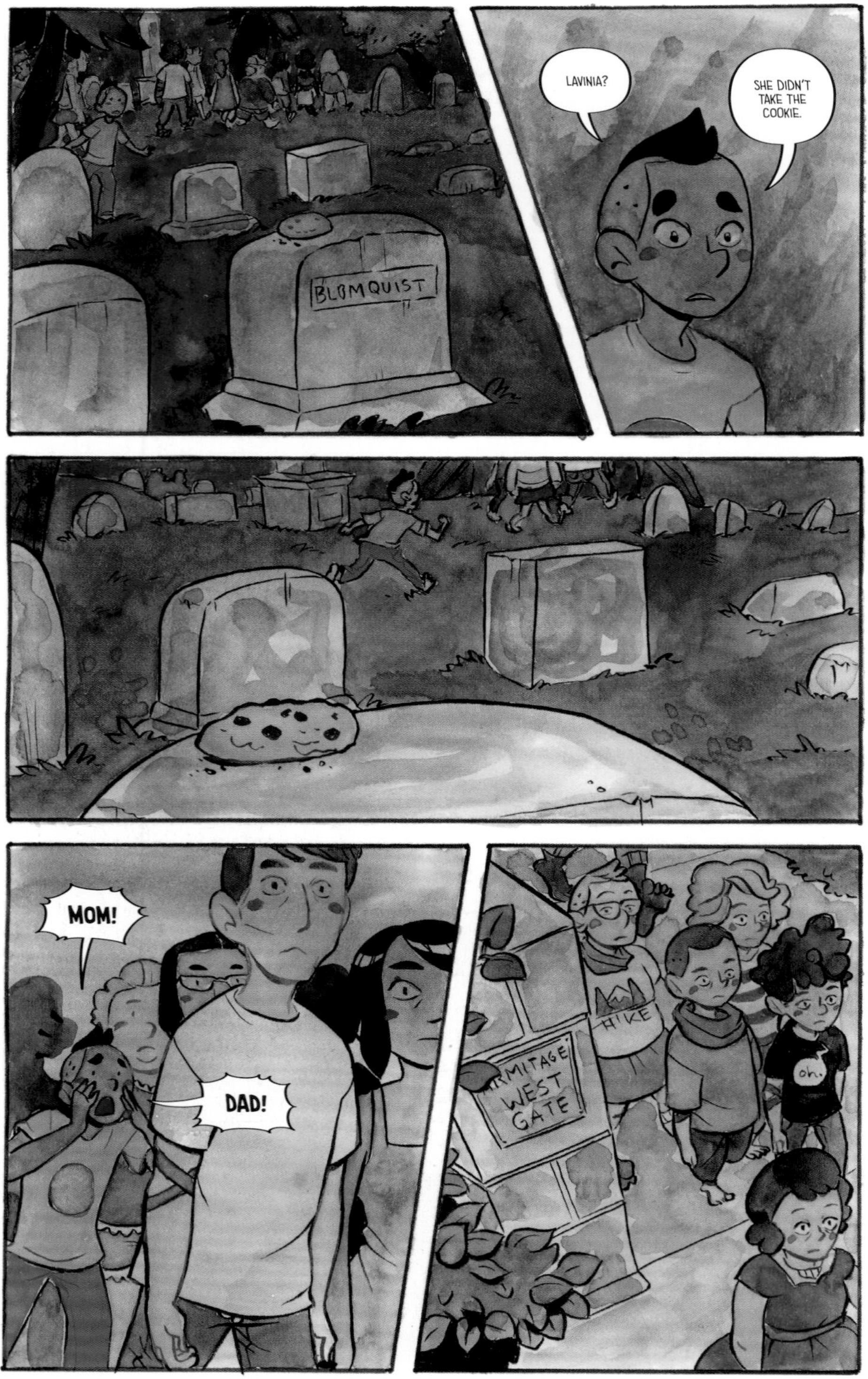
BLOMQUIST
LAVINIA?
SHE DIDN'T TAKE THE COOKIE.
MOM!
DAD!
HIKE
RMITAGE WEST GATE
oh.

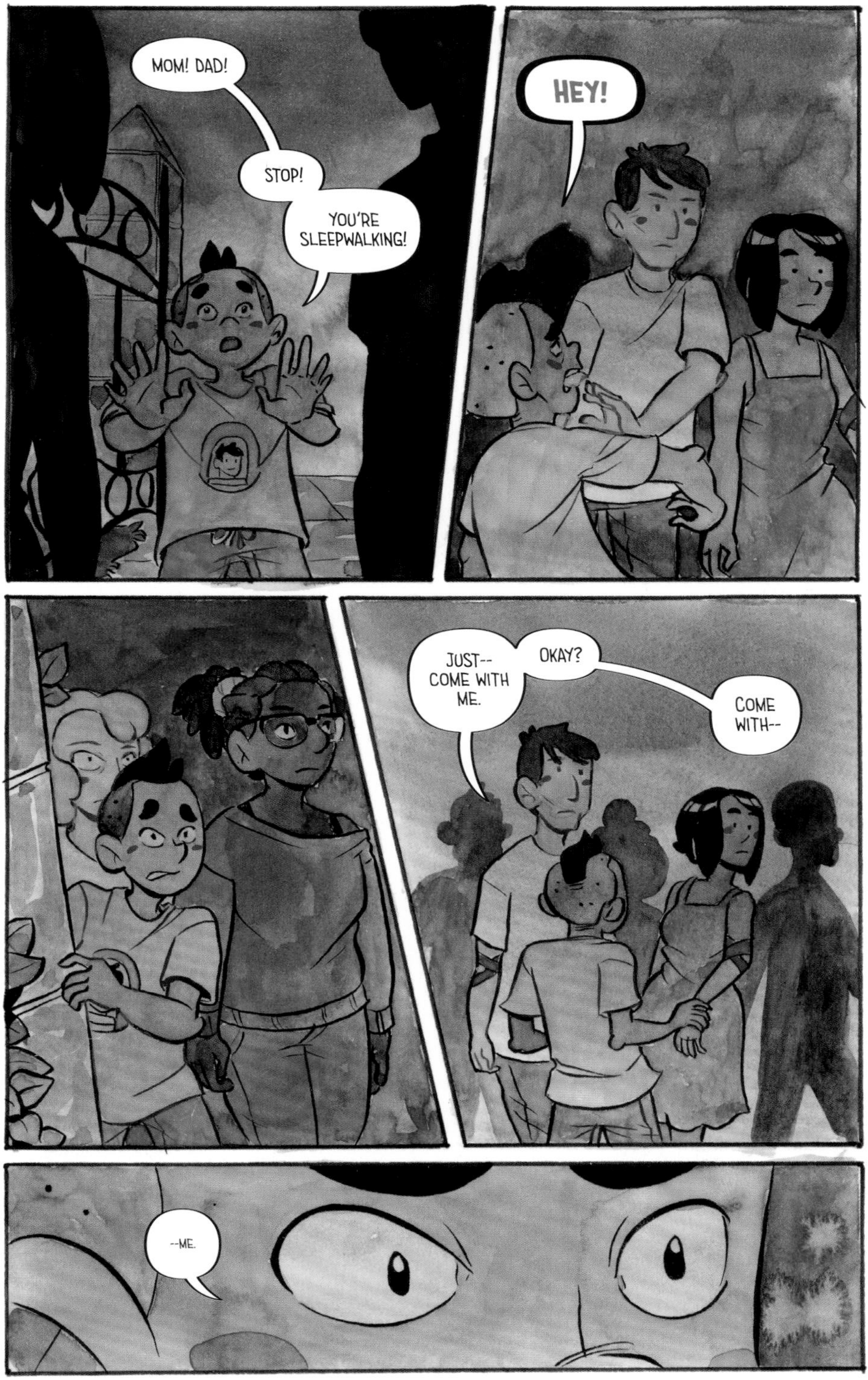
MOM! DAD!
STOP!
YOU'RE SLEEPWALKING!
HEY!
JUST-- COME WITH ME.
OKAY?
COME WITH--
--ME.

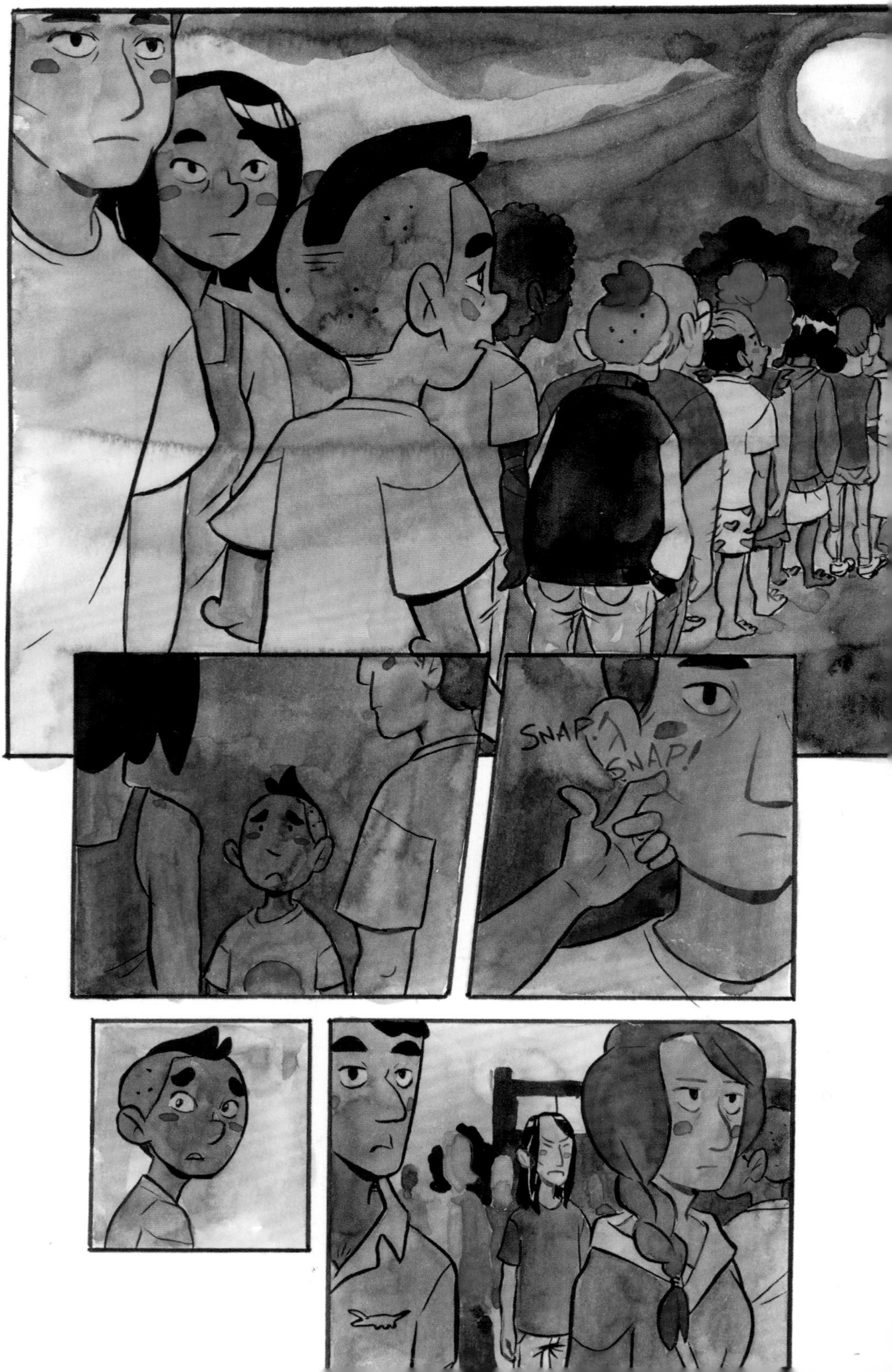
SNAP!
SNAP!

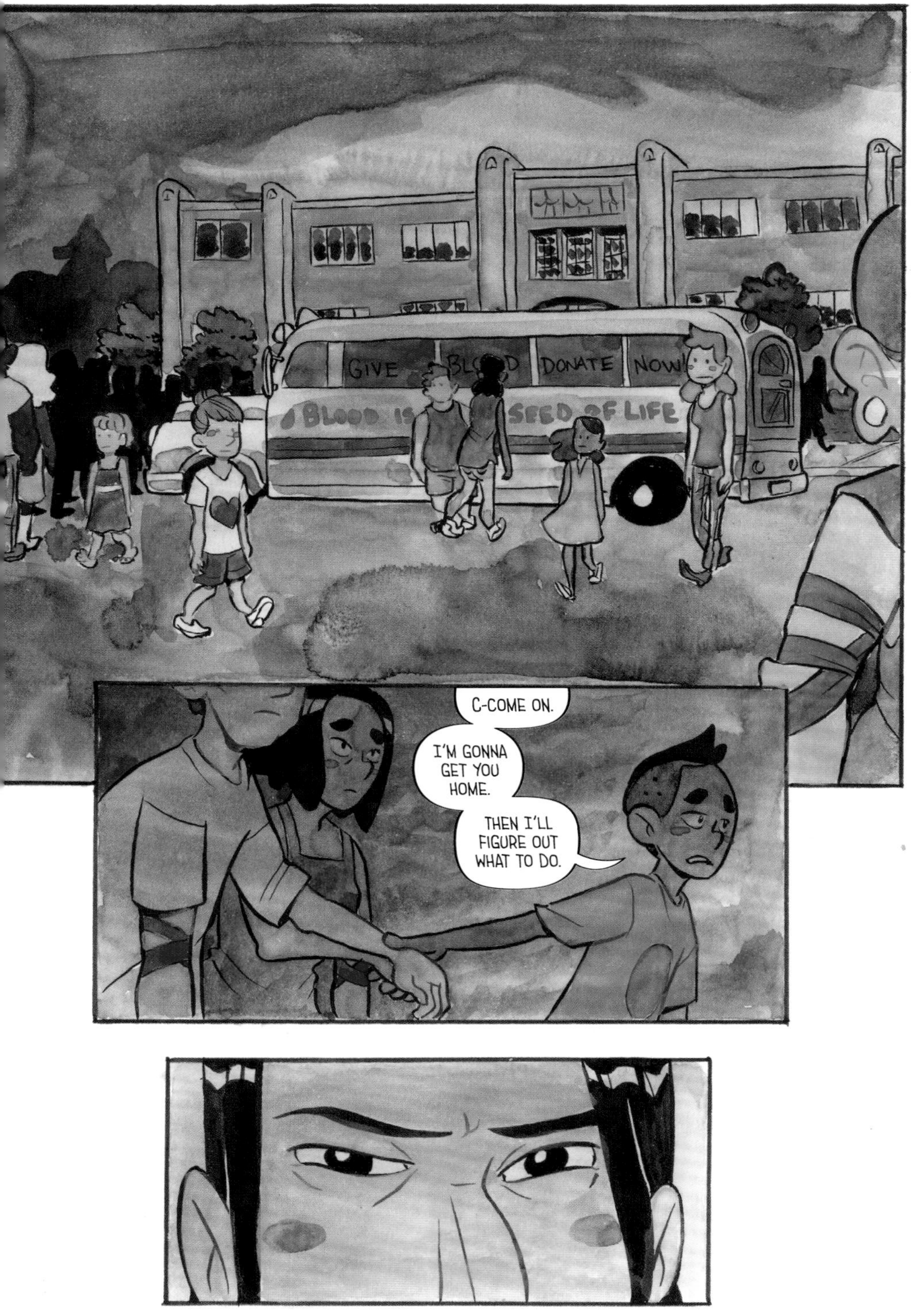
GIVE
DONATE
NOW!
BLOOD IS
SEED OF LIFE
C-COME ON.
I'M GONNA GET YOU HOME.
THEN I'LL FIGURE OUT WHAT TO DO.

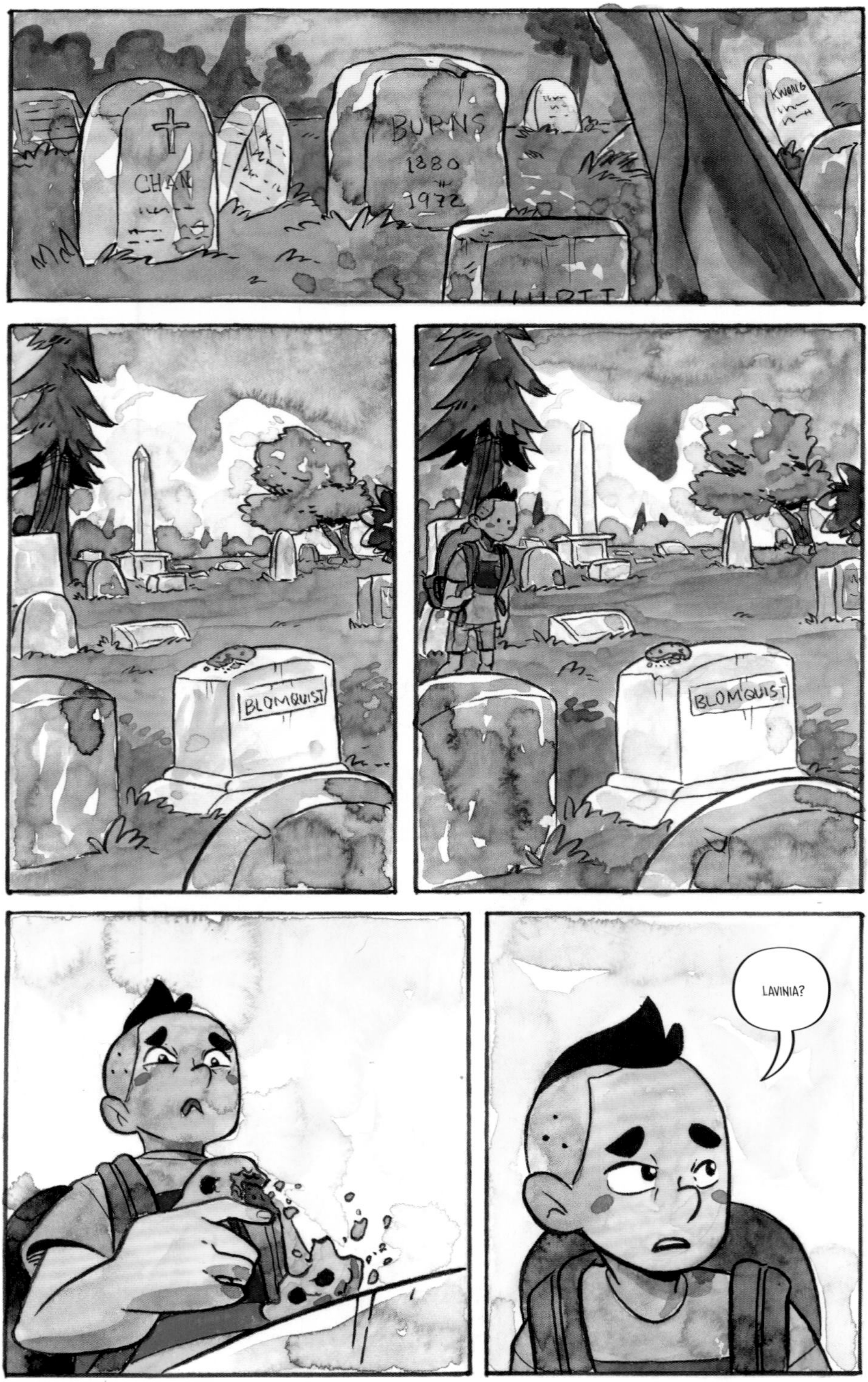
CHAN
BURNS
1880
1972
KWONG
BLOMQUIST
BLOMQUIST
LAVINIA?

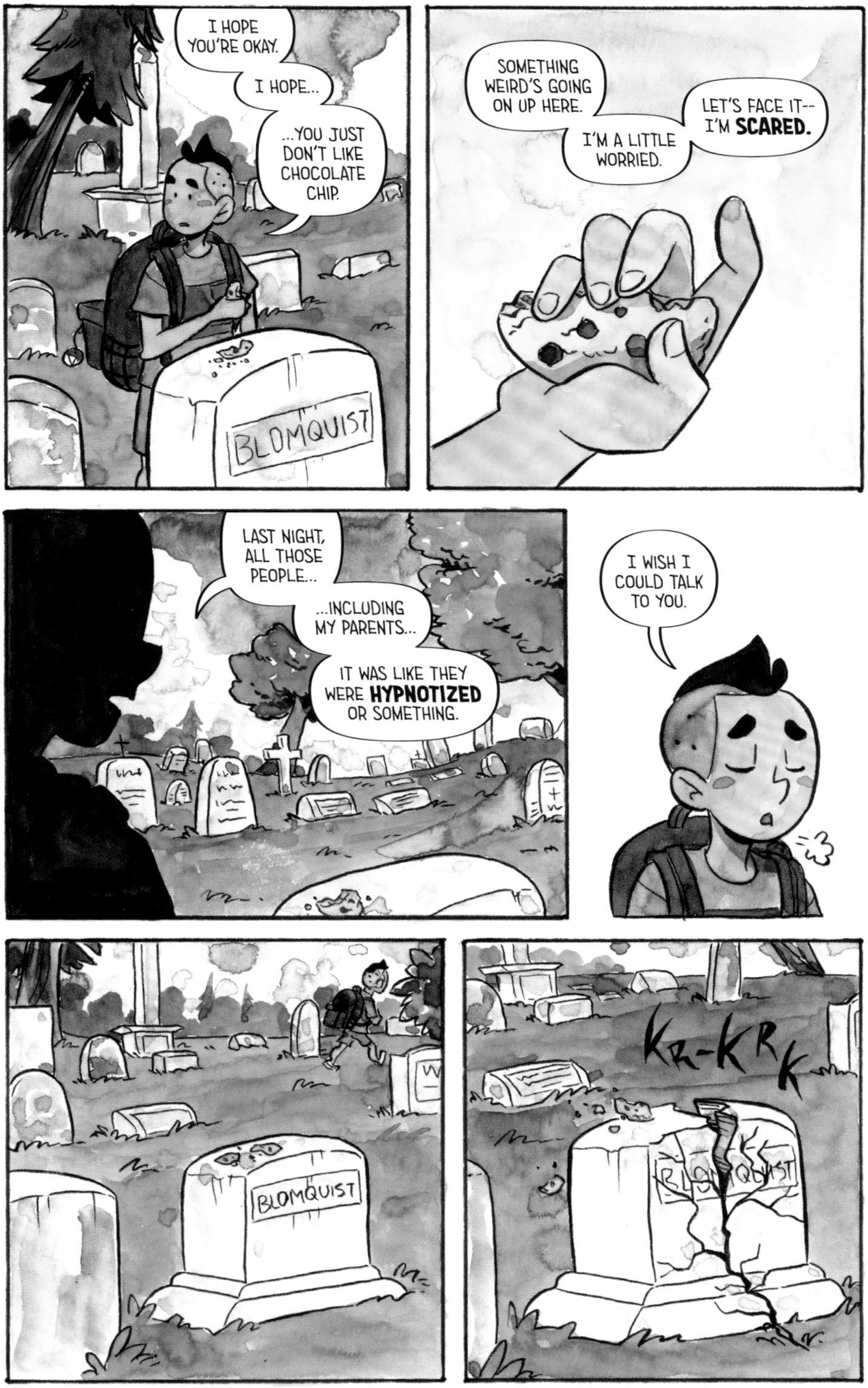

I HOPE YOU'RE OKAY.
I HOPE...
...YOU JUST DON'T LIKE CHOCOLATE CHIP.
BLOMQUIST
SOMETHING WEIRD'S GOING ON UP HERE.
I'M A LITTLE WORRIED.
LET'S FACE IT-- I'M **SCARED.**
LAST NIGHT, ALL THOSE PEOPLE...
...INCLUDING MY PARENTS...
IT WAS LIKE THEY WERE **HYPNOTIZED** OR SOMETHING.
I WISH I COULD TALK TO YOU.
BLOMQUIST
KR-KRRK

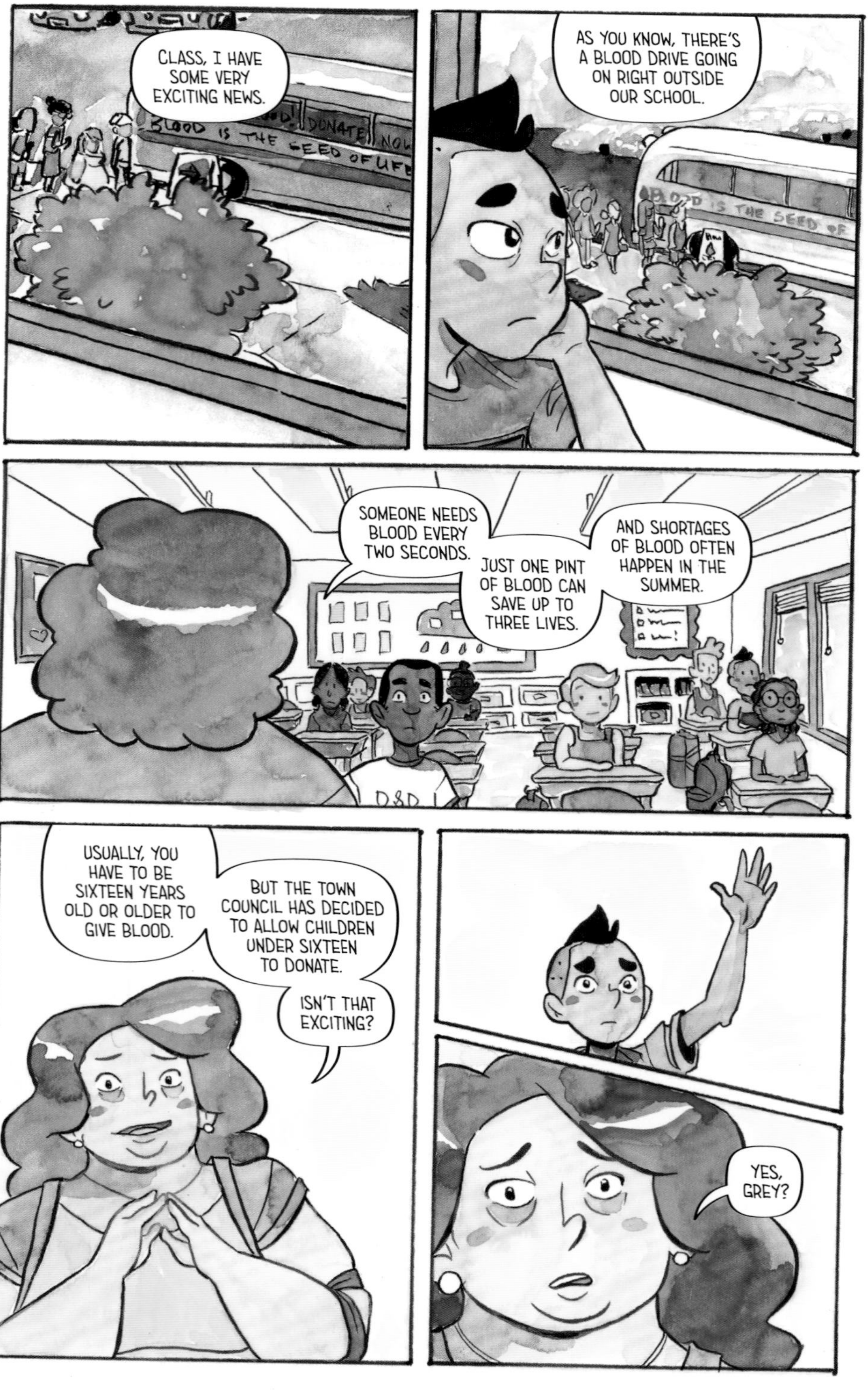
CLASS, I HAVE SOME VERY EXCITING NEWS.
AS YOU KNOW, THERE'S A BLOOD DRIVE GOING ON RIGHT OUTSIDE OUR SCHOOL.
SOMEONE NEEDS BLOOD EVERY TWO SECONDS.
JUST ONE PINT OF BLOOD CAN SAVE UP TO THREE LIVES.
AND SHORTAGES OF BLOOD OFTEN HAPPEN IN THE SUMMER.
USUALLY, YOU HAVE TO BE SIXTEEN YEARS OLD OR OLDER TO GIVE BLOOD.
BUT THE TOWN COUNCIL HAS DECIDED TO ALLOW CHILDREN UNDER SIXTEEN TO DONATE.
ISN'T THAT EXCITING?
YES, GREY?

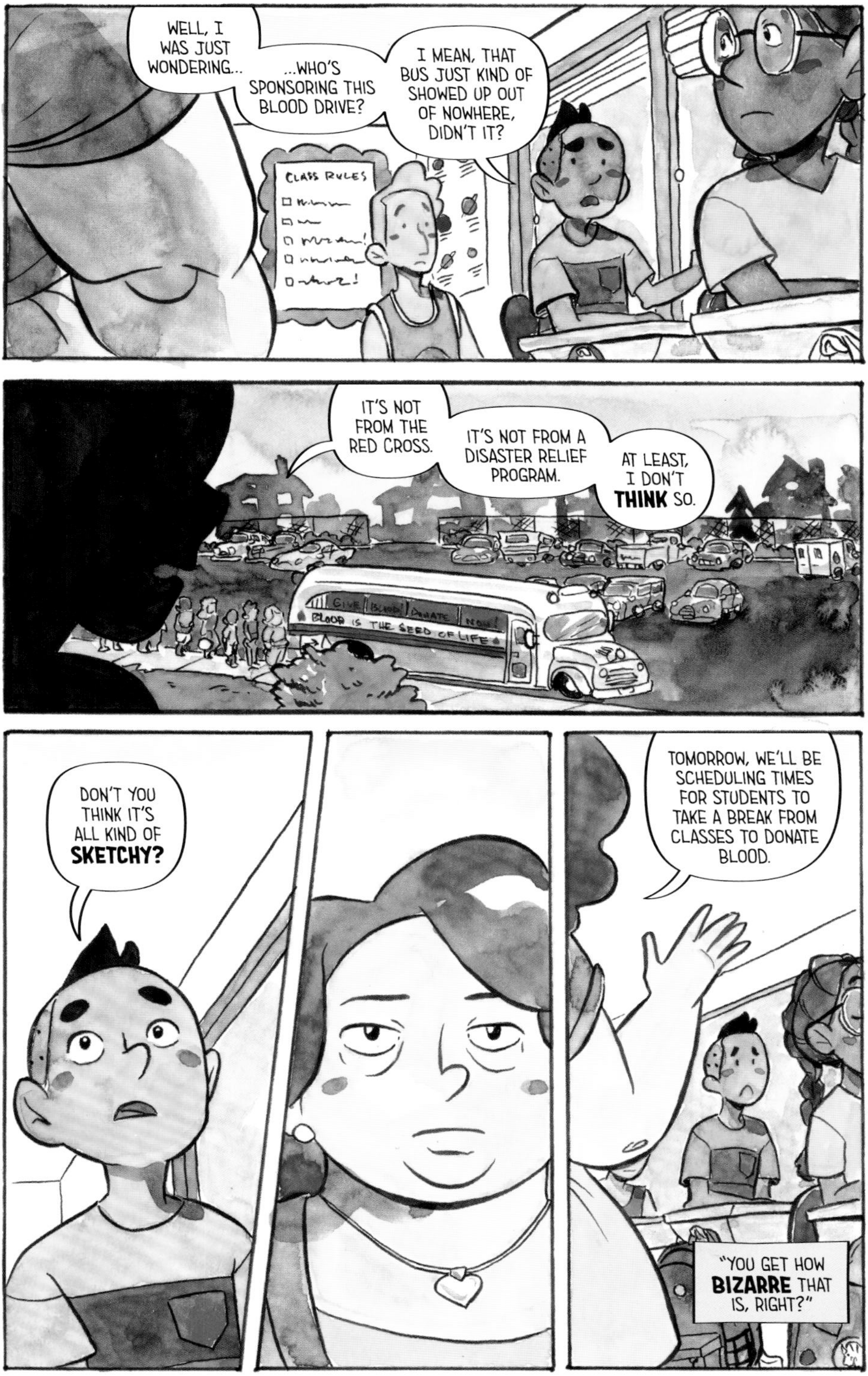

WELL, I WAS JUST WONDERING...
...WHO'S SPONSORING THIS BLOOD DRIVE?
I MEAN, THAT BUS JUST KIND OF SHOWED UP OUT OF NOWHERE, DIDN'T IT?
CLASS RULES
IT'S NOT FROM THE RED CROSS.
IT'S NOT FROM A DISASTER RELIEF PROGRAM.
AT LEAST, I DON'T **THINK** SO.
GIVE BLOOD! DONATE NOW!
BLOOD IS THE SEED OF LIFE
DON'T YOU THINK IT'S ALL KIND OF **SKETCHY?**
TOMORROW, WE'LL BE SCHEDULING TIMES FOR STUDENTS TO TAKE A BREAK FROM CLASSES TO DONATE BLOOD.
"YOU GET HOW **BIZARRE** THAT IS, RIGHT?"

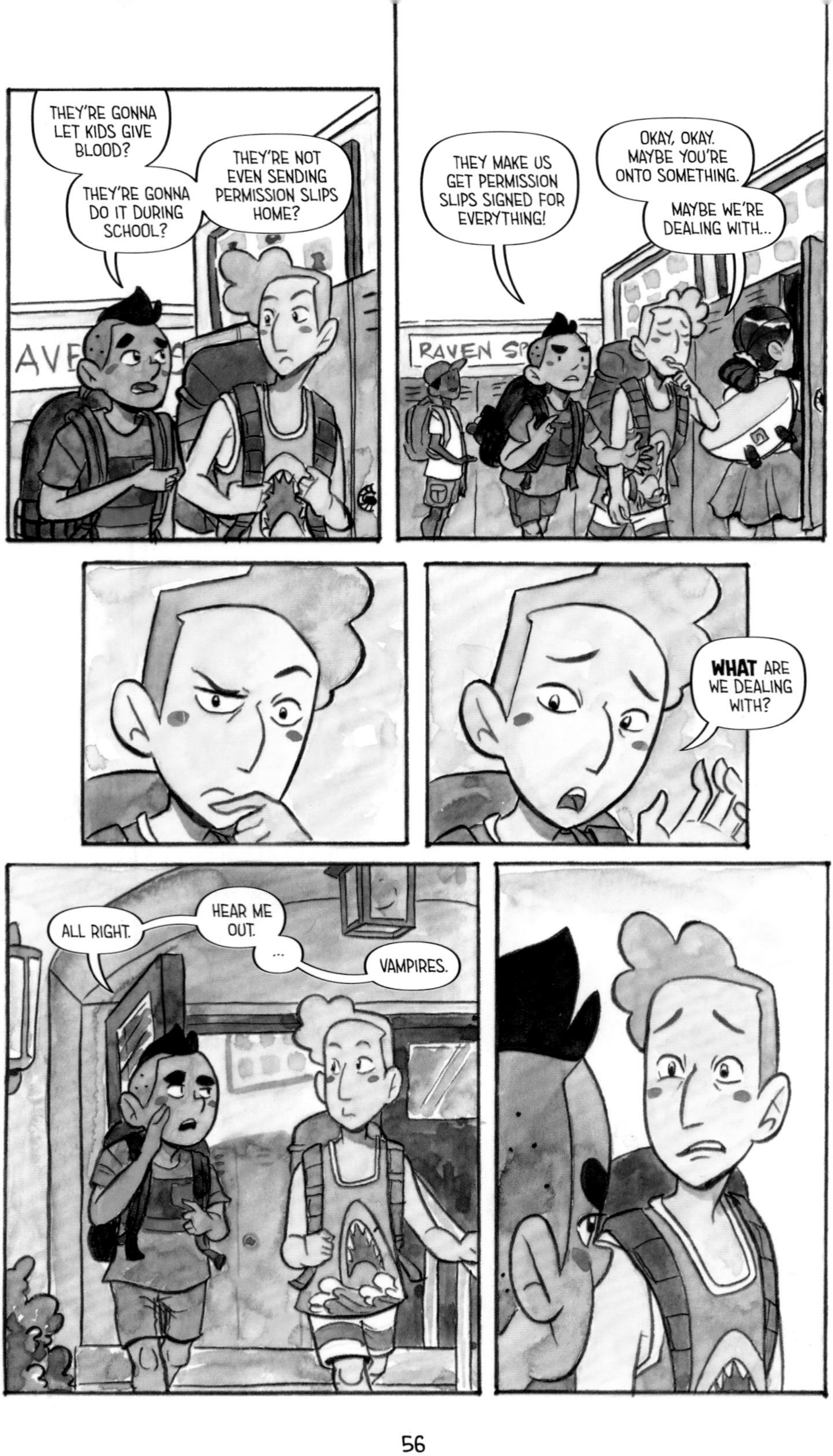
THEY'RE GONNA LET KIDS GIVE BLOOD?
THEY'RE GONNA DO IT DURING SCHOOL?
THEY'RE NOT EVEN SENDING PERMISSION SLIPS HOME?
AVE
THEY MAKE US GET PERMISSION SLIPS SIGNED FOR EVERYTHING!
OKAY, OKAY. MAYBE YOU'RE ONTO SOMETHING.
MAYBE WE'RE DEALING WITH...
RAVEN SP
WHAT ARE WE DEALING WITH?
ALL RIGHT.
HEAR ME OUT.
...
VAMPIRES.

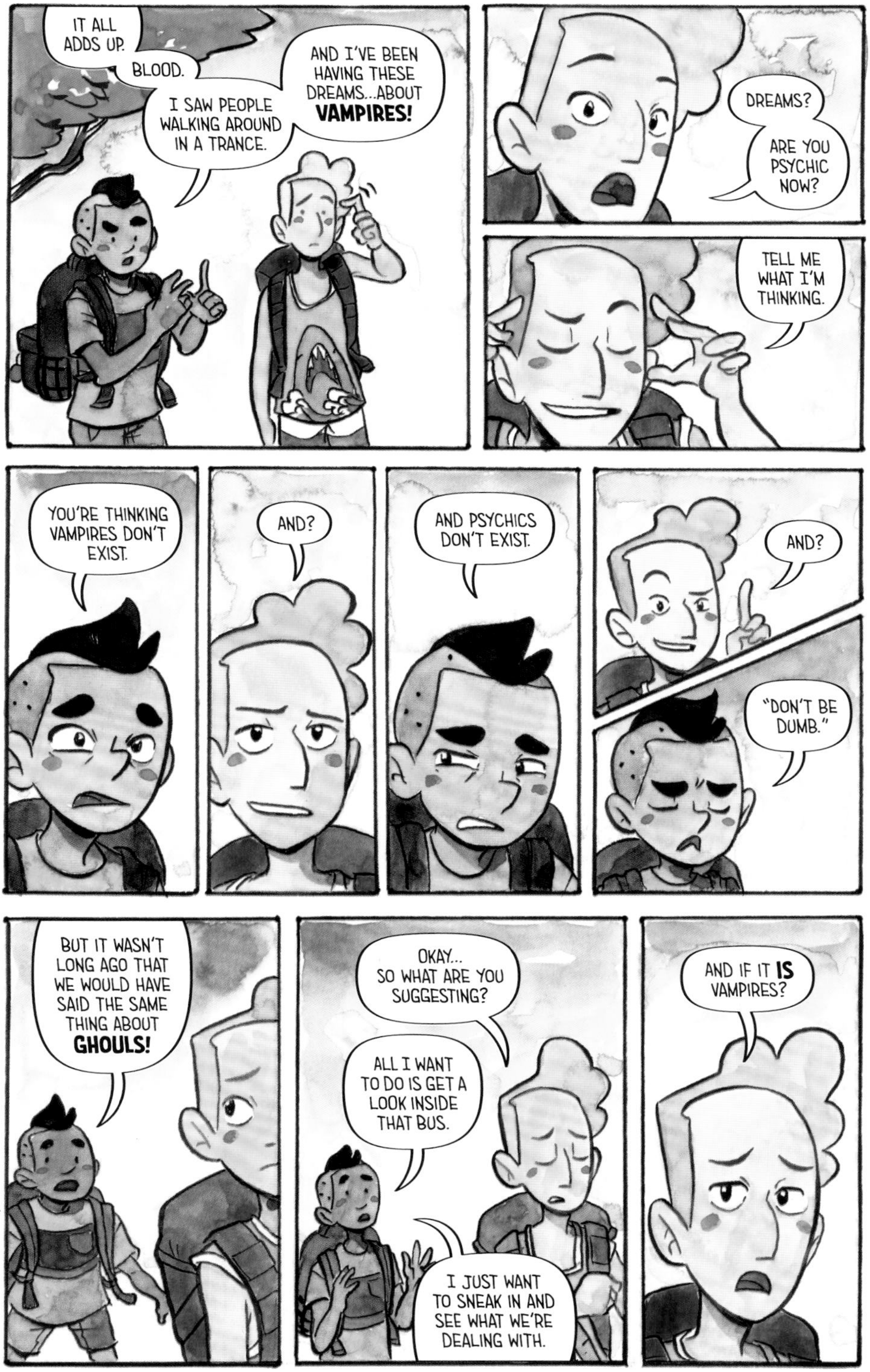
IT ALL ADDS UP.
BLOOD.
I SAW PEOPLE WALKING AROUND IN A TRANCE.
AND I'VE BEEN HAVING THESE DREAMS...ABOUT **VAMPIRES!**
DREAMS?
ARE YOU PSYCHIC NOW?
TELL ME WHAT I'M THINKING.
YOU'RE THINKING VAMPIRES DON'T EXIST.
AND?
AND PSYCHICS DON'T EXIST.
AND?
"DON'T BE DUMB."
BUT IT WASN'T LONG AGO THAT WE WOULD HAVE SAID THE SAME THING ABOUT **GHOULS!**
OKAY... SO WHAT ARE YOU SUGGESTING?
ALL I WANT TO DO IS GET A LOOK INSIDE THAT BUS.
I JUST WANT TO SNEAK IN AND SEE WHAT WE'RE DEALING WITH.
AND IF IT **IS** VAMPIRES?

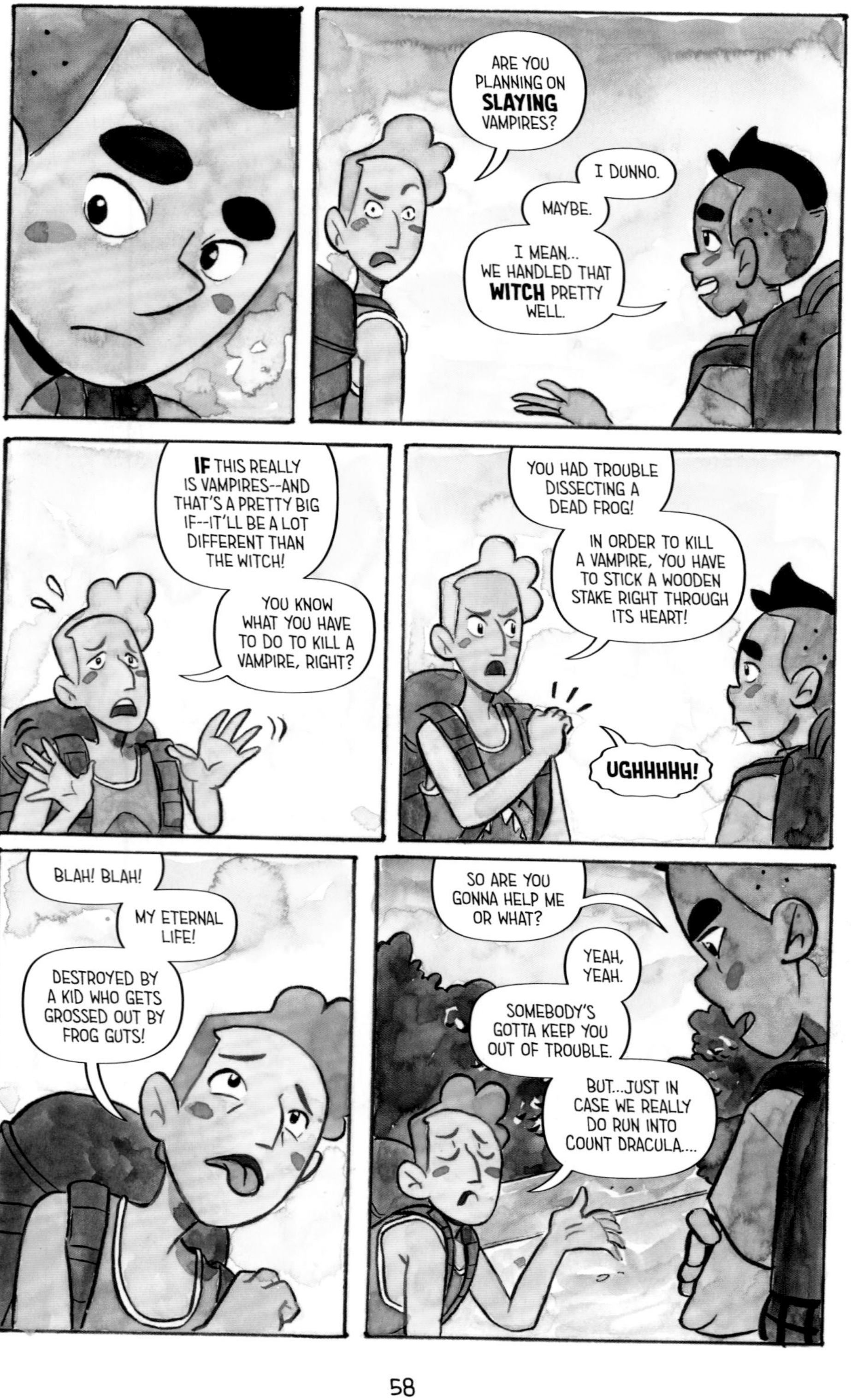

ARE YOU PLANNING ON **SLAYING** VAMPIRES?
I DUNNO.
MAYBE.
I MEAN... WE HANDLED THAT **WITCH** PRETTY WELL.
IF THIS REALLY IS VAMPIRES--AND THAT'S A PRETTY BIG IF--IT'LL BE A LOT DIFFERENT THAN THE WITCH!
YOU KNOW WHAT YOU HAVE TO DO TO KILL A VAMPIRE, RIGHT?
YOU HAD TROUBLE DISSECTING A DEAD FROG!
IN ORDER TO KILL A VAMPIRE, YOU HAVE TO STICK A WOODEN STAKE RIGHT THROUGH ITS HEART!
UGHHHHH!
BLAH! BLAH!
MY ETERNAL LIFE!
DESTROYED BY A KID WHO GETS GROSSED OUT BY FROG GUTS!
SO ARE YOU GONNA HELP ME OR WHAT?
YEAH, YEAH.
SOMEBODY'S GOTTA KEEP YOU OUT OF TROUBLE.
BUT...JUST IN CASE WE REALLY DO RUN INTO COUNT DRACULA....

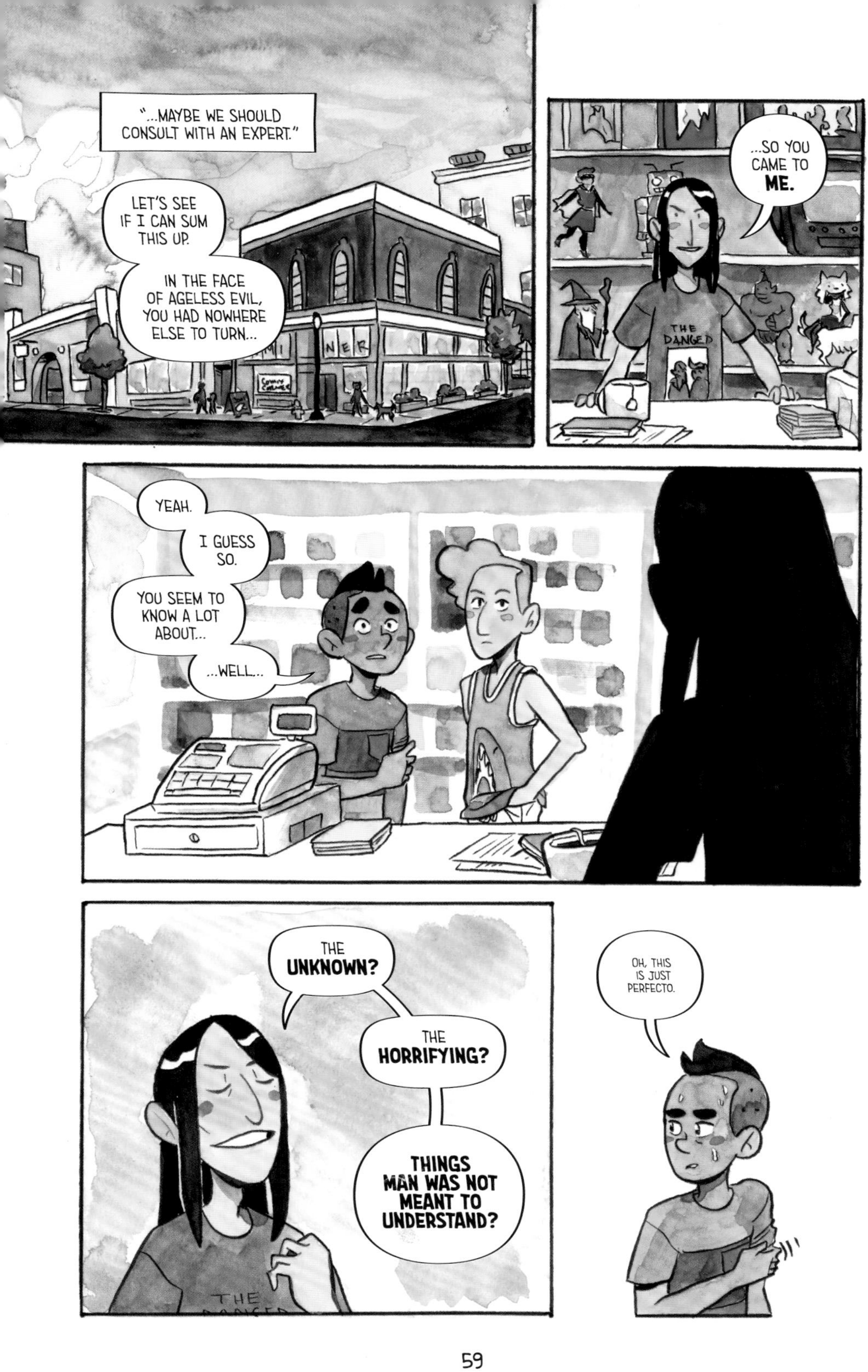
"...MAYBE WE SHOULD CONSULT WITH AN EXPERT."
LET'S SEE IF I CAN SUM THIS UP.
IN THE FACE OF AGELESS EVIL, YOU HAD NOWHERE ELSE TO TURN...
...SO YOU CAME TO **ME.**
THE DANGED
YEAH.
I GUESS SO.
YOU SEEM TO KNOW A LOT ABOUT...
...WELL...
THE **UNKNOWN?**
THE **HORRIFYING?**
THINGS MAN WAS NOT MEANT TO UNDERSTAND?
OH, THIS IS JUST PERFECTO.

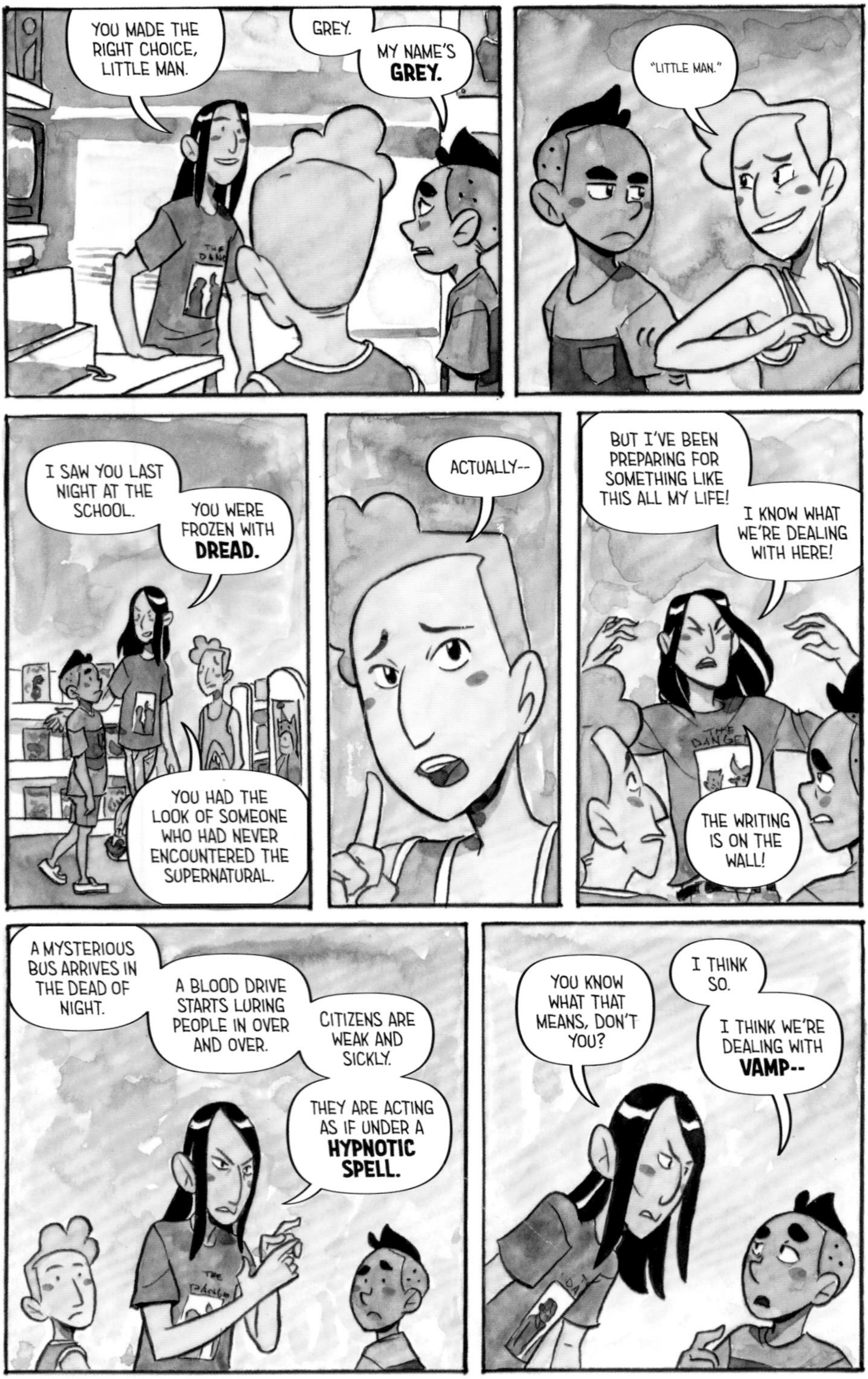
YOU MADE THE RIGHT CHOICE, LITTLE MAN.
GREY.
MY NAME'S **GREY.**
"LITTLE MAN."
I SAW YOU LAST NIGHT AT THE SCHOOL.
YOU WERE FROZEN WITH **DREAD.**
YOU HAD THE LOOK OF SOMEONE WHO HAD NEVER ENCOUNTERED THE SUPERNATURAL.
ACTUALLY--
BUT I'VE BEEN PREPARING FOR SOMETHING LIKE THIS ALL MY LIFE!
I KNOW WHAT WE'RE DEALING WITH HERE!
THE WRITING IS ON THE WALL!
A MYSTERIOUS BUS ARRIVES IN THE DEAD OF NIGHT.
A BLOOD DRIVE STARTS LURING PEOPLE IN OVER AND OVER.
CITIZENS ARE WEAK AND SICKLY.
THEY ARE ACTING AS IF UNDER A **HYPNOTIC SPELL.**
YOU KNOW WHAT THAT MEANS, DON'T YOU?
I THINK SO.
I THINK WE'RE DEALING WITH **VAMP--**

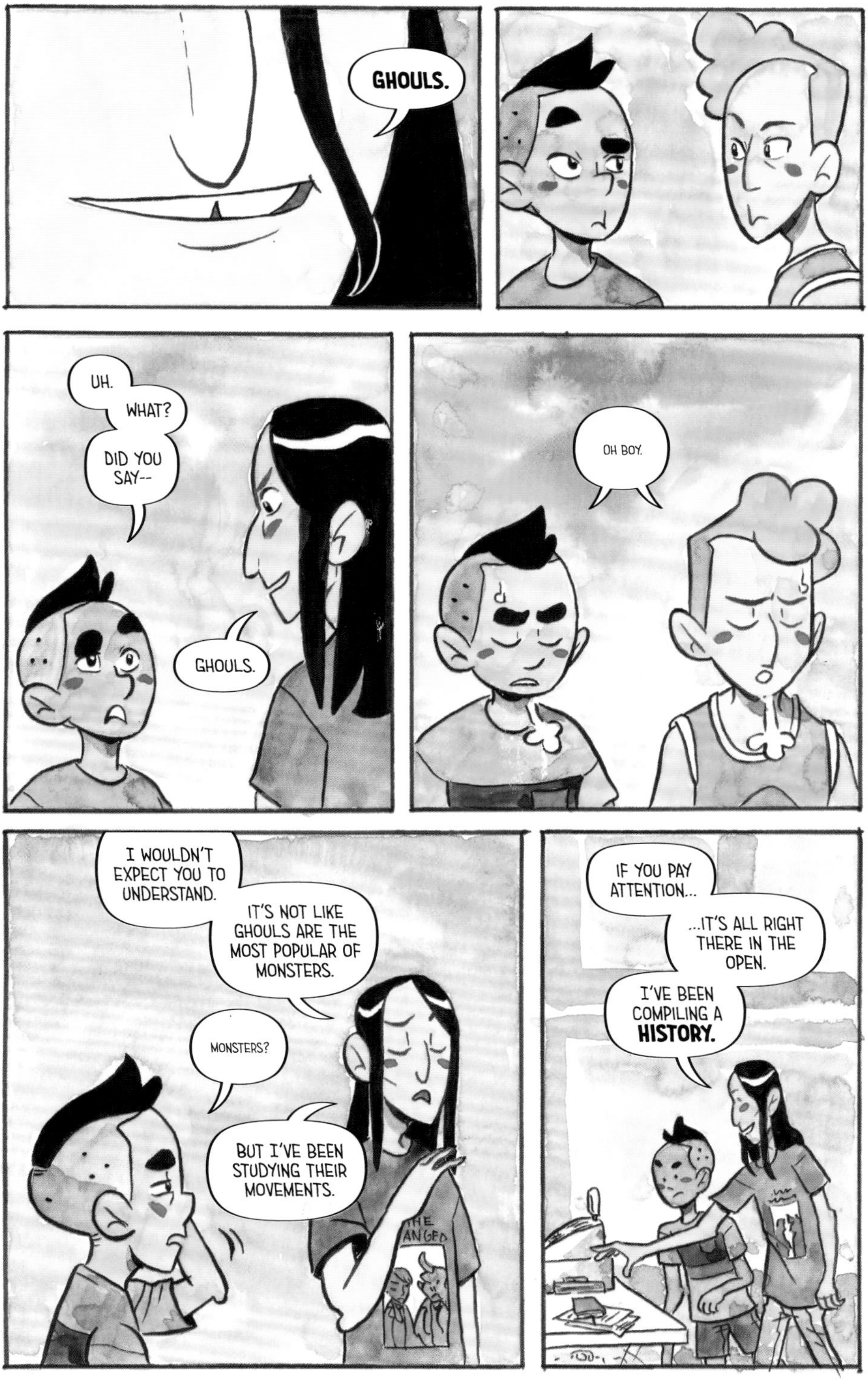
GHOULS.
UH.
WHAT?
DID YOU SAY--
GHOULS.
OH BOY.
I WOULDN'T EXPECT YOU TO UNDERSTAND.
IT'S NOT LIKE GHOULS ARE THE MOST POPULAR OF MONSTERS.
MONSTERS?
BUT I'VE BEEN STUDYING THEIR MOVEMENTS.
IF YOU PAY ATTENTION...
...IT'S ALL RIGHT THERE IN THE OPEN.
I'VE BEEN COMPILING A **HISTORY.**

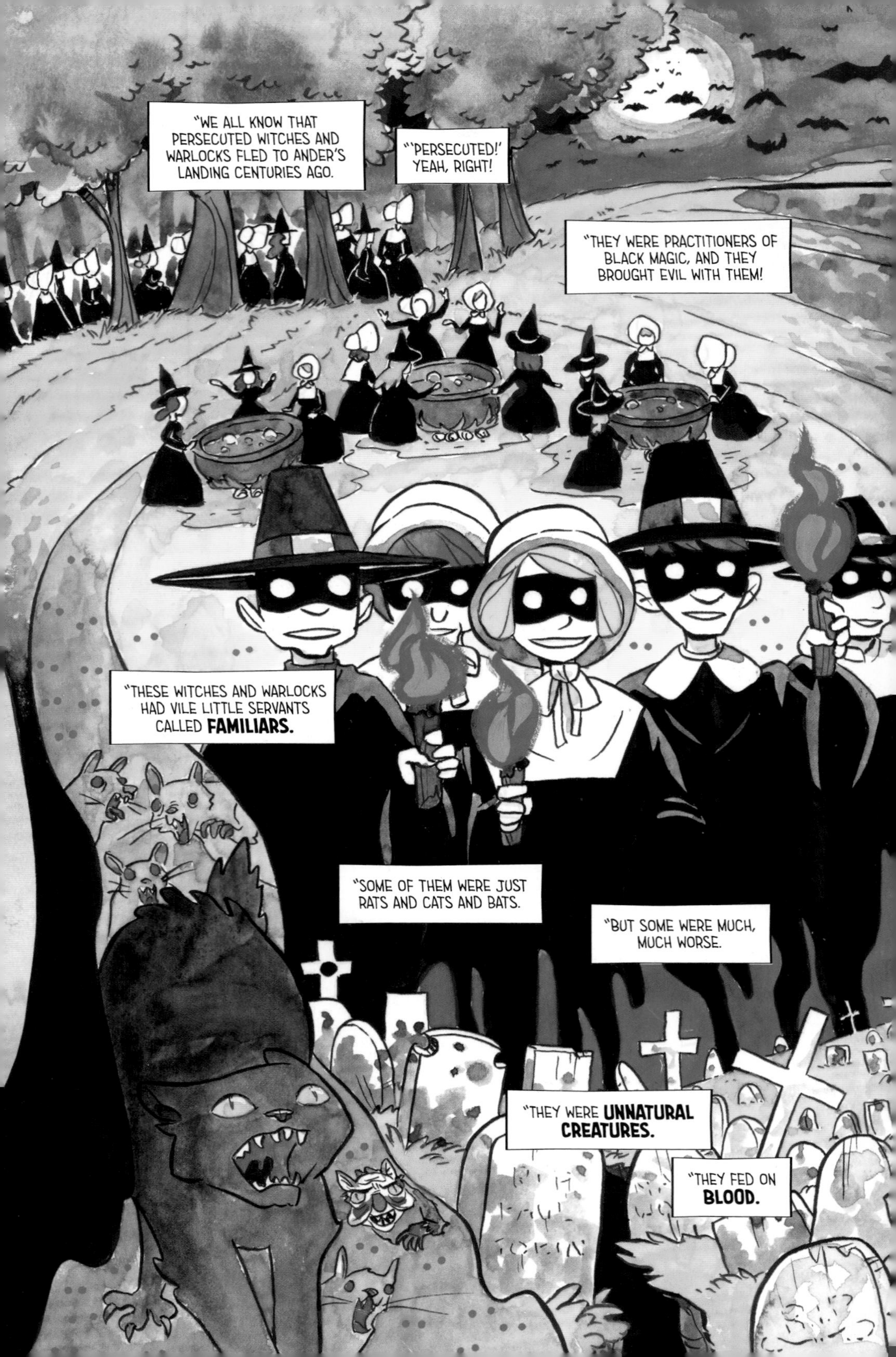
"WE ALL KNOW THAT PERSECUTED WITCHES AND WARLOCKS FLED TO ANDER'S LANDING CENTURIES AGO.
"'PERSECUTED!' YEAH, RIGHT!
"THEY WERE PRACTITIONERS OF BLACK MAGIC, AND THEY BROUGHT EVIL WITH THEM!
"THESE WITCHES AND WARLOCKS HAD VILE LITTLE SERVANTS CALLED **FAMILIARS.**
"SOME OF THEM WERE JUST RATS AND CATS AND BATS.
"BUT SOME WERE MUCH, MUCH WORSE.
"THEY WERE **UNNATURAL CREATURES.**
"THEY FED ON **BLOOD.**

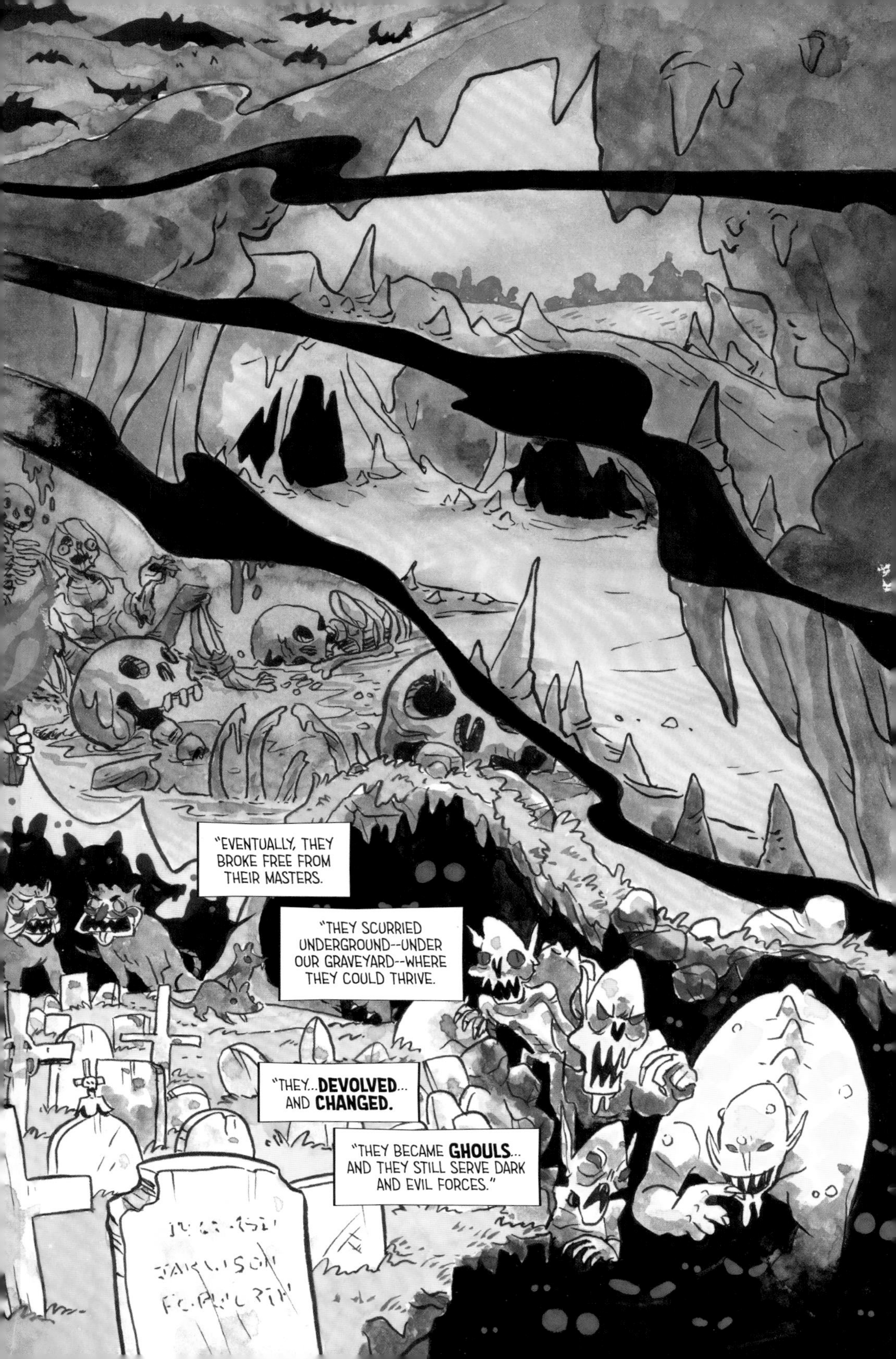
"EVENTUALLY, THEY BROKE FREE FROM THEIR MASTERS.
"THEY SCURRIED UNDERGROUND--UNDER OUR GRAVEYARD--WHERE THEY COULD THRIVE.
"THEY...**DEVOLVED**... AND **CHANGED.**
"THEY BECAME **GHOULS**... AND THEY STILL SERVE DARK AND EVIL FORCES."

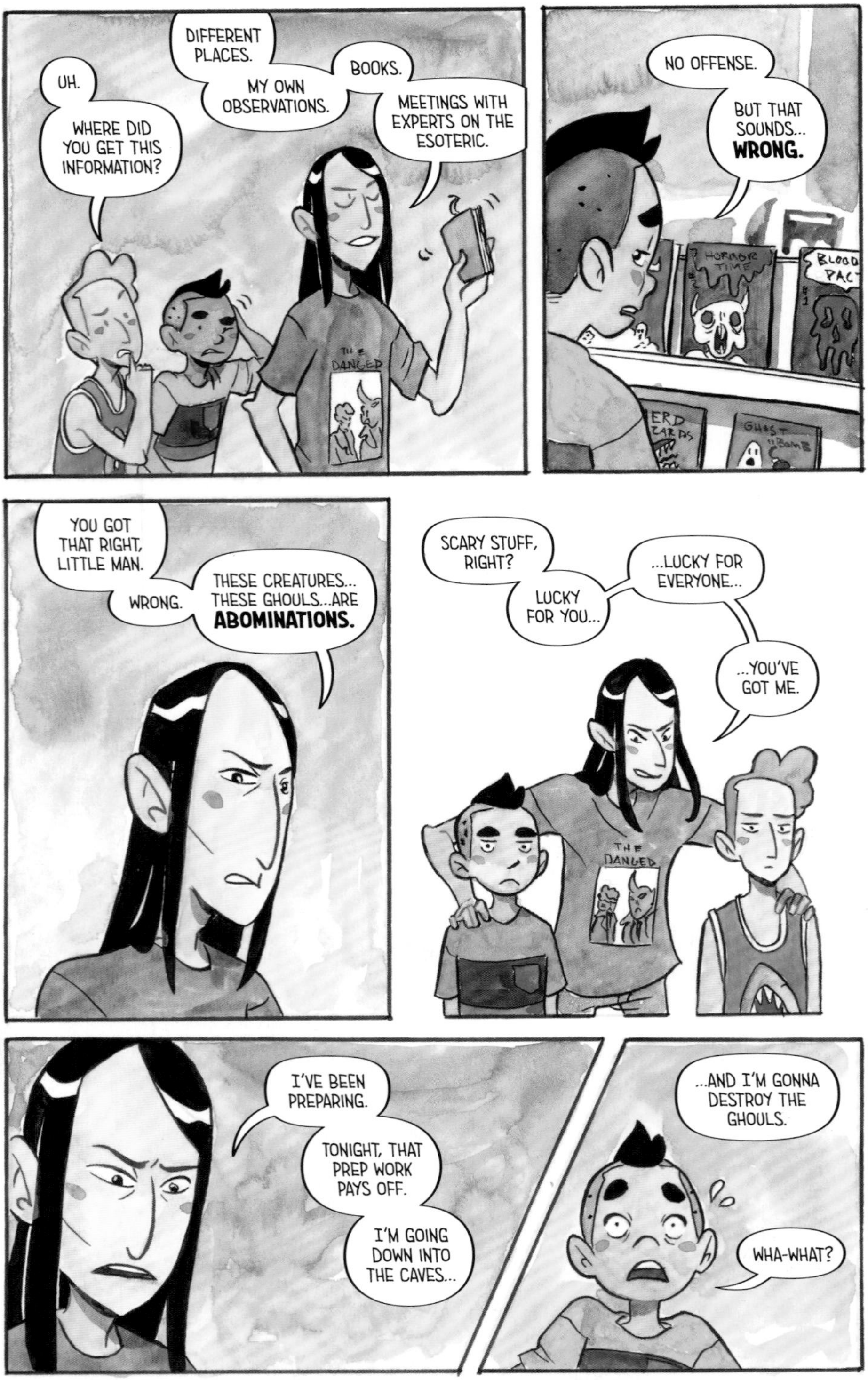
UH.
WHERE DID YOU GET THIS INFORMATION?
DIFFERENT PLACES.
MY OWN OBSERVATIONS.
BOOKS.
MEETINGS WITH EXPERTS ON THE ESOTERIC.
THE DANGED
NO OFFENSE.
BUT THAT SOUNDS... **WRONG.**
HORROR TIME
BLOOD PACT
GHOST
YOU GOT THAT RIGHT, LITTLE MAN.
WRONG.
THESE CREATURES... THESE GHOULS...ARE **ABOMINATIONS.**
SCARY STUFF, RIGHT?
LUCKY FOR YOU...
...LUCKY FOR EVERYONE...
...YOU'VE GOT ME.
THE DANGED
I'VE BEEN PREPARING.
TONIGHT, THAT PREP WORK PAYS OFF.
I'M GOING DOWN INTO THE CAVES...
...AND I'M GONNA DESTROY THE GHOULS.
WHA-WHAT?

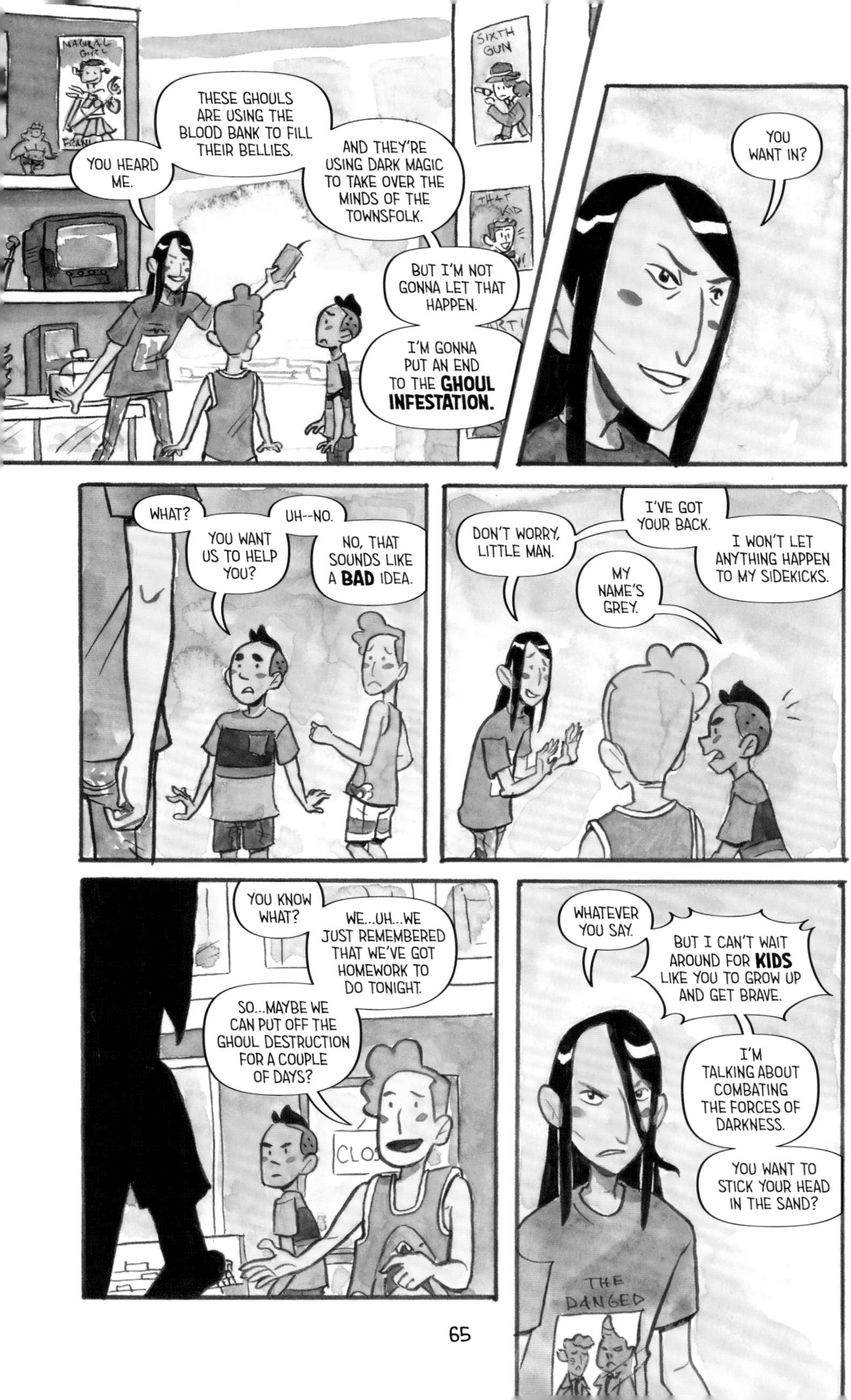
NAGICAL GIRL
SIXTH GUN
THAT KID
YOU HEARD ME.
THESE GHOULS ARE USING THE BLOOD BANK TO FILL THEIR BELLIES.
AND THEY'RE USING DARK MAGIC TO TAKE OVER THE MINDS OF THE TOWNSFOLK.
BUT I'M NOT GONNA LET THAT HAPPEN.
I'M GONNA PUT AN END TO THE **GHOUL INFESTATION.**
YOU WANT IN?
WHAT?
YOU WANT US TO HELP YOU?
UH--NO.
NO, THAT SOUNDS LIKE A **BAD** IDEA.
DON'T WORRY, LITTLE MAN.
I'VE GOT YOUR BACK.
I WON'T LET ANYTHING HAPPEN TO MY SIDEKICKS.
MY NAME'S GREY.
YOU KNOW WHAT?
WE...UH...WE JUST REMEMBERED THAT WE'VE GOT HOMEWORK TO DO TONIGHT.
SO...MAYBE WE CAN PUT OFF THE GHOUL DESTRUCTION FOR A COUPLE OF DAYS?
WHATEVER YOU SAY.
BUT I CAN'T WAIT AROUND FOR **KIDS** LIKE YOU TO GROW UP AND GET BRAVE.
I'M TALKING ABOUT COMBATING THE FORCES OF DARKNESS.
YOU WANT TO STICK YOUR HEAD IN THE SAND?
THE DANGED

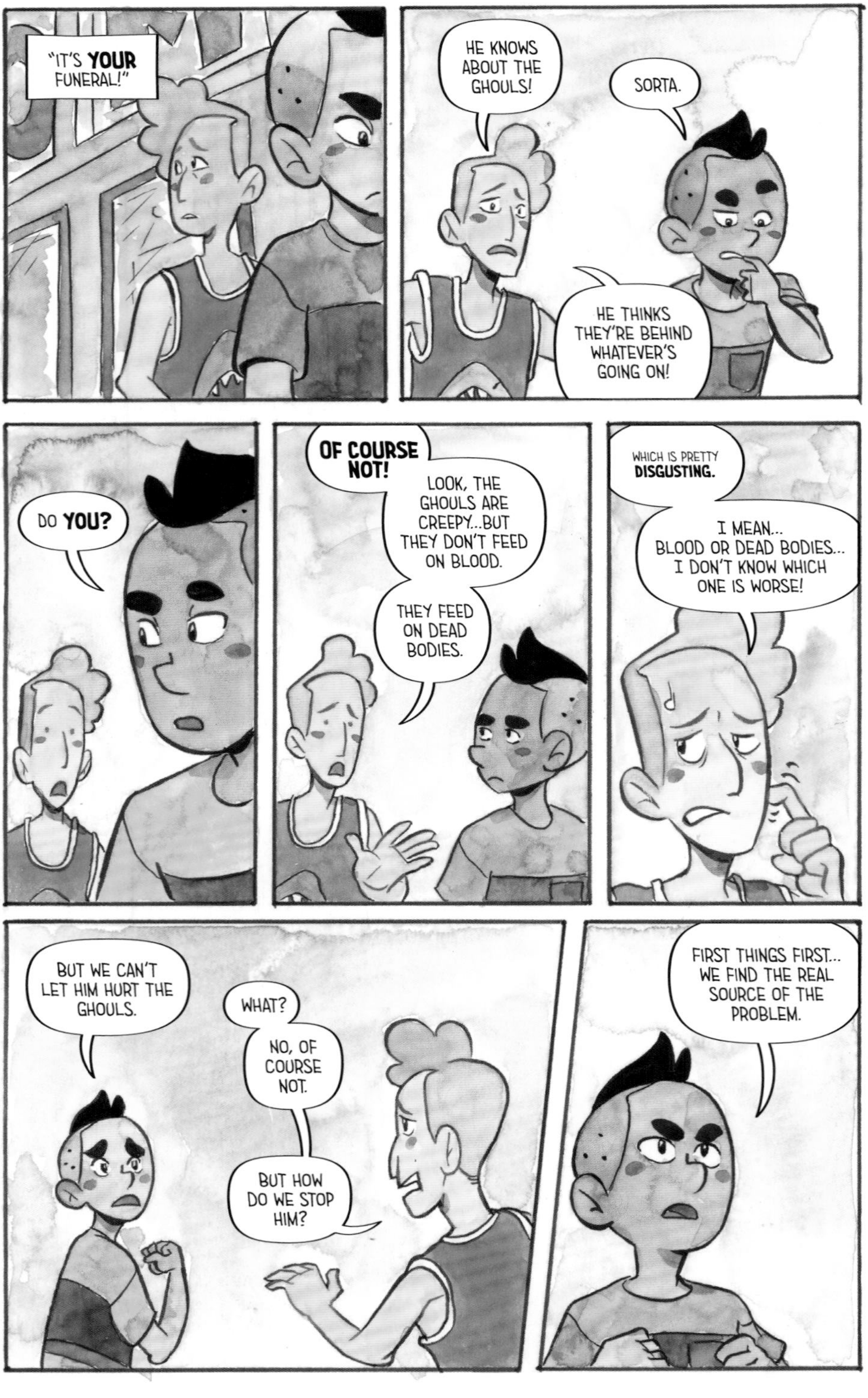
"IT'S **YOUR** FUNERAL!"
HE KNOWS ABOUT THE GHOULS!
SORTA.
HE THINKS THEY'RE BEHIND WHATEVER'S GOING ON!
DO **YOU?**
OF COURSE NOT!
LOOK, THE GHOULS ARE CREEPY...BUT THEY DON'T FEED ON BLOOD.
THEY FEED ON DEAD BODIES.
WHICH IS PRETTY **DISGUSTING.**
I MEAN... BLOOD OR DEAD BODIES... I DON'T KNOW WHICH ONE IS WORSE!
BUT WE CAN'T LET HIM HURT THE GHOULS.
WHAT?
NO, OF COURSE NOT.
BUT HOW DO WE STOP HIM?
FIRST THINGS FIRST... WE FIND THE REAL SOURCE OF THE PROBLEM.

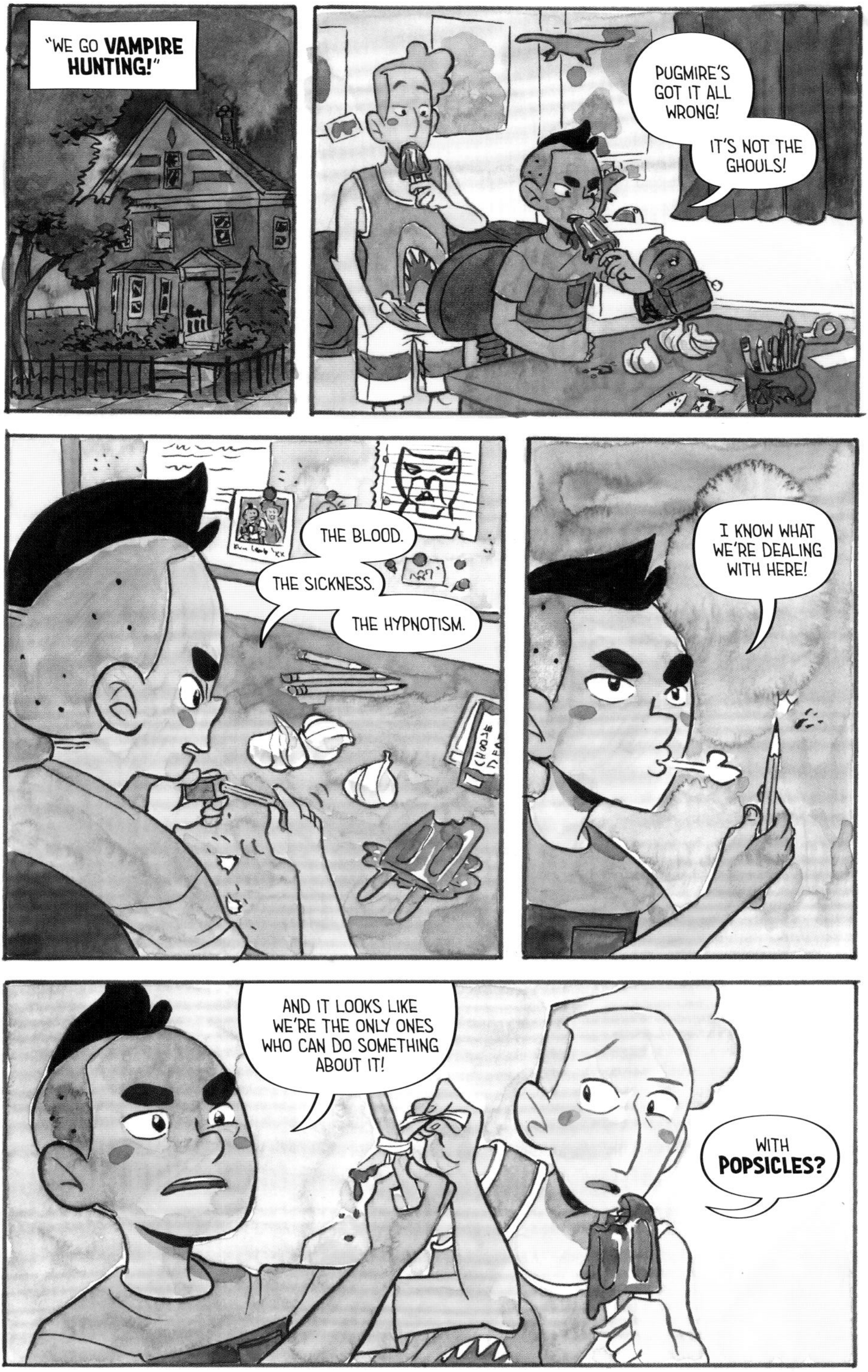
"WE GO VAMPIRE HUNTING!"
PUGMIRE'S GOT IT ALL WRONG!
IT'S NOT THE GHOULS!
THE BLOOD.
THE SICKNESS.
THE HYPNOTISM.
I KNOW WHAT WE'RE DEALING WITH HERE!
AND IT LOOKS LIKE WE'RE THE ONLY ONES WHO CAN DO SOMETHING ABOUT IT!
WITH POPSICLES?

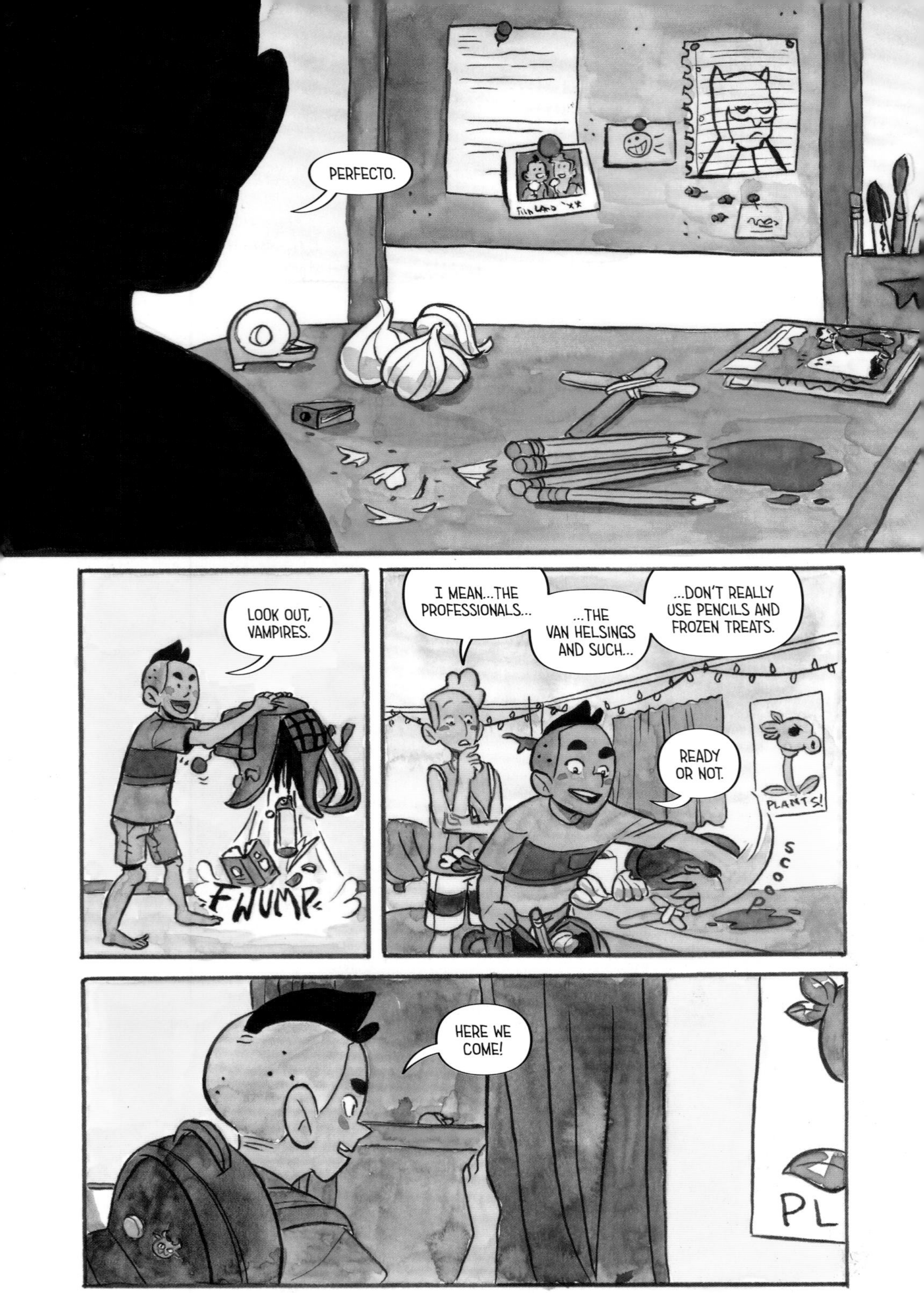
PERFECTO.
LOOK OUT, VAMPIRES.
FWUMP
I MEAN...THE PROFESSIONALS...
...THE VAN HELSINGS AND SUCH...
...DON'T REALLY USE PENCILS AND FROZEN TREATS.
READY OR NOT.
PLANTS!
SCOOOP
HERE WE COME!
PL

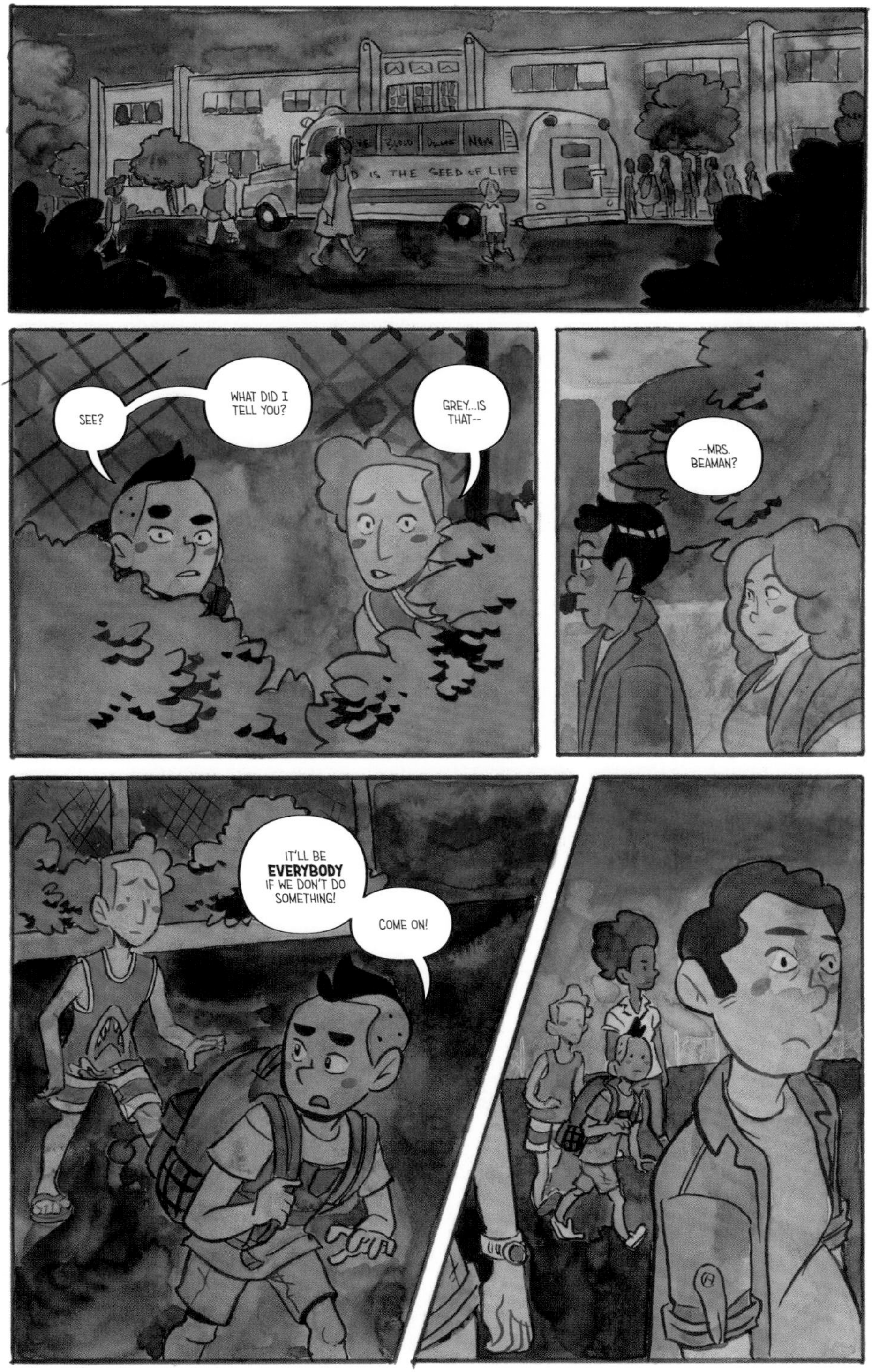
SEE?
WHAT DID I TELL YOU?
GREY...IS THAT--
--MRS. BEAMAN?
IT'LL BE **EVERYBODY** IF WE DON'T DO SOMETHING!
COME ON!

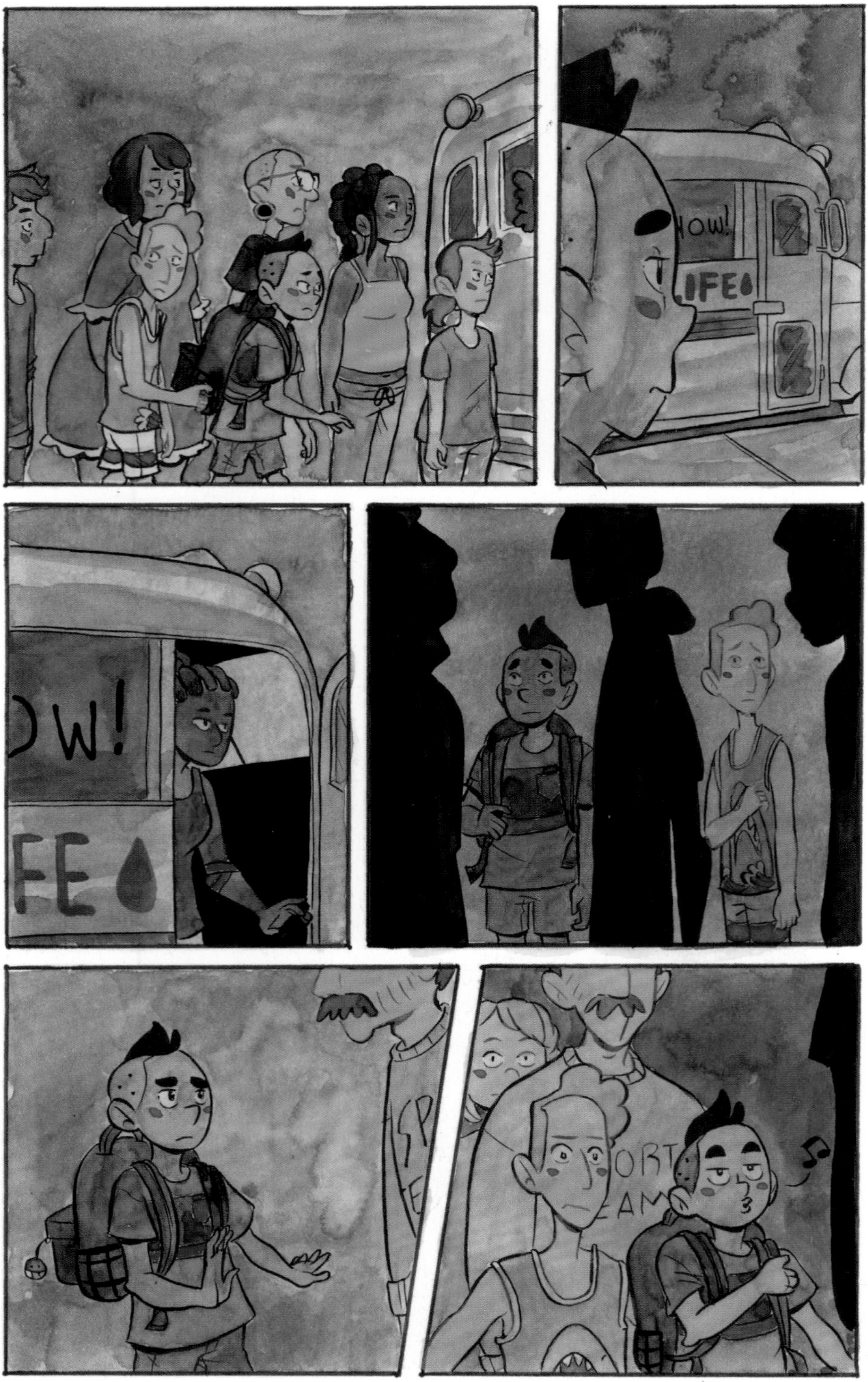
OW!
IFE
OW!
FE
ORT
EAM

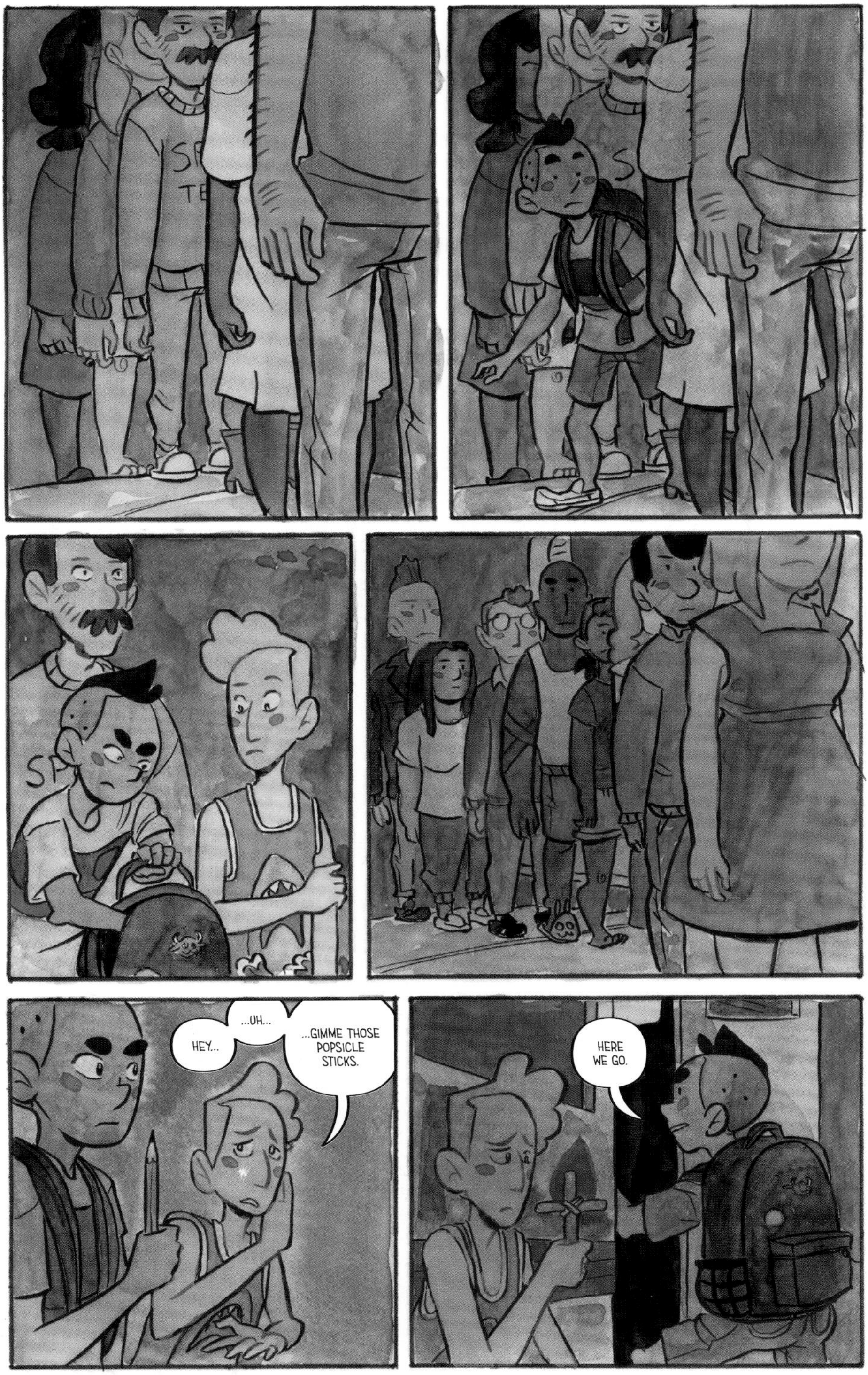
HEY...
...UH...
...GIMME THOSE POPSICLE STICKS.
HERE WE GO.

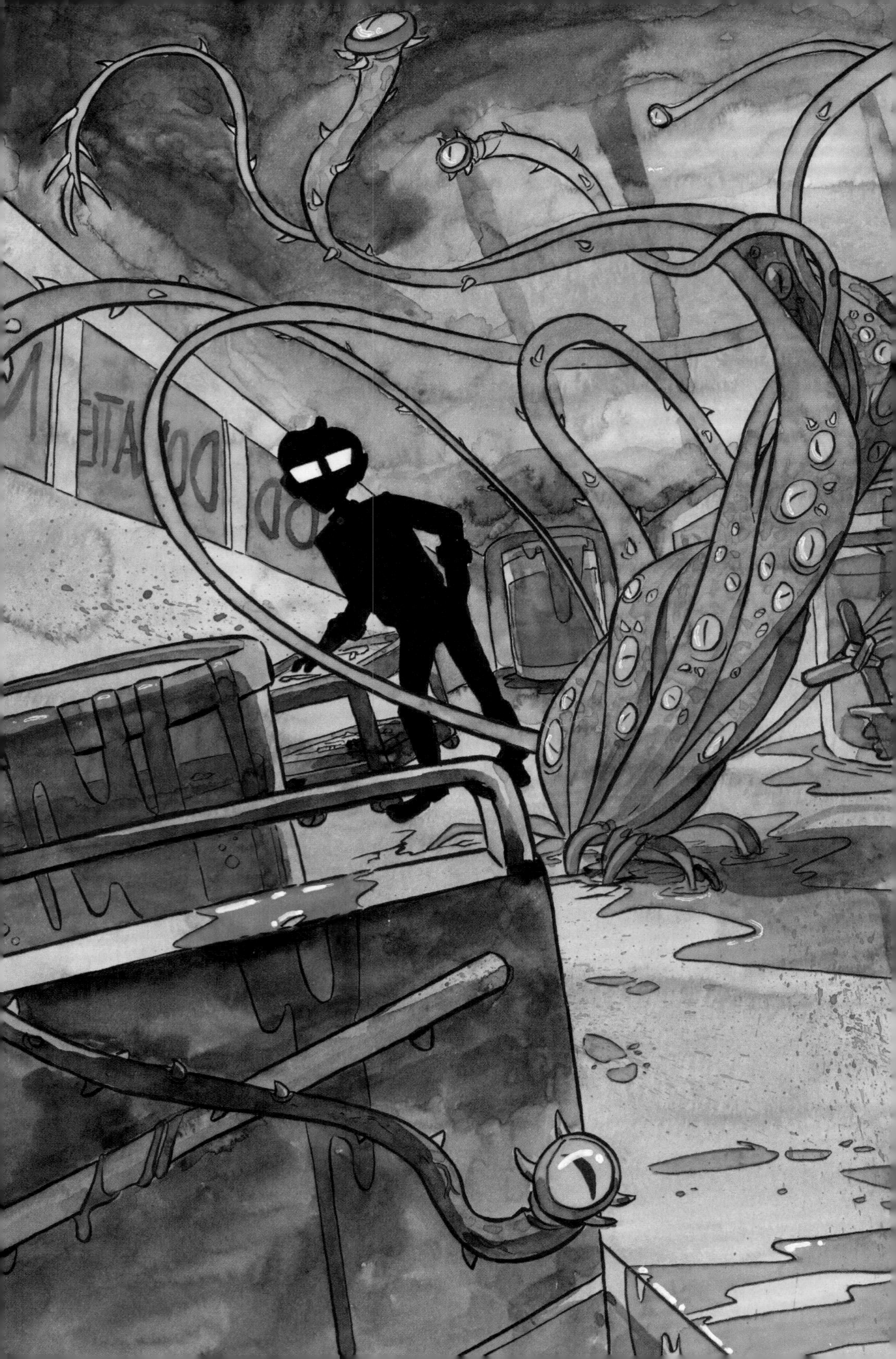

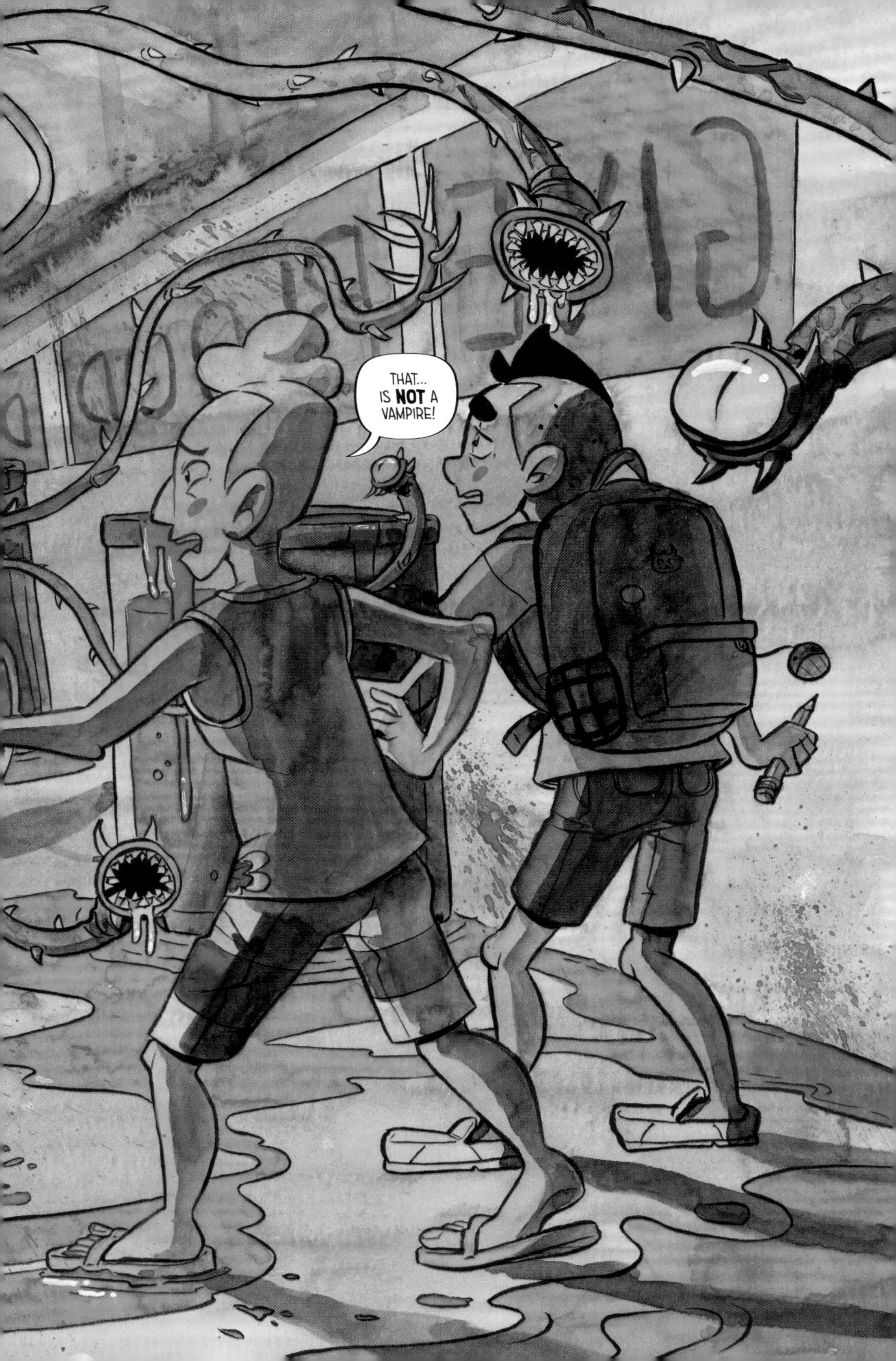
THAT... IS **NOT** A VAMPIRE!

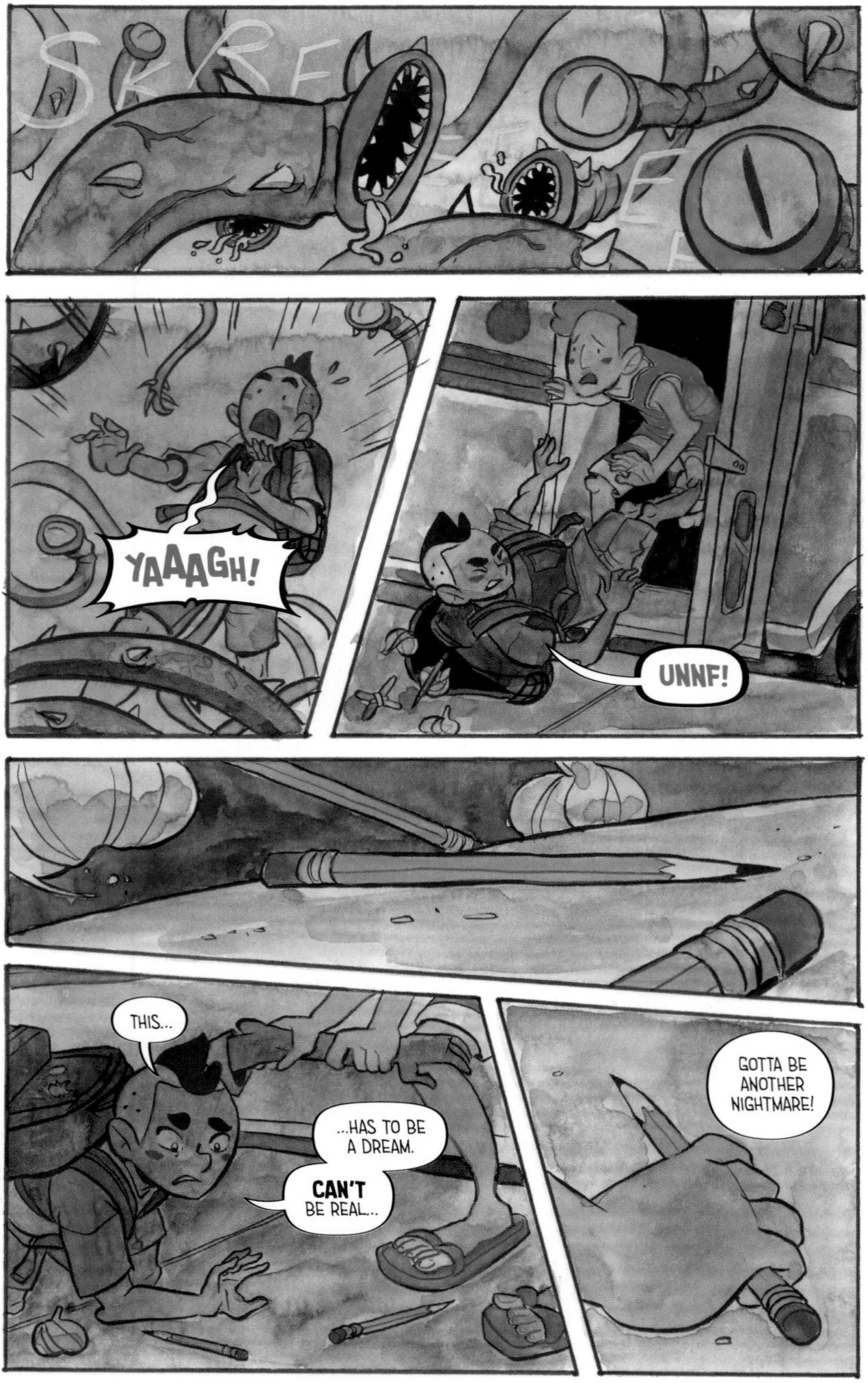
SKREEEE
YAAAGH!
UNNF!
THIS...
...HAS TO BE A DREAM.
CAN'T BE REAL...
GOTTA BE ANOTHER NIGHTMARE!

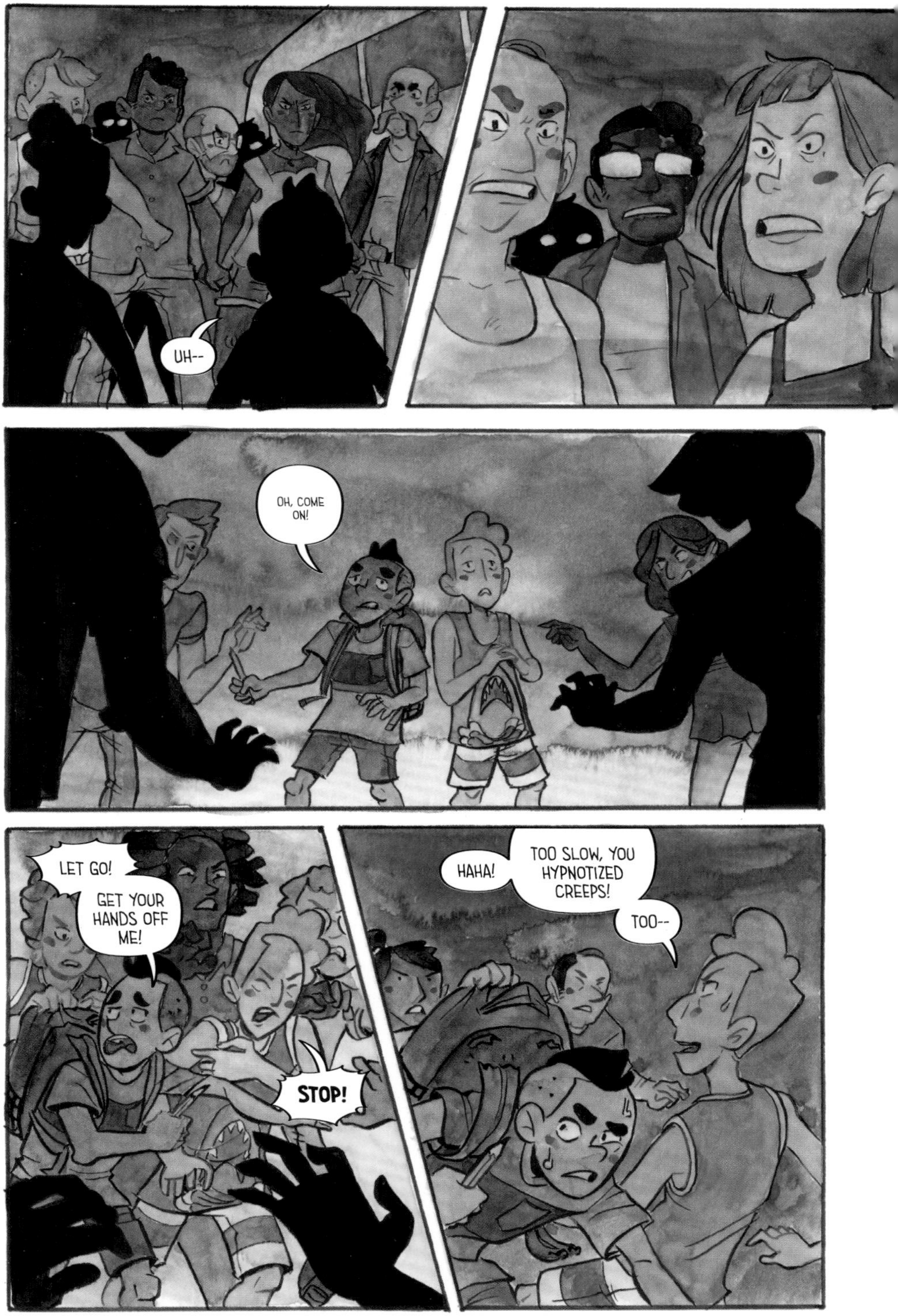
UH--
OH, COME ON!
LET GO!
GET YOUR HANDS OFF ME!
STOP!
HAHA!
TOO SLOW, YOU HYPNOTIZED CREEPS!
TOO--

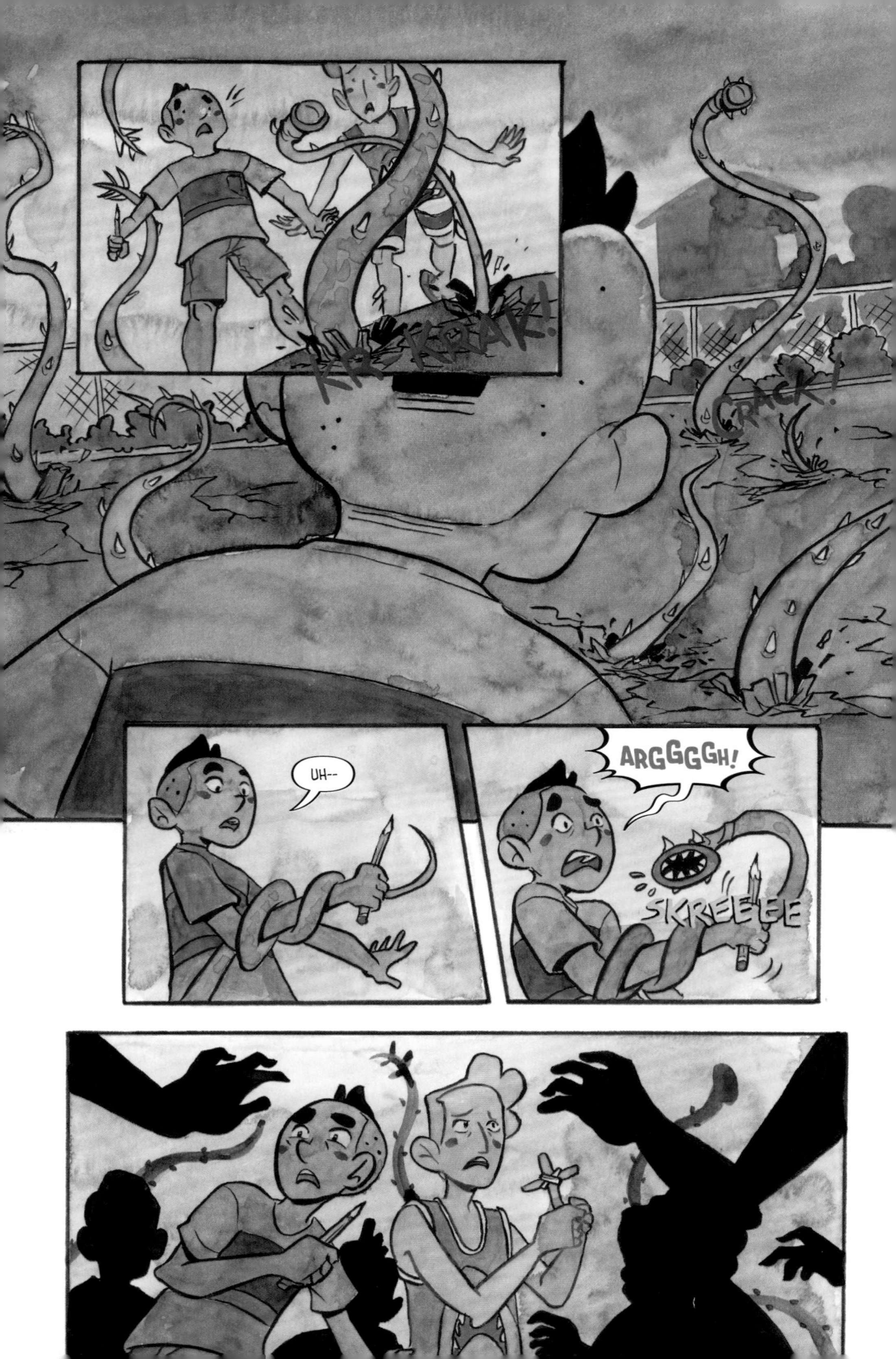
KR-KRAK!
CRACK!
UH--
ARGGGGH!
SKREEEEE

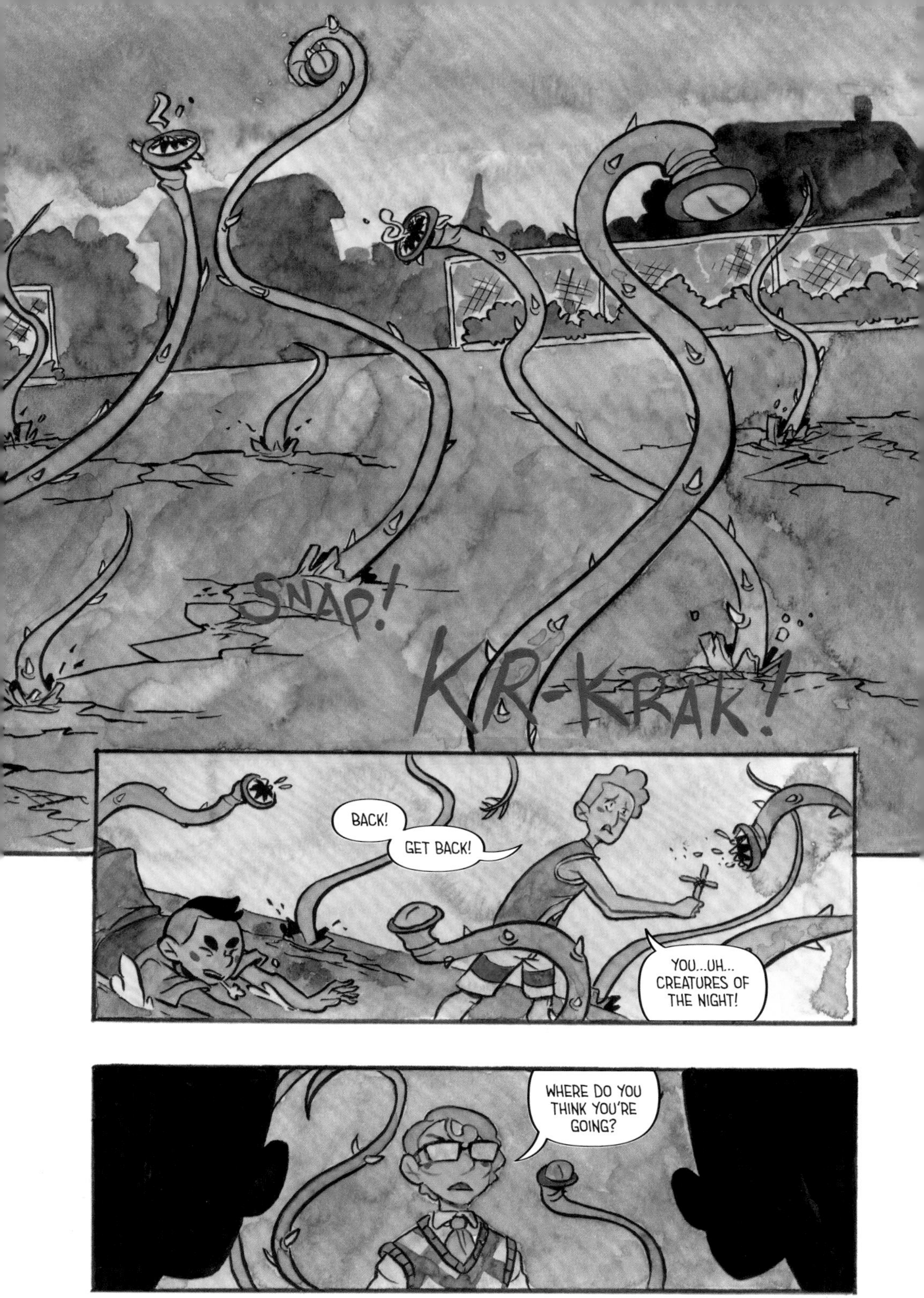
SNAP!
KR-KRAK!
BACK!
GET BACK!
YOU...UH... CREATURES OF THE NIGHT!
WHERE DO YOU THINK YOU'RE GOING?

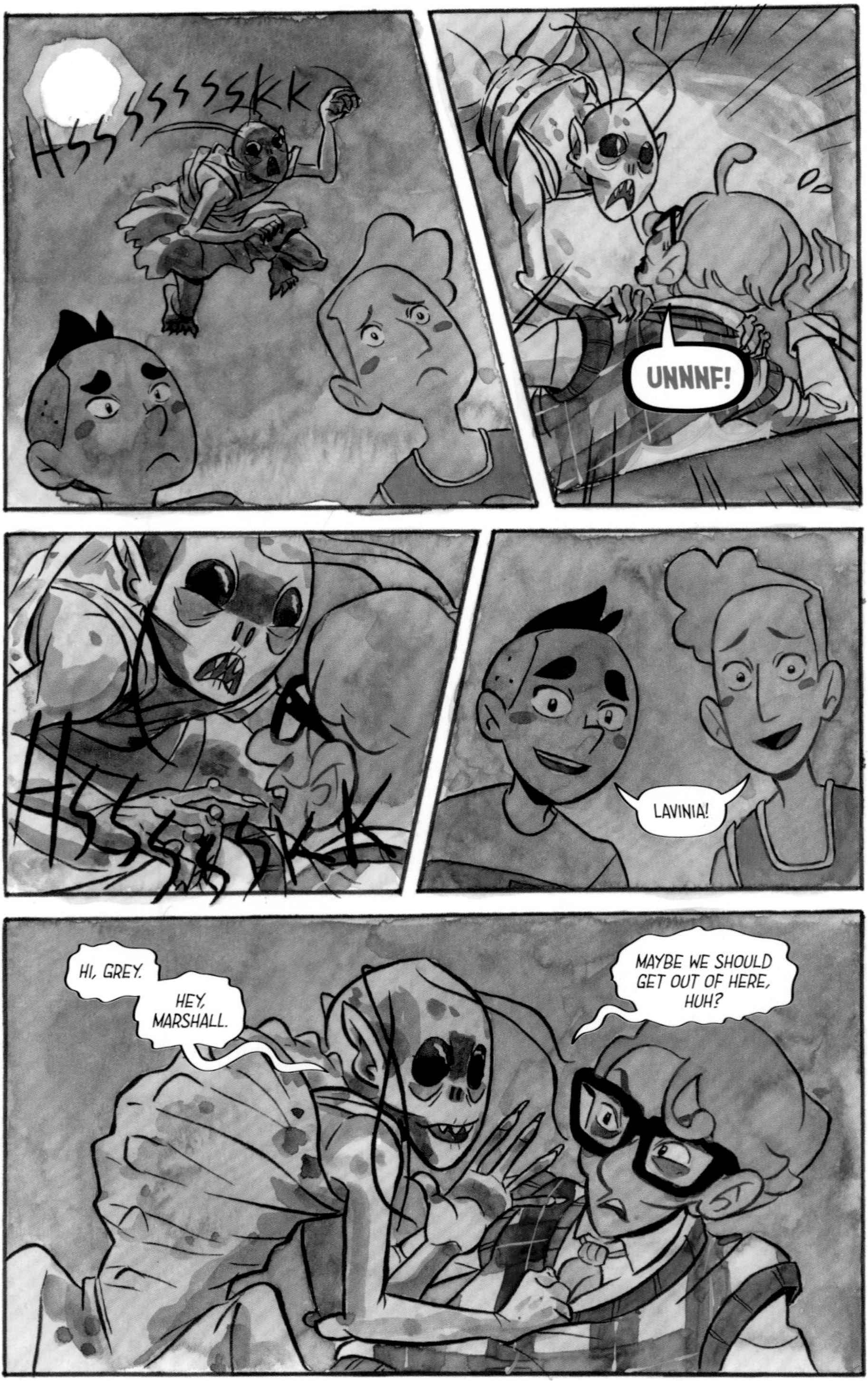
HSSSSSSSKK
UNNNF!
HSSSSSKK
LAVINIA!
HI, GREY.
HEY, MARSHALL.
MAYBE WE SHOULD GET OUT OF HERE, HUH?

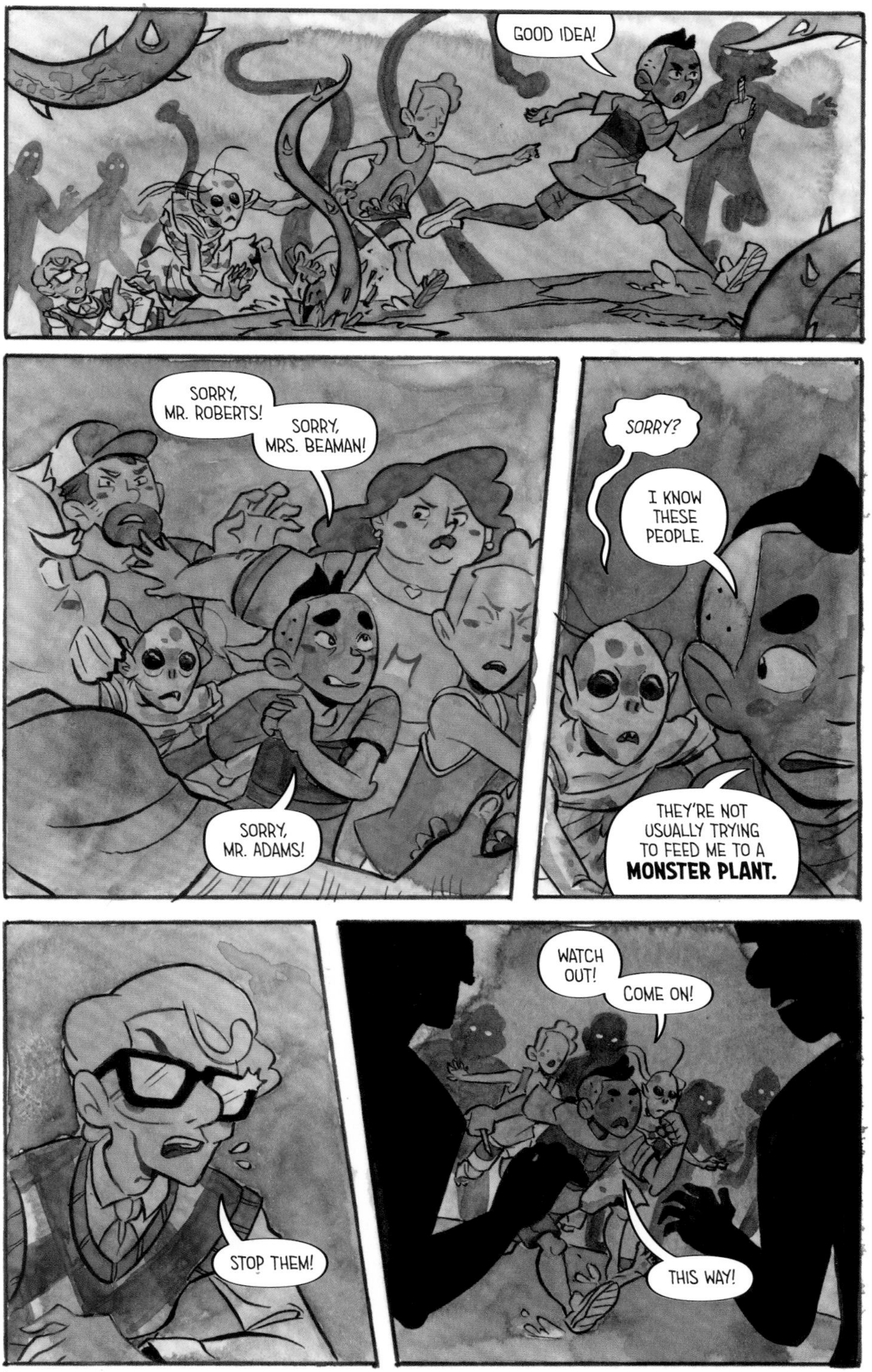
GOOD IDEA!
SORRY, MR. ROBERTS!
SORRY, MRS. BEAMAN!
SORRY, MR. ADAMS!
SORRY?
I KNOW THESE PEOPLE.
THEY'RE NOT USUALLY TRYING TO FEED ME TO A **MONSTER PLANT.**
STOP THEM!
WATCH OUT!
COME ON!
THIS WAY!

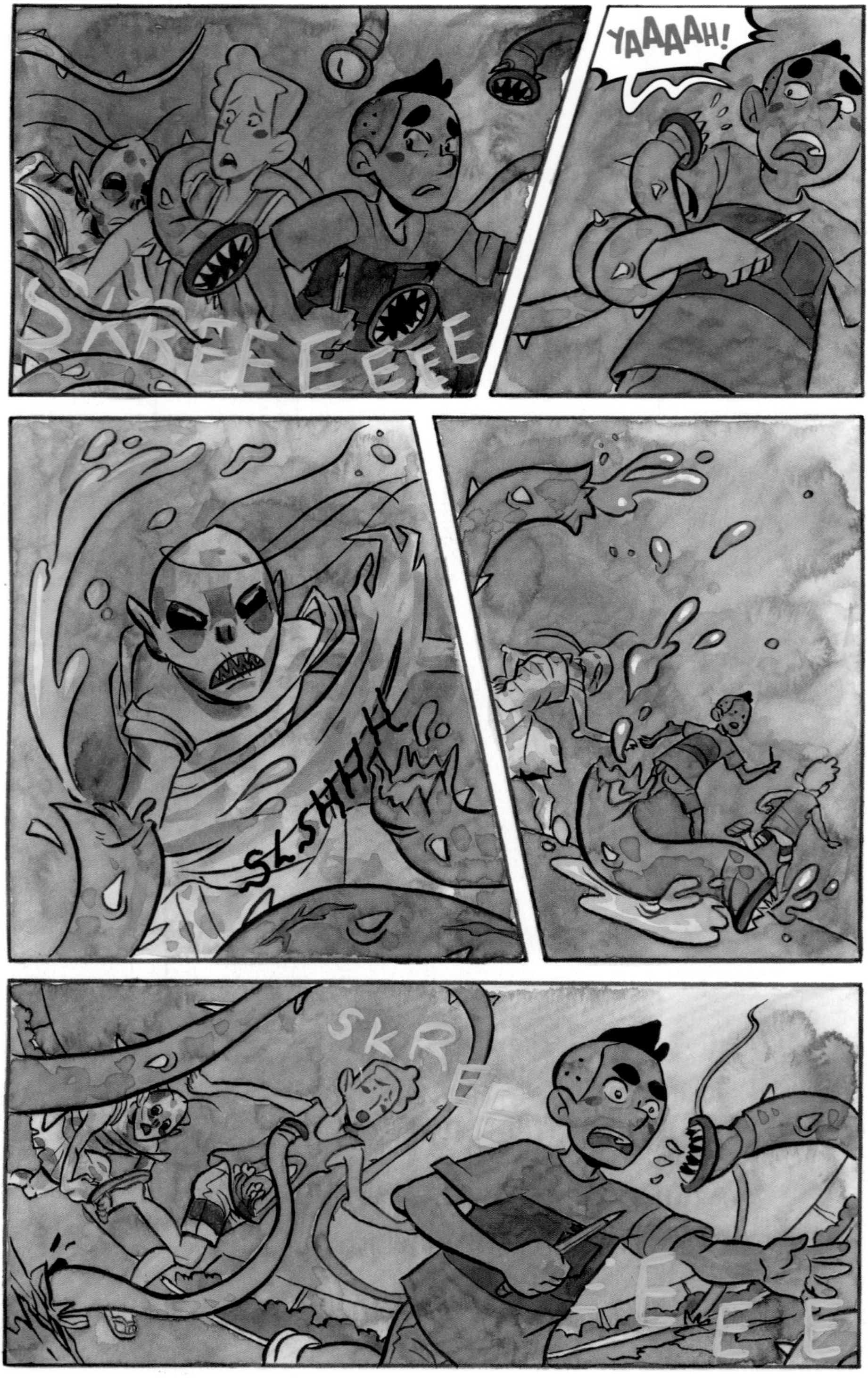
SKREEEEEEE
YAAAAH!
SLSHHH
SKREEEEEE

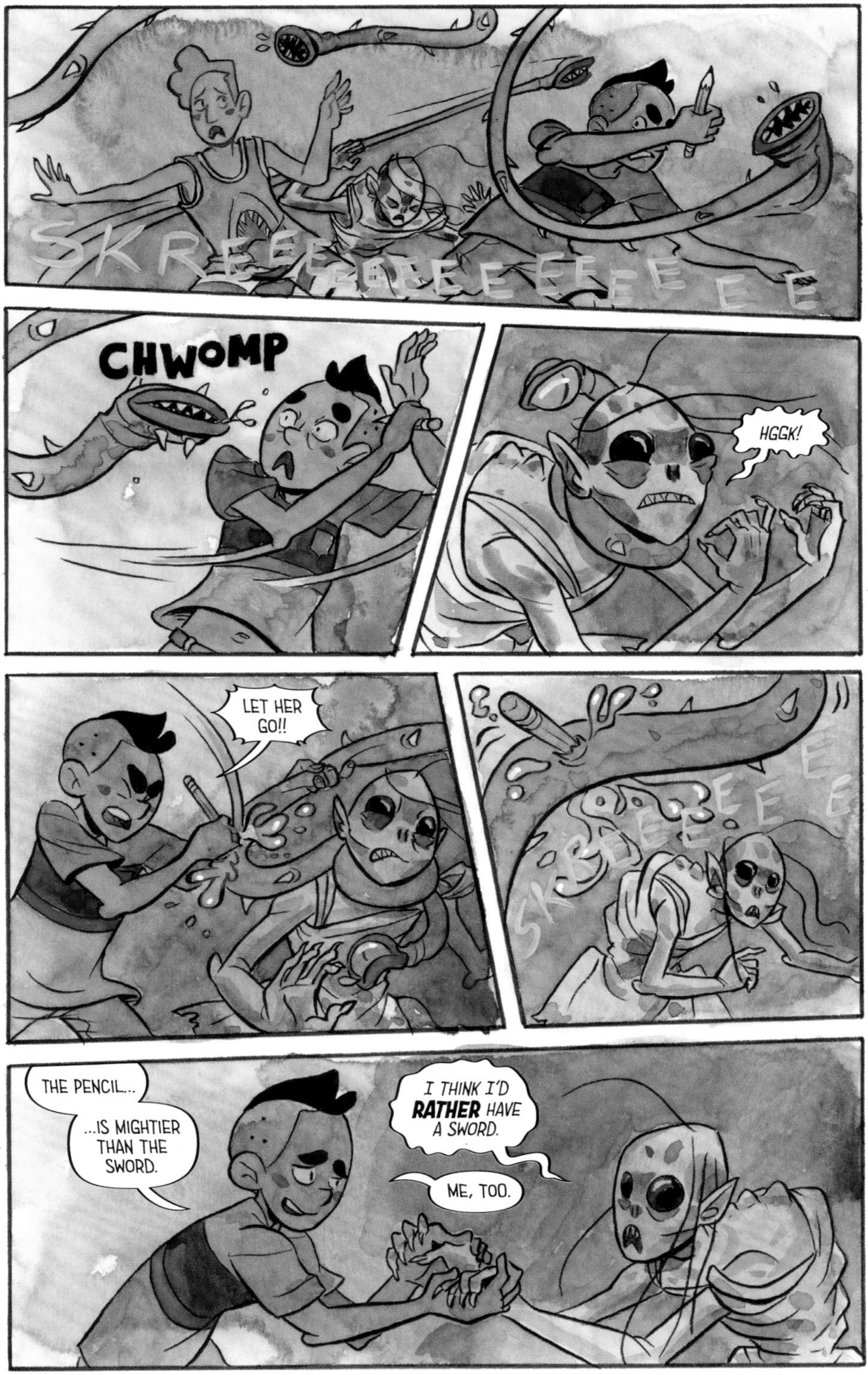
SKREEEEEEEEEEEEEE
CHWOMP
HGGK!
LET HER GO!!
SKREEEEEEE
THE PENCIL...
...IS MIGHTIER THAN THE SWORD.
I THINK I'D **RATHER** HAVE A SWORD.
ME, TOO.

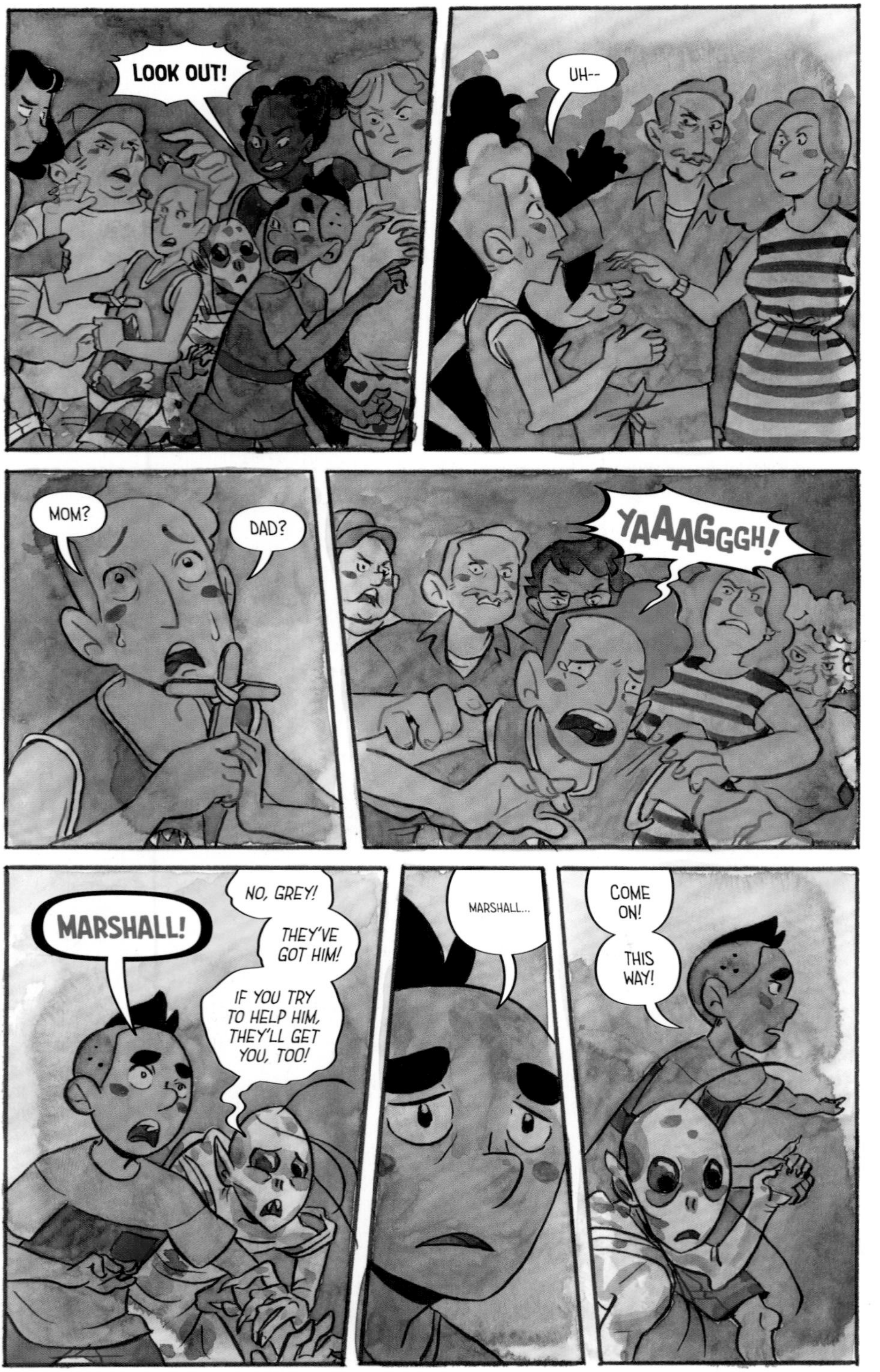
LOOK OUT!
UH--
MOM?
DAD?
YAAAGGGH!
MARSHALL!
NO, GREY!
THEY'VE GOT HIM!
IF YOU TRY TO HELP HIM, THEY'LL GET YOU, TOO!
MARSHALL...
COME ON!
THIS WAY!

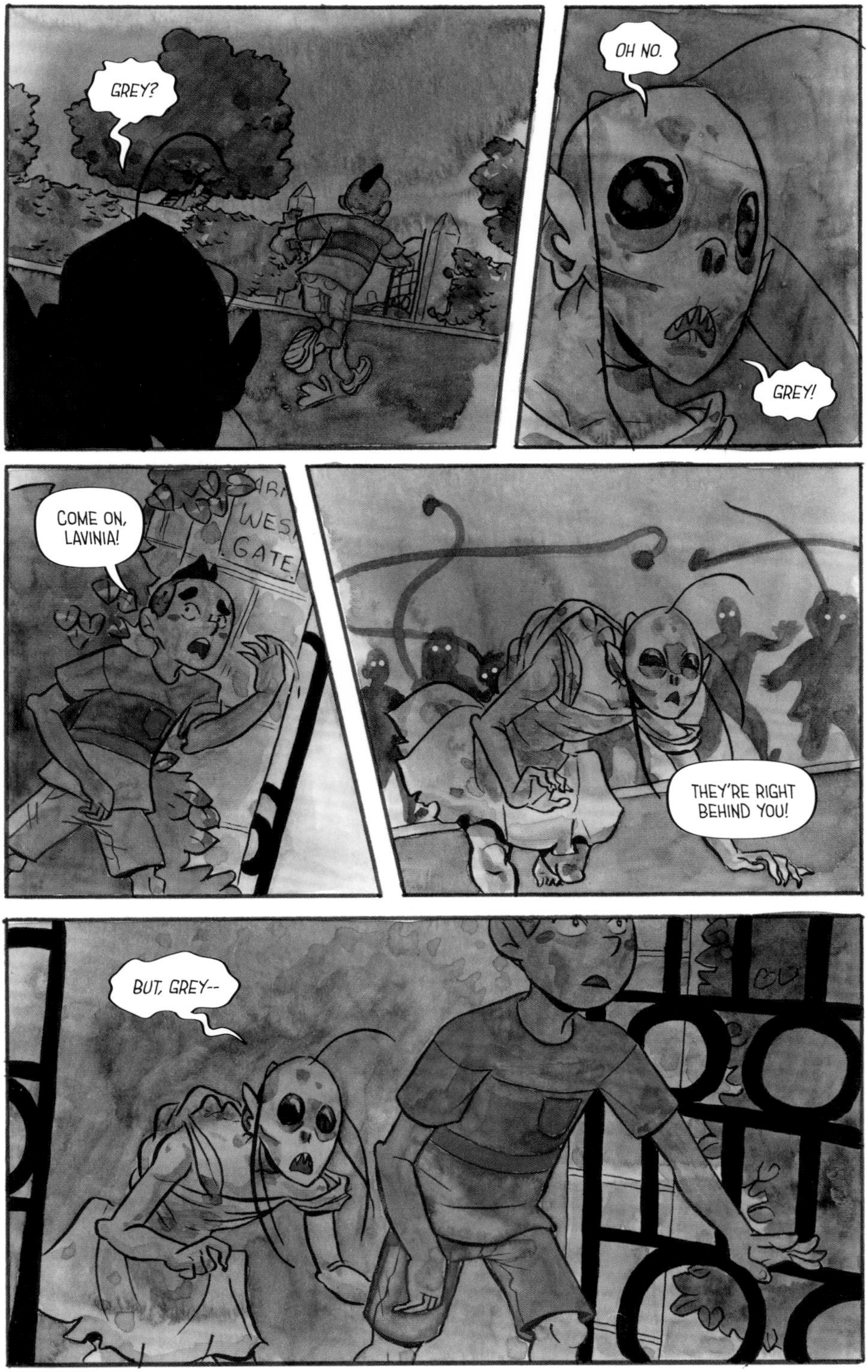
GREY?
OH NO.
GREY!
COME ON, LAVINIA!
WEST GATE
THEY'RE RIGHT BEHIND YOU!
BUT, GREY--

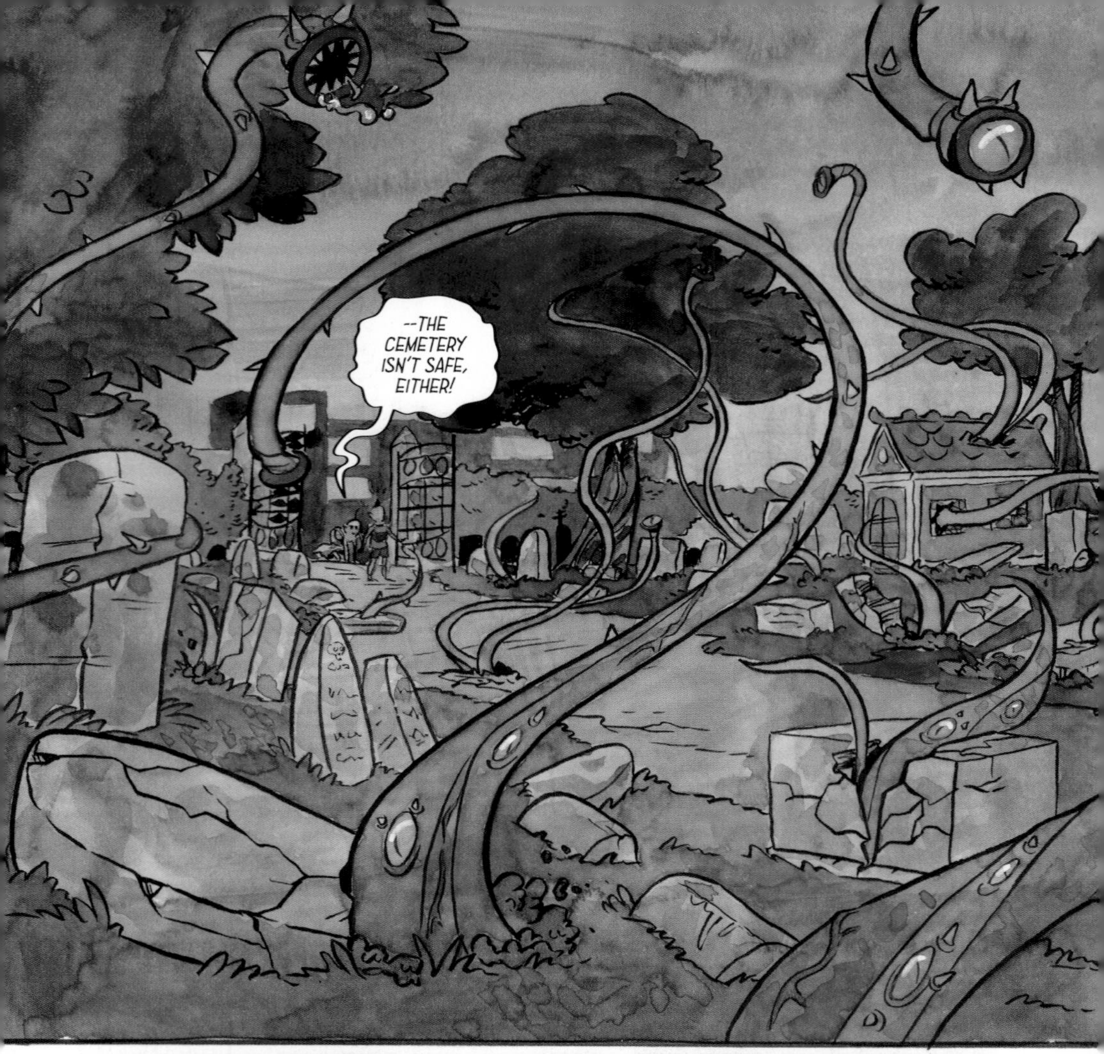
--THE CEMETERY ISN'T SAFE, EITHER!

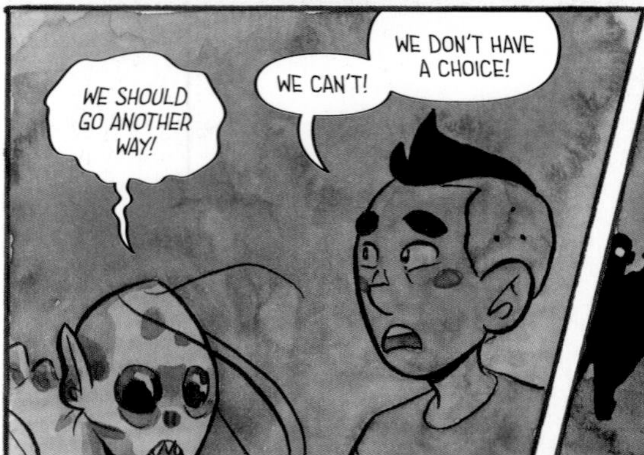
WE SHOULD GO ANOTHER WAY!
WE CAN'T!
WE DON'T HAVE A CHOICE!

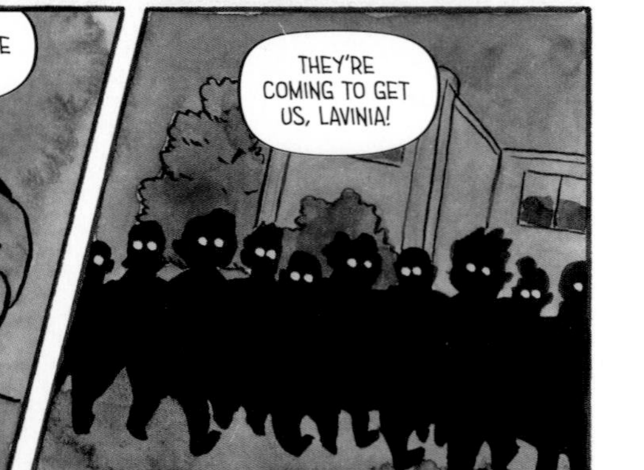
THEY'RE COMING TO GET US, LAVINIA!

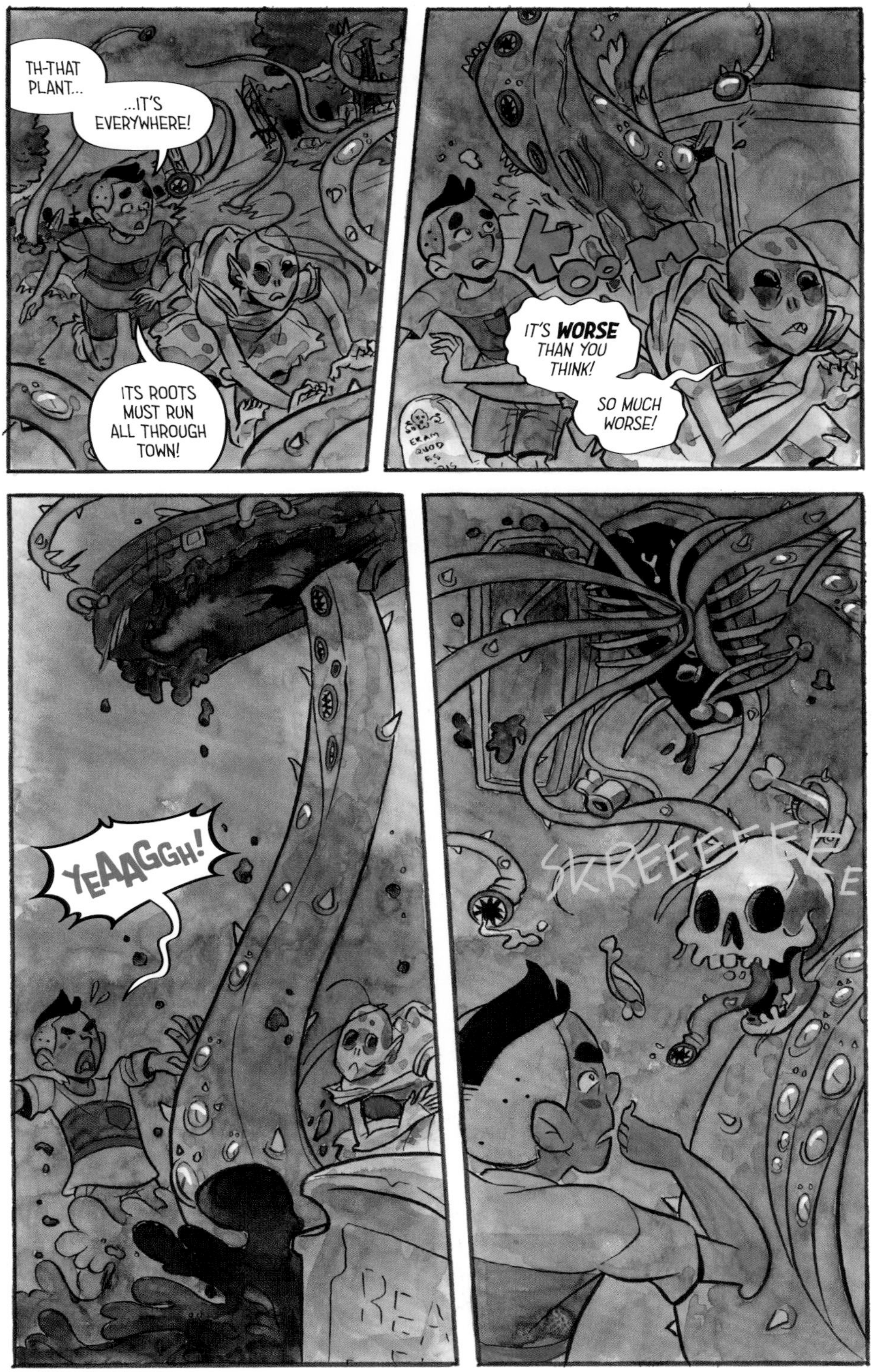
TH-THAT PLANT...
...IT'S EVERYWHERE!
ITS ROOTS MUST RUN ALL THROUGH TOWN!
IT'S **WORSE** THAN YOU THINK!
SO MUCH WORSE!
ERAM QUOD ES
YEAAGGH!

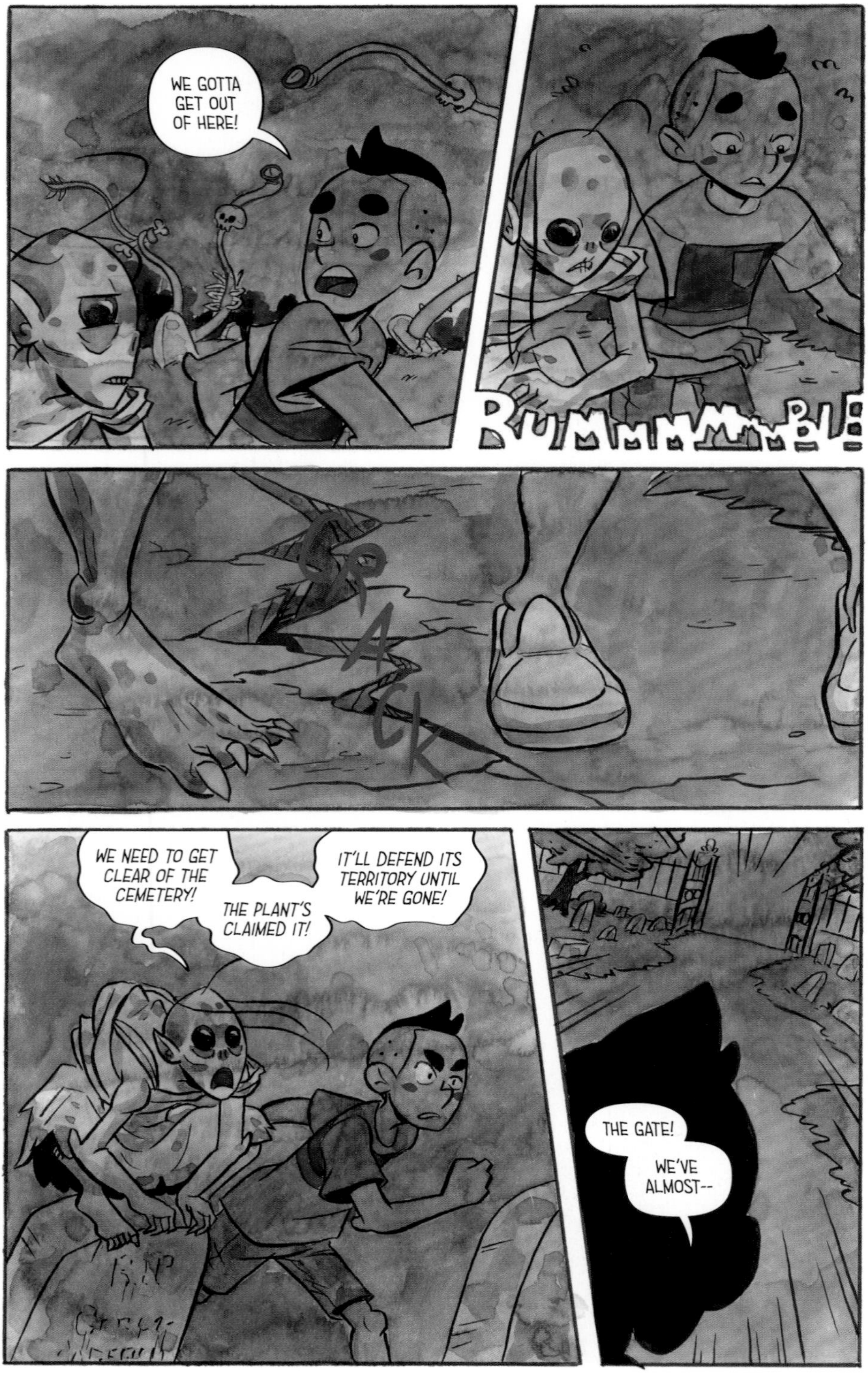
WE GOTTA GET OUT OF HERE!
RUMMMMMMBLE!
CRACK
WE NEED TO GET CLEAR OF THE CEMETERY!
THE PLANT'S CLAIMED IT!
IT'LL DEFEND ITS TERRITORY UNTIL WE'RE GONE!
THE GATE!
WE'VE ALMOST--

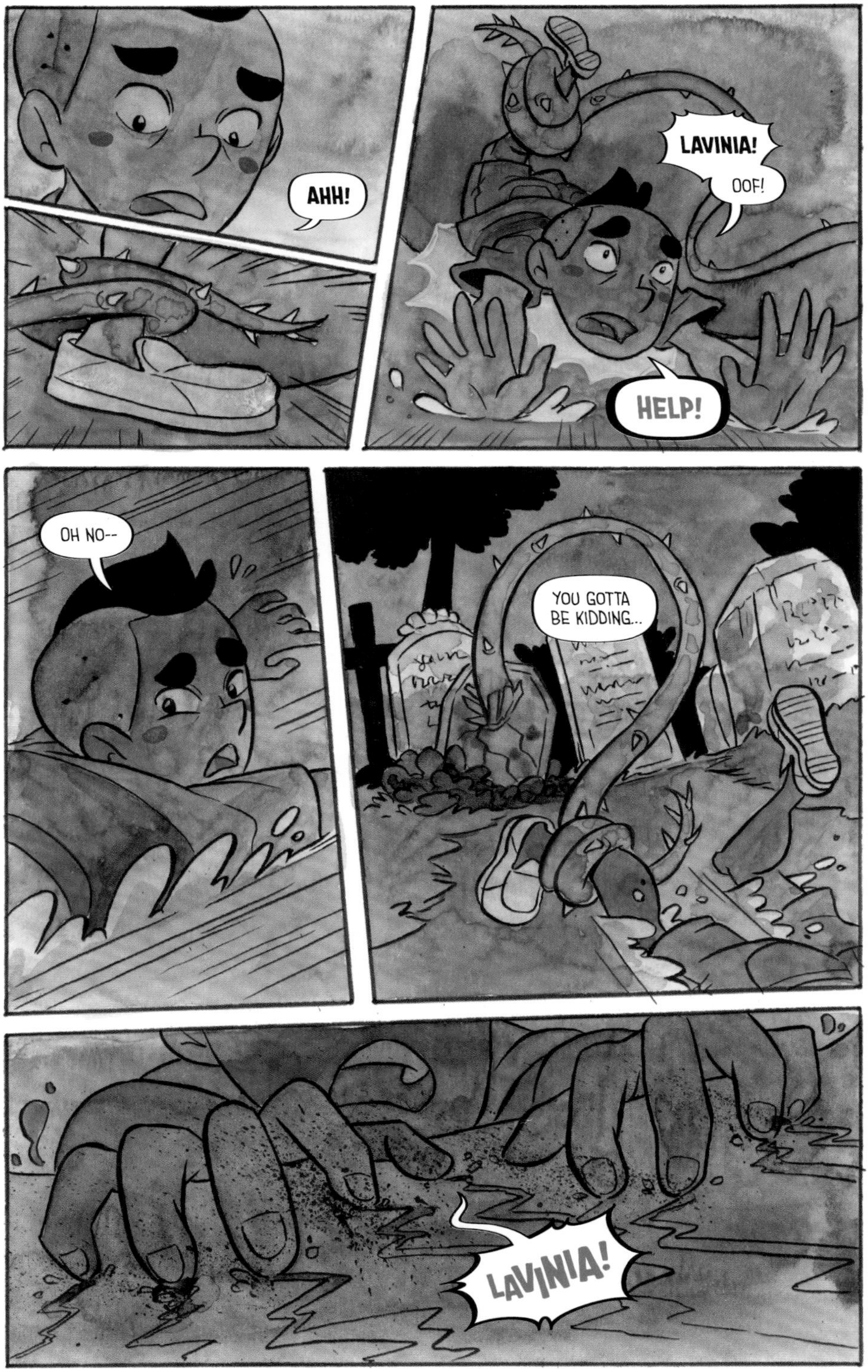
AHH!
LAVINIA!
OOF!
HELP!
OH NO--
YOU GOTTA BE KIDDING...
LAVINIA!

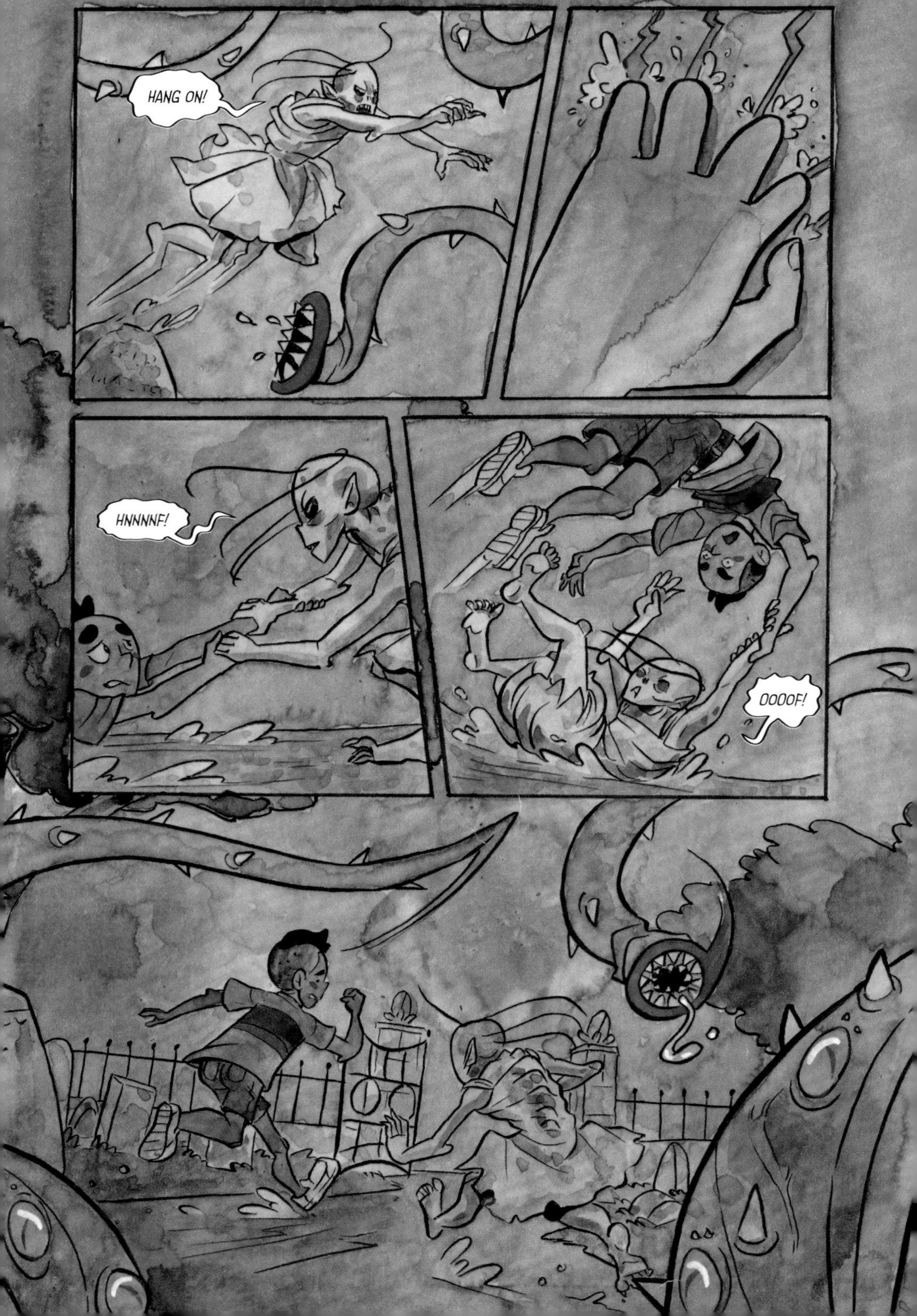
HANG ON!
HNNNNF!
OOOOF!

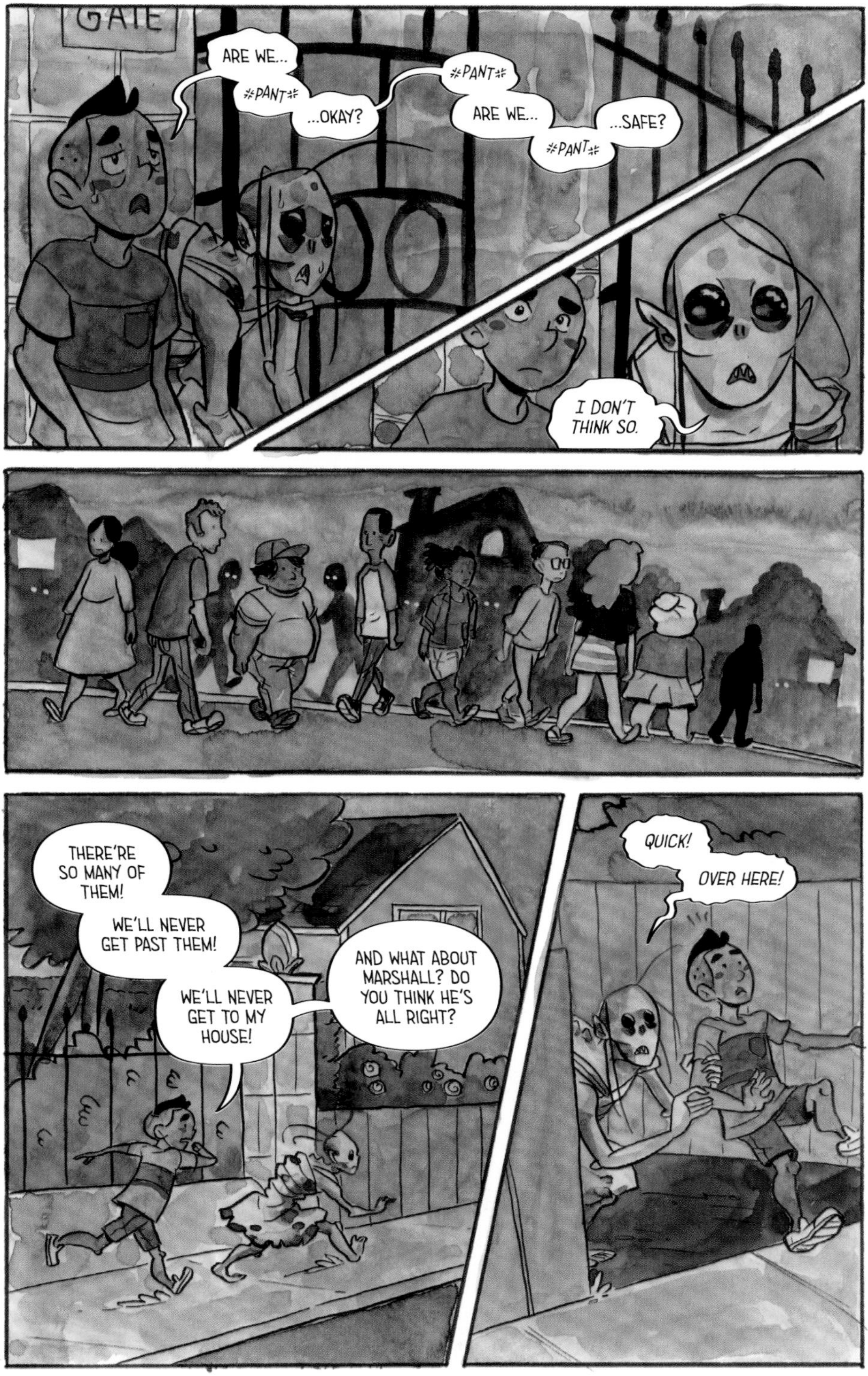
GATE
ARE WE...
#PANT#
...OKAY?
#PANT#
ARE WE...
#PANT#
...SAFE?
I DON'T THINK SO.
THERE'RE SO MANY OF THEM!
WE'LL NEVER GET PAST THEM!
WE'LL NEVER GET TO MY HOUSE!
AND WHAT ABOUT MARSHALL? DO YOU THINK HE'S ALL RIGHT?
QUICK!
OVER HERE!

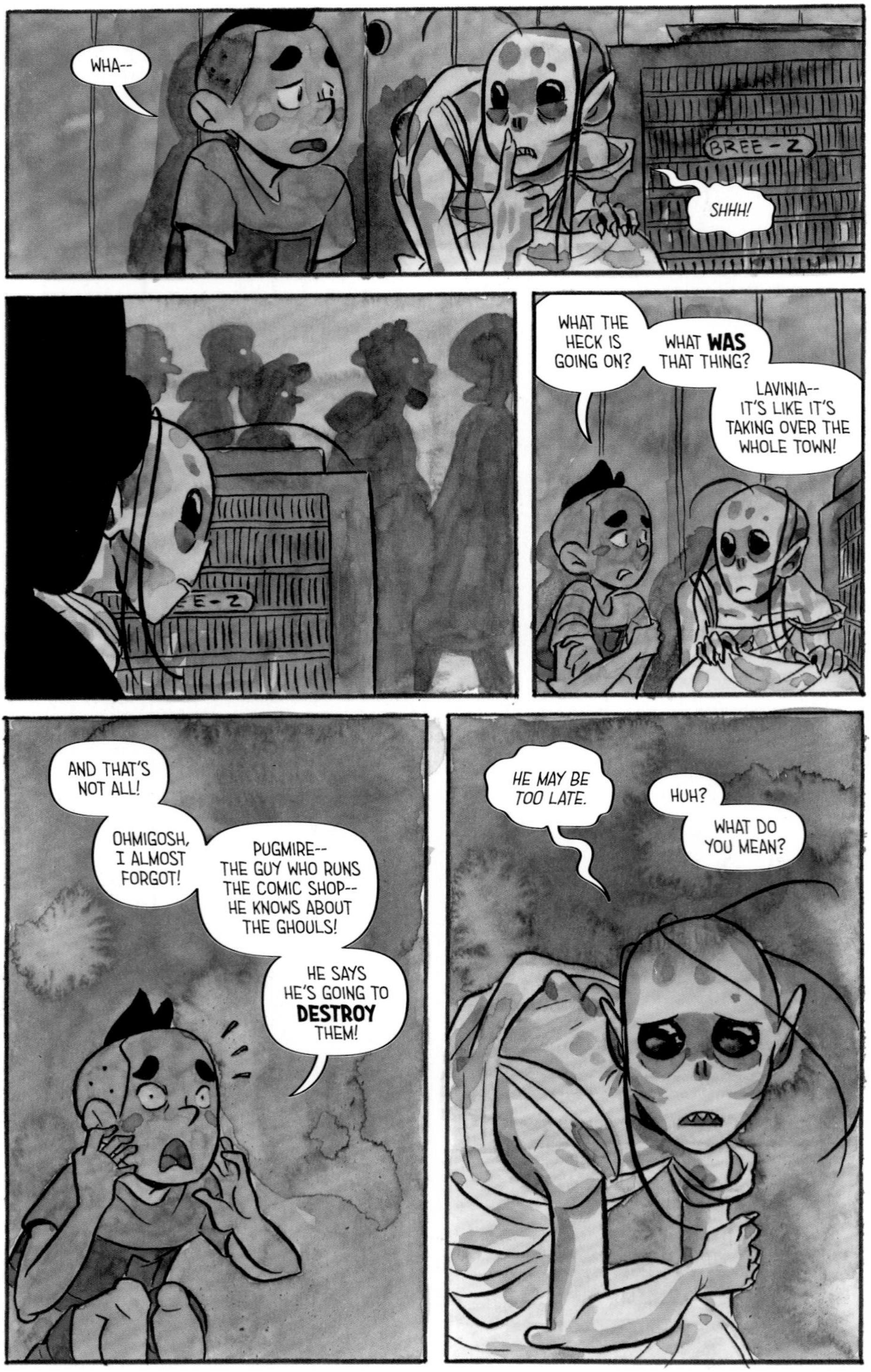
WHA--
BREE-Z
SHHH!
WHAT THE HECK IS GOING ON?
WHAT **WAS** THAT THING?
LAVINIA-- IT'S LIKE IT'S TAKING OVER THE WHOLE TOWN!
AND THAT'S NOT ALL!
OHMIGOSH, I ALMOST FORGOT!
PUGMIRE-- THE GUY WHO RUNS THE COMIC SHOP-- HE KNOWS ABOUT THE GHOULS!
HE SAYS HE'S GOING TO **DESTROY** THEM!
HE MAY BE TOO LATE.
HUH?
WHAT DO YOU MEAN?

THIS THING... THIS PLANT... IS ATTACKING THE GHOULS, TOO.

I *BARELY* ESCAPED NECROPOLIS.

ARE THOSE... **BITES?**

I'M ALL RIGHT.

GHOULS... HEAL QUICKLY.

BUT A LOT OF OTHERS WEREN'T SO LUCKY.

WHAT DO YOU KNOW ABOUT THIS PLANT-CREATURE?

I THOUGHT MAYBE A VAMPIRE HAD COME TO ANDER'S LANDING.

BUT THIS THING--

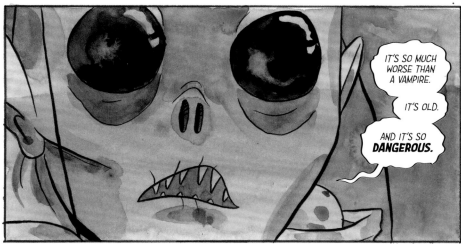

IT'S SO MUCH WORSE THAN A VAMPIRE.

IT'S OLD.

AND IT'S SO **DANGEROUS.**

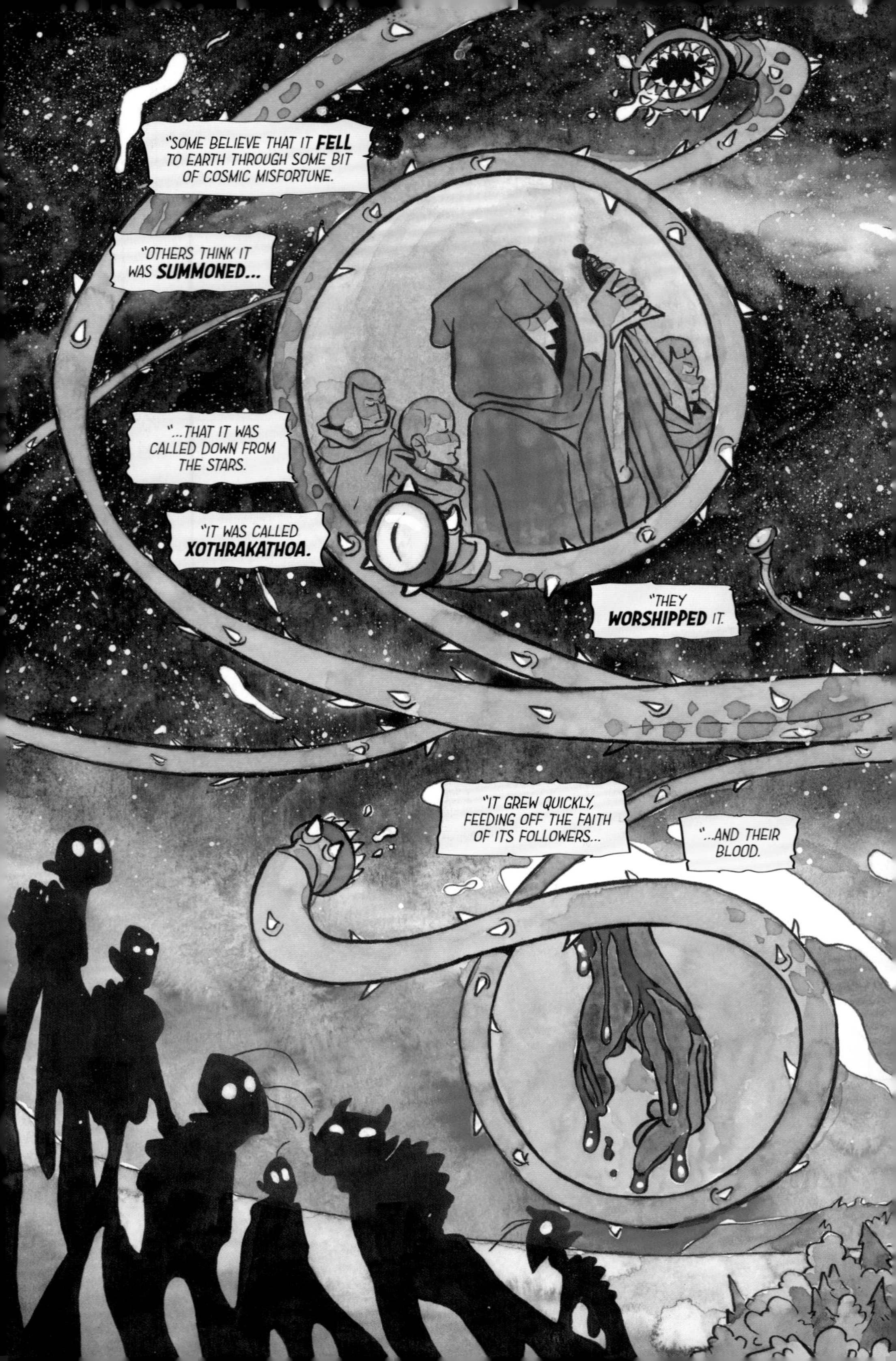
"SOME BELIEVE THAT IT **FELL** TO EARTH THROUGH SOME BIT OF COSMIC MISFORTUNE.
"OTHERS THINK IT WAS **SUMMONED...**
"...THAT IT WAS CALLED DOWN FROM THE STARS.
"IT WAS CALLED **XOTHRAKATHOA.**
"THEY **WORSHIPPED** IT.
"IT GREW QUICKLY, FEEDING OFF THE FAITH OF ITS FOLLOWERS...
"...AND THEIR BLOOD.

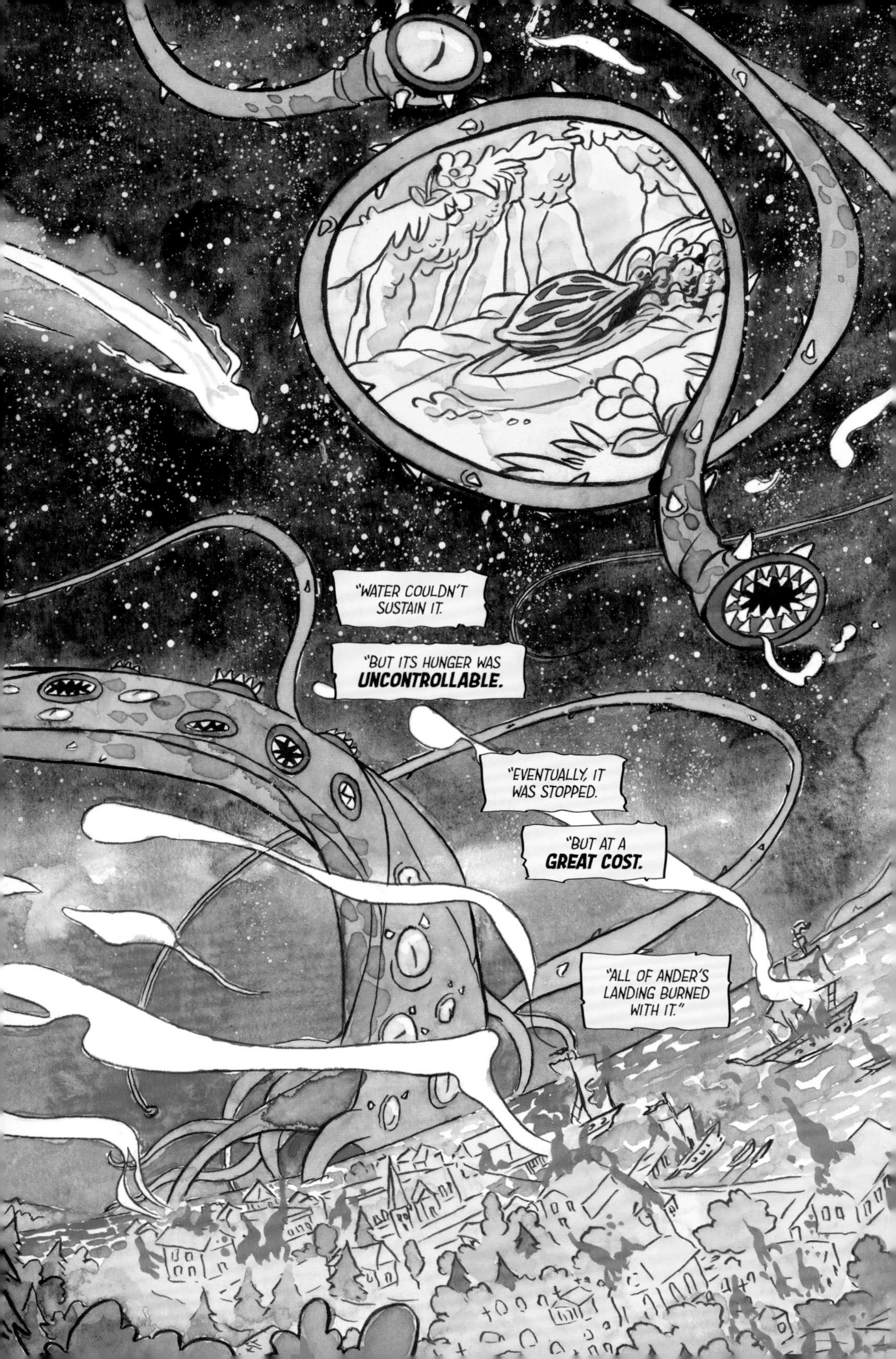
"WATER COULDN'T SUSTAIN IT.
"BUT ITS HUNGER WAS UNCONTROLLABLE.
"EVENTUALLY, IT WAS STOPPED.
"BUT AT A GREAT COST.
"ALL OF ANDER'S LANDING BURNED WITH IT."

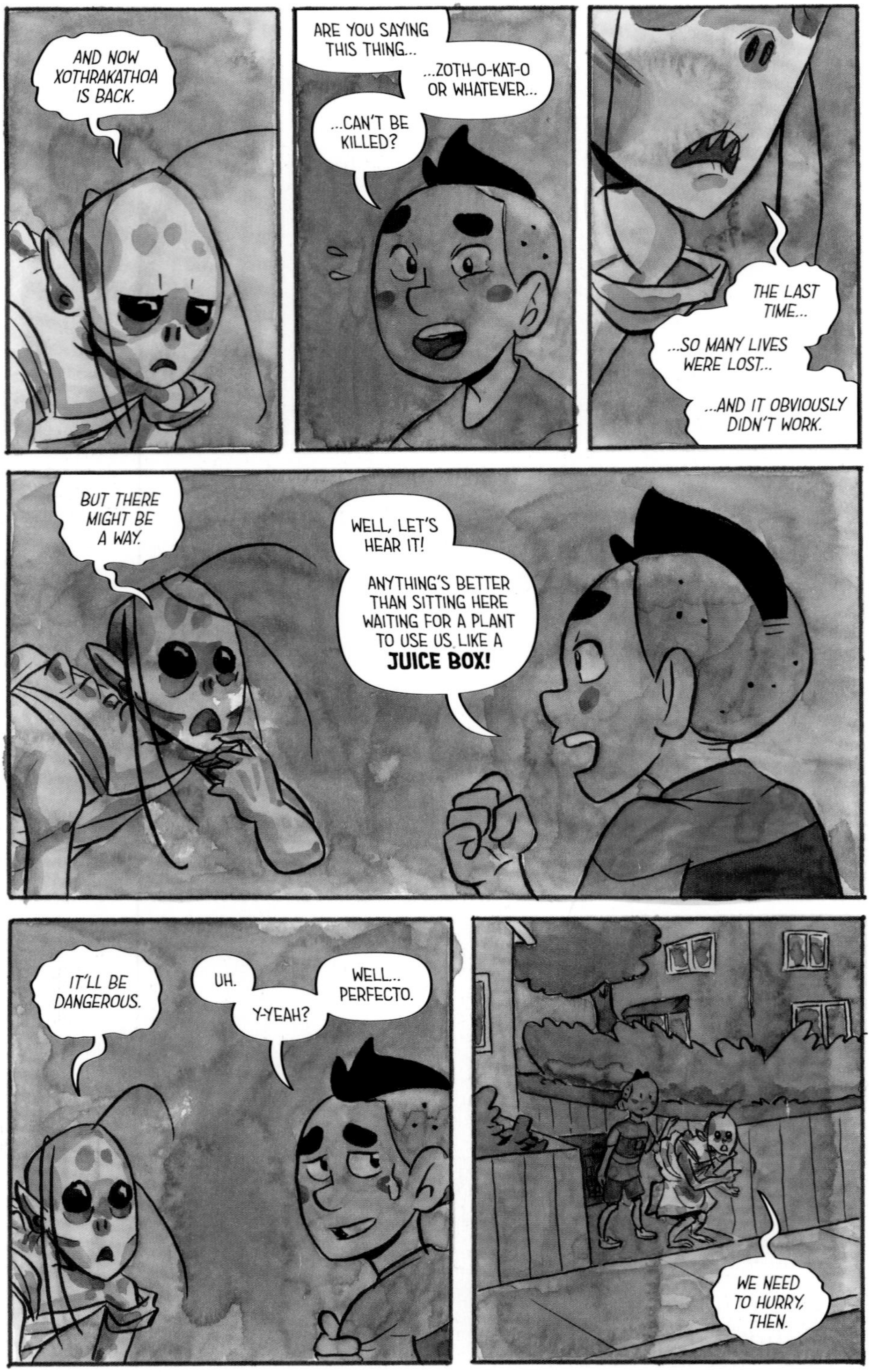
AND NOW XOTHRAKATHOA IS BACK.
ARE YOU SAYING THIS THING...
...ZOTH-O-KAT-O OR WHATEVER...
...CAN'T BE KILLED?
THE LAST TIME...
...SO MANY LIVES WERE LOST...
...AND IT OBVIOUSLY DIDN'T WORK.
BUT THERE MIGHT BE A WAY.
WELL, LET'S HEAR IT!
ANYTHING'S BETTER THAN SITTING HERE WAITING FOR A PLANT TO USE US LIKE A **JUICE BOX!**
IT'LL BE DANGEROUS.
UH.
Y-YEAH?
WELL... PERFECTO.
WE NEED TO HURRY, THEN.

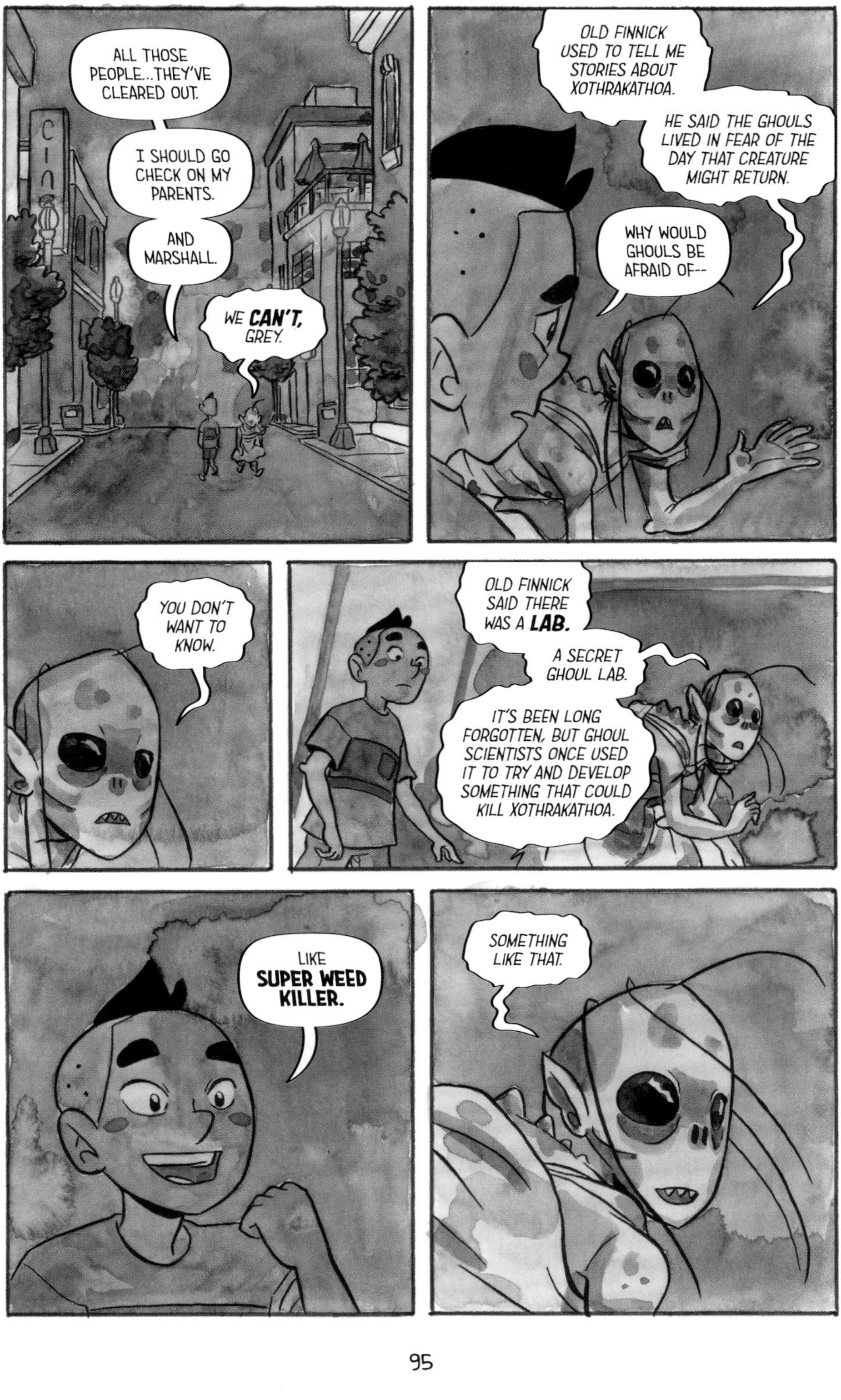
ALL THOSE PEOPLE...THEY'VE CLEARED OUT.
I SHOULD GO CHECK ON MY PARENTS.
AND MARSHALL.
WE CAN'T, GREY.
OLD FINNICK USED TO TELL ME STORIES ABOUT XOTHRAKATHOA.
HE SAID THE GHOULS LIVED IN FEAR OF THE DAY THAT CREATURE MIGHT RETURN.
WHY WOULD GHOULS BE AFRAID OF--
YOU DON'T WANT TO KNOW.
OLD FINNICK SAID THERE WAS A LAB.
A SECRET GHOUL LAB.
IT'S BEEN LONG FORGOTTEN, BUT GHOUL SCIENTISTS ONCE USED IT TO TRY AND DEVELOP SOMETHING THAT COULD KILL XOTHRAKATHOA.
LIKE SUPER WEED KILLER.
SOMETHING LIKE THAT.

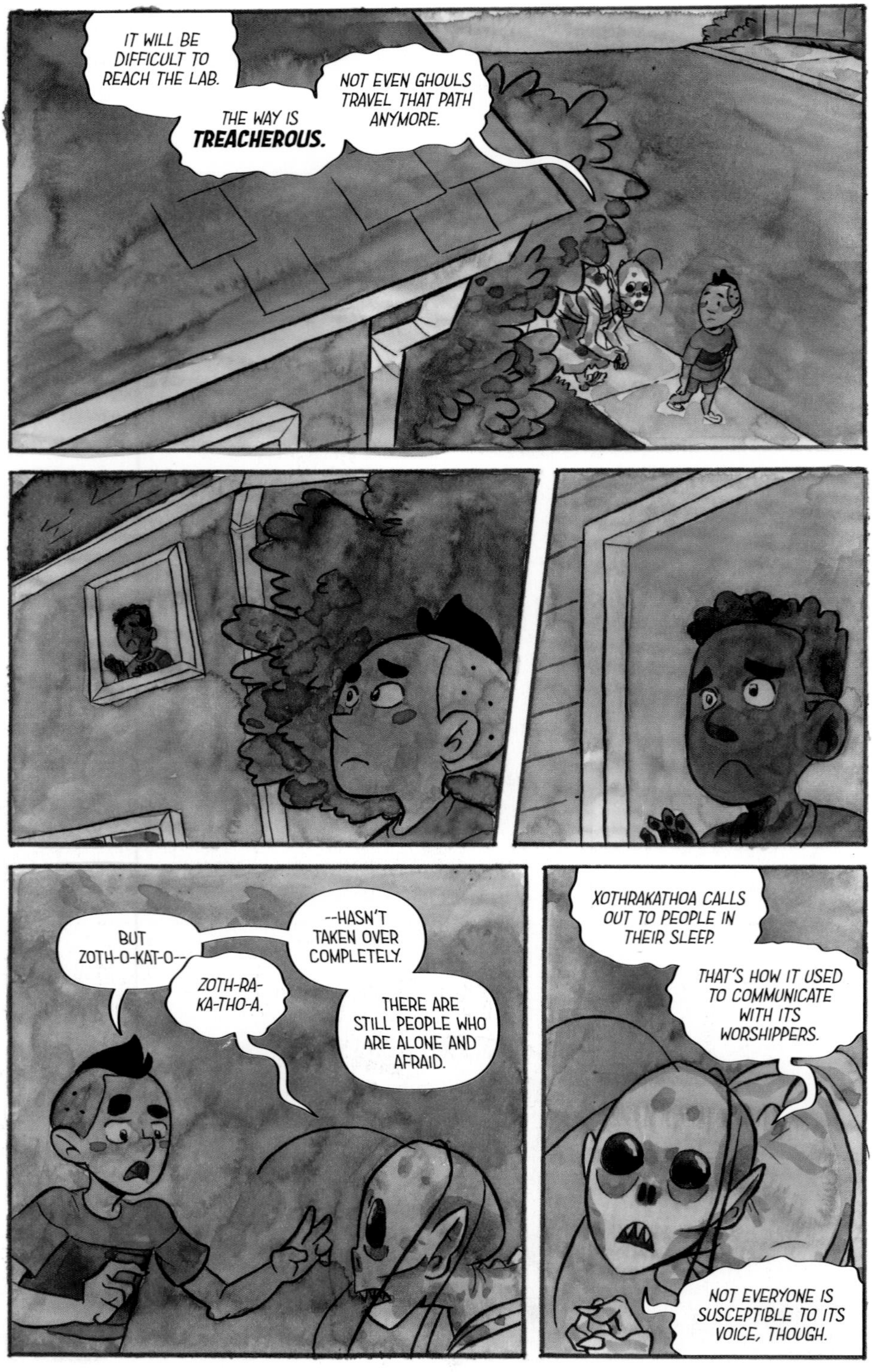
IT WILL BE DIFFICULT TO REACH THE LAB.
THE WAY IS **TREACHEROUS.**
NOT EVEN GHOULS TRAVEL THAT PATH ANYMORE.
BUT ZOTH-O-KAT-O--
ZOTH-RA-KA-THO-A.
--HASN'T TAKEN OVER COMPLETELY.
THERE ARE STILL PEOPLE WHO ARE ALONE AND AFRAID.
XOTHRAKATHOA CALLS OUT TO PEOPLE IN THEIR SLEEP.
THAT'S HOW IT USED TO COMMUNICATE WITH ITS WORSHIPPERS.
NOT EVERYONE IS SUSCEPTIBLE TO ITS VOICE, THOUGH.

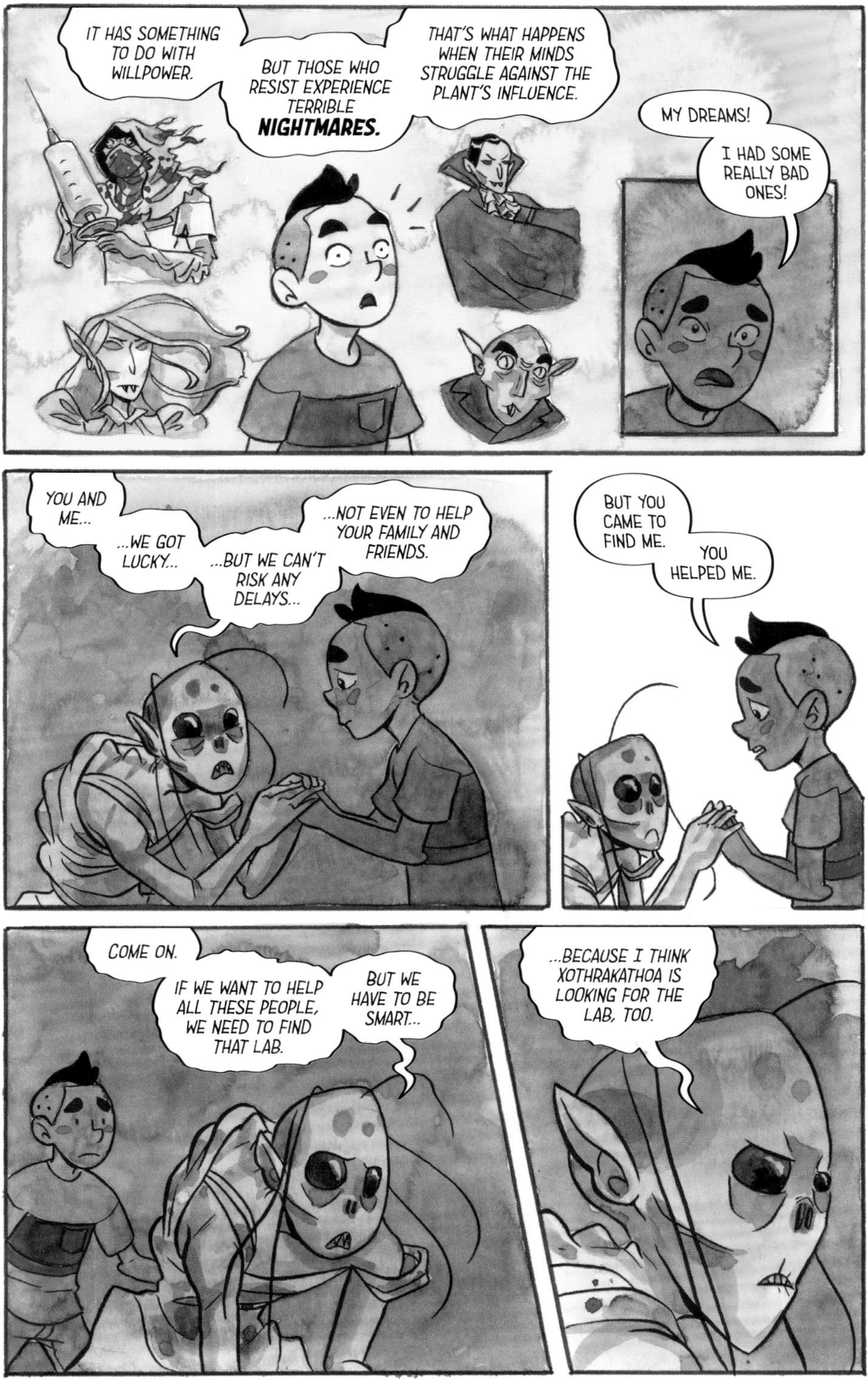
IT HAS SOMETHING TO DO WITH WILLPOWER.
BUT THOSE WHO RESIST EXPERIENCE TERRIBLE **NIGHTMARES.**
THAT'S WHAT HAPPENS WHEN THEIR MINDS STRUGGLE AGAINST THE PLANT'S INFLUENCE.
MY DREAMS!
I HAD SOME REALLY BAD ONES!
YOU AND ME...
...WE GOT LUCKY...
...BUT WE CAN'T RISK ANY DELAYS...
...NOT EVEN TO HELP YOUR FAMILY AND FRIENDS.
BUT YOU CAME TO FIND ME.
YOU HELPED ME.
COME ON.
IF WE WANT TO HELP ALL THESE PEOPLE, WE NEED TO FIND THAT LAB.
BUT WE HAVE TO BE SMART...
...BECAUSE I THINK XOTHRAKATHOA IS LOOKING FOR THE LAB, TOO.

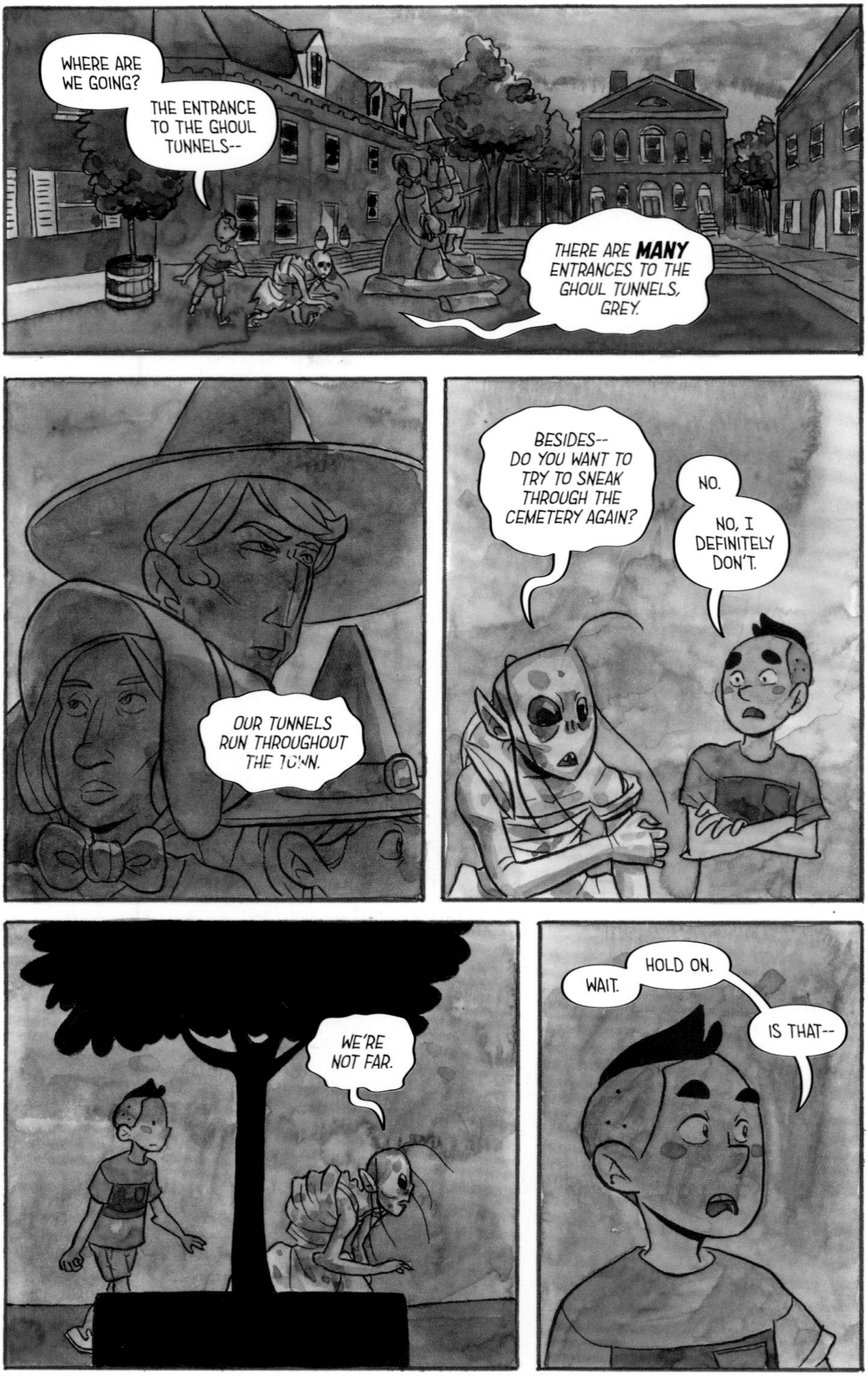
WHERE ARE WE GOING?
THE ENTRANCE TO THE GHOUL TUNNELS--
THERE ARE **MANY** ENTRANCES TO THE GHOUL TUNNELS, GREY.
OUR TUNNELS RUN THROUGHOUT THE TOWN.
BESIDES-- DO YOU WANT TO TRY TO SNEAK THROUGH THE CEMETERY AGAIN?
NO.
NO, I DEFINITELY DON'T.
WE'RE NOT FAR.
WAIT.
HOLD ON.
IS THAT--

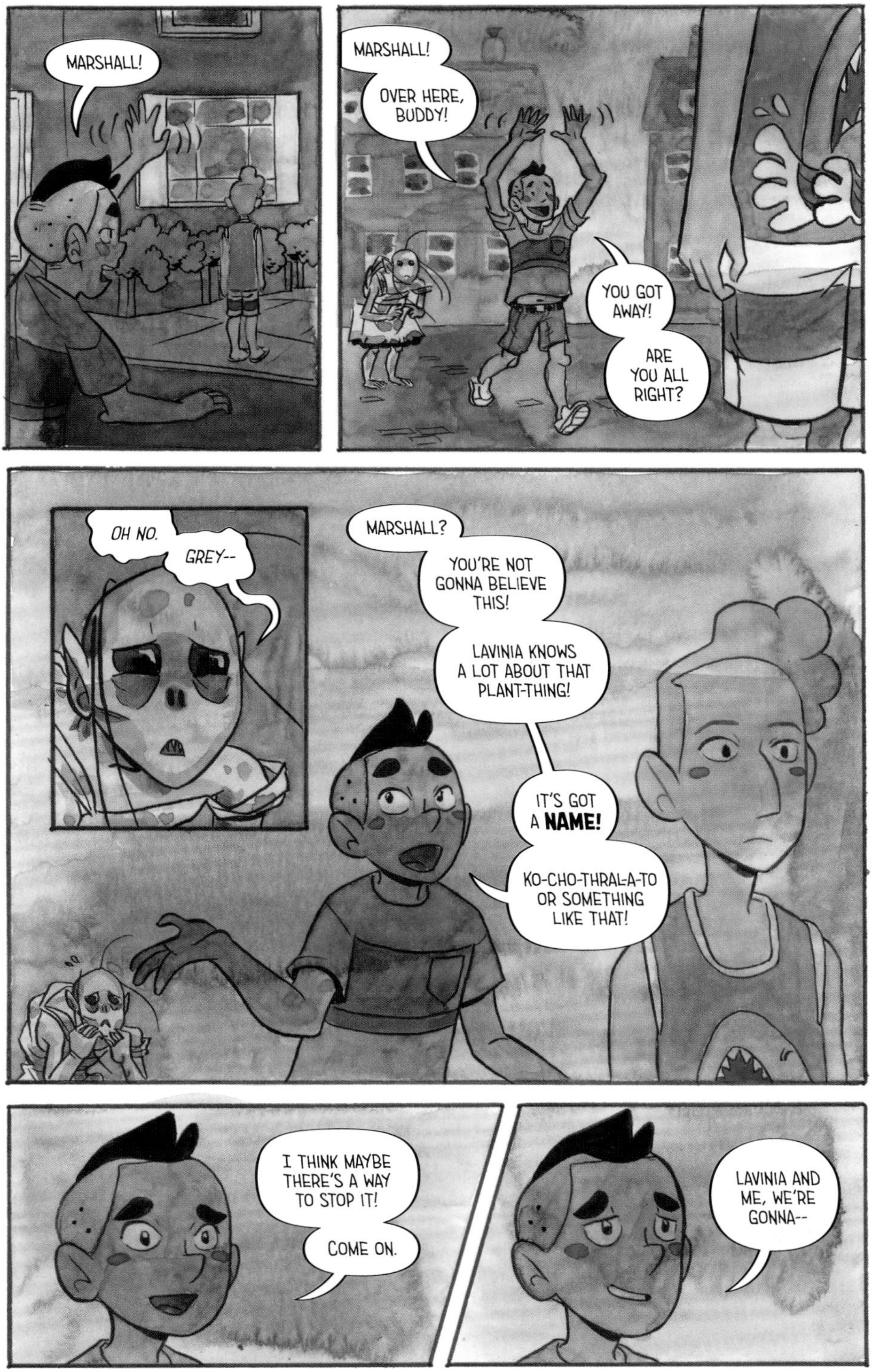
MARSHALL!
MARSHALL!
OVER HERE, BUDDY!
YOU GOT AWAY!
ARE YOU ALL RIGHT?
OH NO.
GREY--
MARSHALL?
YOU'RE NOT GONNA BELIEVE THIS!
LAVINIA KNOWS A LOT ABOUT THAT PLANT-THING!
IT'S GOT A **NAME!**
KO-CHO-THRAL-A-TO OR SOMETHING LIKE THAT!
I THINK MAYBE THERE'S A WAY TO STOP IT!
COME ON.
LAVINIA AND ME, WE'RE GONNA--

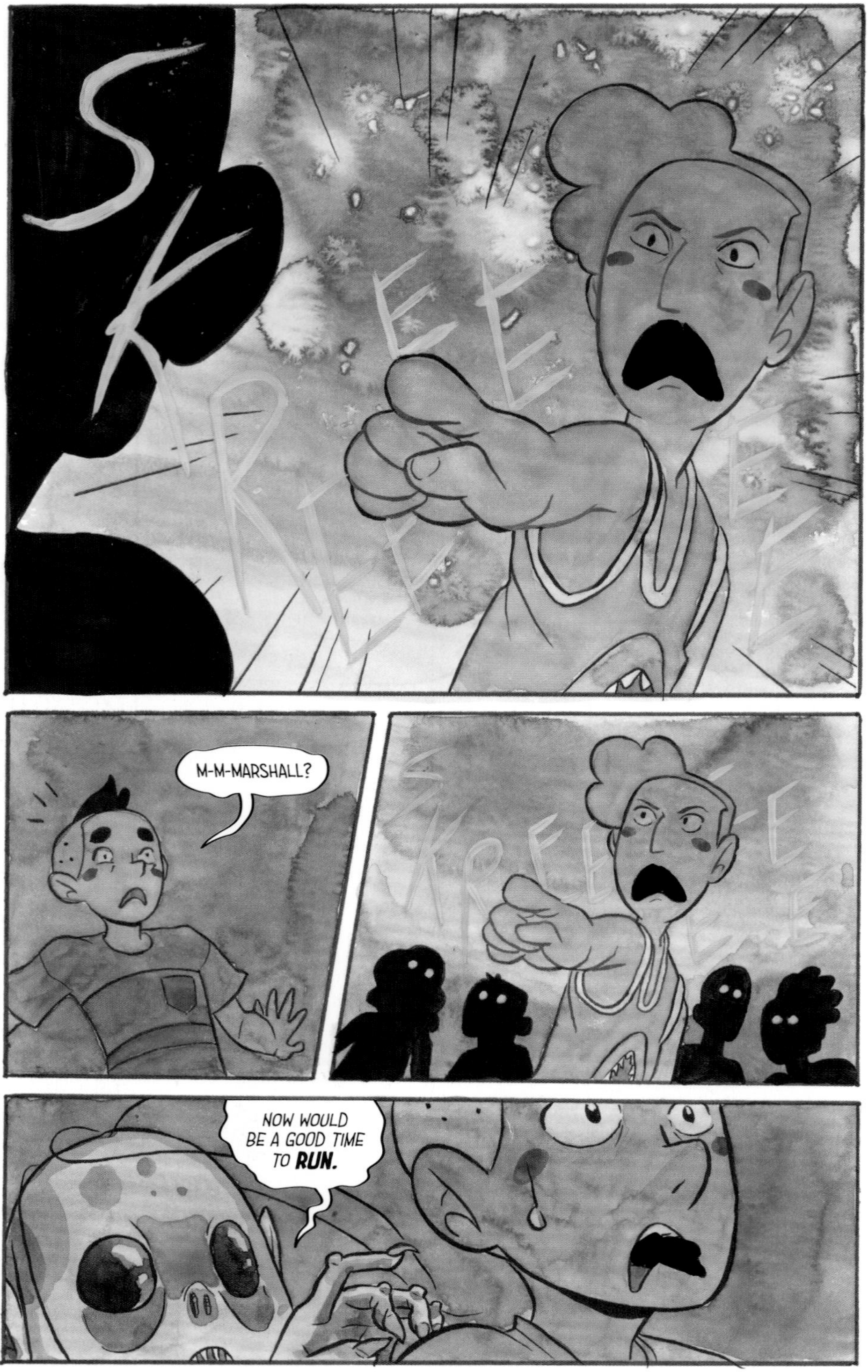
M-M-MARSHALL?
NOW WOULD BE A GOOD TIME TO **RUN.**

THAT...WASN'T MARSHALL.

IT WAS, BUT HE'S UNDER XOTHRAKATHOA'S CONTROL.

WE CAN SAVE HIM.

WE JUST NEED TO--

KILL THE PLANT.

I WAS GONNA SAY "FIND THE LAB."

BUT...YEAH.

WE GOTTA KILL THE PLANT.

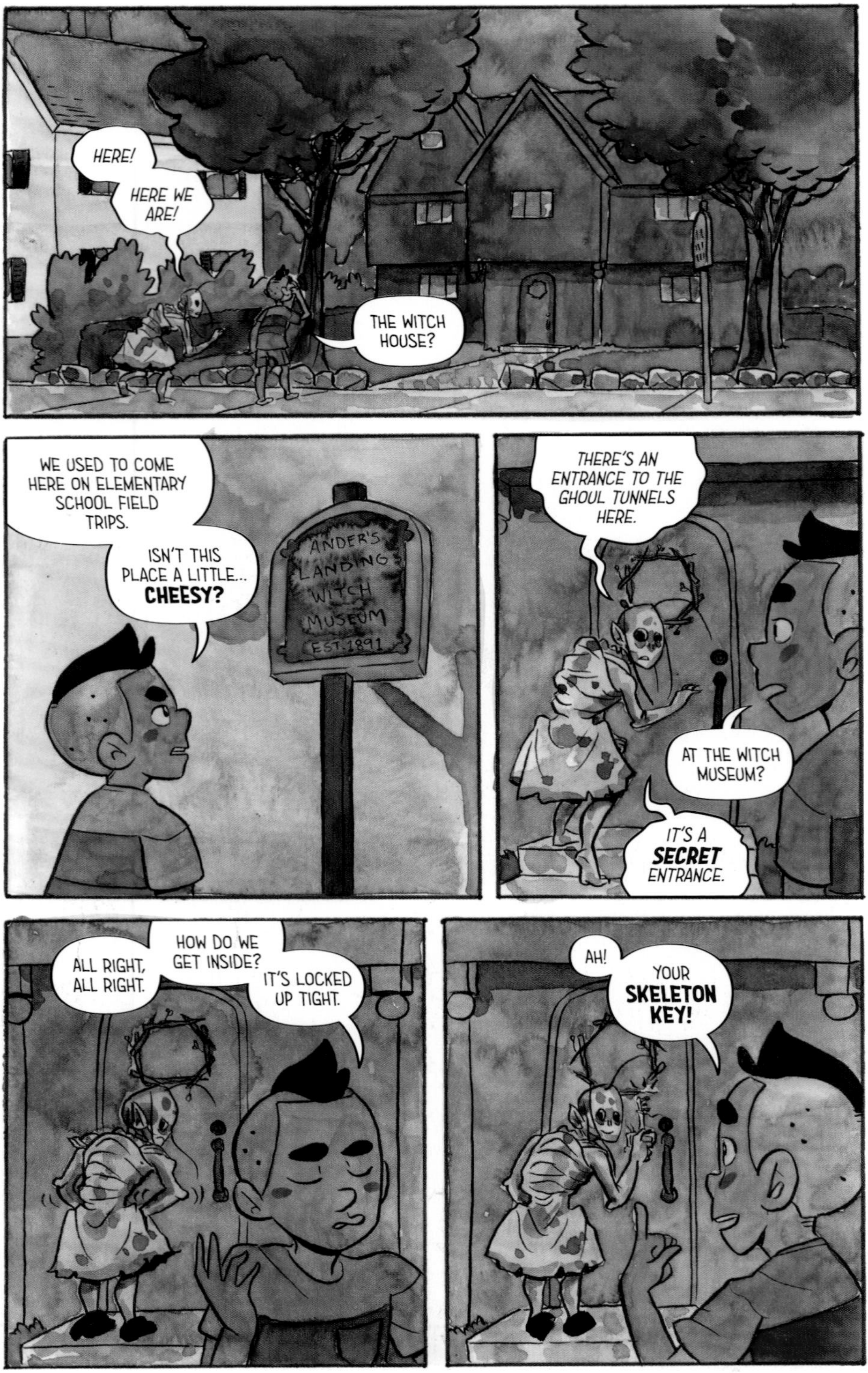
HERE!
HERE WE ARE!
THE WITCH HOUSE?
WE USED TO COME HERE ON ELEMENTARY SCHOOL FIELD TRIPS.
ISN'T THIS PLACE A LITTLE... **CHEESY?**
ANDER'S LANDING WITCH MUSEUM EST. 1891
THERE'S AN ENTRANCE TO THE GHOUL TUNNELS HERE.
AT THE WITCH MUSEUM?
IT'S A **SECRET** ENTRANCE.
ALL RIGHT, ALL RIGHT.
HOW DO WE GET INSIDE?
IT'S LOCKED UP TIGHT.
AH!
YOUR **SKELETON KEY!**

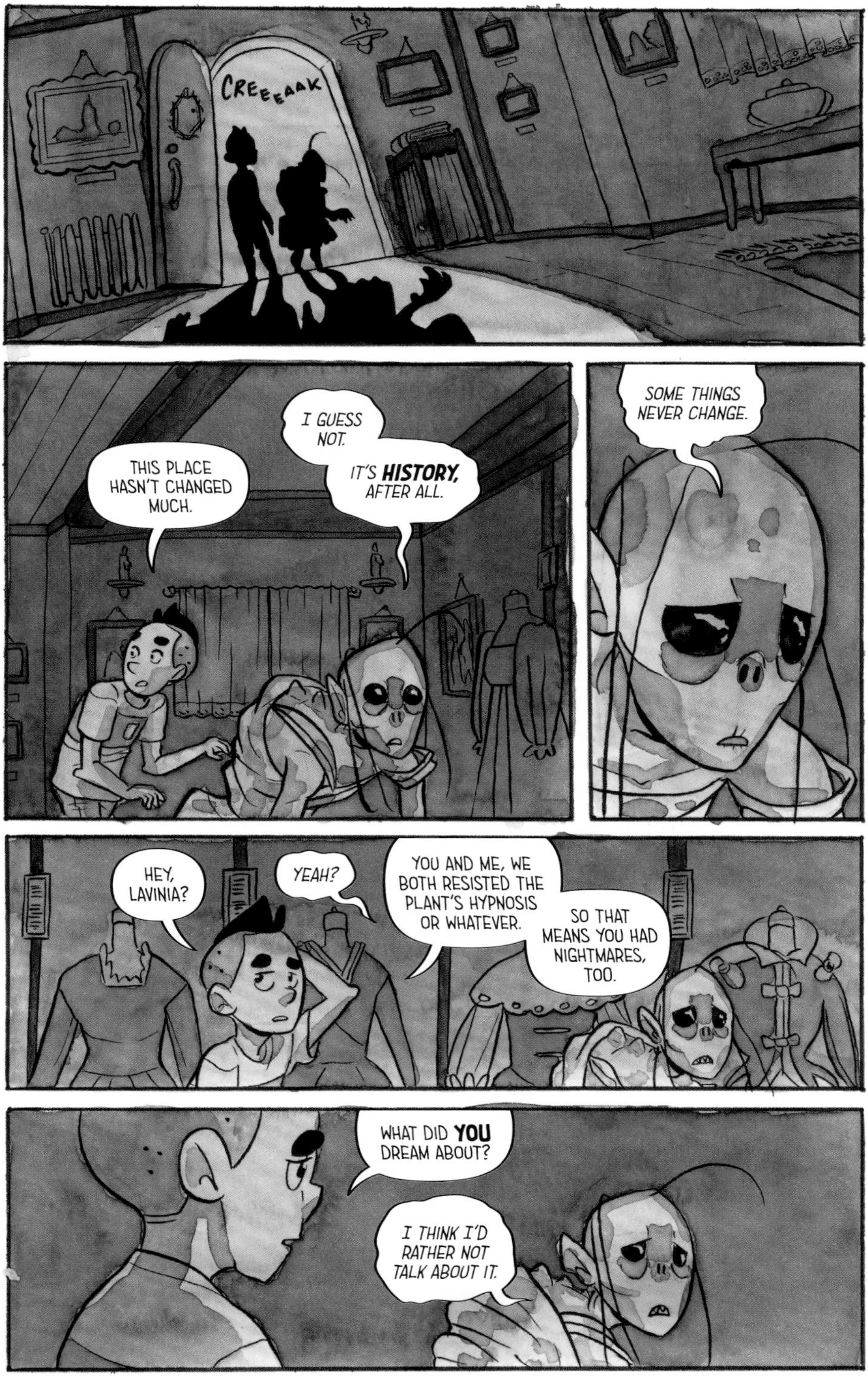
CREEEAAK
THIS PLACE HASN'T CHANGED MUCH.
I GUESS NOT.
IT'S **HISTORY,** AFTER ALL.
SOME THINGS NEVER CHANGE.
HEY, LAVINIA?
YEAH?
YOU AND ME, WE BOTH RESISTED THE PLANT'S HYPNOSIS OR WHATEVER.
SO THAT MEANS YOU HAD NIGHTMARES, TOO.
WHAT DID **YOU** DREAM ABOUT?
I THINK I'D RATHER NOT TALK ABOUT IT.

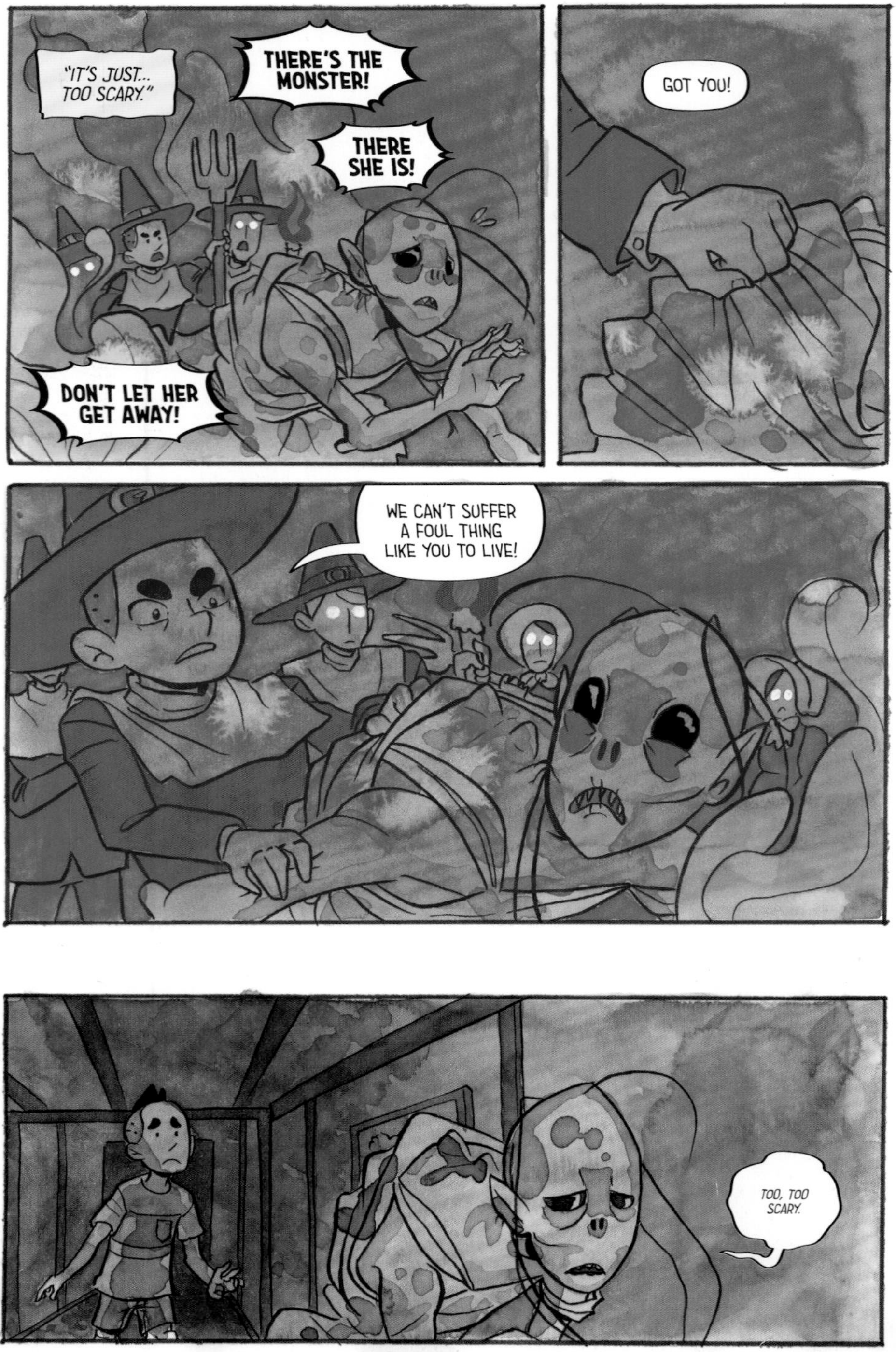
"IT'S JUST... TOO SCARY."
THERE'S THE MONSTER!
THERE SHE IS!
DON'T LET HER GET AWAY!
GOT YOU!
WE CAN'T SUFFER A FOUL THING LIKE YOU TO LIVE!
TOO, TOO SCARY.

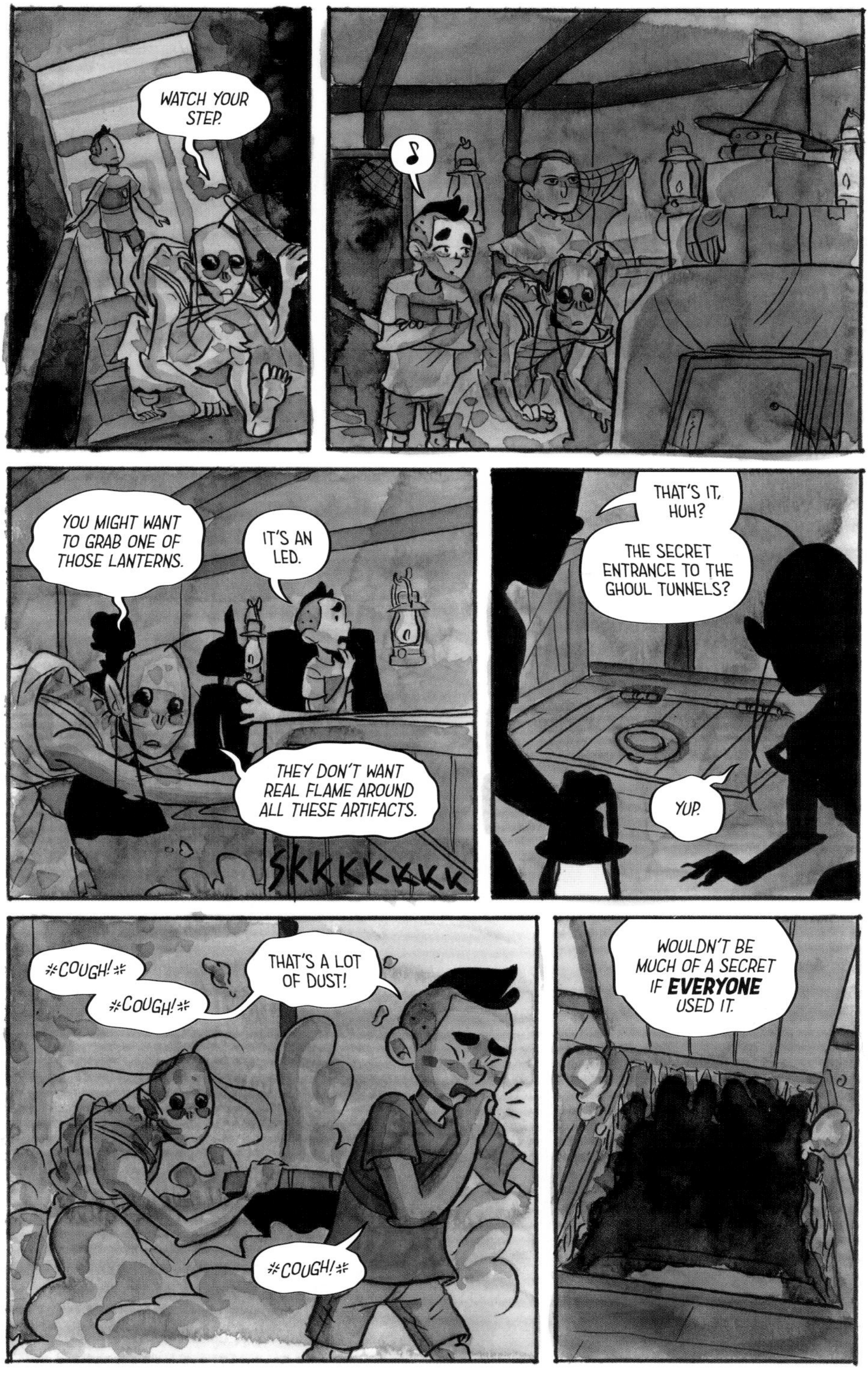
WATCH YOUR STEP.
♪
YOU MIGHT WANT TO GRAB ONE OF THOSE LANTERNS.
IT'S AN LED.
THEY DON'T WANT REAL FLAME AROUND ALL THESE ARTIFACTS.
SKKKKKKK
THAT'S IT, HUH?
THE SECRET ENTRANCE TO THE GHOUL TUNNELS?
YUP.
COUGH!
COUGH!
THAT'S A LOT OF DUST!
COUGH!
WOULDN'T BE MUCH OF A SECRET IF **EVERYONE** USED IT.

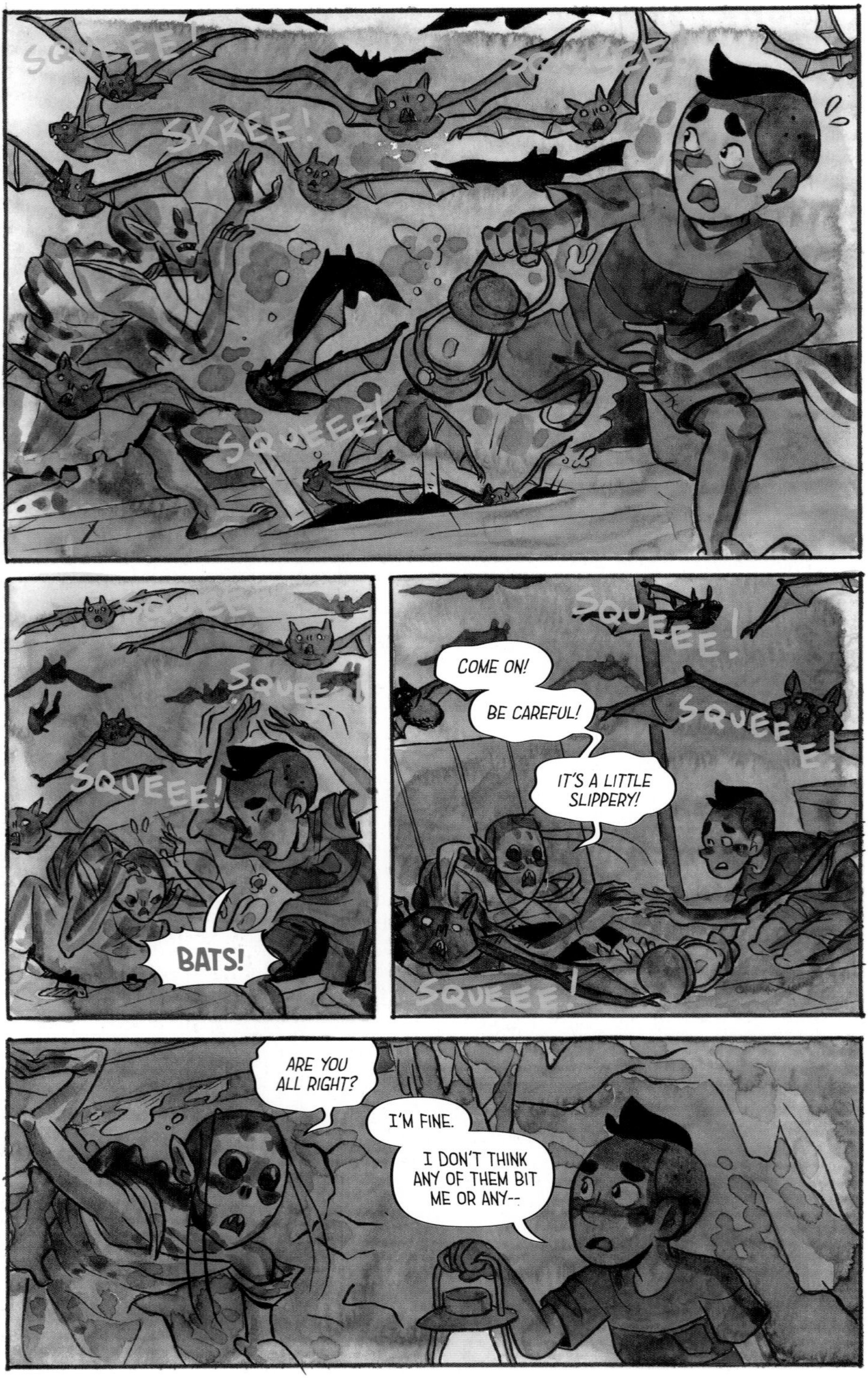
SQUEEE!
SKREE!
SQUEEE!
SQUEEE!
SQUEEE!
SQUEEE!
SQUEEE!
BATS!
SQUEEE!
COME ON!
BE CAREFUL!
SQUEEEE!
IT'S A LITTLE SLIPPERY!
SQUEEE!
ARE YOU ALL RIGHT?
I'M FINE.
I DON'T THINK ANY OF THEM BIT ME OR ANY--

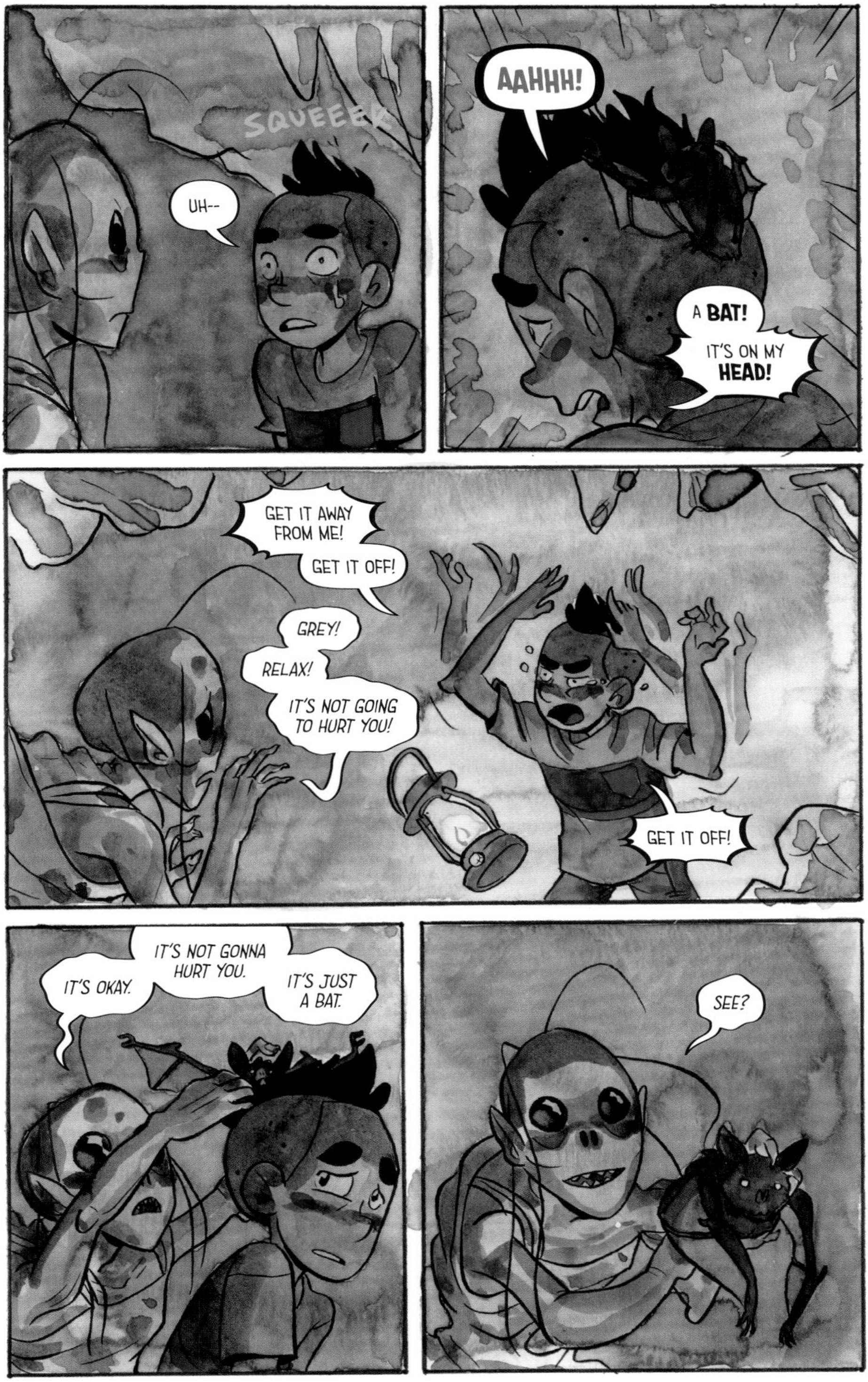
SQUEEEK
UH--
AAHHH!
A **BAT!**
IT'S ON MY **HEAD!**
GET IT AWAY FROM ME!
GET IT OFF!
GREY!
RELAX!
IT'S NOT GOING TO HURT YOU!
GET IT OFF!
IT'S OKAY.
IT'S NOT GONNA HURT YOU.
IT'S JUST A BAT.
SEE?

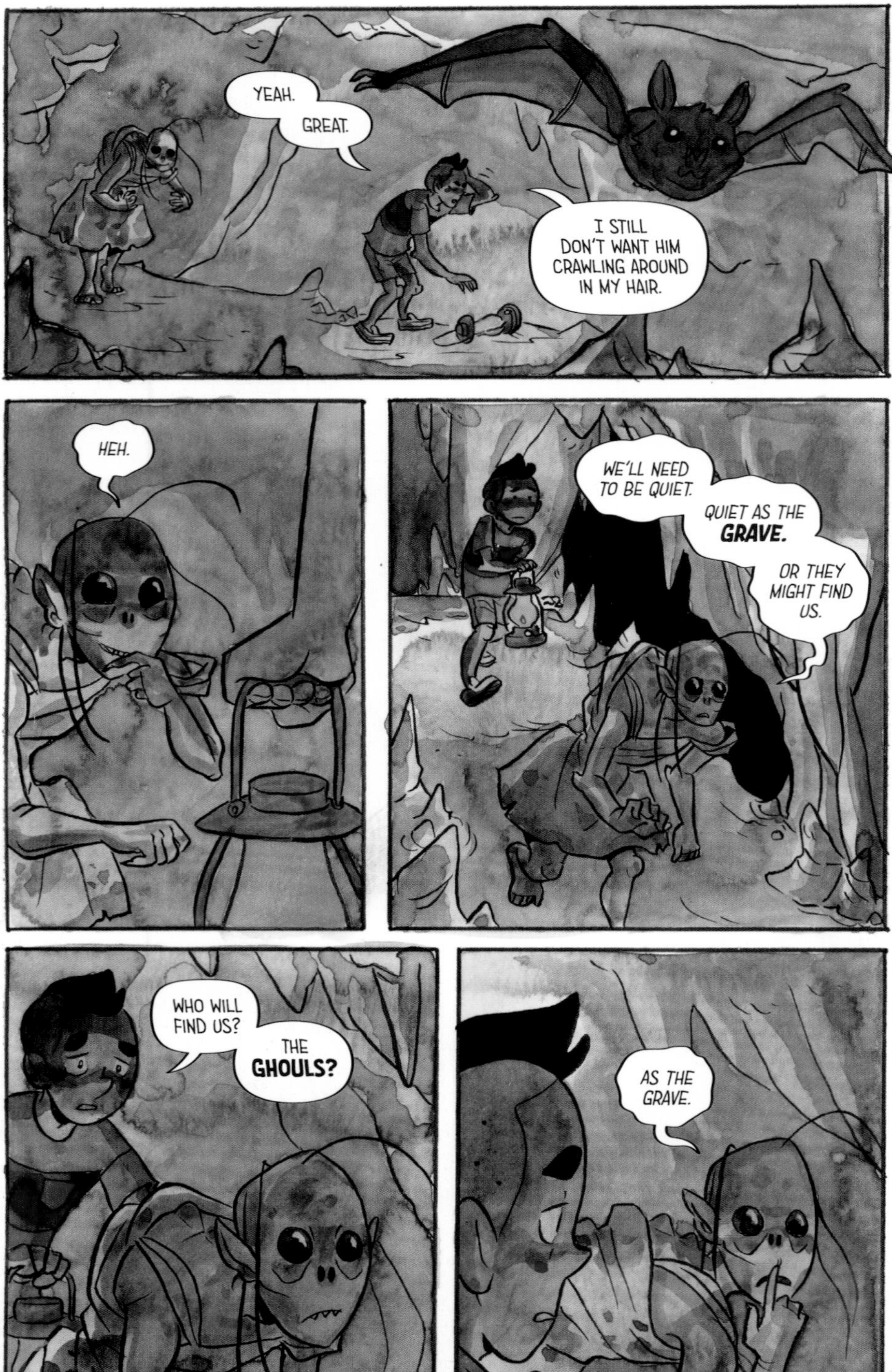

YEAH.
GREAT.
I STILL DON'T WANT HIM CRAWLING AROUND IN MY HAIR.
HEH.
WE'LL NEED TO BE QUIET.
QUIET AS THE **GRAVE.**
OR THEY MIGHT FIND US.
WHO WILL FIND US?
THE **GHOULS?**
AS THE GRAVE.

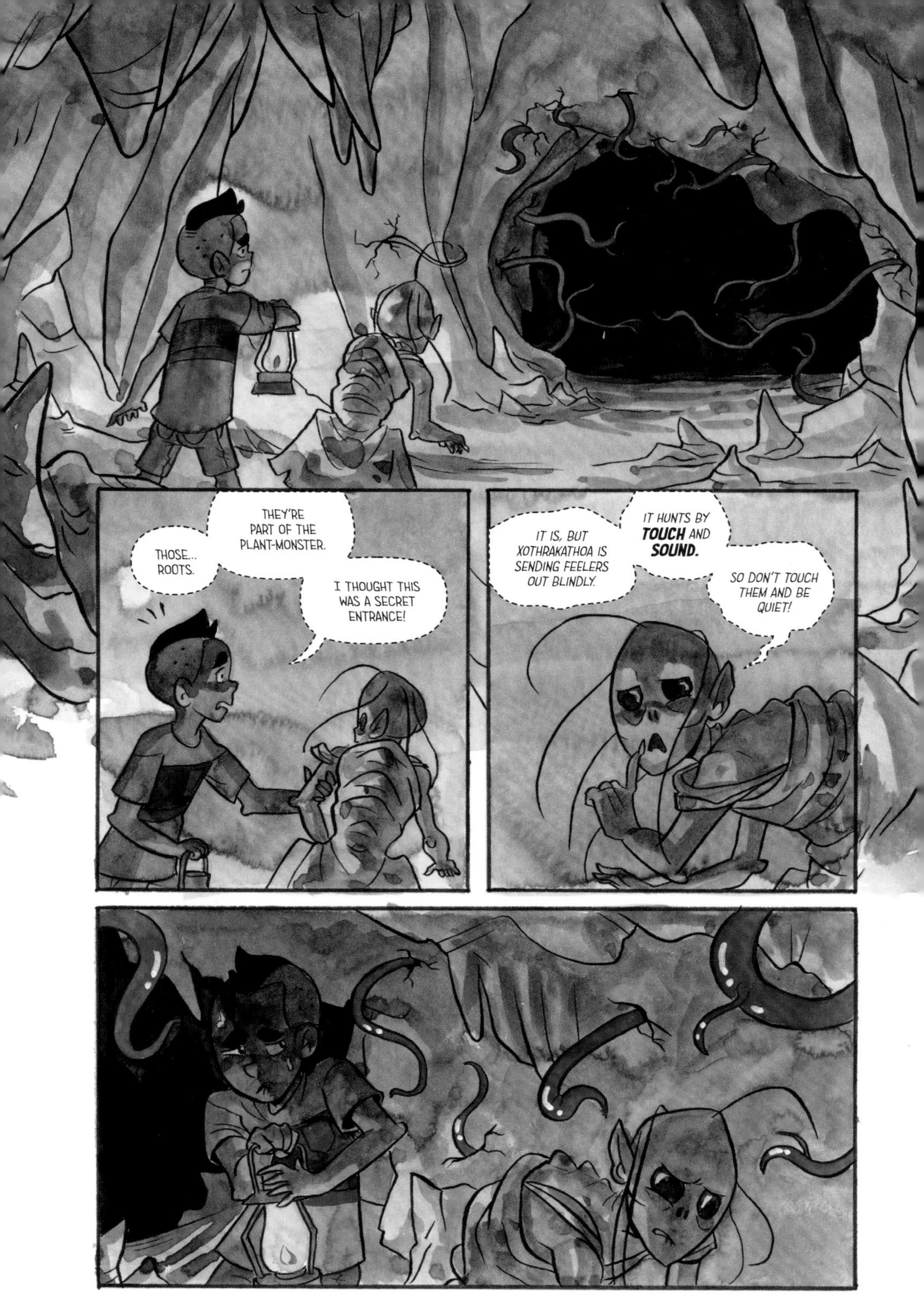
THOSE... ROOTS.
THEY'RE PART OF THE PLANT-MONSTER.
I THOUGHT THIS WAS A SECRET ENTRANCE!
IT IS, BUT XOTHRAKATHOA IS SENDING FEELERS OUT BLINDLY.
IT HUNTS BY TOUCH AND SOUND.
SO DON'T TOUCH THEM AND BE QUIET!

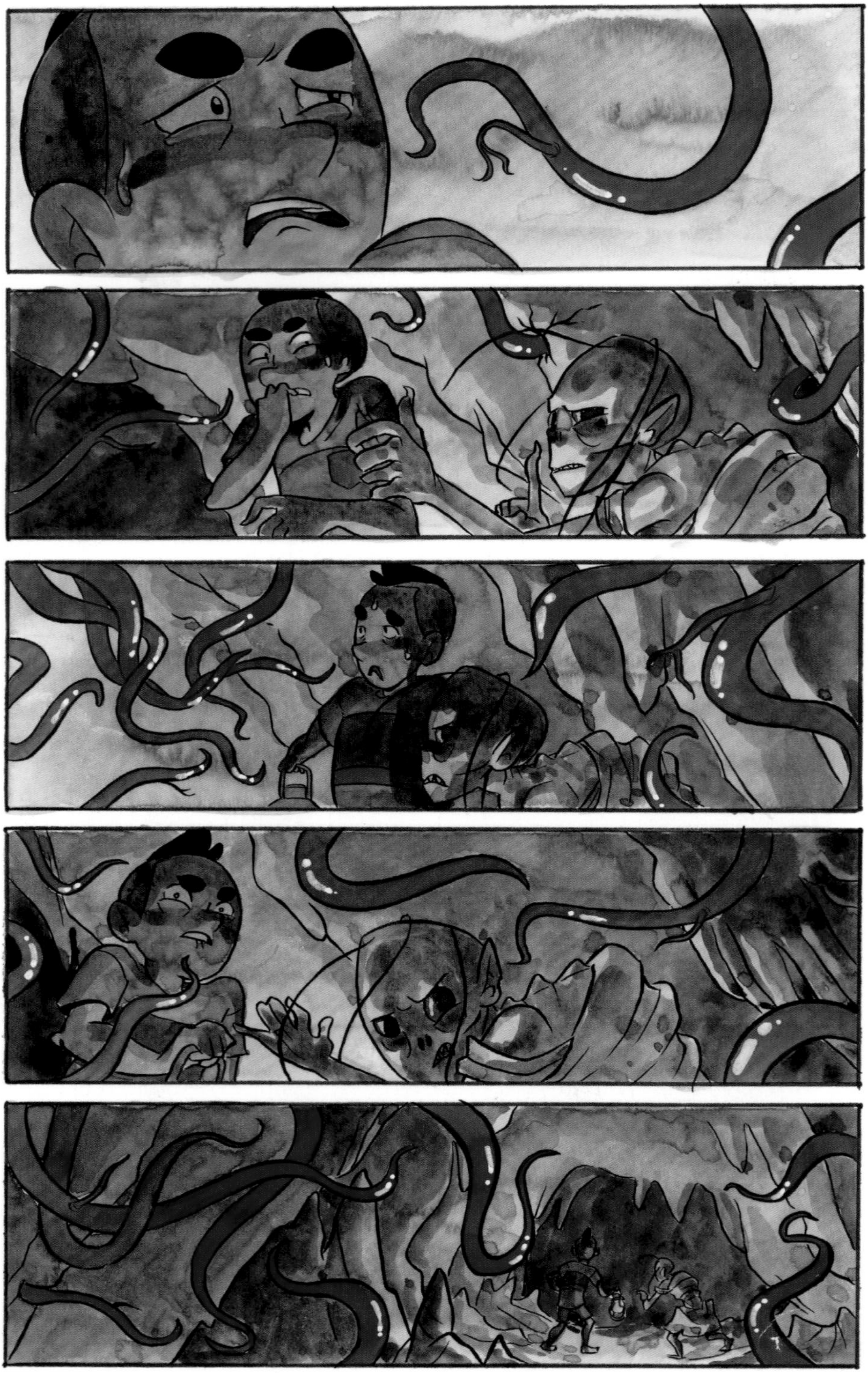

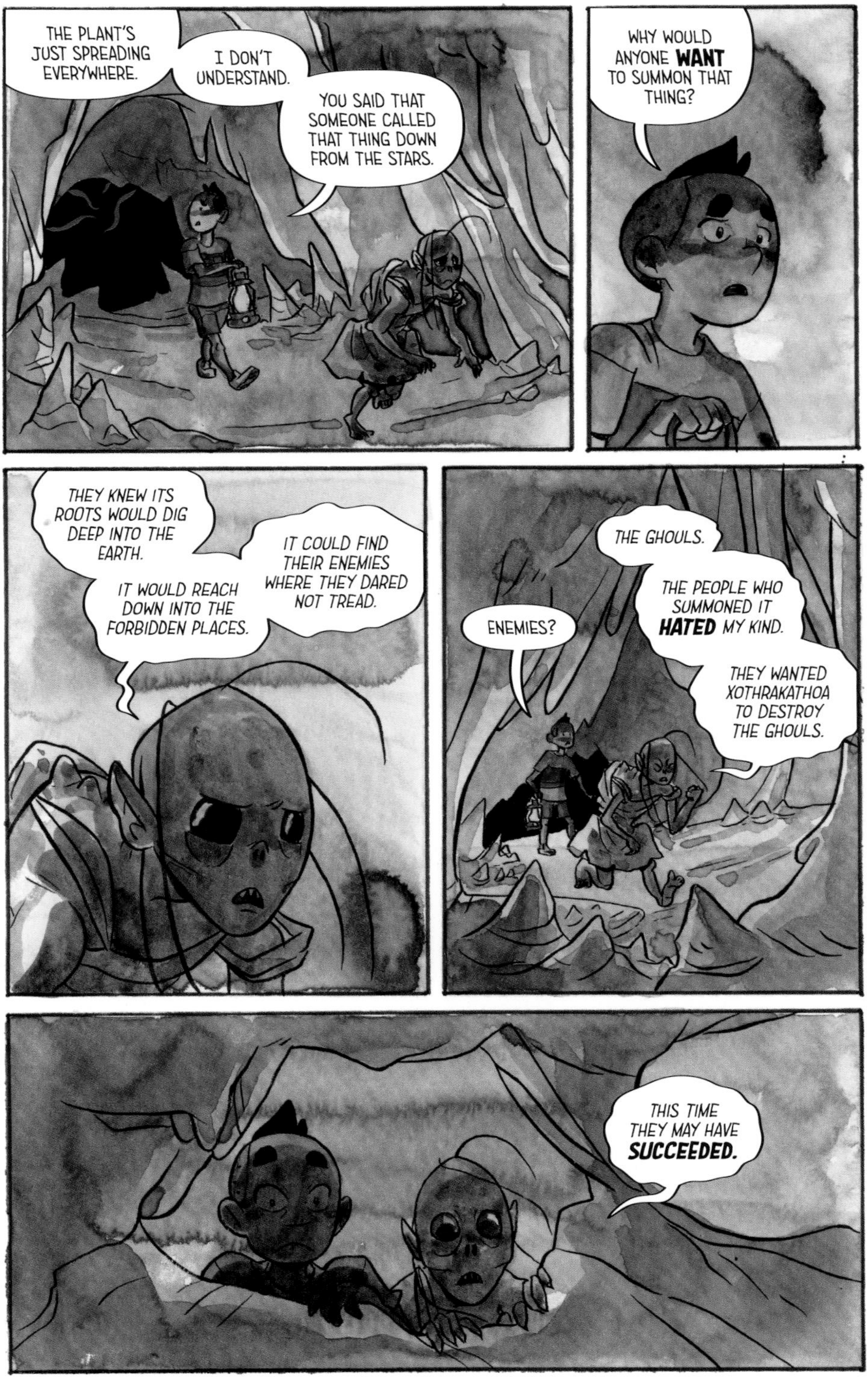
THE PLANT'S JUST SPREADING EVERYWHERE.
I DON'T UNDERSTAND.
YOU SAID THAT SOMEONE CALLED THAT THING DOWN FROM THE STARS.
WHY WOULD ANYONE **WANT** TO SUMMON THAT THING?
THEY KNEW ITS ROOTS WOULD DIG DEEP INTO THE EARTH.
IT WOULD REACH DOWN INTO THE FORBIDDEN PLACES.
IT COULD FIND THEIR ENEMIES WHERE THEY DARED NOT TREAD.
ENEMIES?
THE GHOULS.
*THE PEOPLE WHO SUMMONED IT **HATED** MY KIND.*
THEY WANTED XOTHRAKATHOA TO DESTROY THE GHOULS.
*THIS TIME THEY MAY HAVE **SUCCEEDED.***

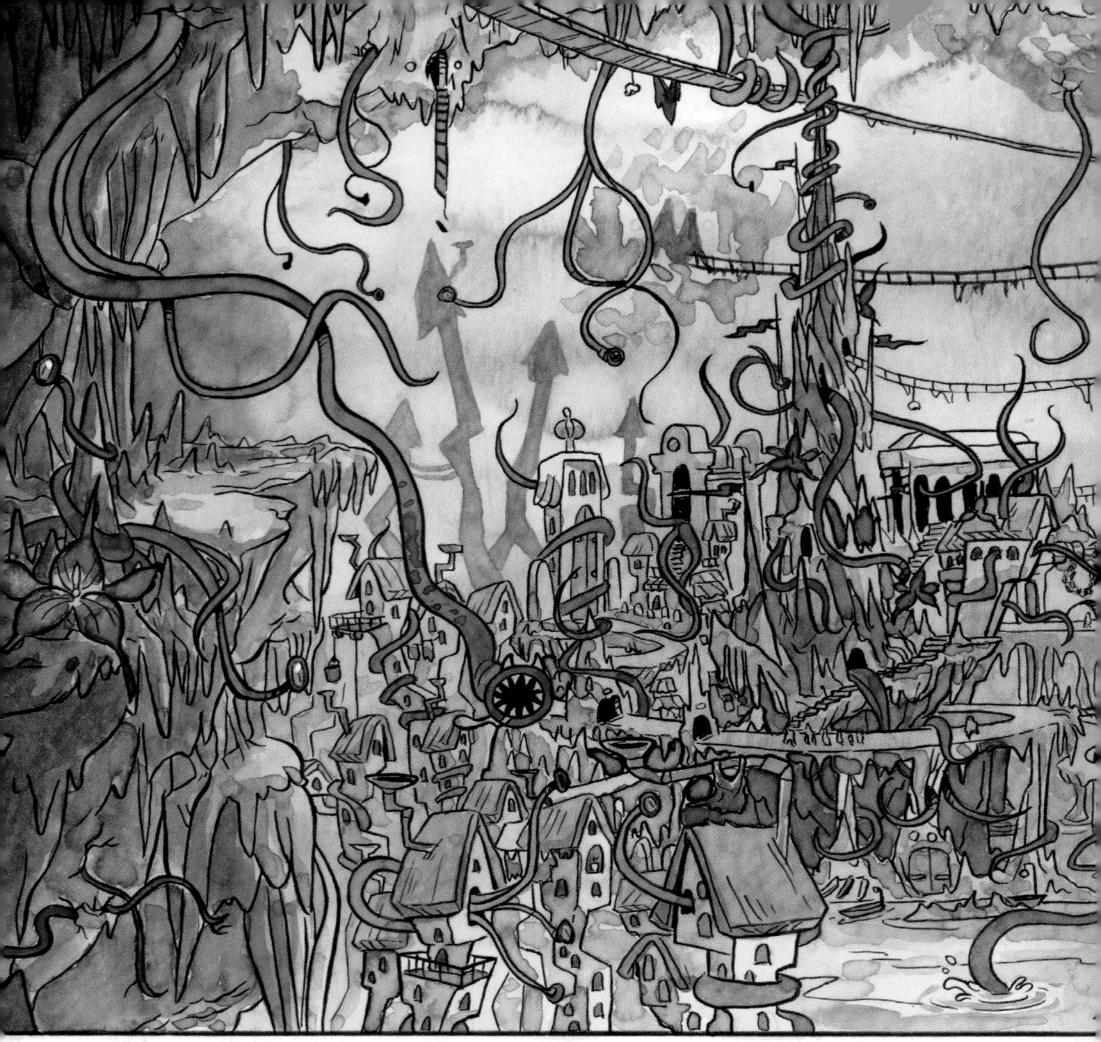

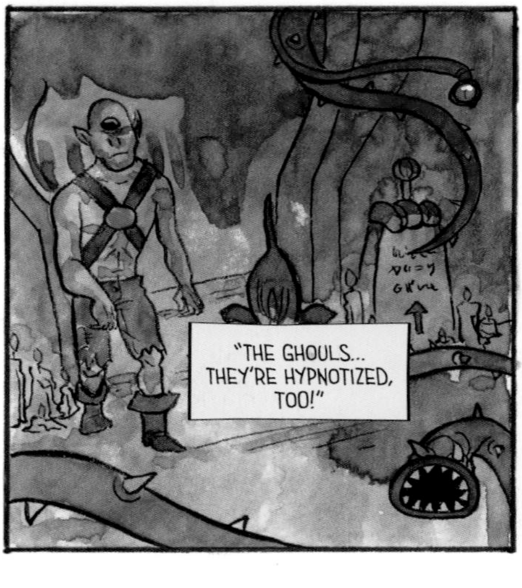

"THE GHOULS... THEY'RE HYPNOTIZED, TOO!"

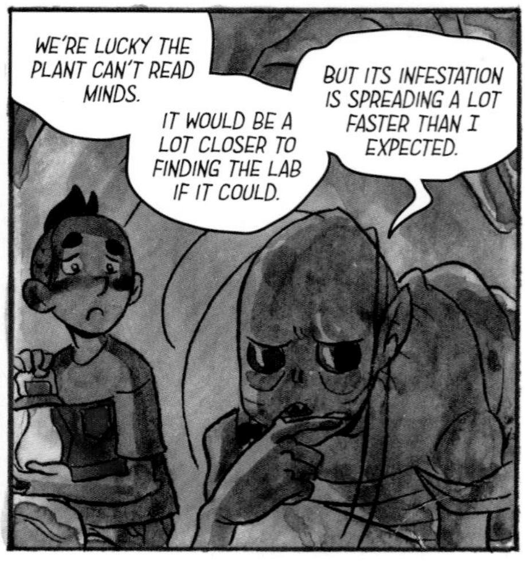

WE'RE LUCKY THE PLANT CAN'T READ MINDS.
IT WOULD BE A LOT CLOSER TO FINDING THE LAB IF IT COULD.
BUT ITS INFESTATION IS SPREADING A LOT FASTER THAN I EXPECTED.

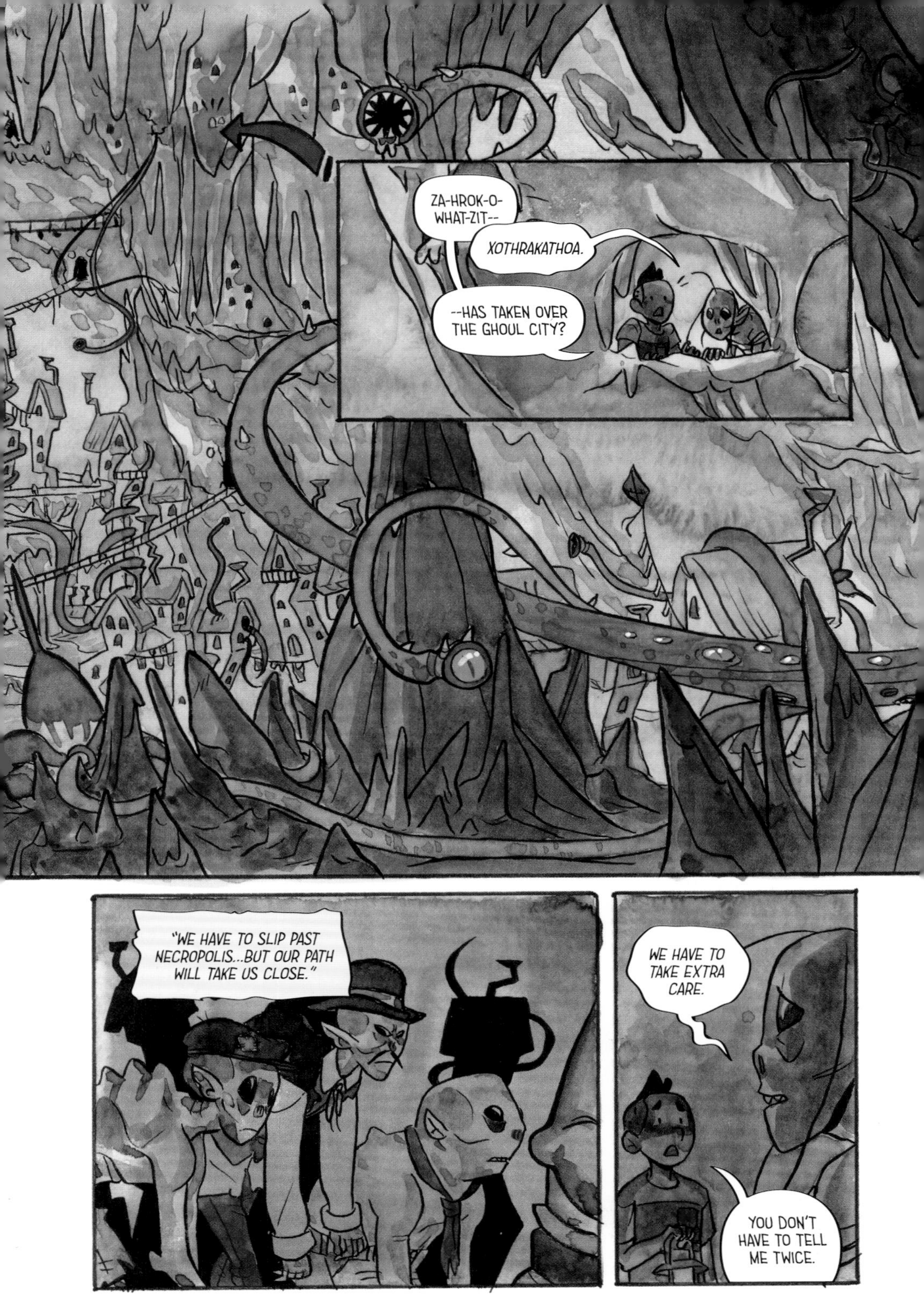
ZA-HROK-O-WHAT-ZIT--
XOTHRAKATHOA.
--HAS TAKEN OVER THE GHOUL CITY?
"WE HAVE TO SLIP PAST NECROPOLIS...BUT OUR PATH WILL TAKE US CLOSE."
WE HAVE TO TAKE EXTRA CARE.
YOU DON'T HAVE TO TELL ME TWICE.

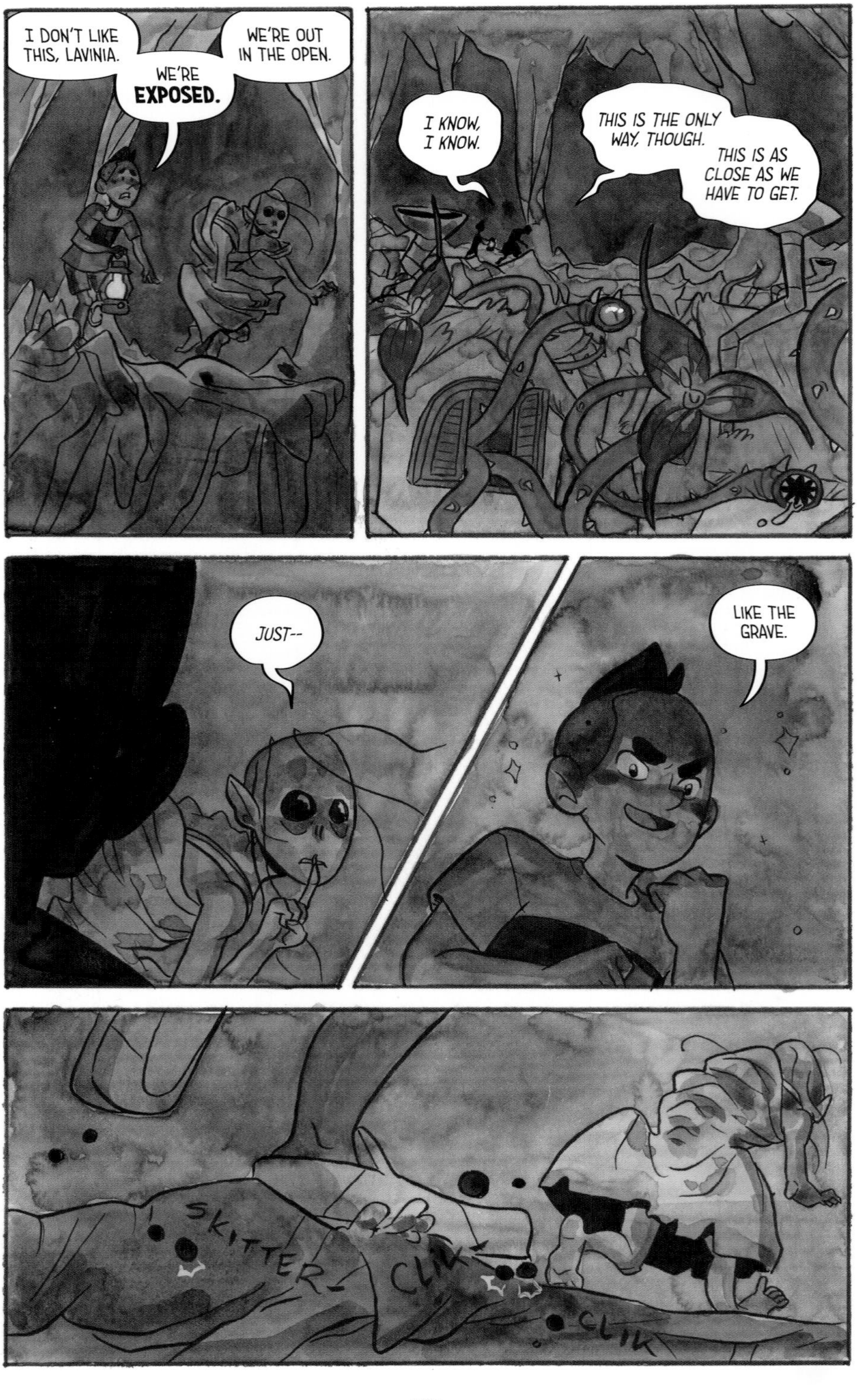
I DON'T LIKE THIS, LAVINIA.
WE'RE OUT IN THE OPEN.
WE'RE **EXPOSED.**
I KNOW, I KNOW.
THIS IS THE ONLY WAY, THOUGH.
THIS IS AS CLOSE AS WE HAVE TO GET.
JUST--
LIKE THE GRAVE.
SKITTER--
CLIK
CLIK

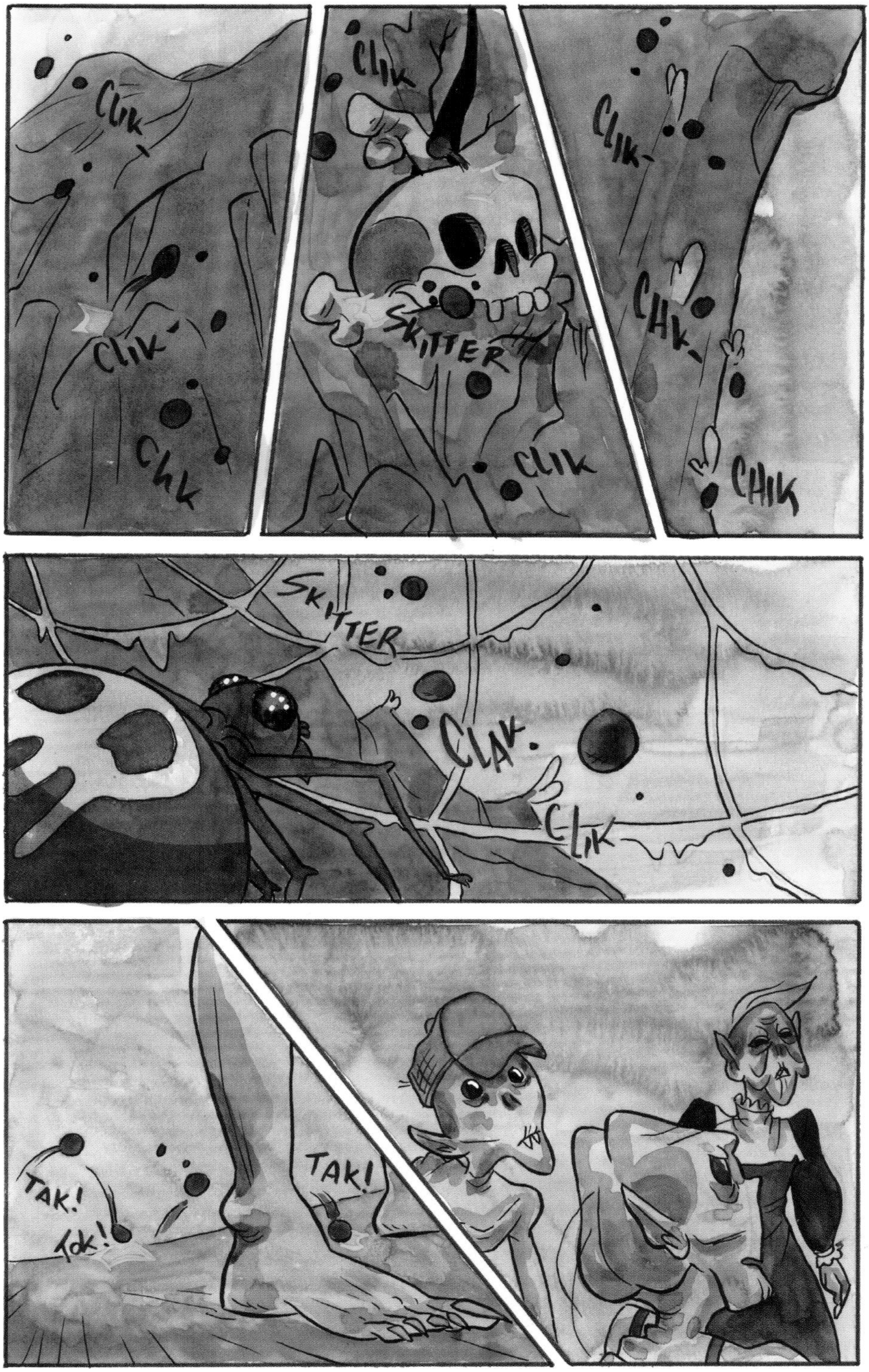
CLIK-
CLIK-
CHK
CLIK
SKITTER
CLIK
CLIK-
CHK-
CHIK
SKITTER
CLAK.
CLIK
TAK!
TOK!
TAK!

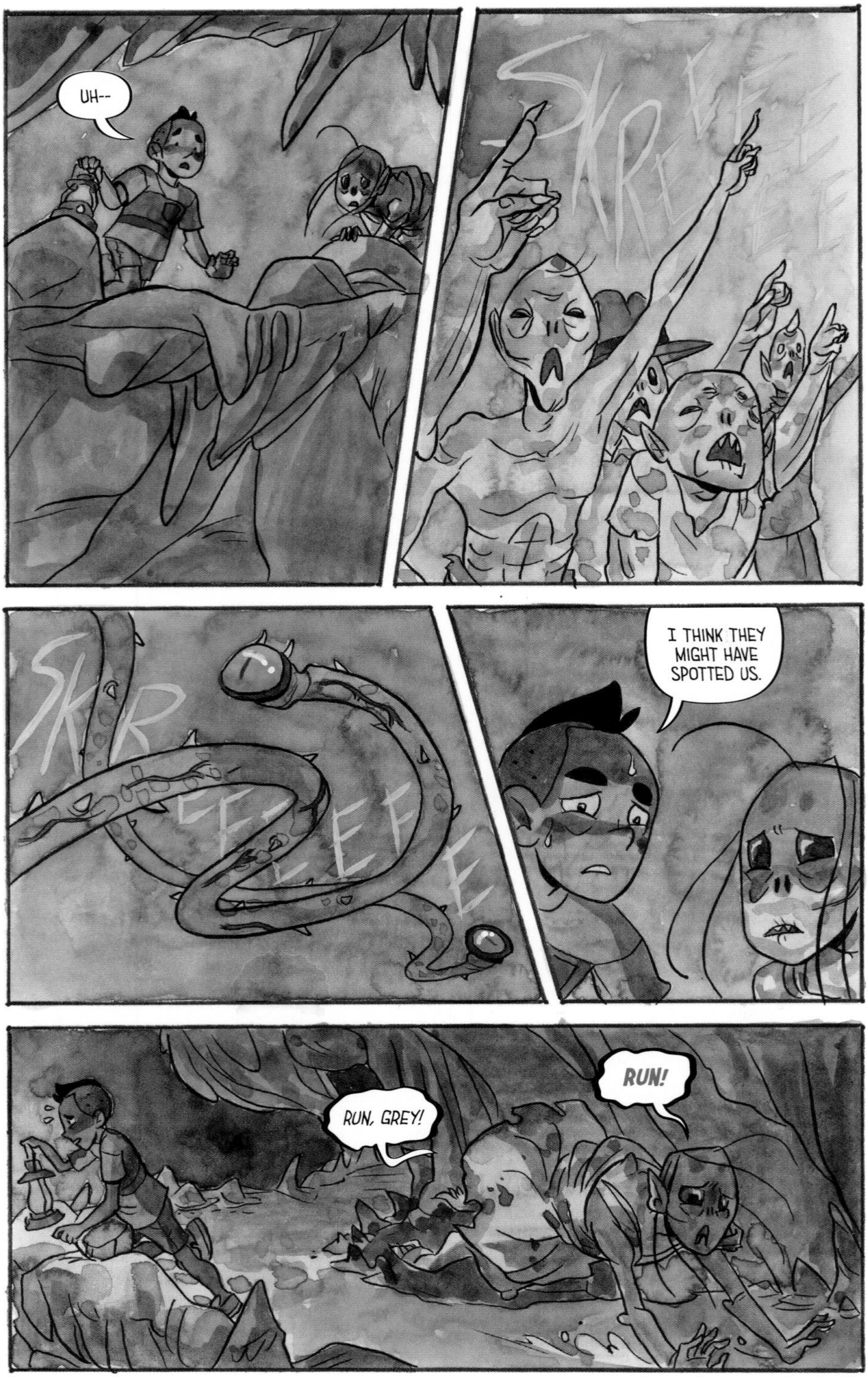
UH--
SKREEEEEE
SKREEEEE
I THINK THEY MIGHT HAVE SPOTTED US.
RUN, GREY!
RUN!

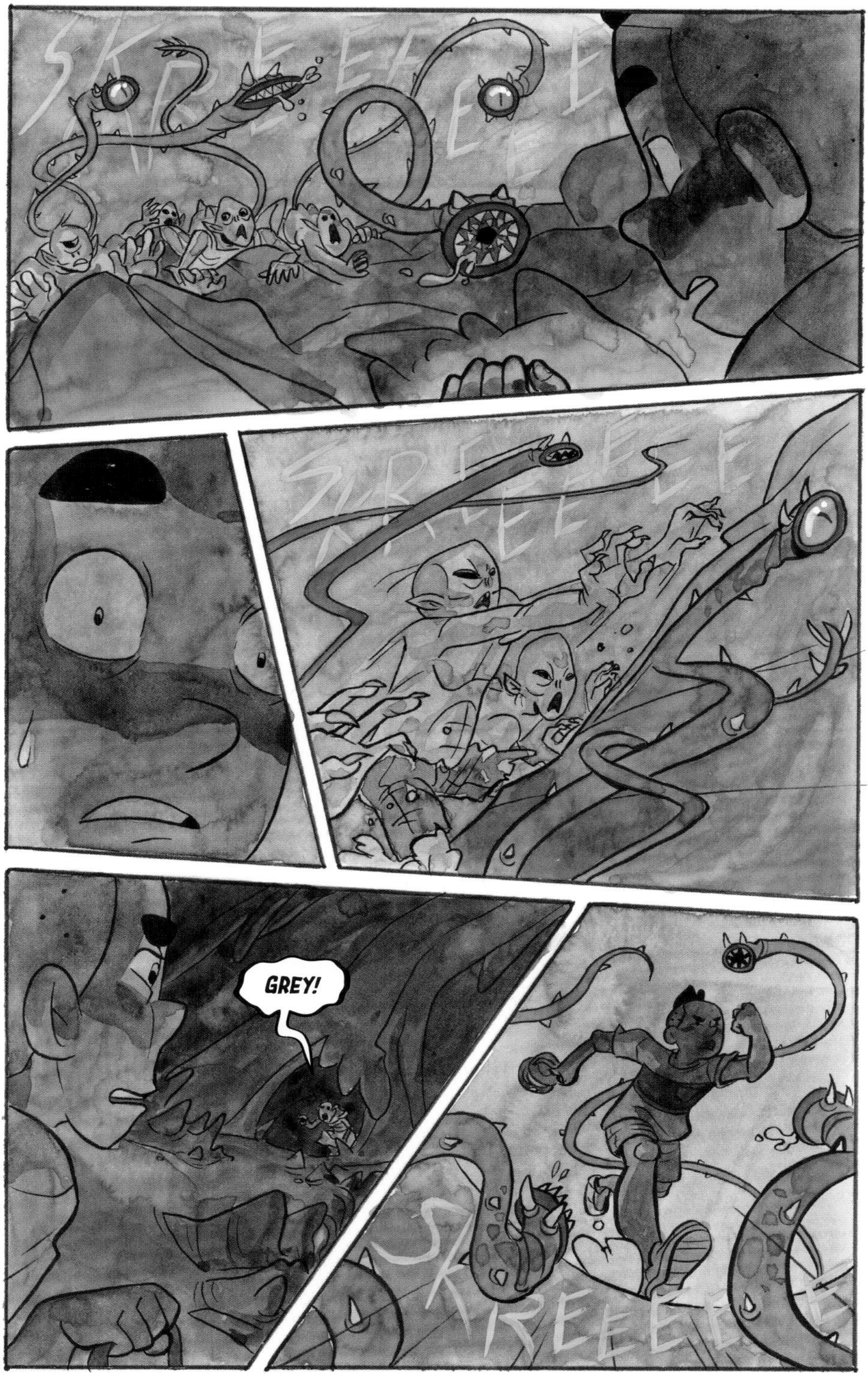
SKREEEEEEE
SKREEEEEE
GREY!
SKREEEEEE

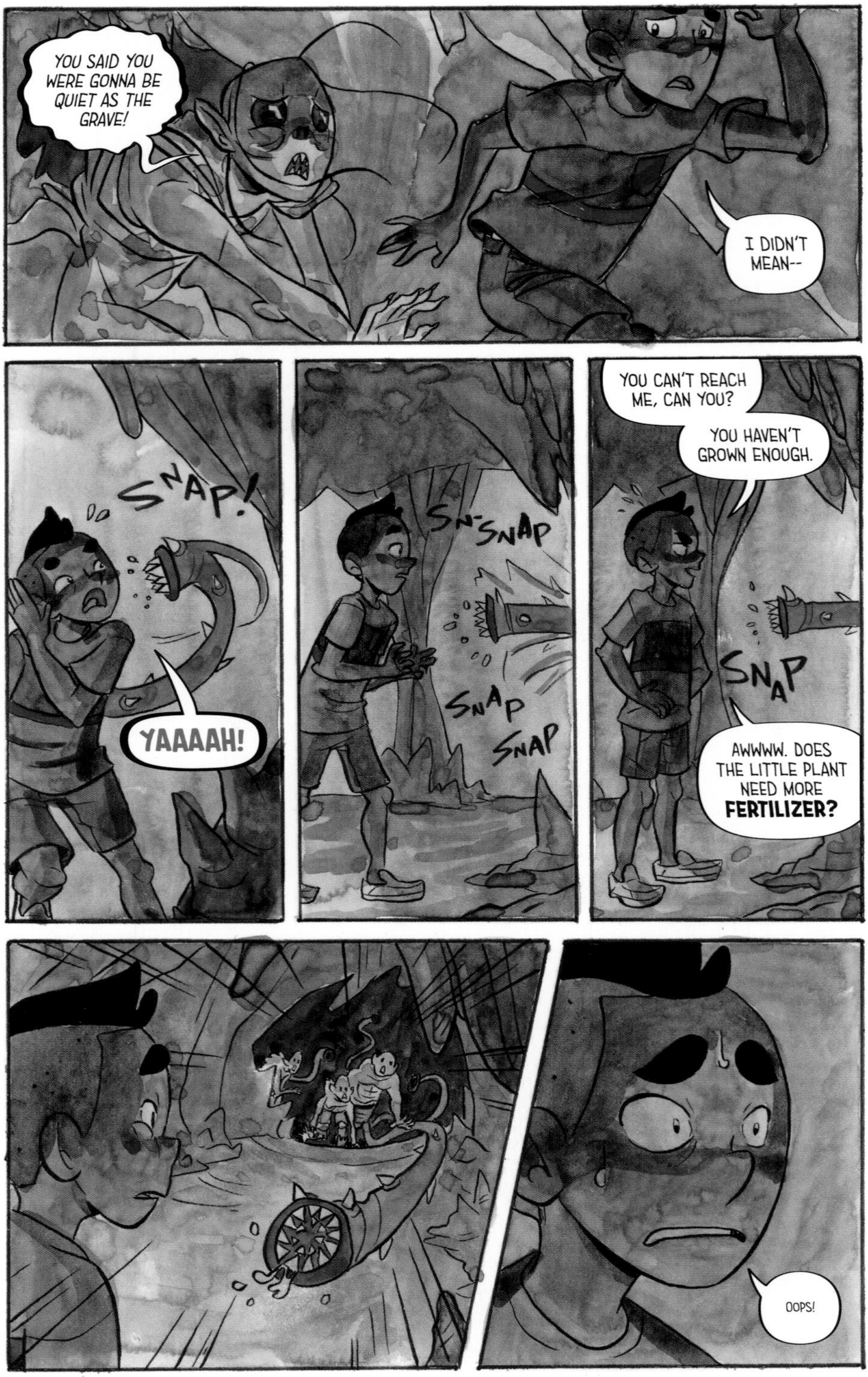
YOU SAID YOU WERE GONNA BE QUIET AS THE GRAVE!
I DIDN'T MEAN--
SNAP!
YAAAAH!
SN-SNAP
SNAP
SNAP
YOU CAN'T REACH ME, CAN YOU?
YOU HAVEN'T GROWN ENOUGH.
SNAP
AWWWW. DOES THE LITTLE PLANT NEED MORE **FERTILIZER?**
OOPS!

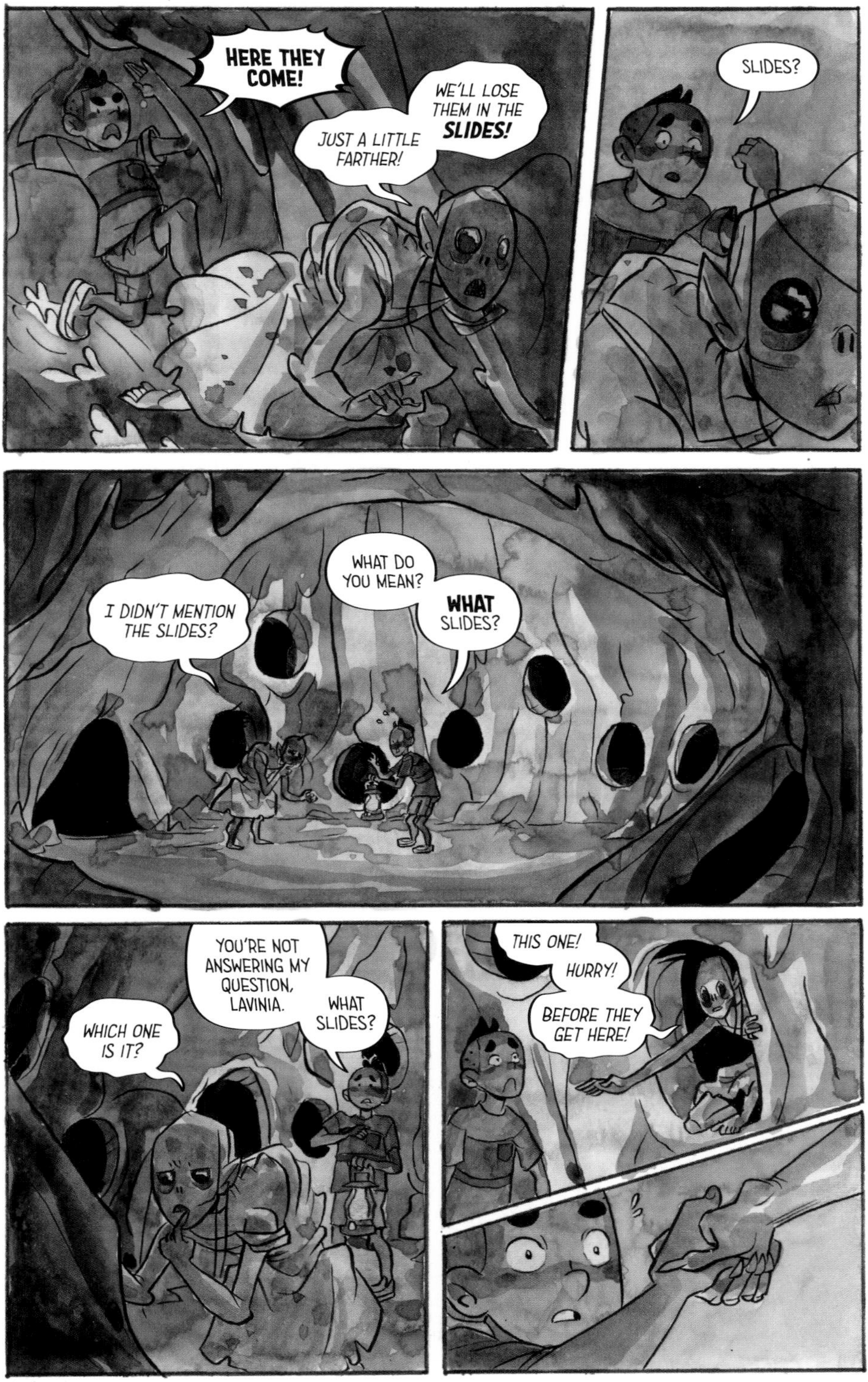
HERE THEY COME!
WE'LL LOSE THEM IN THE SLIDES!
JUST A LITTLE FARTHER!
SLIDES?
I DIDN'T MENTION THE SLIDES?
WHAT DO YOU MEAN?
WHAT SLIDES?
YOU'RE NOT ANSWERING MY QUESTION, LAVINIA.
WHAT SLIDES?
WHICH ONE IS IT?
THIS ONE!
HURRY!
BEFORE THEY GET HERE!

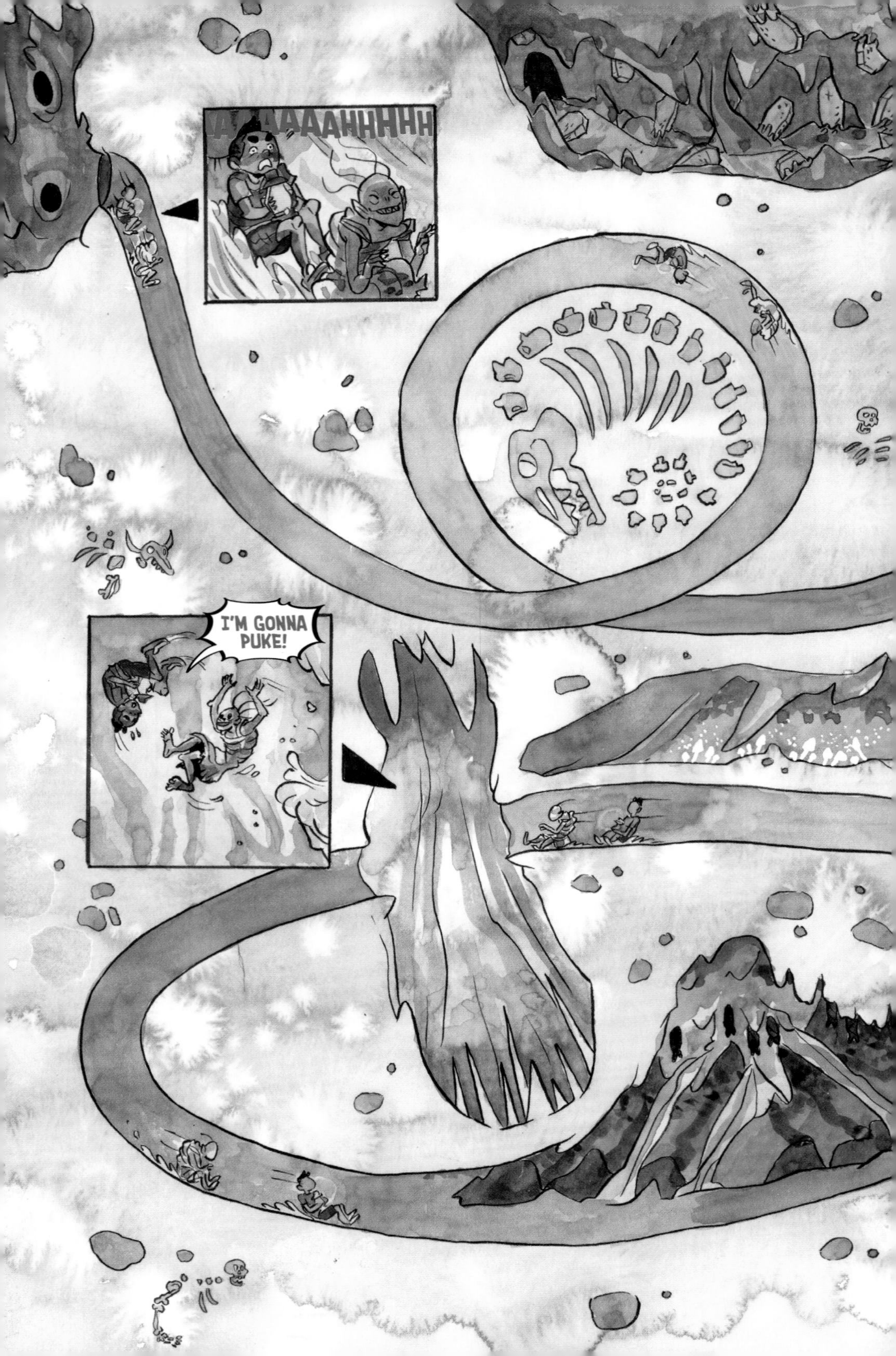
AAAAAAHHHHH
I'M GONNA PUKE!

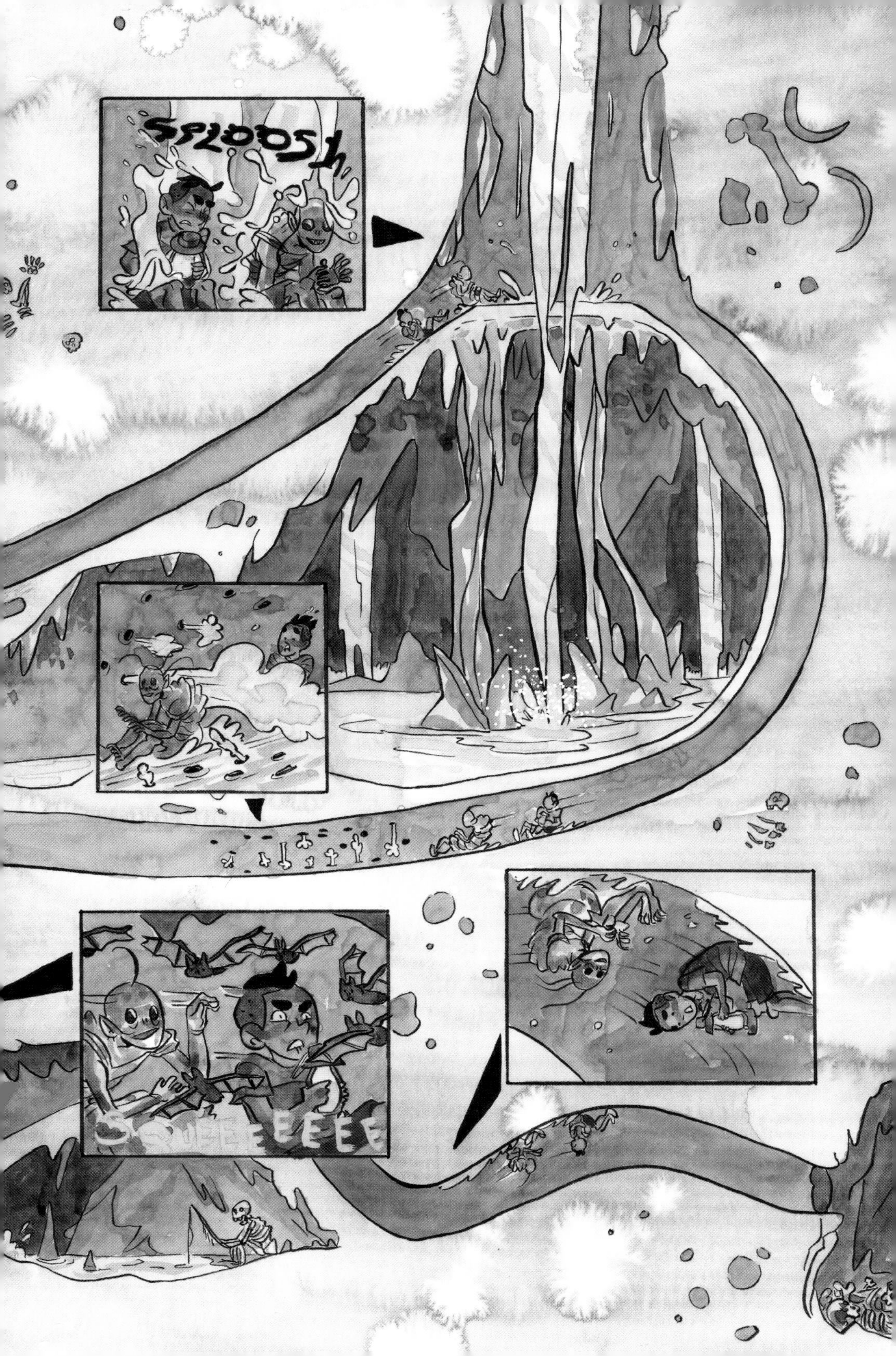
SPLOOSH
SQUEEEEEEE

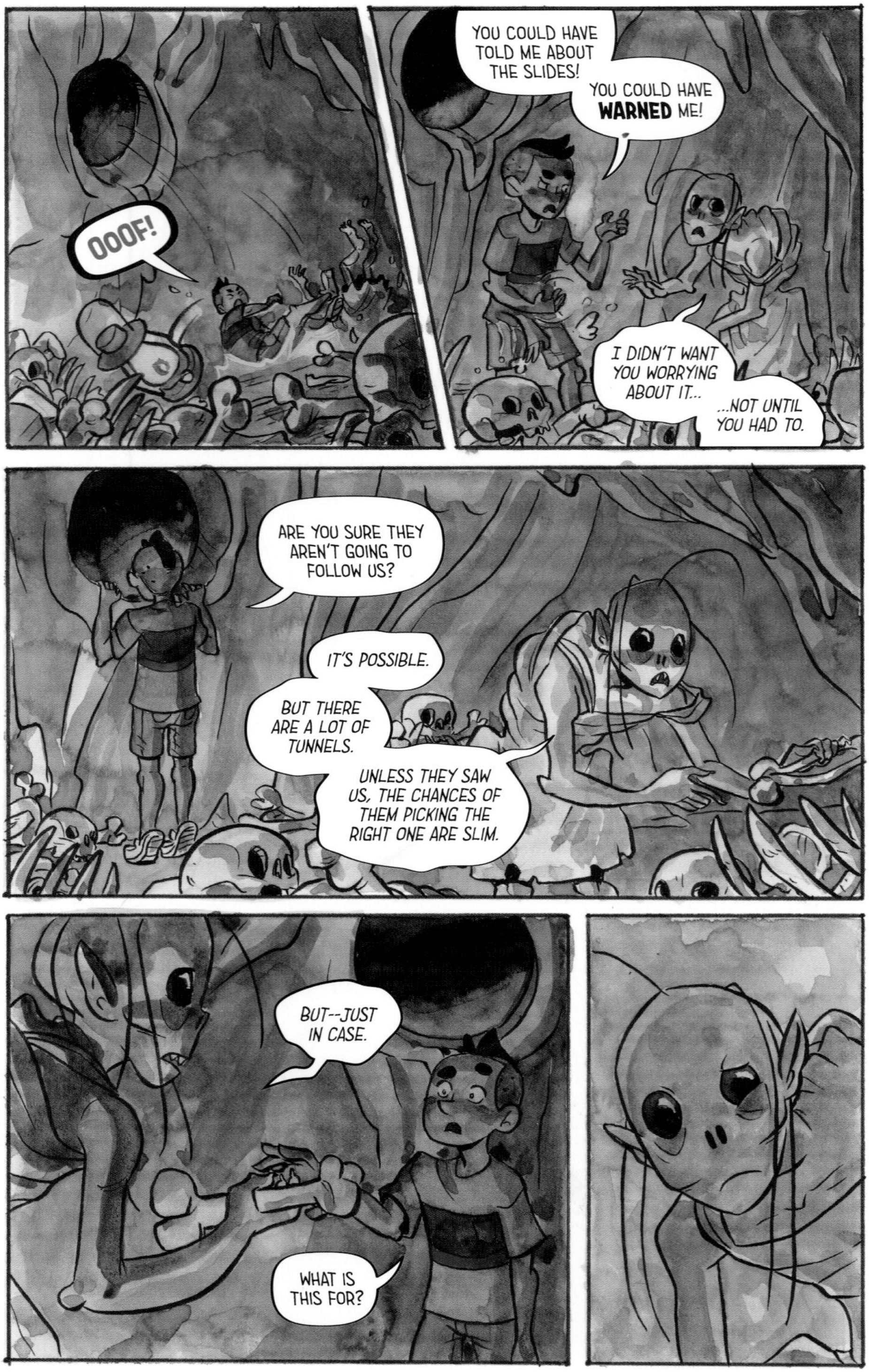

OOOF!
YOU COULD HAVE TOLD ME ABOUT THE SLIDES!
YOU COULD HAVE **WARNED** ME!
I DIDN'T WANT YOU WORRYING ABOUT IT...
...NOT UNTIL YOU HAD TO.
ARE YOU SURE THEY AREN'T GOING TO FOLLOW US?
IT'S POSSIBLE.
BUT THERE ARE A LOT OF TUNNELS.
UNLESS THEY SAW US, THE CHANCES OF THEM PICKING THE RIGHT ONE ARE SLIM.
BUT--JUST IN CASE.
WHAT IS THIS FOR?

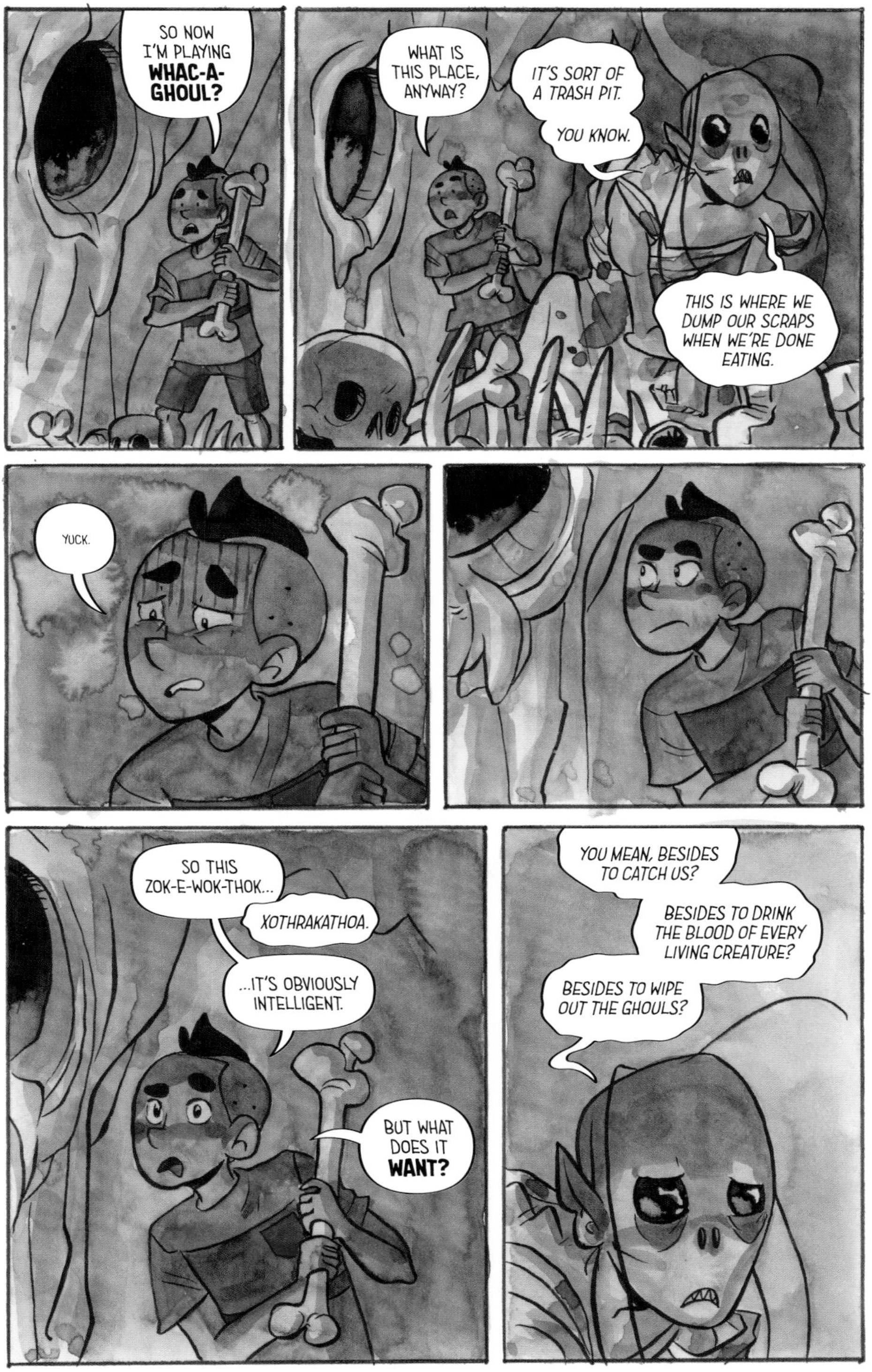
SO NOW I'M PLAYING WHAC-A-GHOUL?
WHAT IS THIS PLACE, ANYWAY?
IT'S SORT OF A TRASH PIT.
YOU KNOW.
THIS IS WHERE WE DUMP OUR SCRAPS WHEN WE'RE DONE EATING.
YUCK.
SO THIS ZOK-E-WOK-THOK...
XOTHRAKATHOA.
...IT'S OBVIOUSLY INTELLIGENT.
BUT WHAT DOES IT WANT?
YOU MEAN, BESIDES TO CATCH US?
BESIDES TO DRINK THE BLOOD OF EVERY LIVING CREATURE?
BESIDES TO WIPE OUT THE GHOULS?

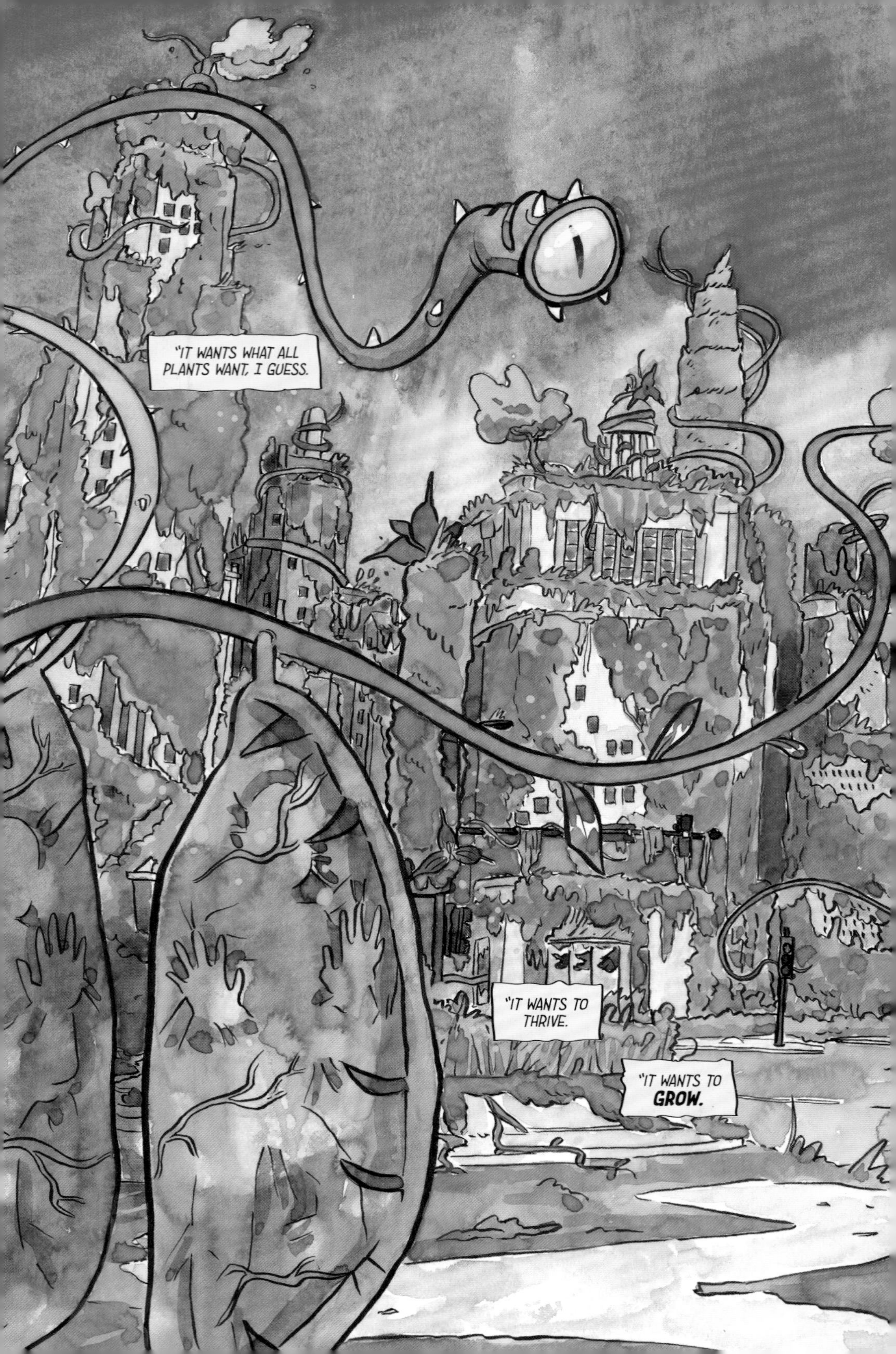
"IT WANTS WHAT ALL PLANTS WANT, I GUESS.
"IT WANTS TO THRIVE.
"IT WANTS TO **GROW.**

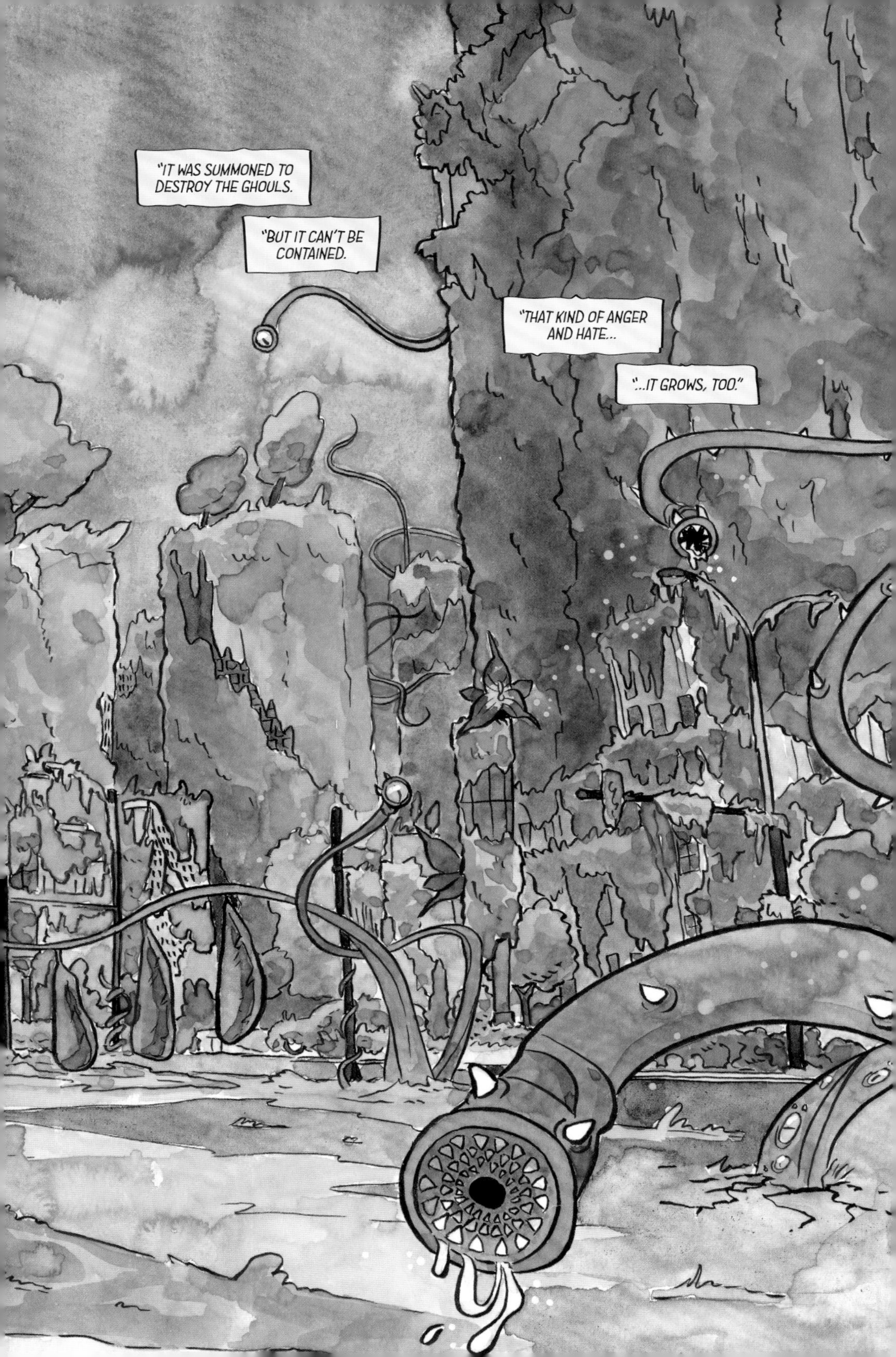
"IT WAS SUMMONED TO DESTROY THE GHOULS.
"BUT IT CAN'T BE CONTAINED.
"THAT KIND OF ANGER AND HATE...
"...IT GROWS, TOO."

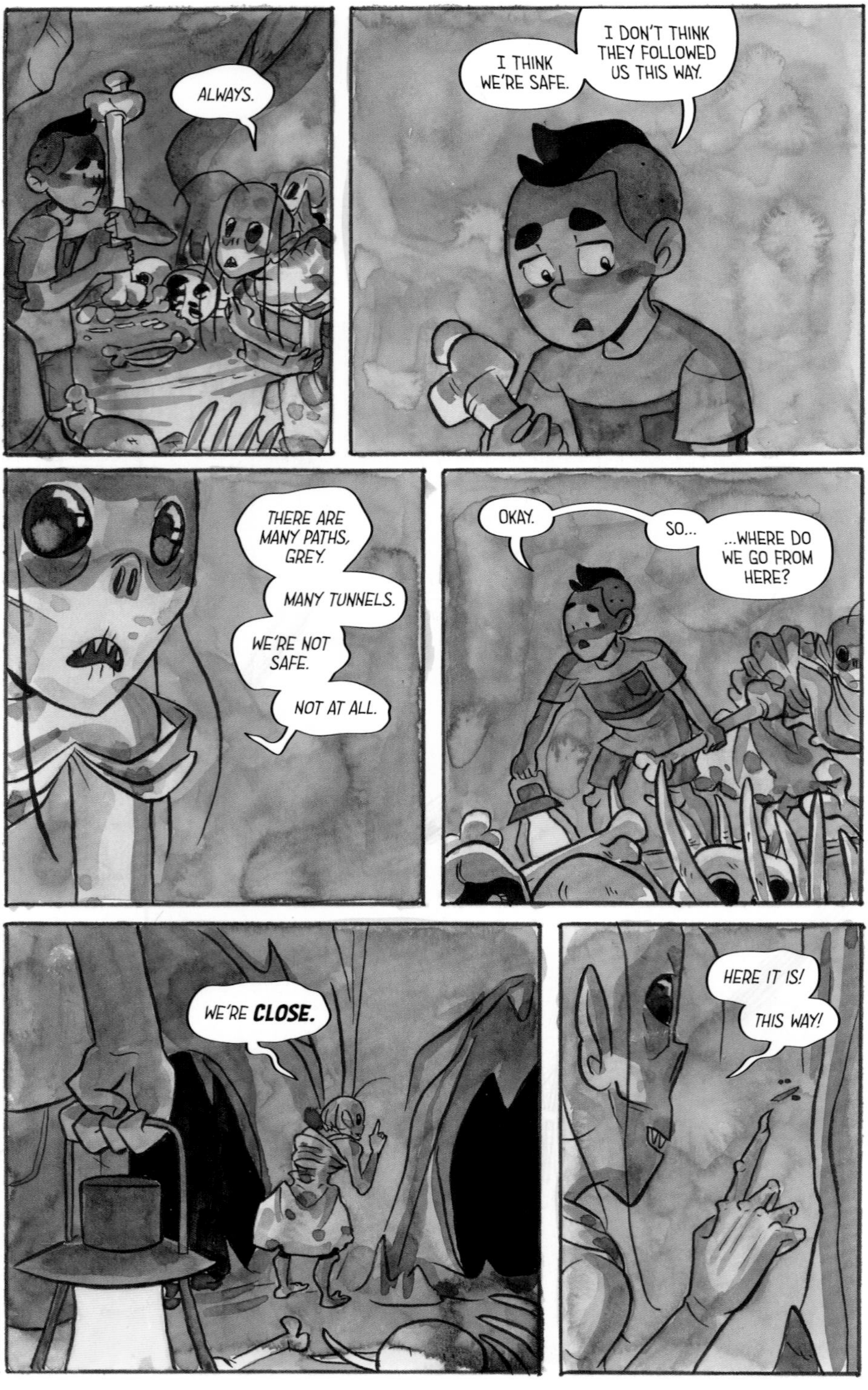
ALWAYS.
I THINK WE'RE SAFE.
I DON'T THINK THEY FOLLOWED US THIS WAY.
THERE ARE MANY PATHS, GREY.
MANY TUNNELS.
WE'RE NOT SAFE.
NOT AT ALL.
OKAY.
SO...
...WHERE DO WE GO FROM HERE?
WE'RE **CLOSE.**
HERE IT IS!
THIS WAY!

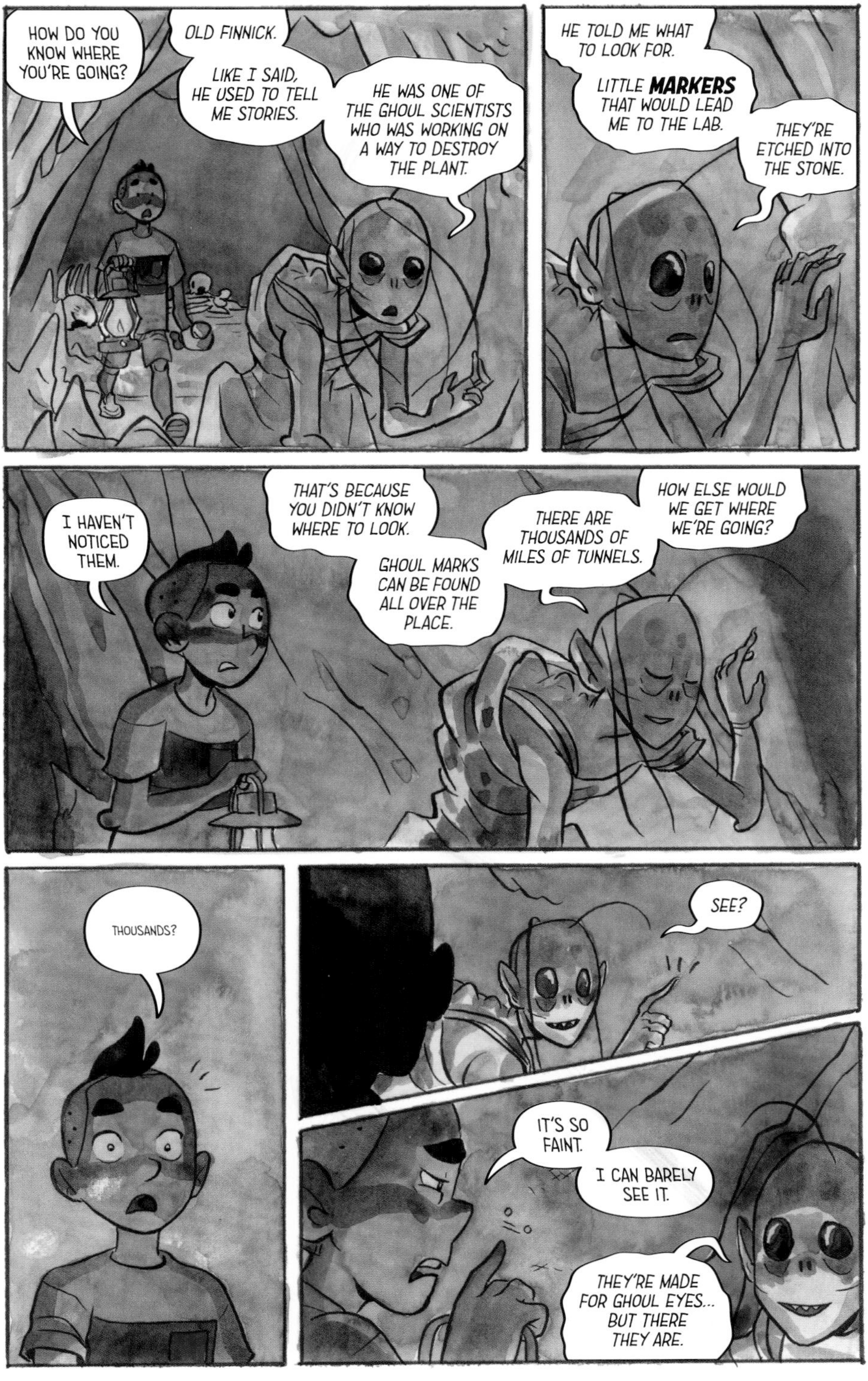
HOW DO YOU KNOW WHERE YOU'RE GOING?
OLD FINNICK.
LIKE I SAID, HE USED TO TELL ME STORIES.
HE WAS ONE OF THE GHOUL SCIENTISTS WHO WAS WORKING ON A WAY TO DESTROY THE PLANT.
HE TOLD ME WHAT TO LOOK FOR.
LITTLE **MARKERS** THAT WOULD LEAD ME TO THE LAB.
THEY'RE ETCHED INTO THE STONE.
I HAVEN'T NOTICED THEM.
THAT'S BECAUSE YOU DIDN'T KNOW WHERE TO LOOK.
GHOUL MARKS CAN BE FOUND ALL OVER THE PLACE.
THERE ARE THOUSANDS OF MILES OF TUNNELS.
HOW ELSE WOULD WE GET WHERE WE'RE GOING?
THOUSANDS?
SEE?
IT'S SO FAINT.
I CAN BARELY SEE IT.
THEY'RE MADE FOR GHOUL EYES... BUT THERE THEY ARE.

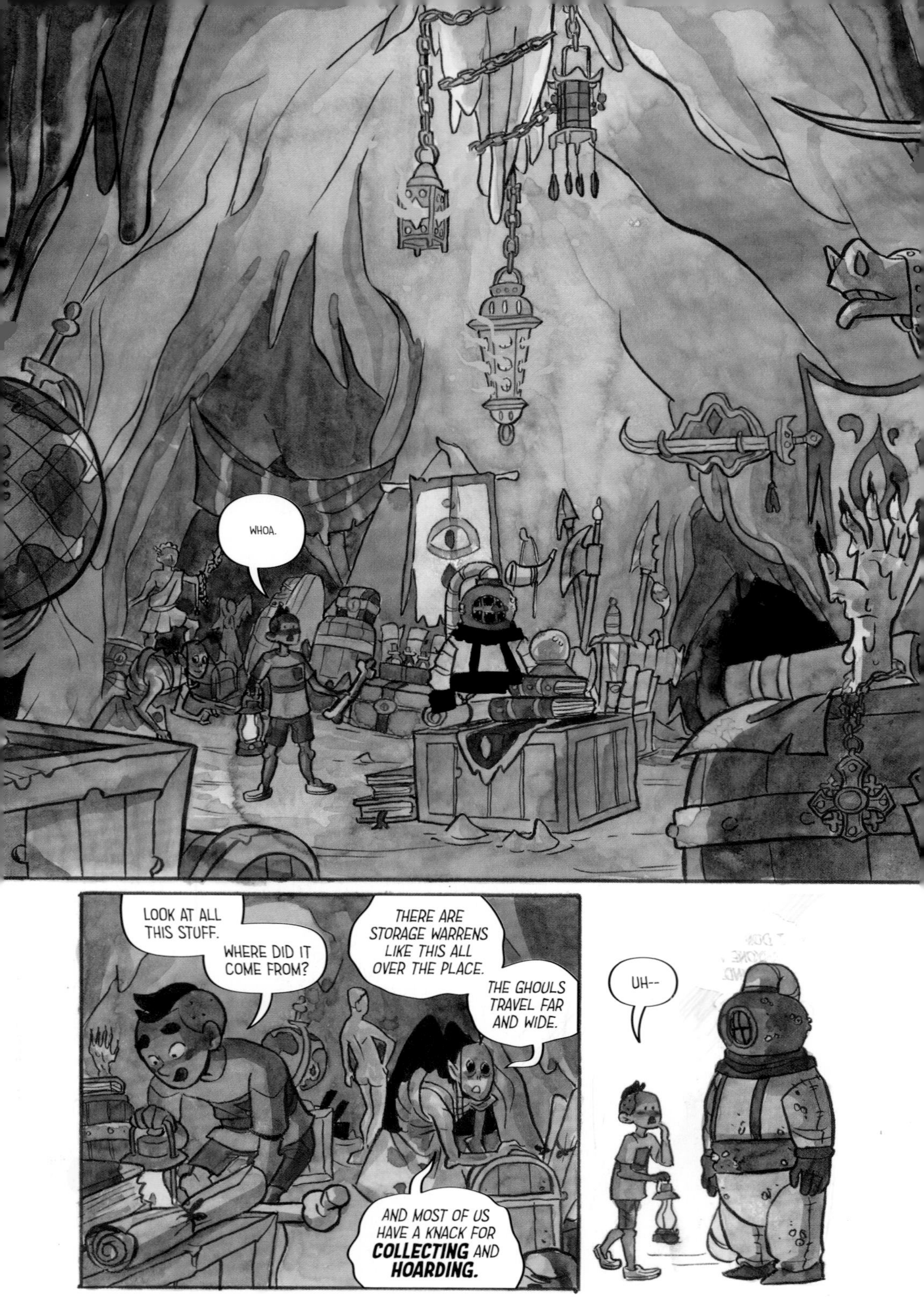
WHOA.
LOOK AT ALL THIS STUFF.
WHERE DID IT COME FROM?
THERE ARE STORAGE WARRENS LIKE THIS ALL OVER THE PLACE.
THE GHOULS TRAVEL FAR AND WIDE.
AND MOST OF US HAVE A KNACK FOR **COLLECTING** AND **HOARDING.**
UH--

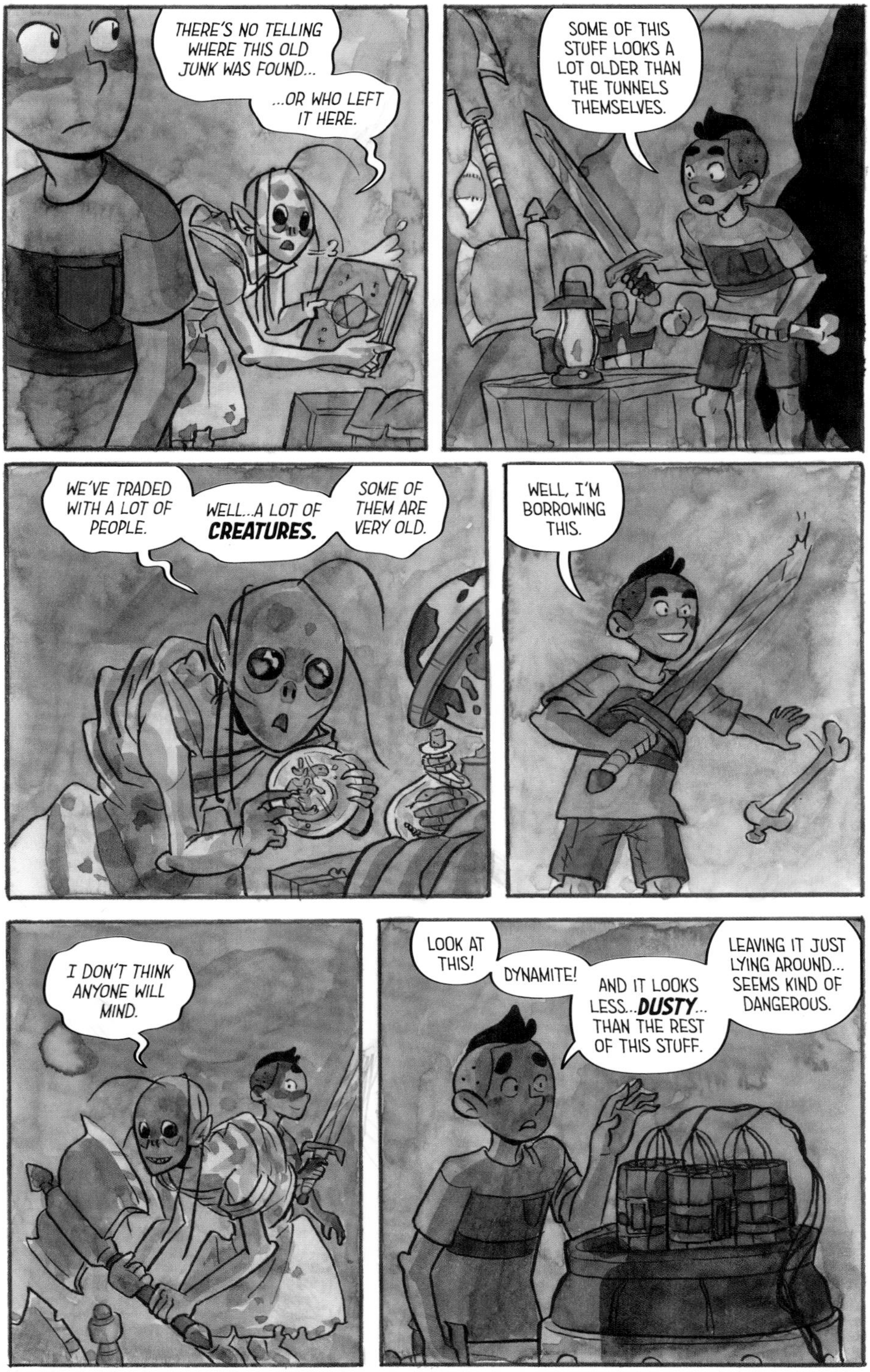
THERE'S NO TELLING WHERE THIS OLD JUNK WAS FOUND...
...OR WHO LEFT IT HERE.
SOME OF THIS STUFF LOOKS A LOT OLDER THAN THE TUNNELS THEMSELVES.
WE'VE TRADED WITH A LOT OF PEOPLE.
WELL...A LOT OF **CREATURES.**
SOME OF THEM ARE VERY OLD.
WELL, I'M BORROWING THIS.
I DON'T THINK ANYONE WILL MIND.
LOOK AT THIS!
DYNAMITE!
AND IT LOOKS LESS...**DUSTY**... THAN THE REST OF THIS STUFF.
LEAVING IT JUST LYING AROUND... SEEMS KIND OF DANGEROUS.

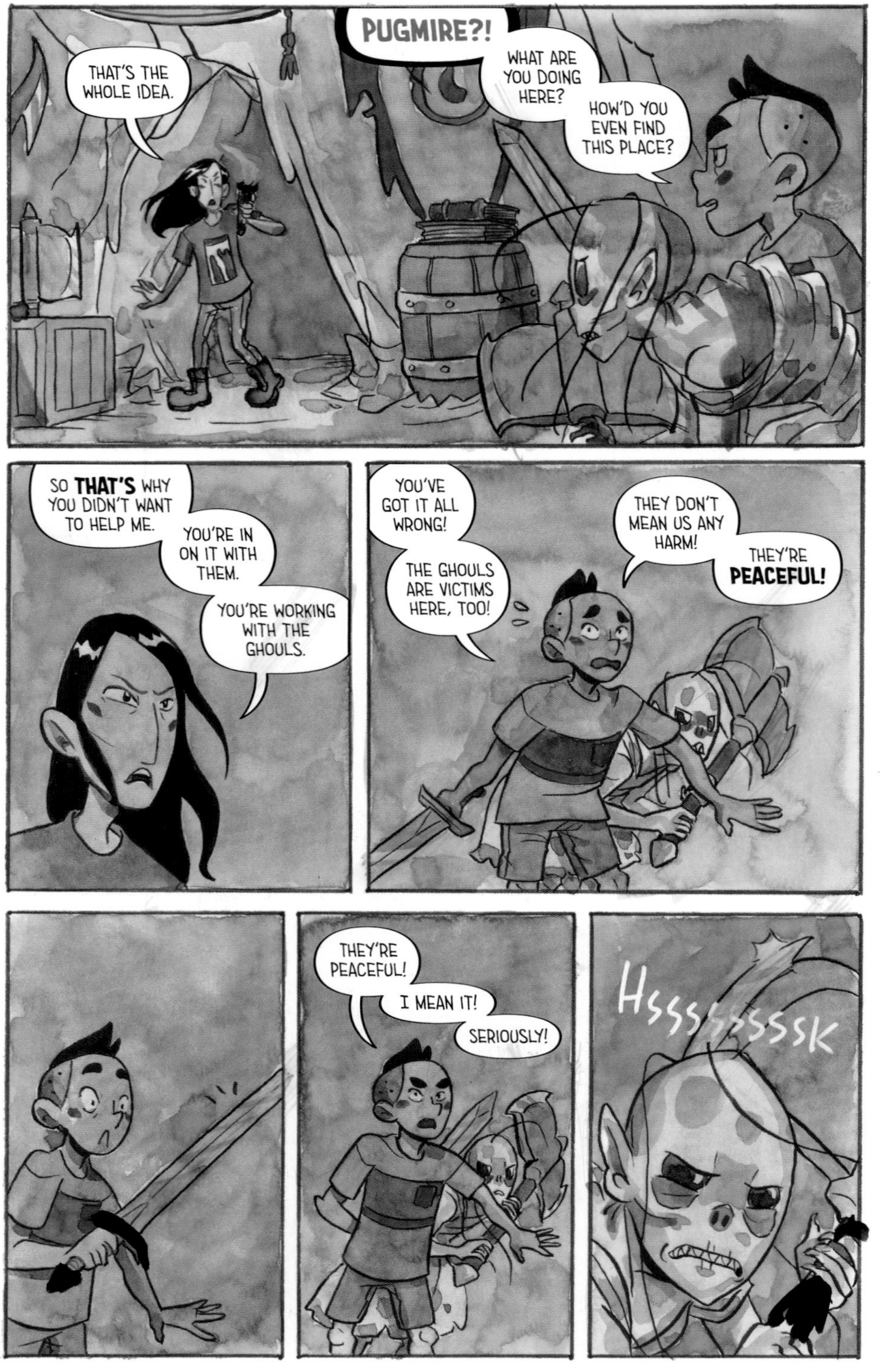
THAT'S THE WHOLE IDEA.
PUGMIRE?!
WHAT ARE YOU DOING HERE?
HOW'D YOU EVEN FIND THIS PLACE?
SO **THAT'S** WHY YOU DIDN'T WANT TO HELP ME.
YOU'RE IN ON IT WITH THEM.
YOU'RE WORKING WITH THE GHOULS.
YOU'VE GOT IT ALL WRONG!
THE GHOULS ARE VICTIMS HERE, TOO!
THEY DON'T MEAN US ANY HARM!
THEY'RE **PEACEFUL!**
THEY'RE PEACEFUL!
I MEAN IT!
SERIOUSLY!
HSSSSSSSSK

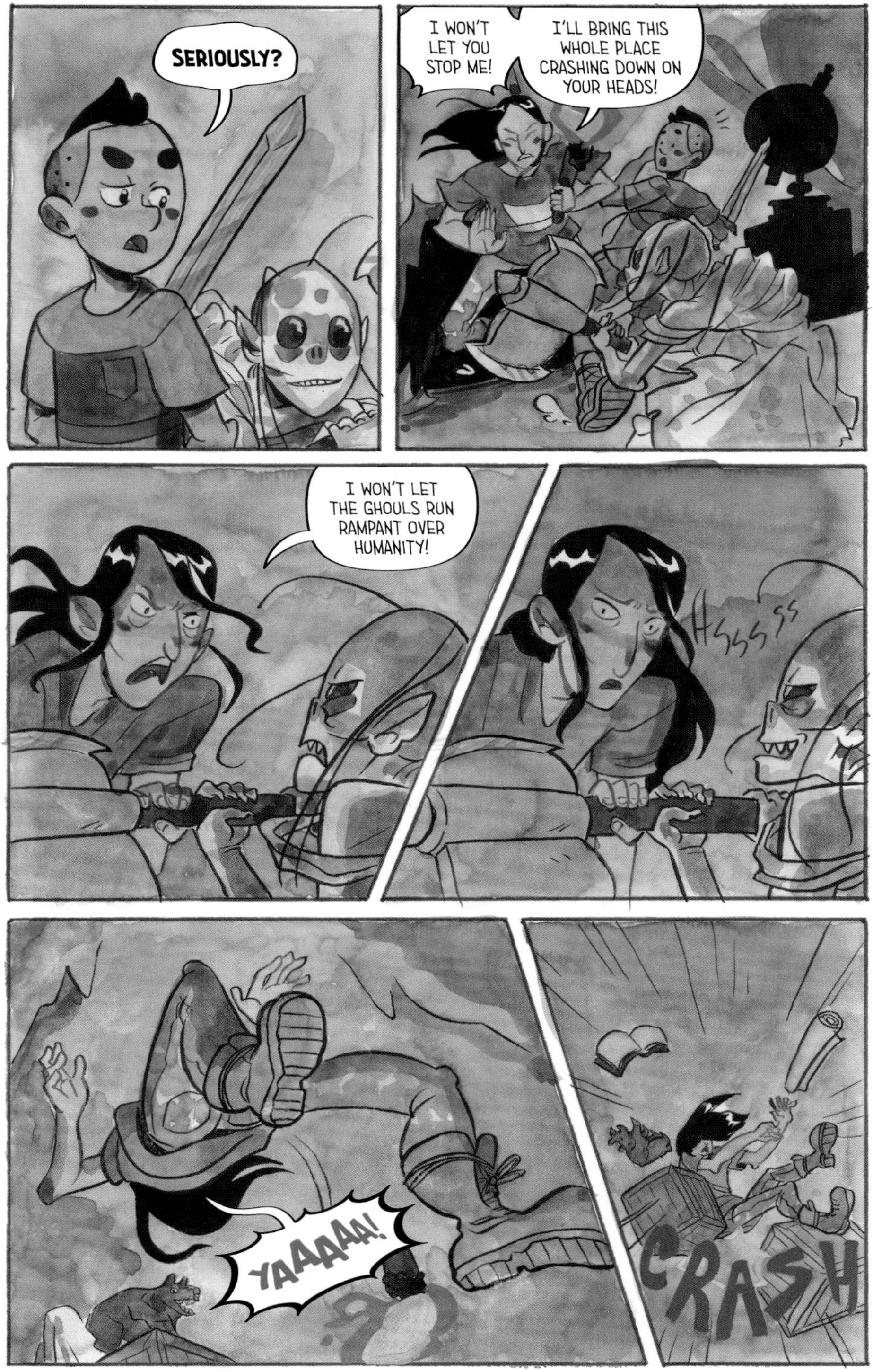
SERIOUSLY?
I WON'T LET YOU STOP ME!
I'LL BRING THIS WHOLE PLACE CRASHING DOWN ON YOUR HEADS!
I WON'T LET THE GHOULS RUN RAMPANT OVER HUMANITY!
HSSSSS
YAAAAA!
CRASH

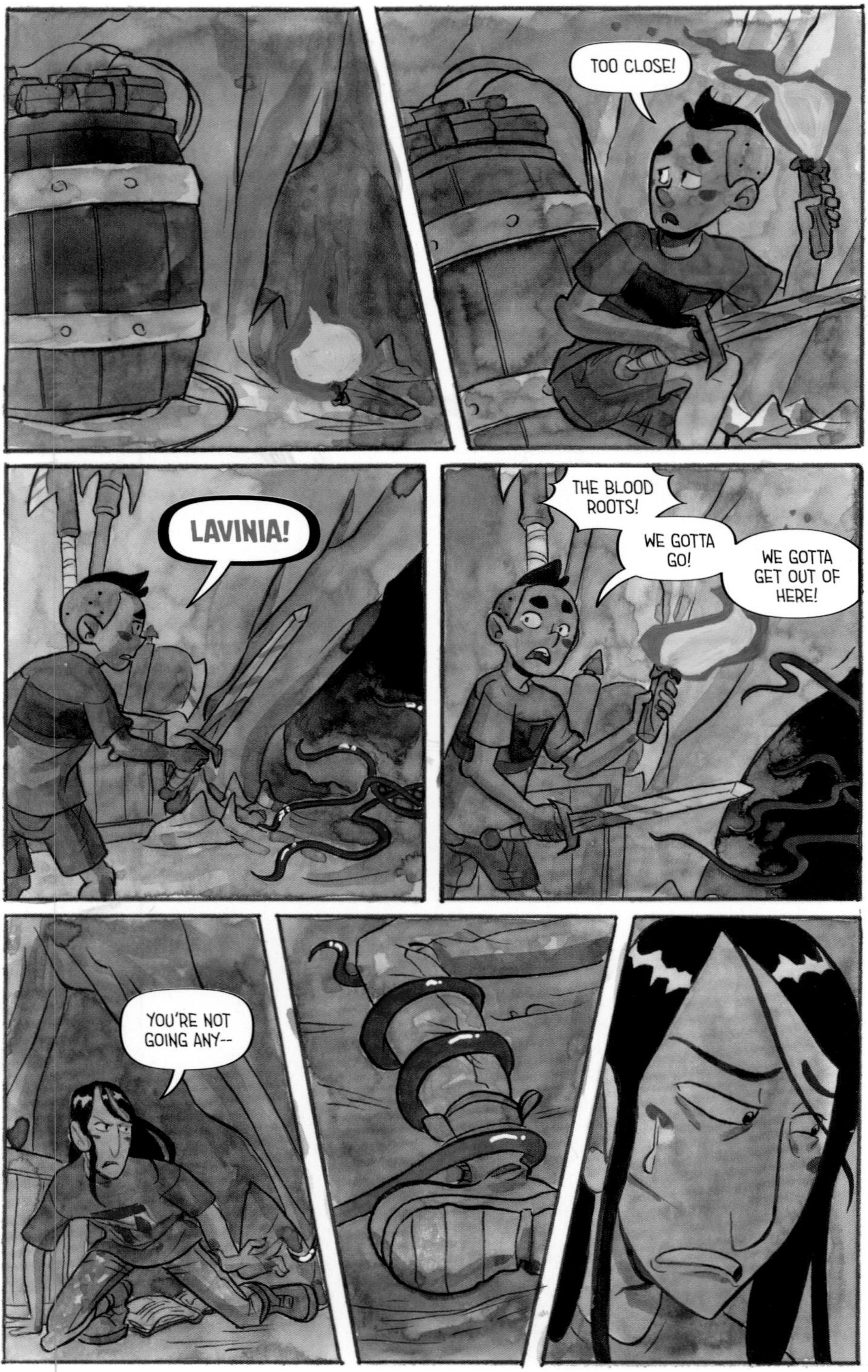
TOO CLOSE!
LAVINIA!
THE BLOOD ROOTS!
WE GOTTA GO!
WE GOTTA GET OUT OF HERE!
YOU'RE NOT GOING ANY--

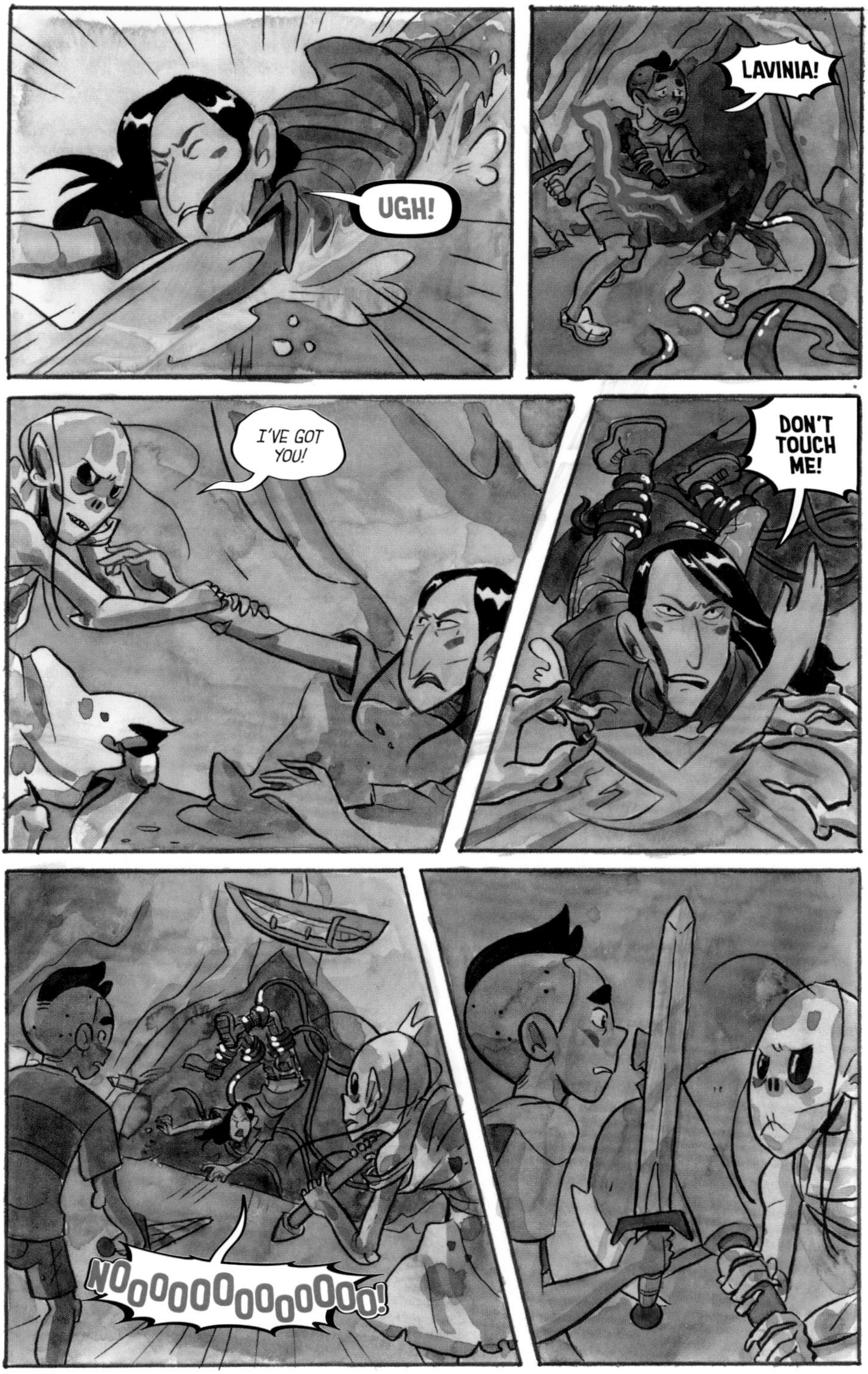
UGH!
LAVINIA!
I'VE GOT YOU!
DON'T TOUCH ME!
NOOOOOOOOOOOOOO!

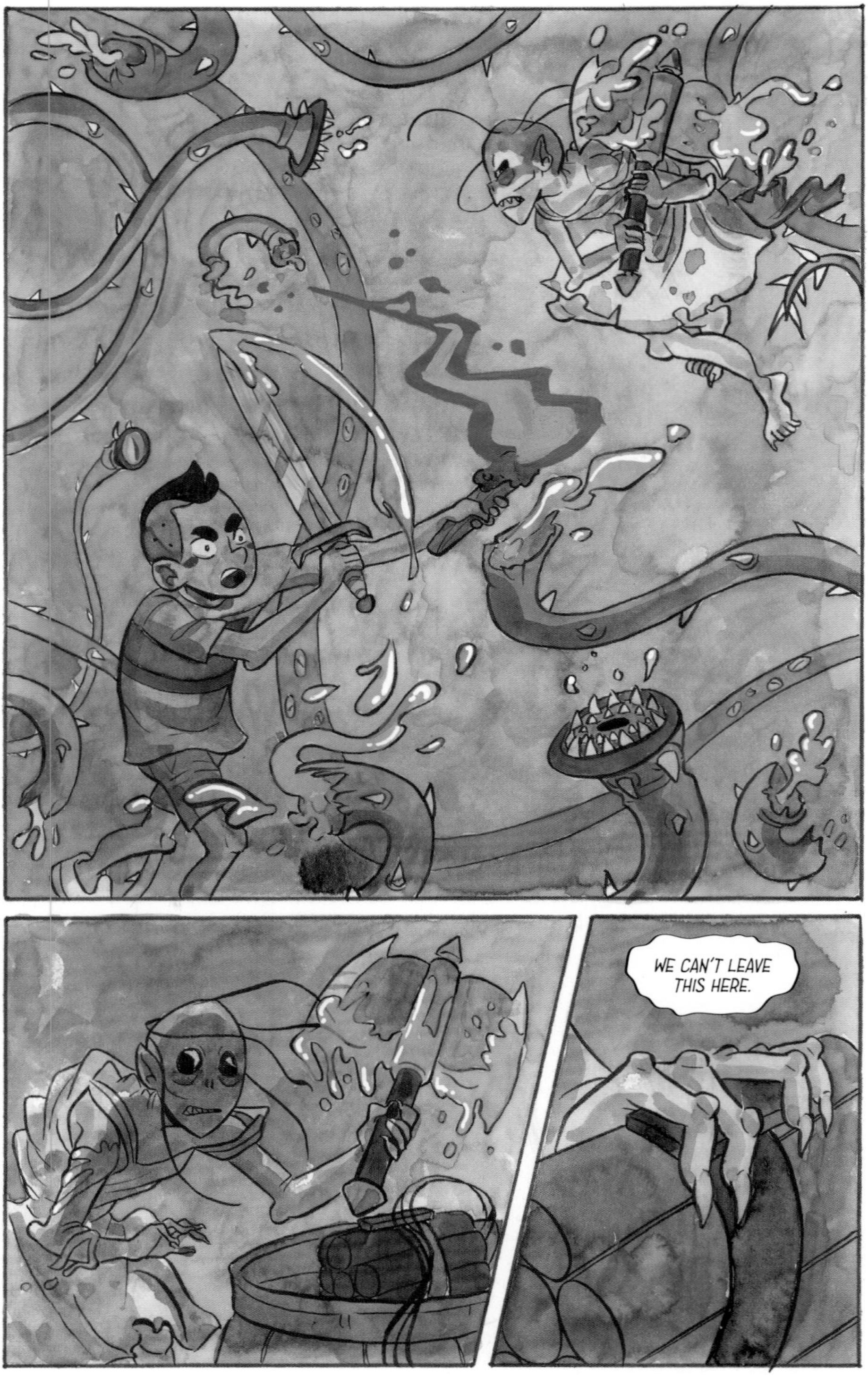
WE CAN'T LEAVE
THIS HERE.

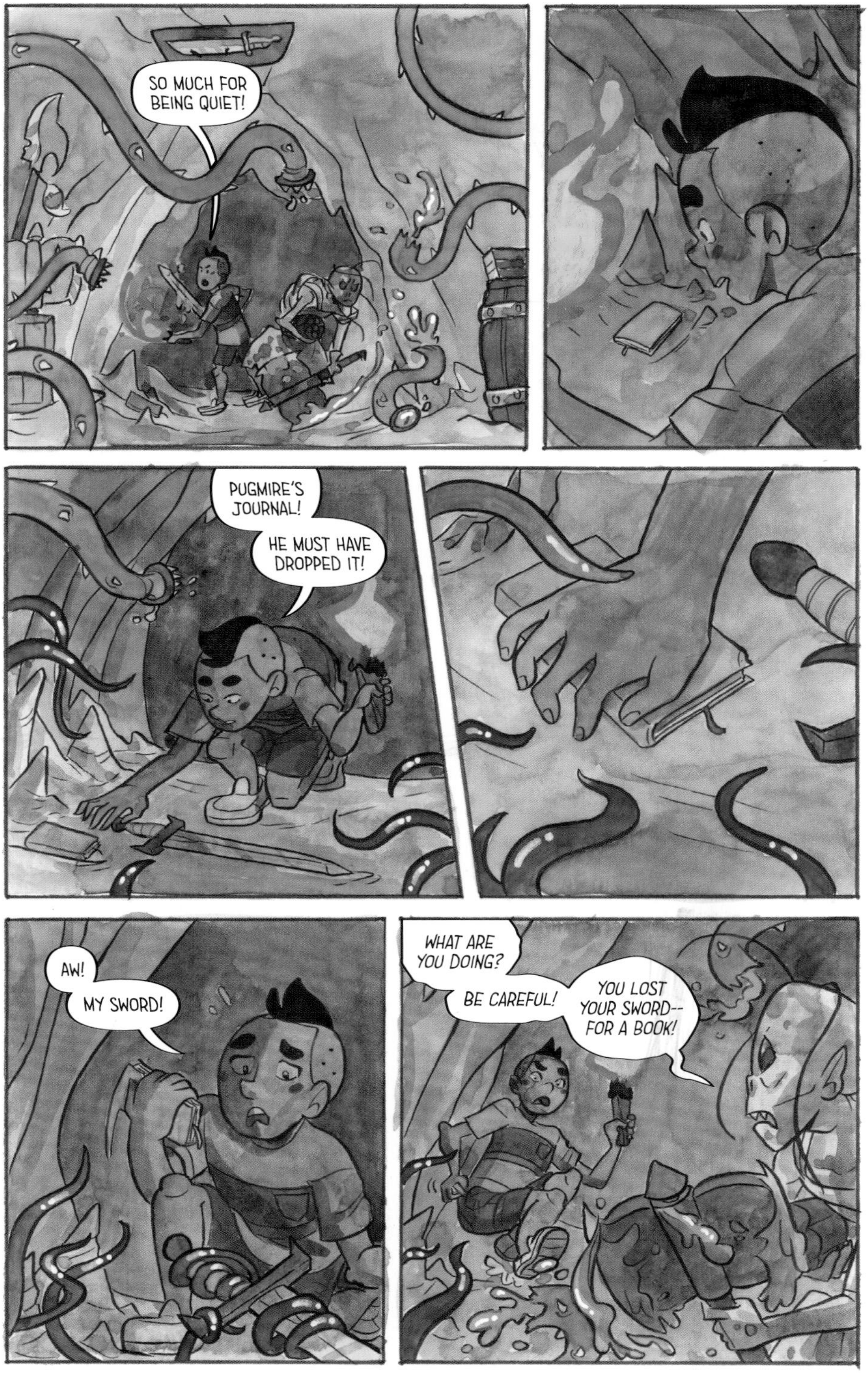
SO MUCH FOR BEING QUIET!
PUGMIRE'S JOURNAL!
HE MUST HAVE DROPPED IT!
AW!
MY SWORD!
WHAT ARE YOU DOING?
BE CAREFUL!
YOU LOST YOUR SWORD-- FOR A BOOK!

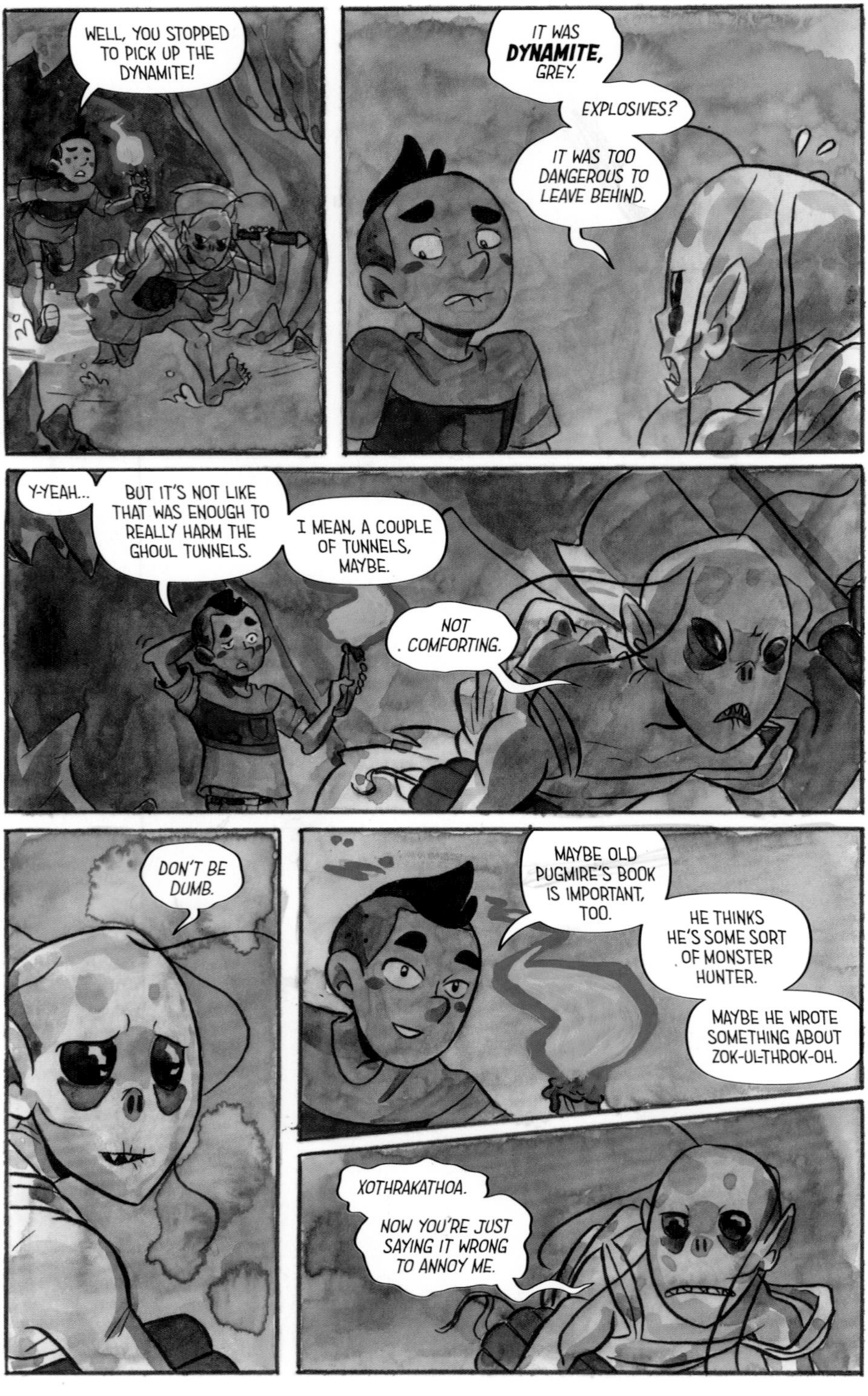
WELL, YOU STOPPED TO PICK UP THE DYNAMITE!
IT WAS **DYNAMITE,** GREY.
EXPLOSIVES?
IT WAS TOO DANGEROUS TO LEAVE BEHIND.
Y-YEAH...
BUT IT'S NOT LIKE THAT WAS ENOUGH TO REALLY HARM THE GHOUL TUNNELS.
I MEAN, A COUPLE OF TUNNELS, MAYBE.
NOT COMFORTING.
DON'T BE DUMB.
MAYBE OLD PUGMIRE'S BOOK IS IMPORTANT, TOO.
HE THINKS HE'S SOME SORT OF MONSTER HUNTER.
MAYBE HE WROTE SOMETHING ABOUT ZOK-UL-THROK-OH.
XOTHRAKATHOA.
NOW YOU'RE JUST SAYING IT WRONG TO ANNOY ME.

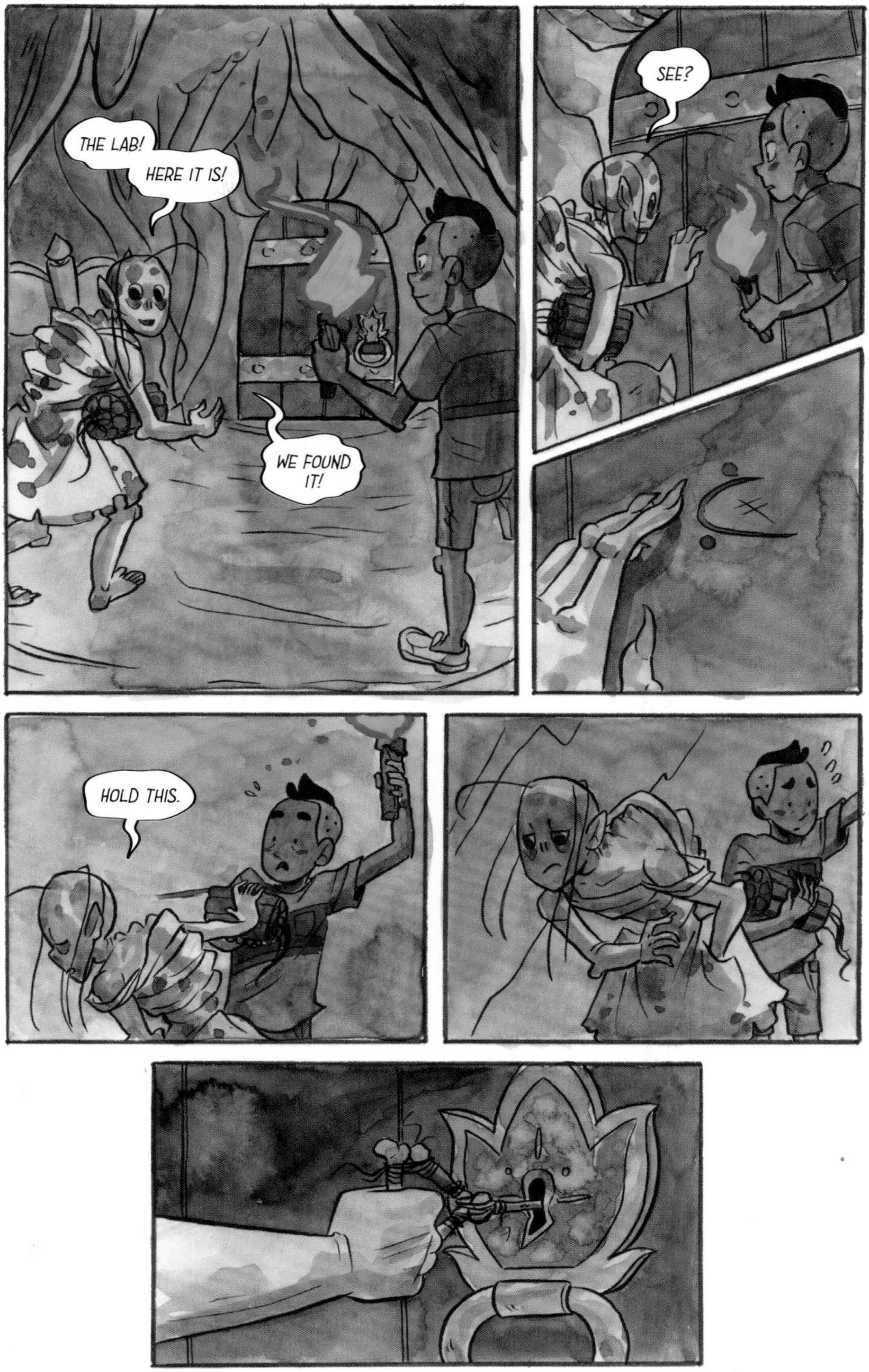
THE LAB!
HERE IT IS!
WE FOUND IT!
SEE?
HOLD THIS.

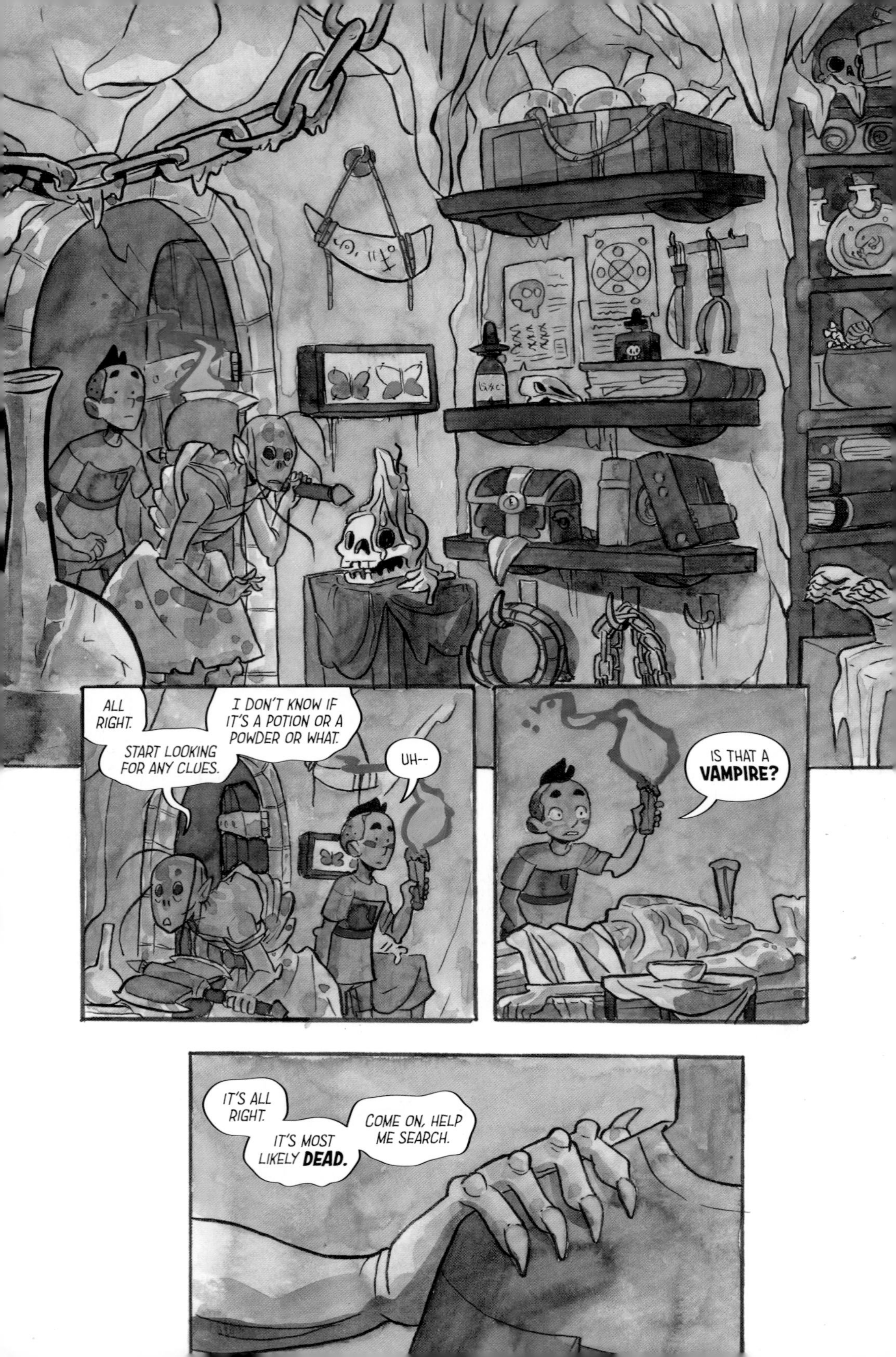
ALL RIGHT.
START LOOKING FOR ANY CLUES.
I DON'T KNOW IF IT'S A POTION OR A POWDER OR WHAT.
UH--
IS THAT A **VAMPIRE?**
IT'S ALL RIGHT.
IT'S MOST LIKELY **DEAD.**
COME ON, HELP ME SEARCH.

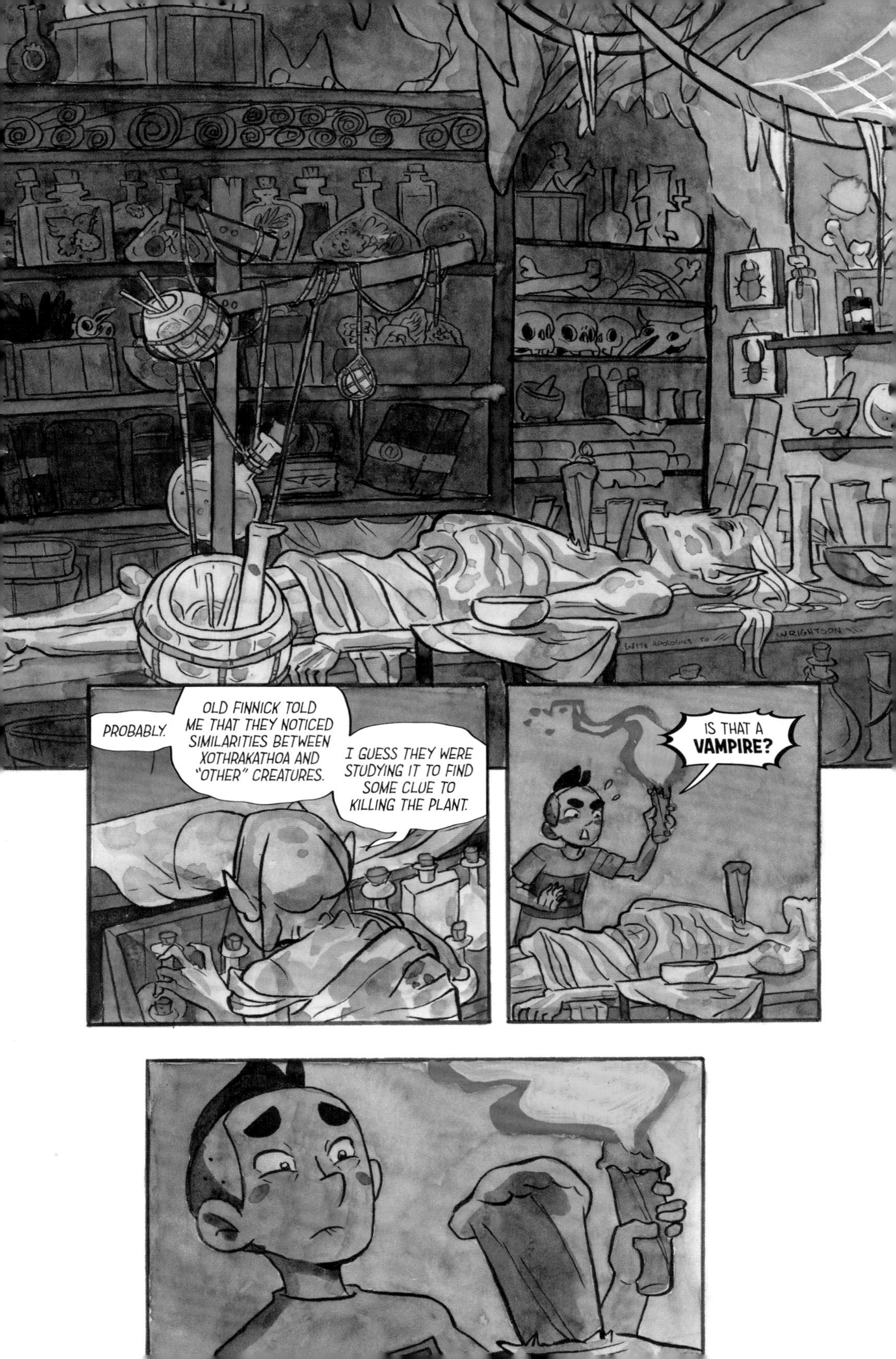
WITH APOLOGIES TO WRIGHTSON
PROBABLY.
OLD FINNICK TOLD ME THAT THEY NOTICED SIMILARITIES BETWEEN XOTHRAKATHOA AND "OTHER" CREATURES.
I GUESS THEY WERE STUDYING IT TO FIND SOME CLUE TO KILLING THE PLANT.
IS THAT A **VAMPIRE?**

MAYBE ONE OF THESE OLD SCROLLS HOLDS THE KEY.
THERE'S JUST... SO MANY OF THEM.
THIS WOULD BE A LOT EASIER IF--
HOLD ON A SECOND!
THIS IS IT!
IT'S A RECIPE!
THE GHOULS MIGHT HAVE FIGURED OUT A WAY TO STOP THE PLANT IF IT EVER RETURNED!
I THINK THIS IS SOME SORT OF POISON!

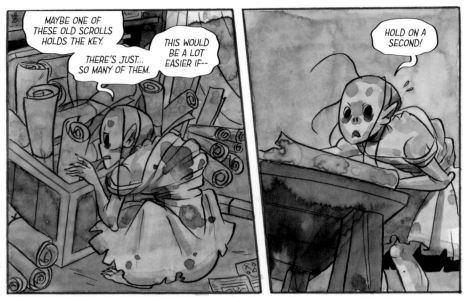

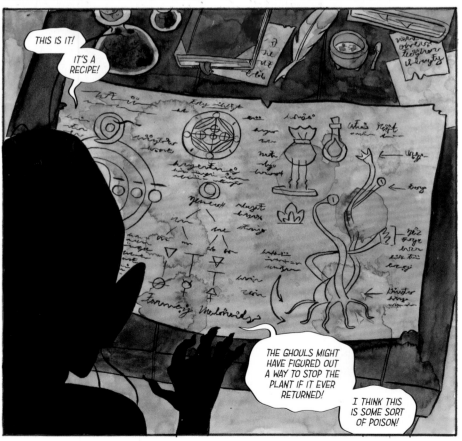

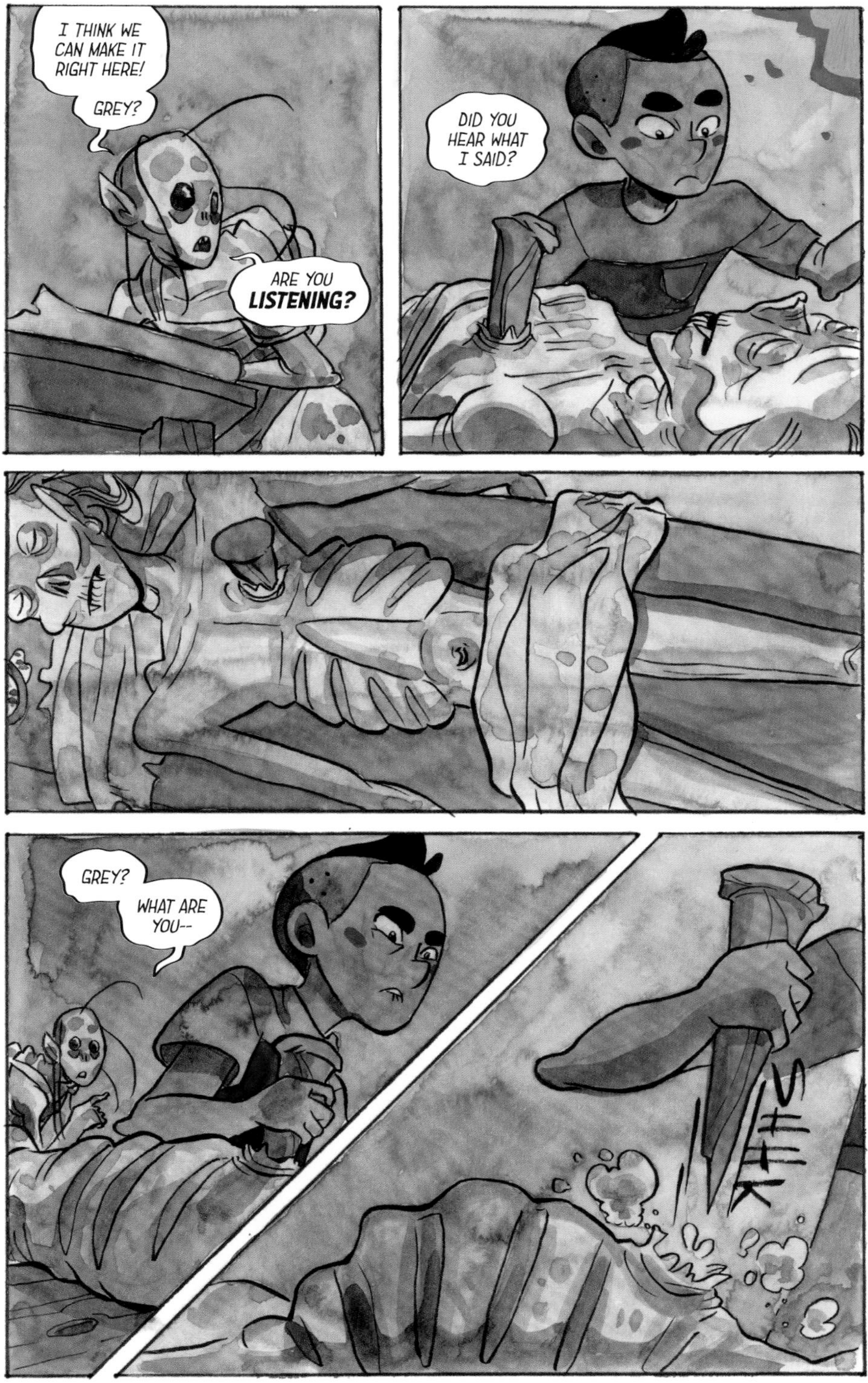
I THINK WE CAN MAKE IT RIGHT HERE!
GREY?
ARE YOU **LISTENING?**
DID YOU HEAR WHAT I SAID?
GREY?
WHAT ARE YOU--

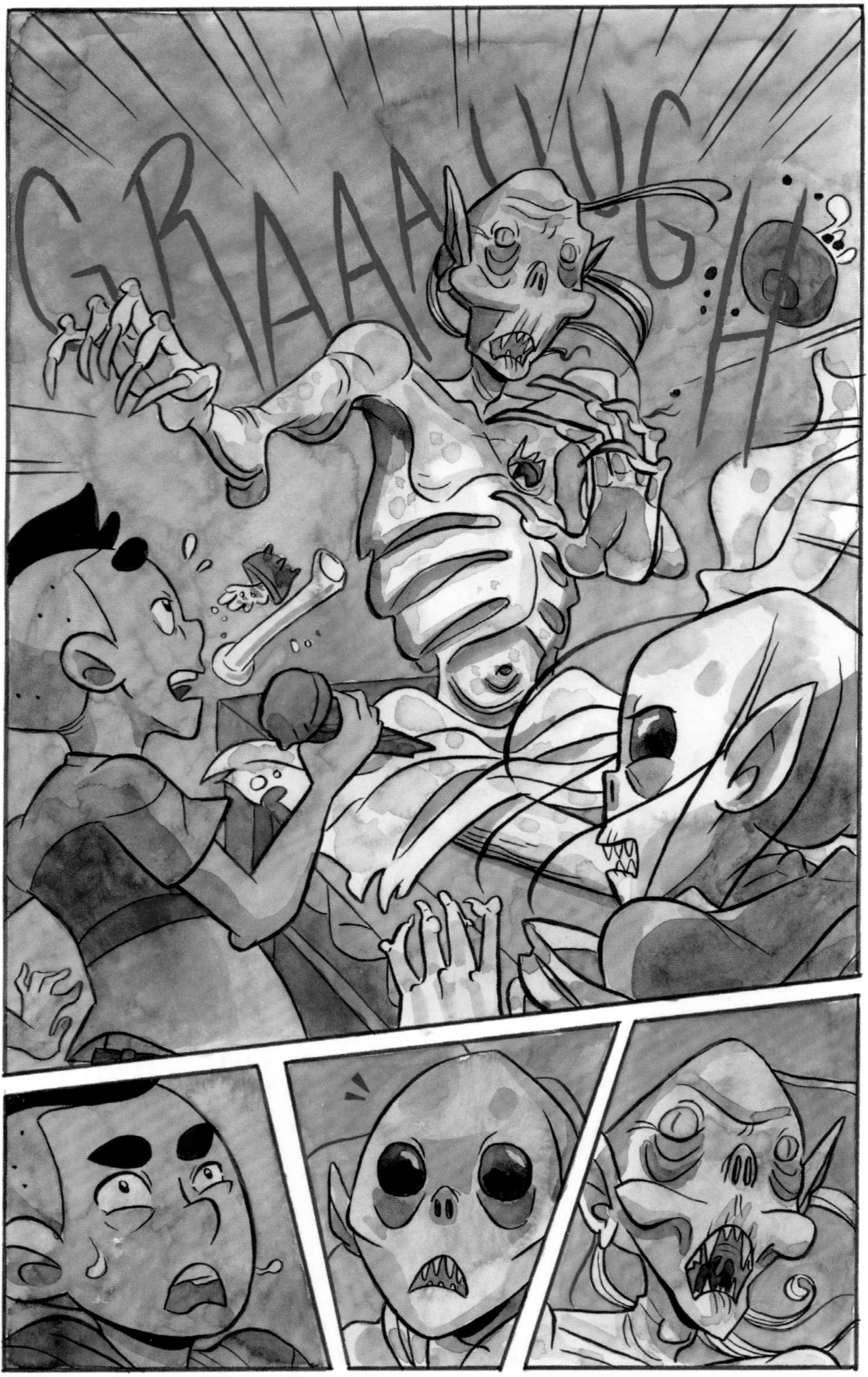
GRAAAWUGH

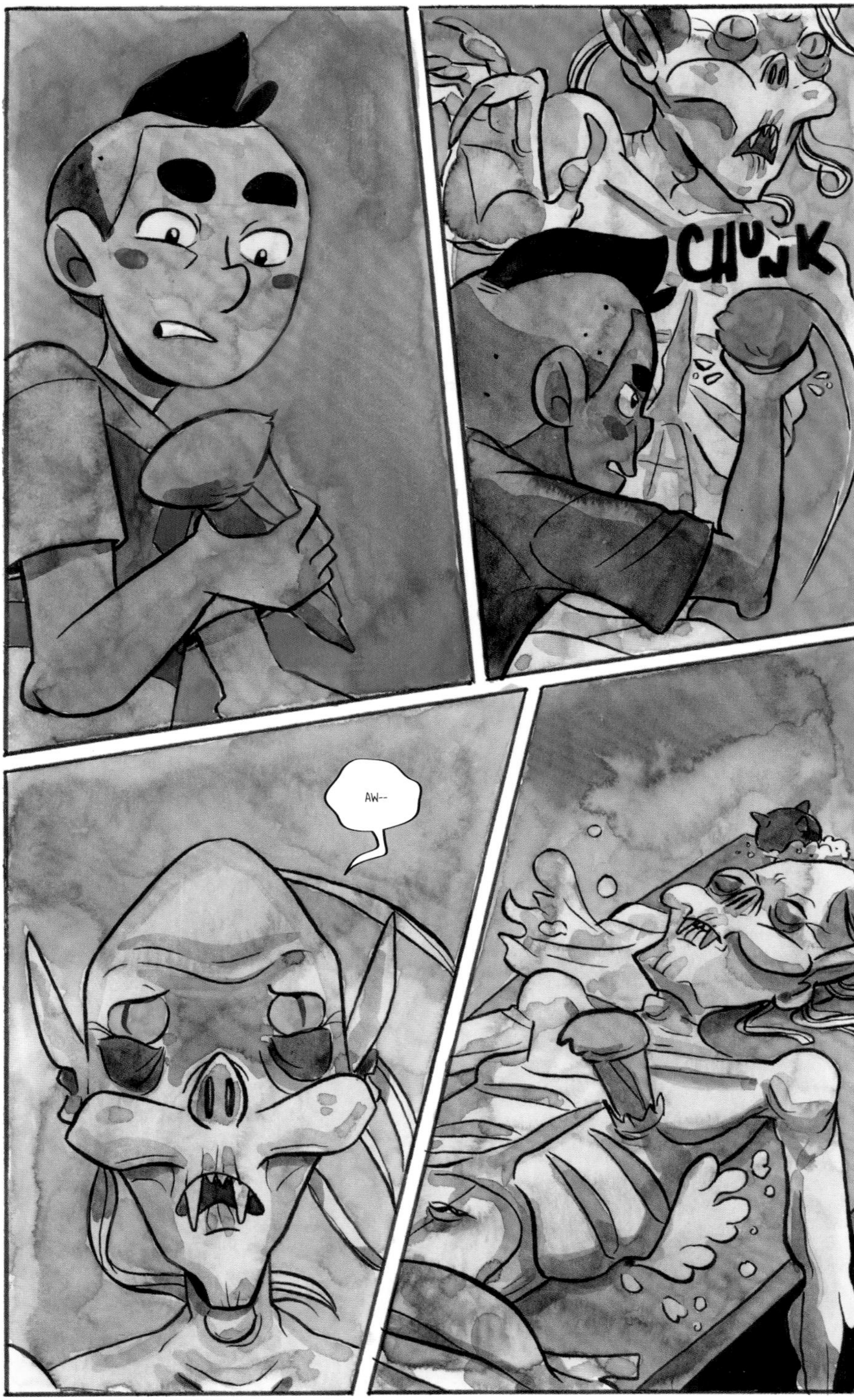
CHUNK
AW--

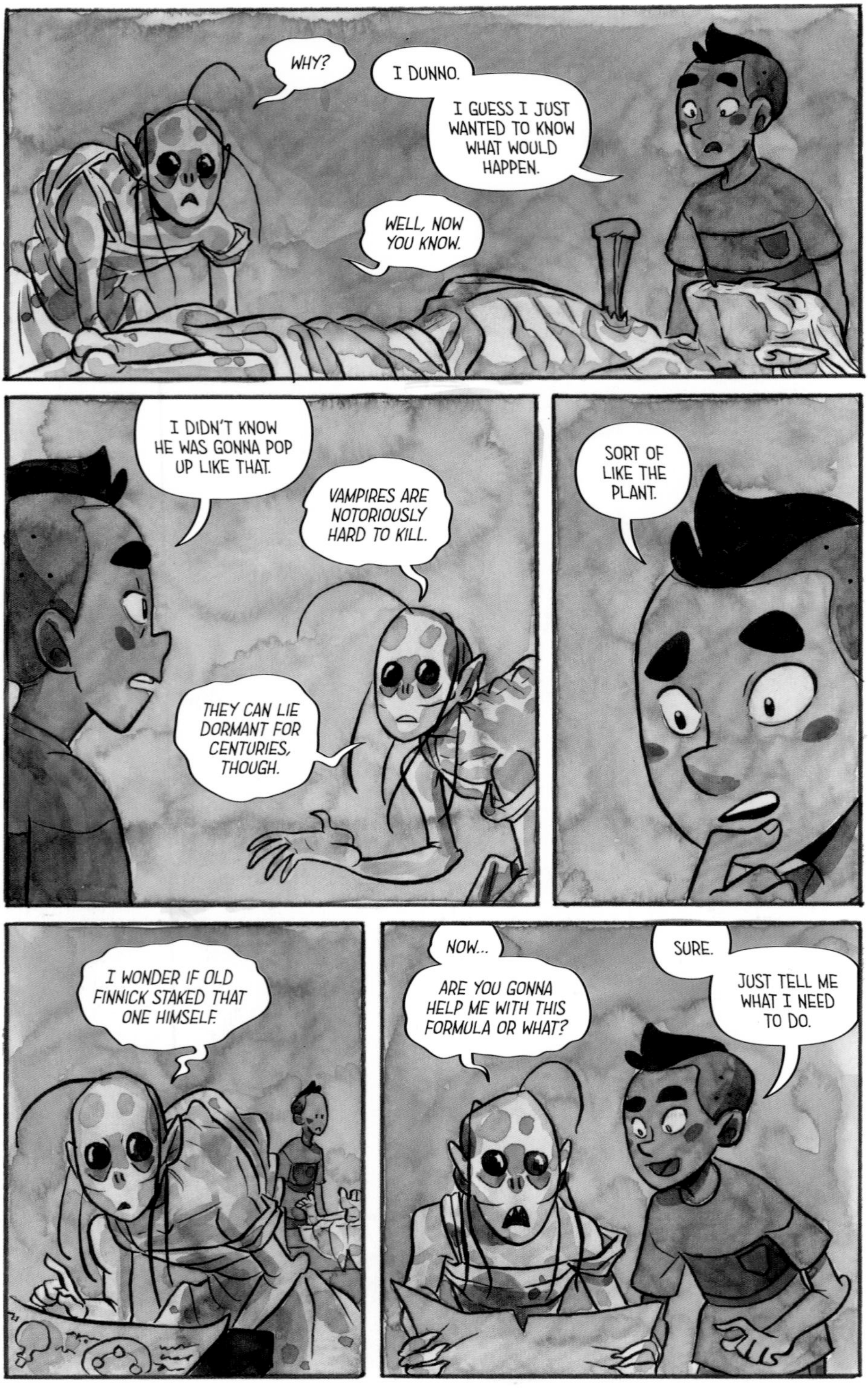
WHY?
I DUNNO.
I GUESS I JUST WANTED TO KNOW WHAT WOULD HAPPEN.
WELL, NOW YOU KNOW.
I DIDN'T KNOW HE WAS GONNA POP UP LIKE THAT.
VAMPIRES ARE NOTORIOUSLY HARD TO KILL.
THEY CAN LIE DORMANT FOR CENTURIES, THOUGH.
SORT OF LIKE THE PLANT.
I WONDER IF OLD FINNICK STAKED THAT ONE HIMSELF.
NOW...
ARE YOU GONNA HELP ME WITH THIS FORMULA OR WHAT?
SURE.
JUST TELL ME WHAT I NEED TO DO.

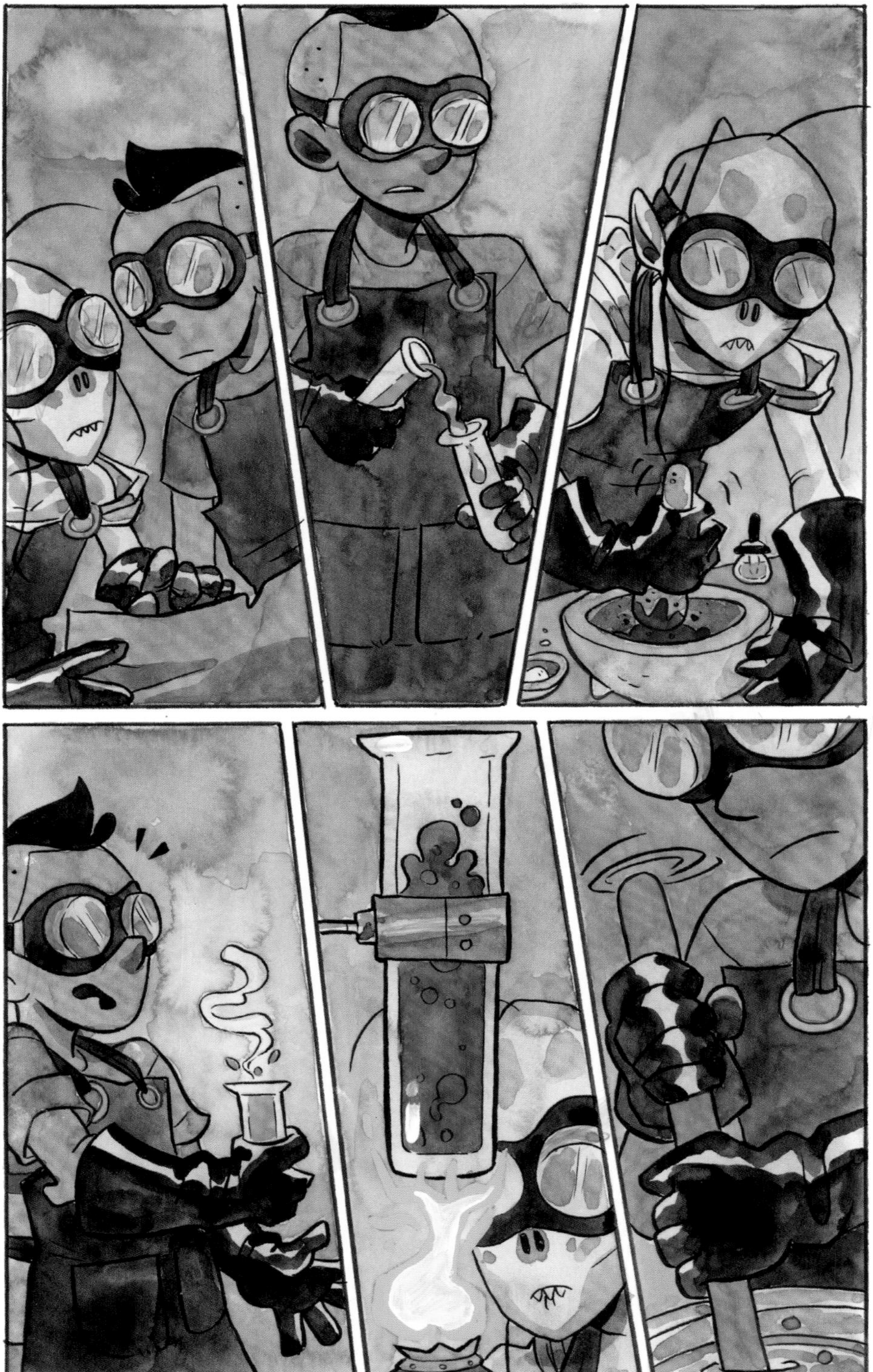

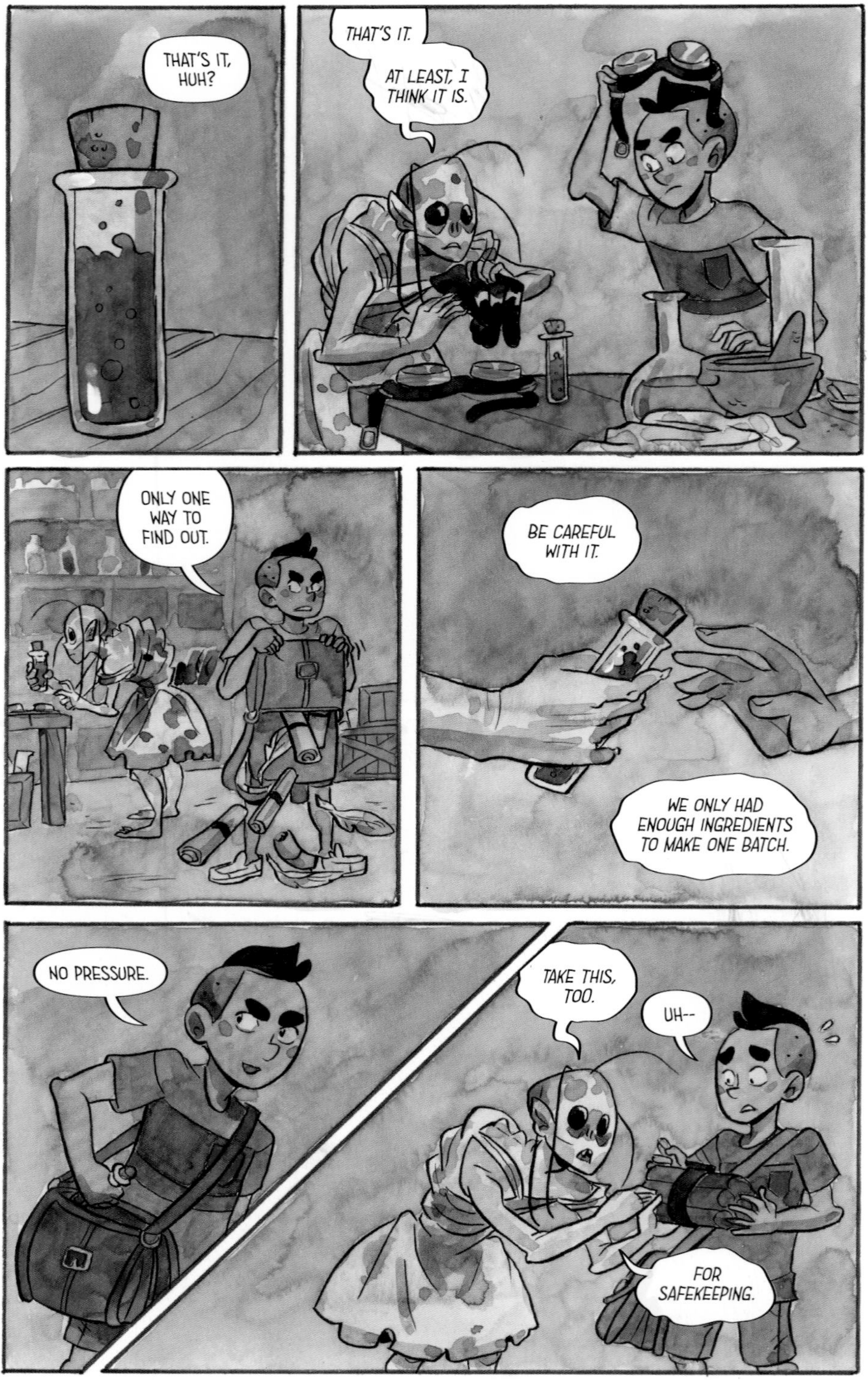
THAT'S IT, HUH?
THAT'S IT.
AT LEAST, I THINK IT IS.
ONLY ONE WAY TO FIND OUT.
BE CAREFUL WITH IT.
WE ONLY HAD ENOUGH INGREDIENTS TO MAKE ONE BATCH.
NO PRESSURE.
TAKE THIS, TOO.
UH--
FOR SAFEKEEPING.

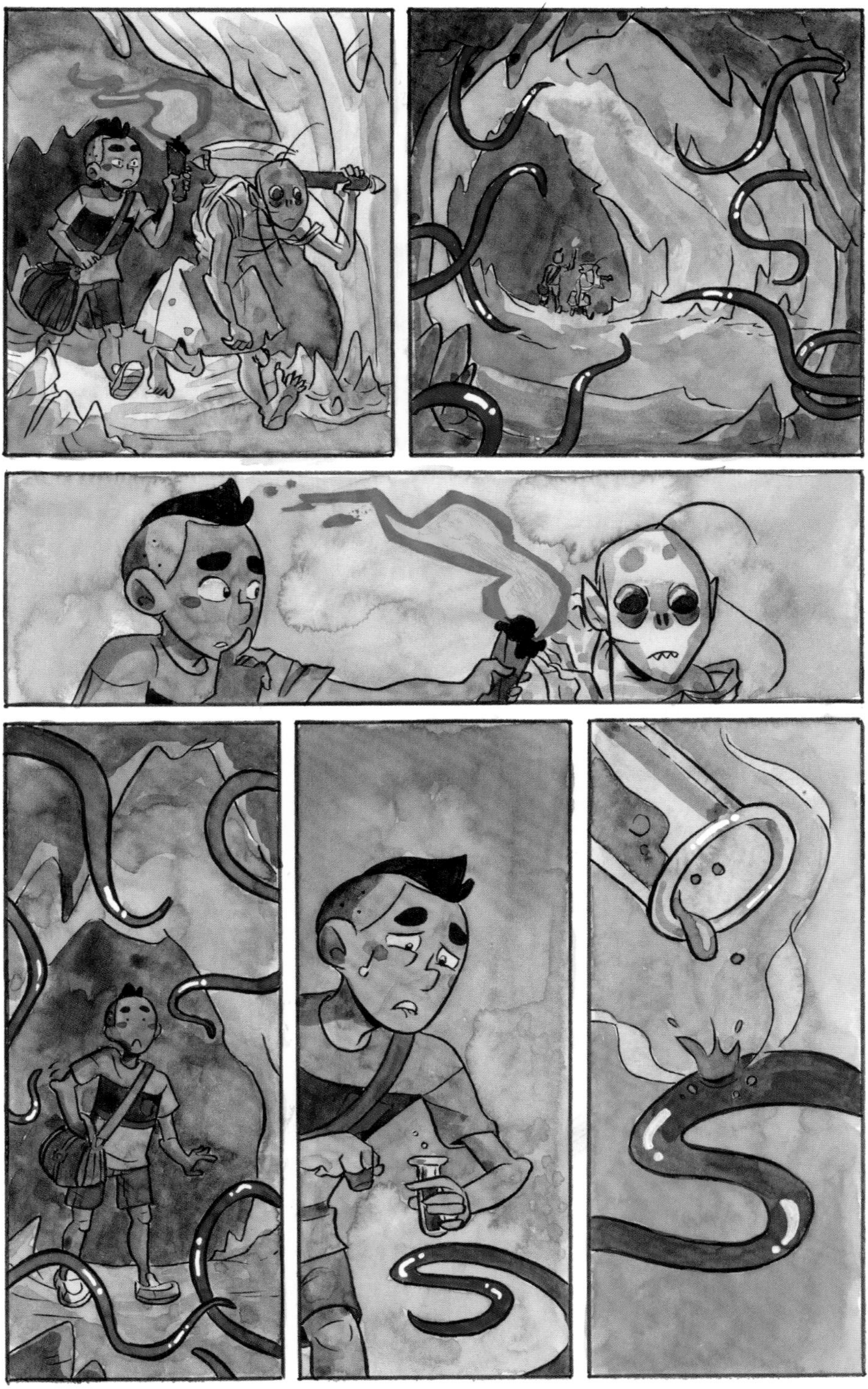

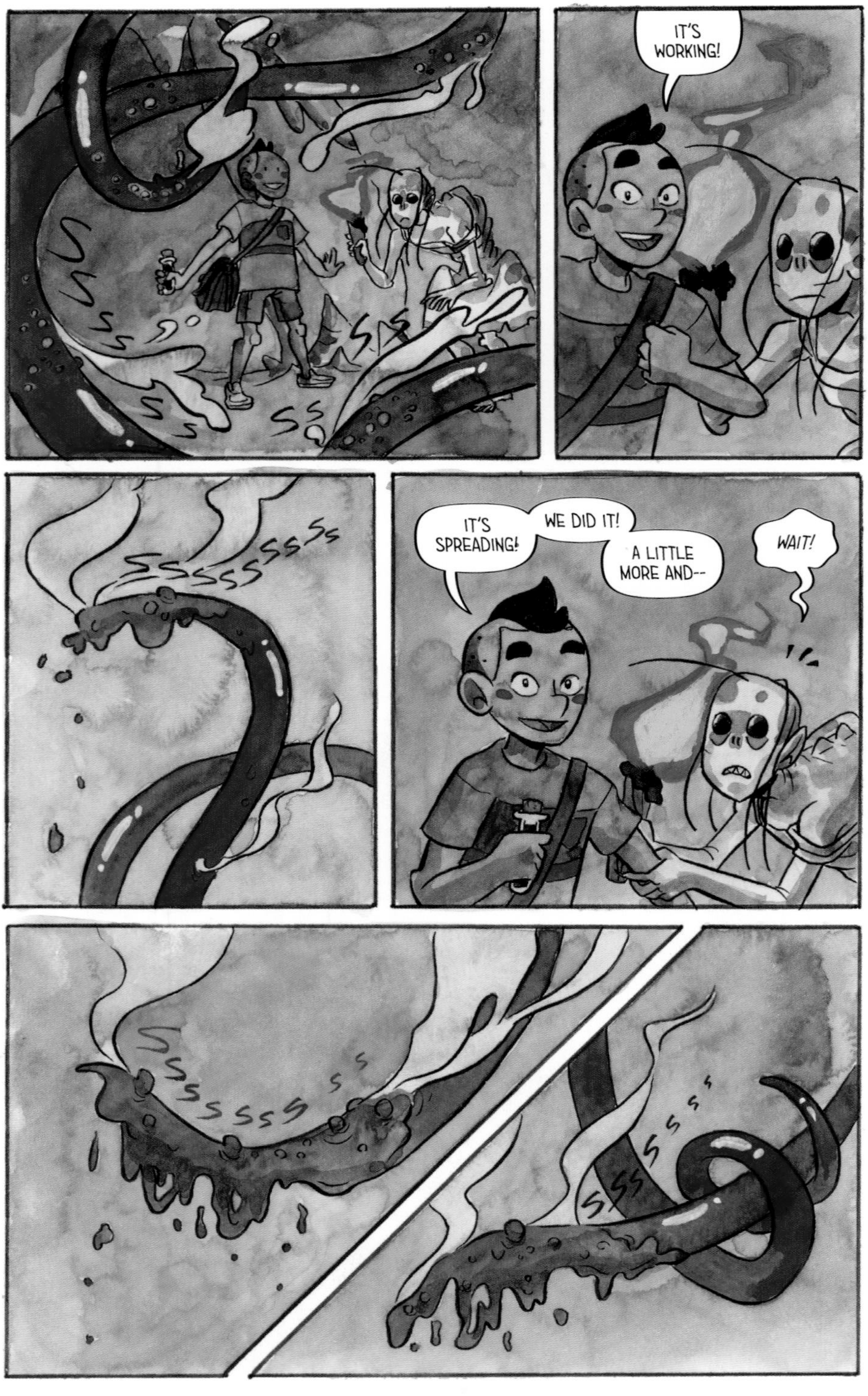
IT'S WORKING!
IT'S SPREADING!
WE DID IT!
A LITTLE MORE AND--
WAIT!

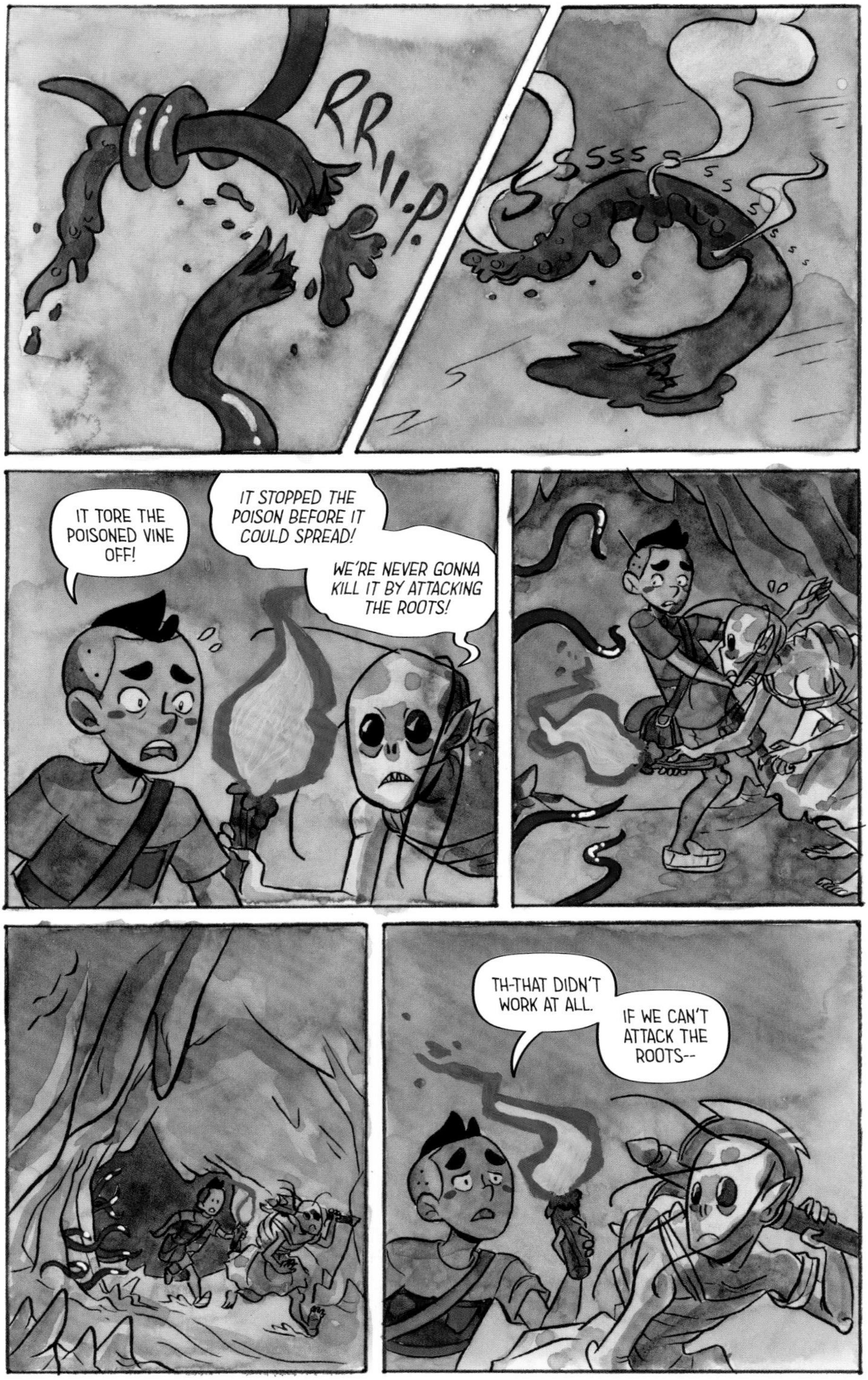
RRIIP
SSSSSSSSSSS
IT TORE THE POISONED VINE OFF!
IT STOPPED THE POISON BEFORE IT COULD SPREAD!
WE'RE NEVER GONNA KILL IT BY ATTACKING THE ROOTS!
TH-THAT DIDN'T WORK AT ALL.
IF WE CAN'T ATTACK THE ROOTS--

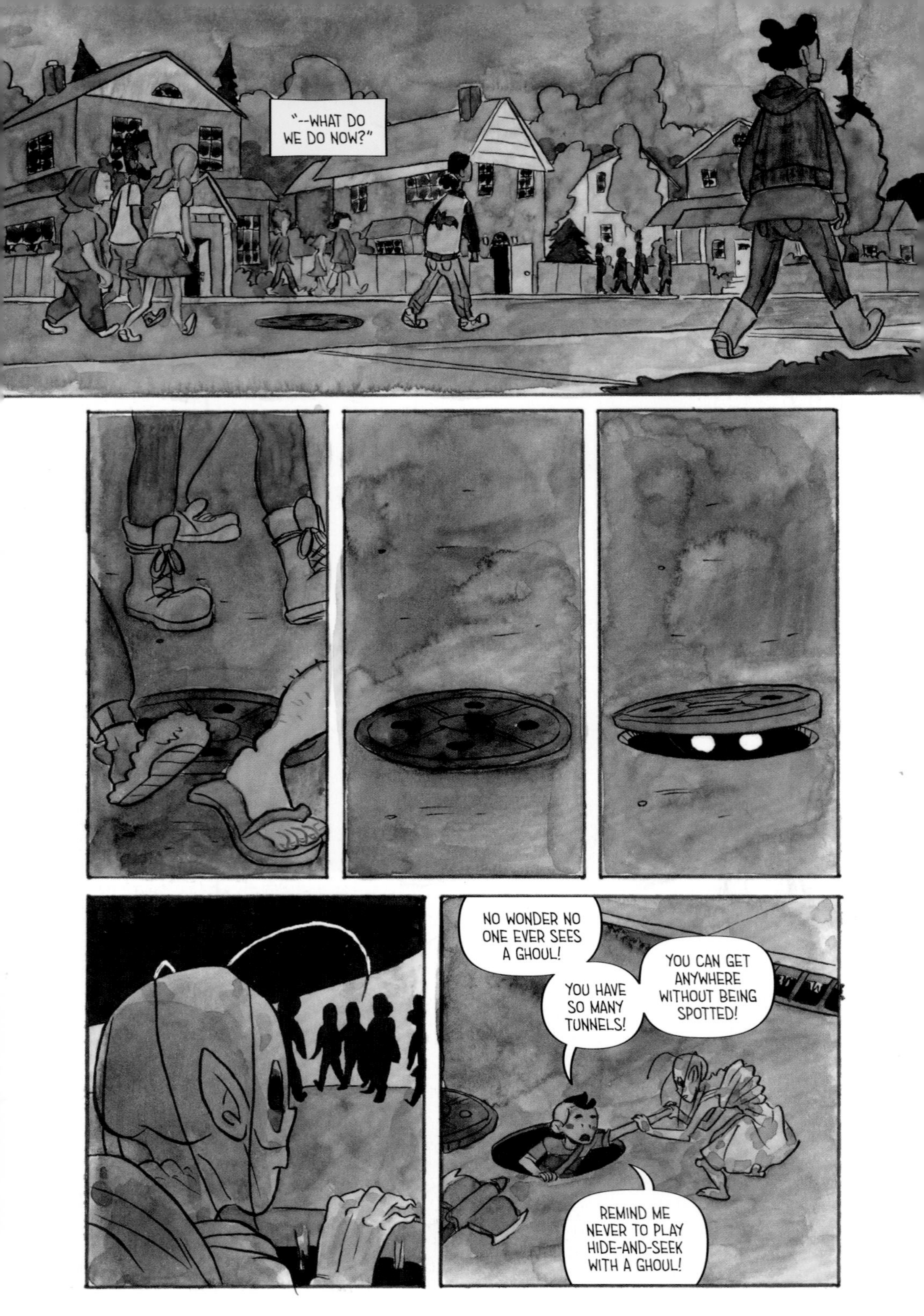
"--WHAT DO WE DO NOW?"
NO WONDER NO ONE EVER SEES A GHOUL!
YOU HAVE SO MANY TUNNELS!
YOU CAN GET ANYWHERE WITHOUT BEING SPOTTED!
REMIND ME NEVER TO PLAY HIDE-AND-SEEK WITH A GHOUL!

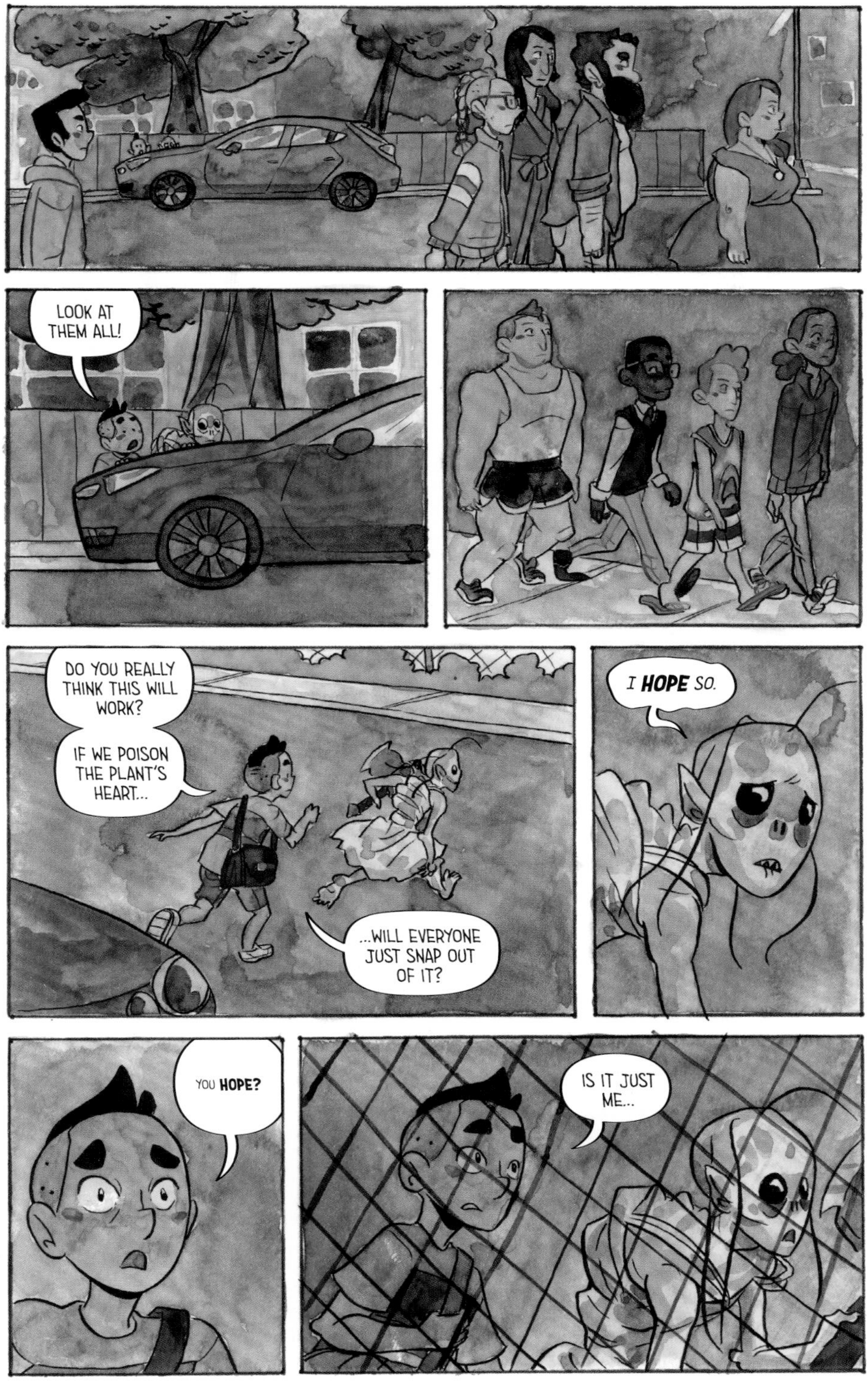
LOOK AT THEM ALL!
DO YOU REALLY THINK THIS WILL WORK?
IF WE POISON THE PLANT'S HEART...
...WILL EVERYONE JUST SNAP OUT OF IT?
I HOPE SO.
YOU HOPE?
IS IT JUST ME...

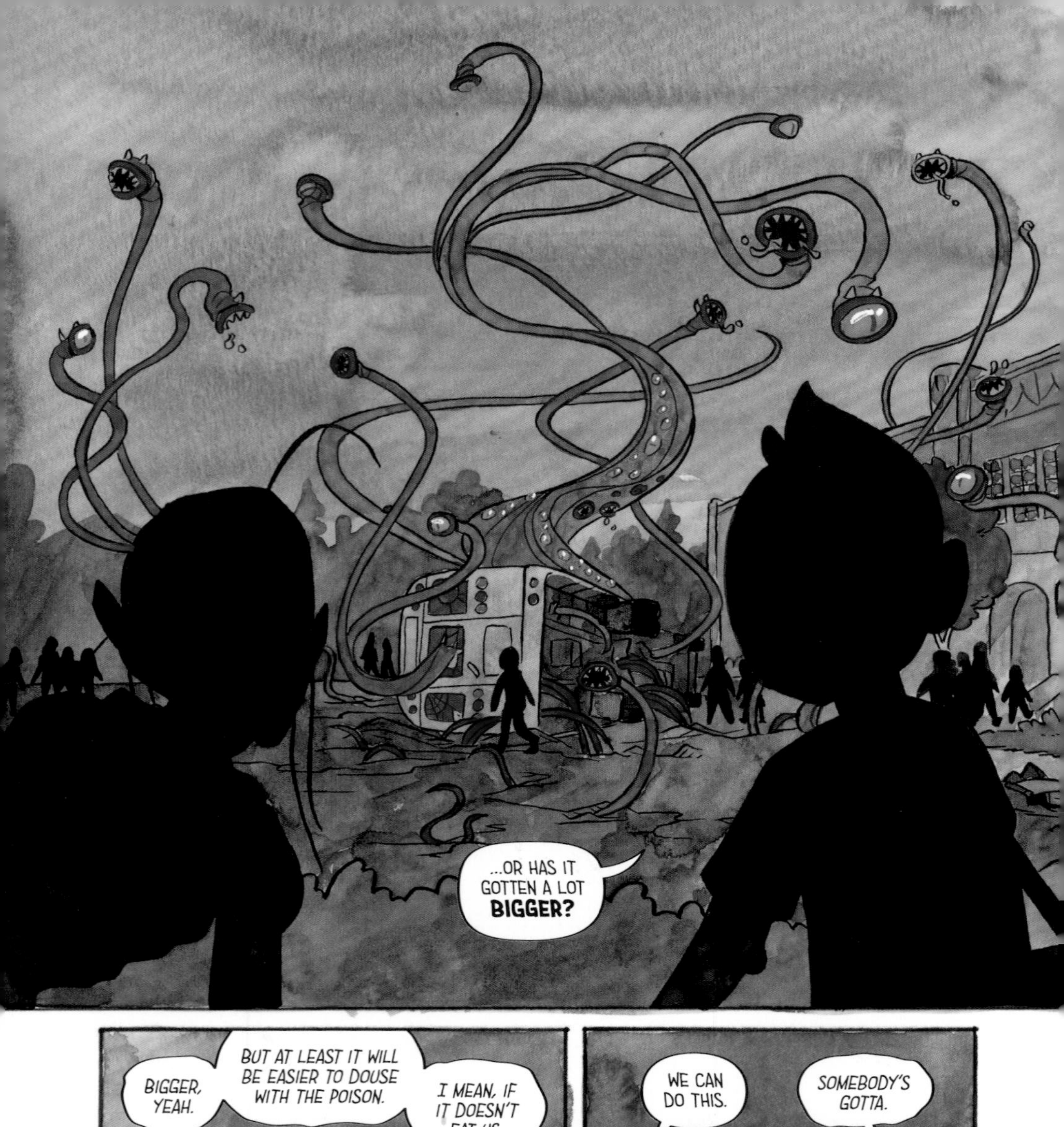
...OR HAS IT GOTTEN A LOT **BIGGER?**

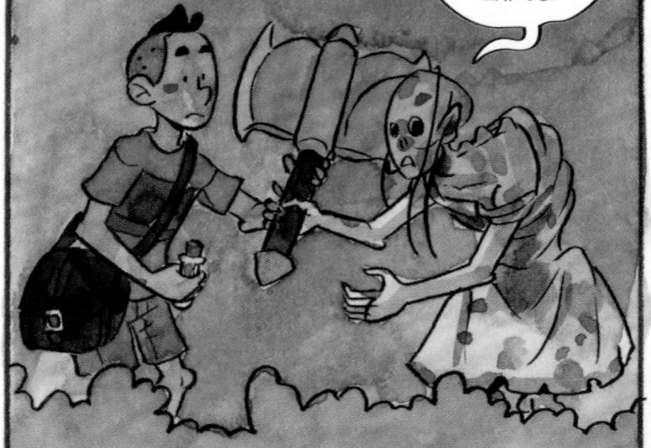
BIGGER, YEAH.
BUT AT LEAST IT WILL BE EASIER TO DOUSE WITH THE POISON.
I MEAN, IF IT DOESN'T EAT US.

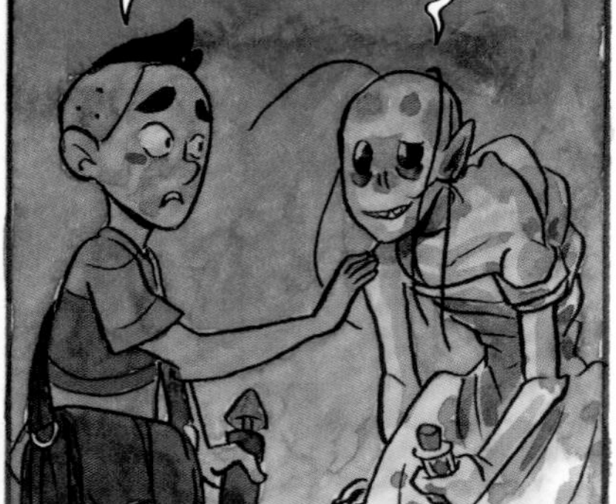
WE CAN DO THIS.
SOMEBODY'S GOTTA.

COVER ME FOR AS LONG AS YOU CAN!
I WANT TO GET AS CLOSE AS POSSIBLE TO XOTHRAKATHOA.
ZOTTO-WOK-KO.
LET'S GO!
GET BACK!
ALL OF YOU!
I DON'T WANT TO HURT YOU!

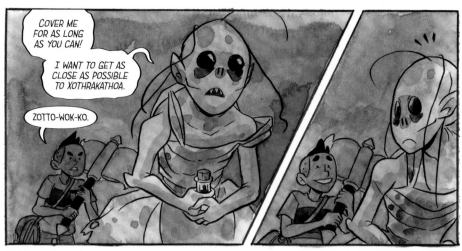

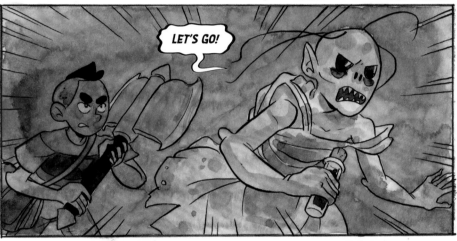

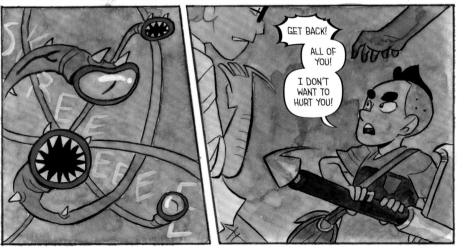

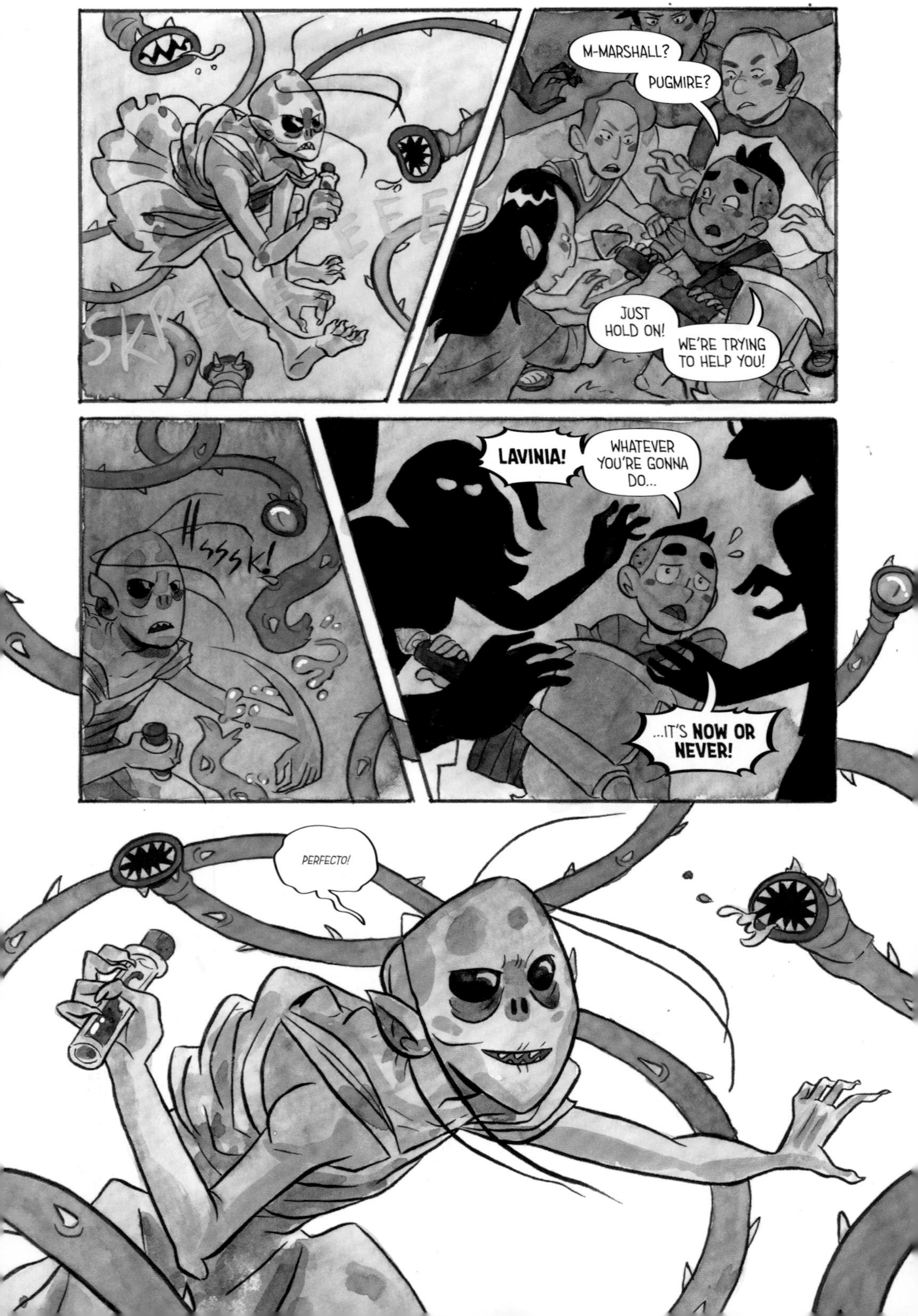
SKREEEEEEE
M-MARSHALL?
PUGMIRE?
JUST HOLD ON!
WE'RE TRYING TO HELP YOU!
HSSSK!
LAVINIA!
WHATEVER YOU'RE GONNA DO...
...IT'S NOW OR NEVER!
PERFECTO!

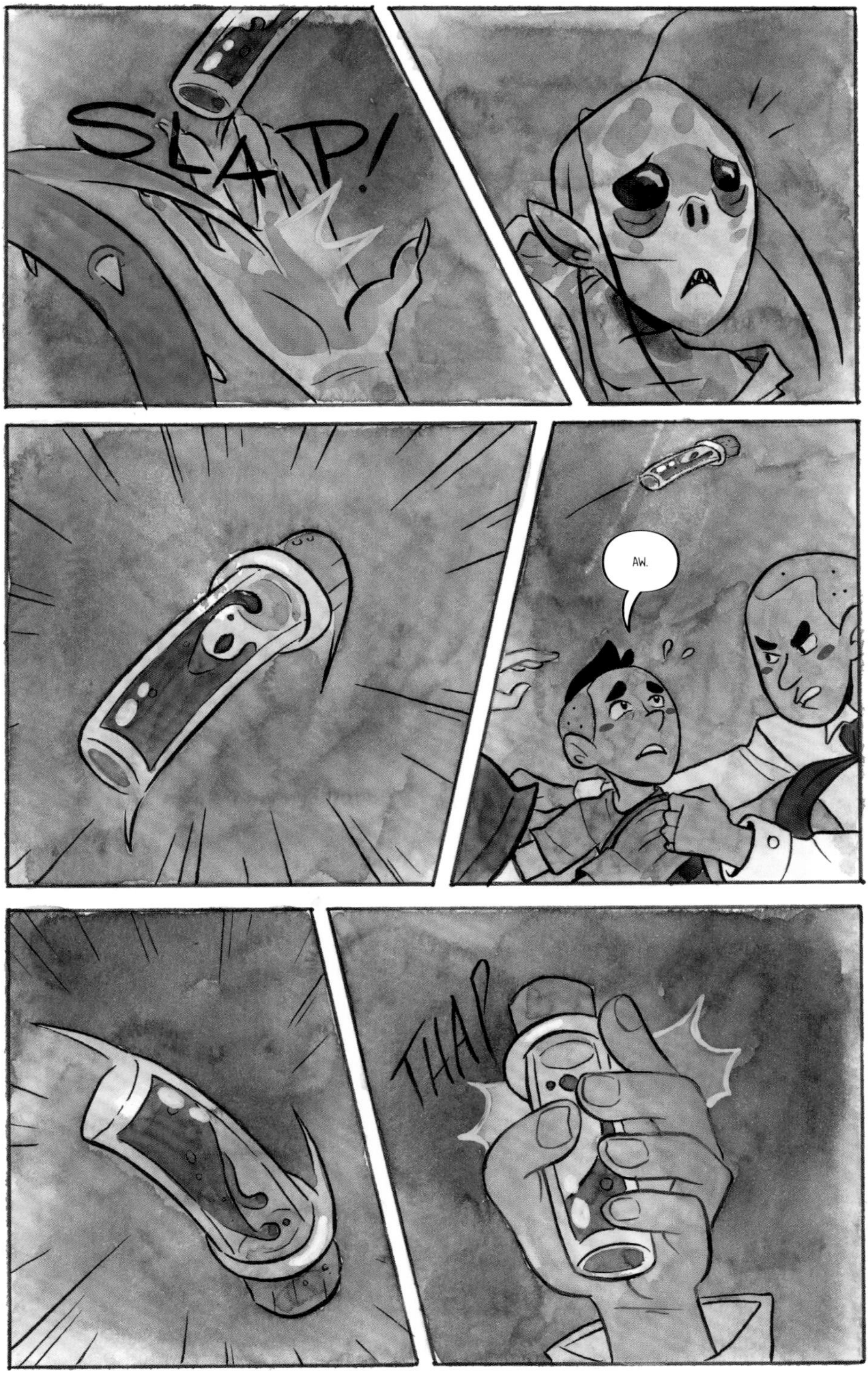
SLAP!
AW.
THAP

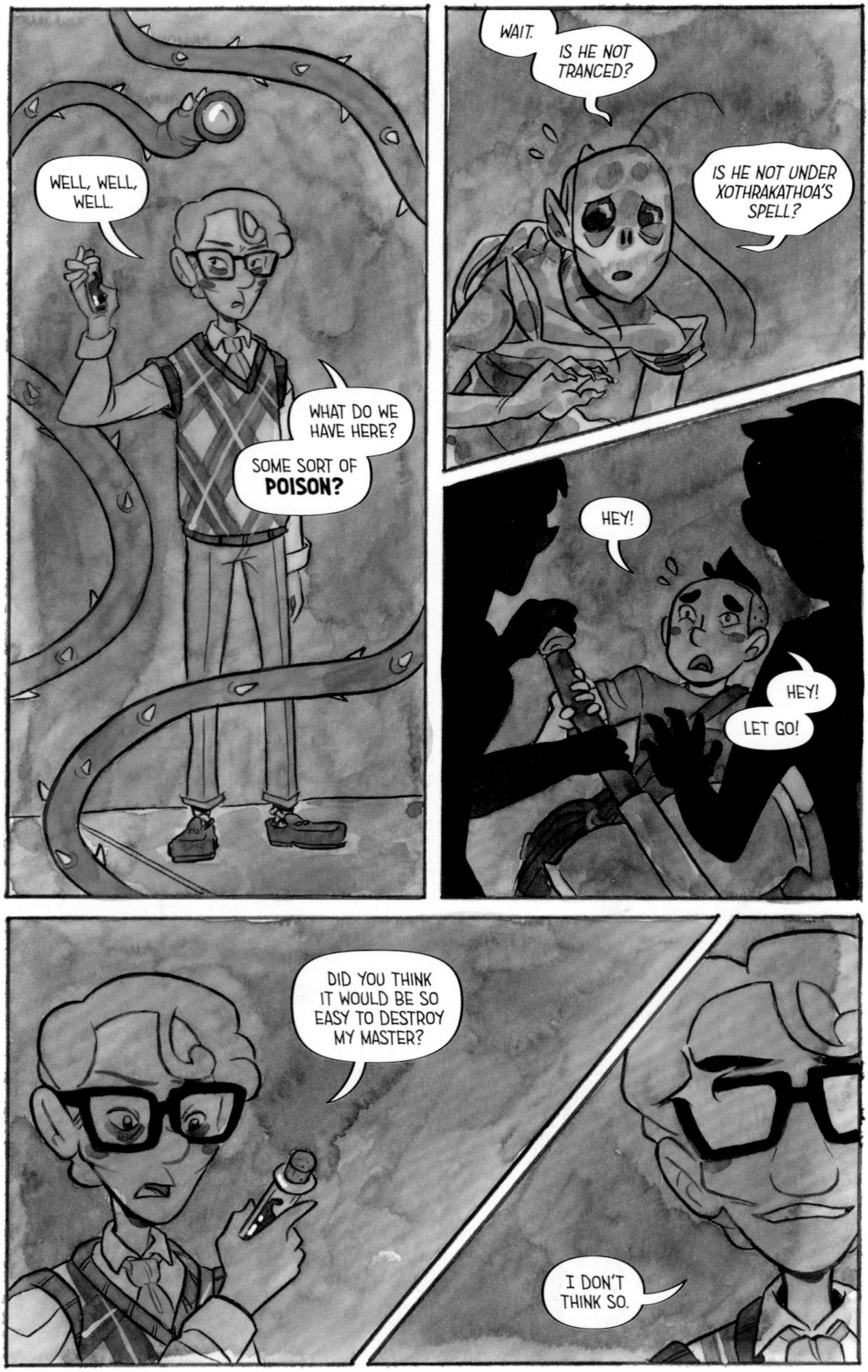
WELL, WELL, WELL.
WHAT DO WE HAVE HERE?
SOME SORT OF **POISON?**
WAIT.
IS HE NOT TRANCED?
IS HE NOT UNDER XOTHRAKATHOA'S SPELL?
HEY!
HEY!
LET GO!
DID YOU THINK IT WOULD BE SO EASY TO DESTROY MY MASTER?
I DON'T THINK SO.

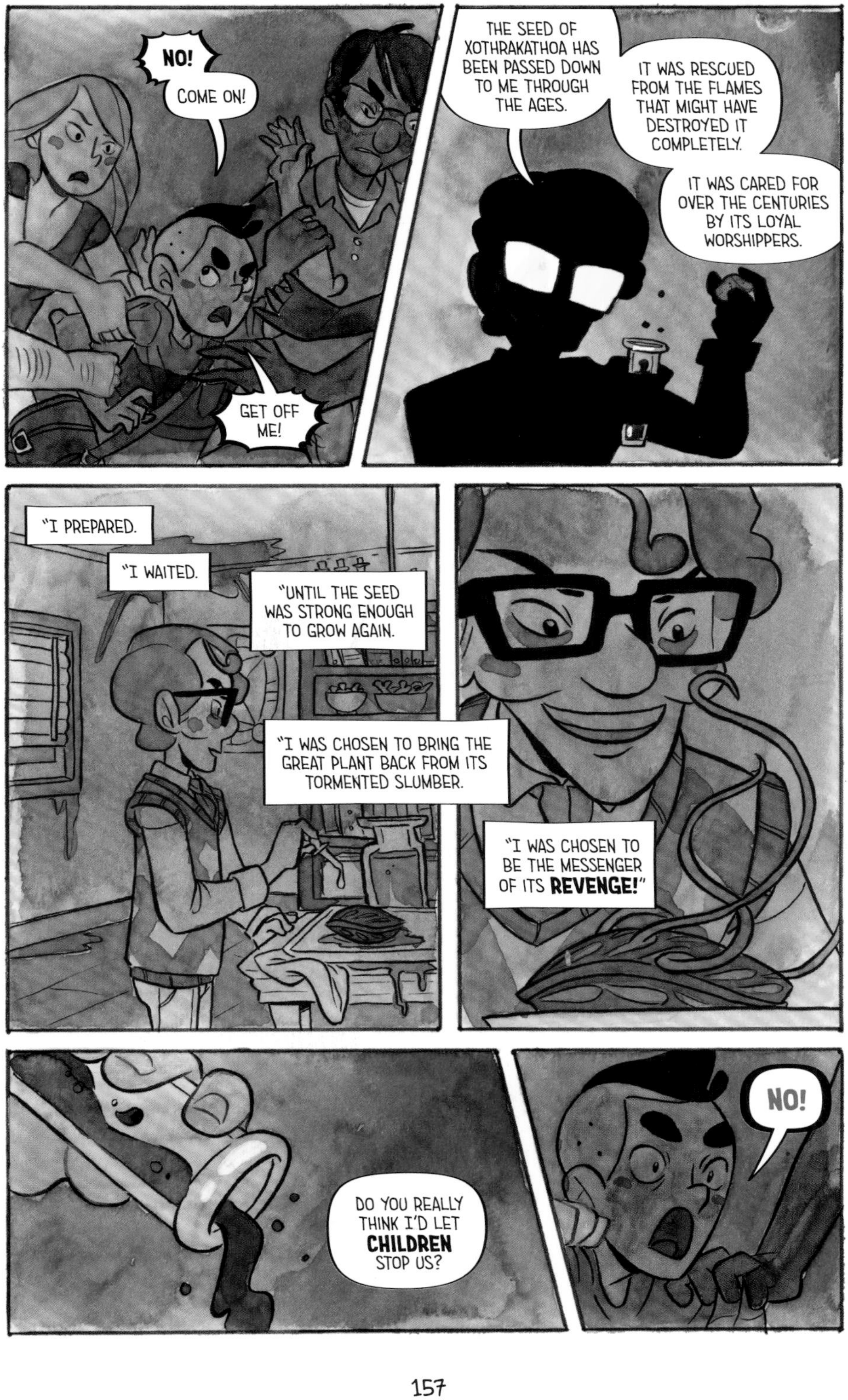
NO!
COME ON!
GET OFF ME!
THE SEED OF XOTHRAKATHOA HAS BEEN PASSED DOWN TO ME THROUGH THE AGES.
IT WAS RESCUED FROM THE FLAMES THAT MIGHT HAVE DESTROYED IT COMPLETELY.
IT WAS CARED FOR OVER THE CENTURIES BY ITS LOYAL WORSHIPPERS.
"I PREPARED.
"I WAITED.
"UNTIL THE SEED WAS STRONG ENOUGH TO GROW AGAIN.
"I WAS CHOSEN TO BRING THE GREAT PLANT BACK FROM ITS TORMENTED SLUMBER.
"I WAS CHOSEN TO BE THE MESSENGER OF ITS **REVENGE!**"
DO YOU REALLY THINK I'D LET **CHILDREN** STOP US?
NO!

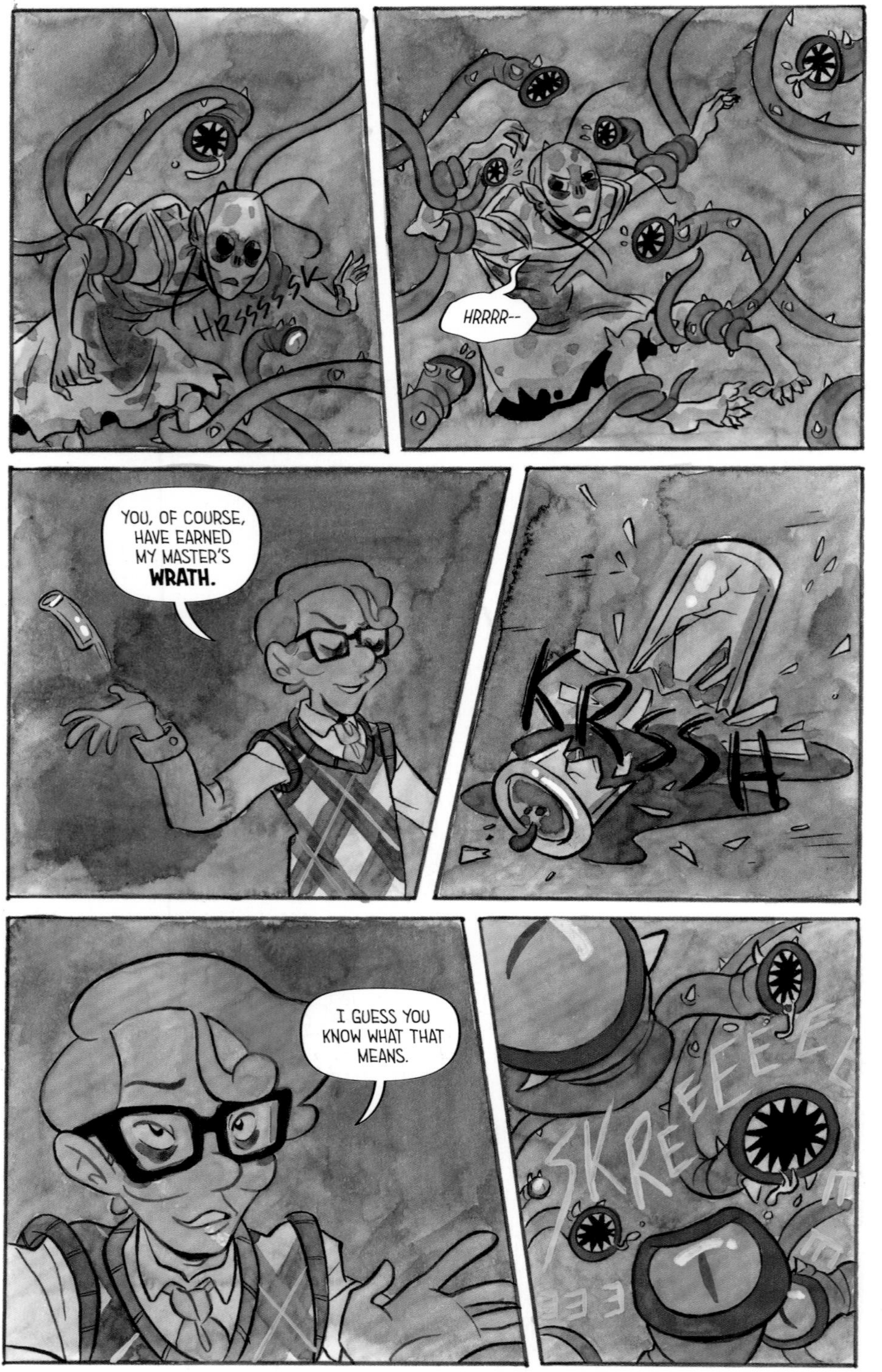
HRSSSSSSK
HRRRR--
YOU, OF COURSE, HAVE EARNED MY MASTER'S **WRATH.**
KRSSH
I GUESS YOU KNOW WHAT THAT MEANS.
SKREEEEEEEEE

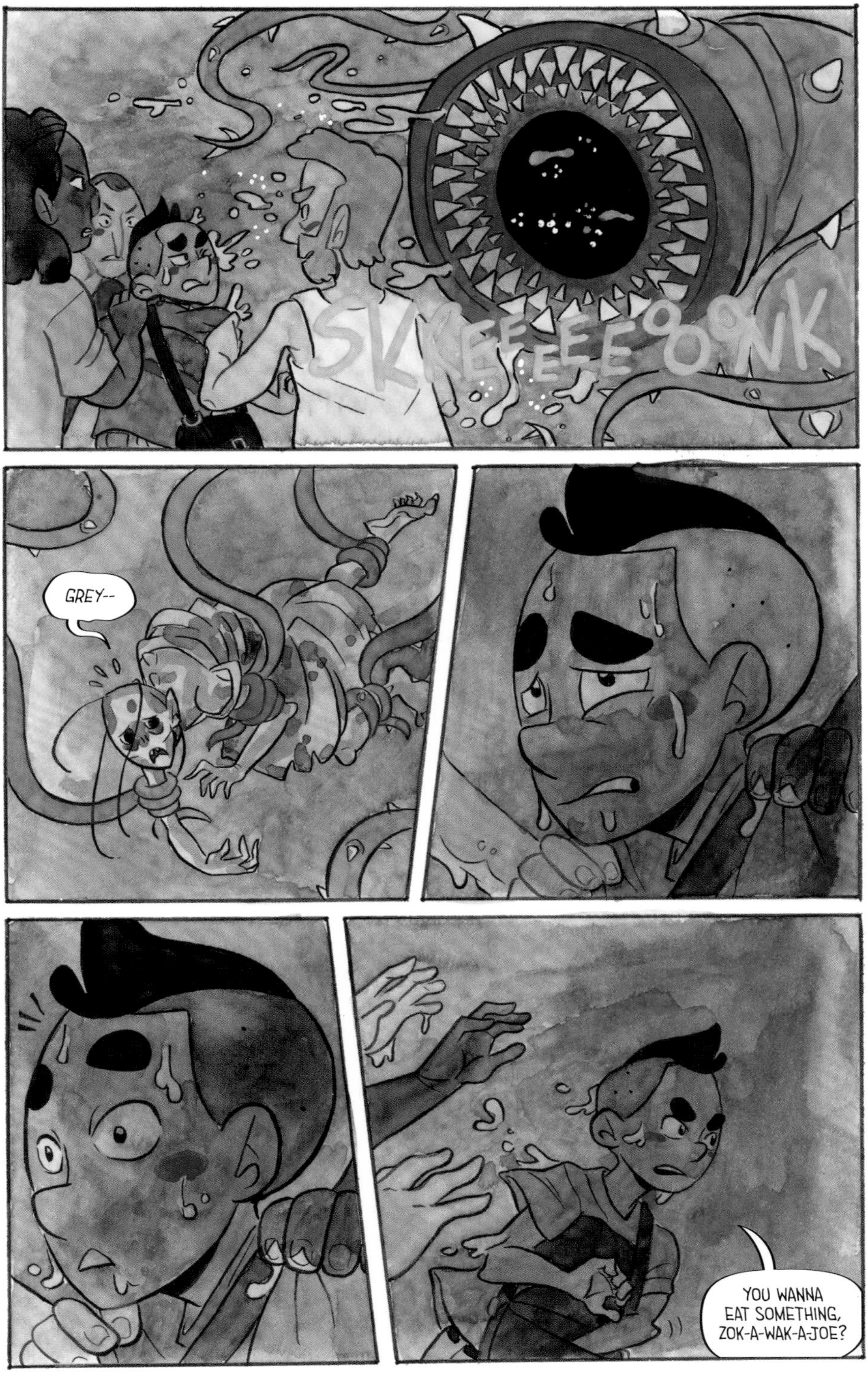
SKREEEEEOONK
GREY--
YOU WANNA EAT SOMETHING, ZOK-A-WAK-A-JOE?

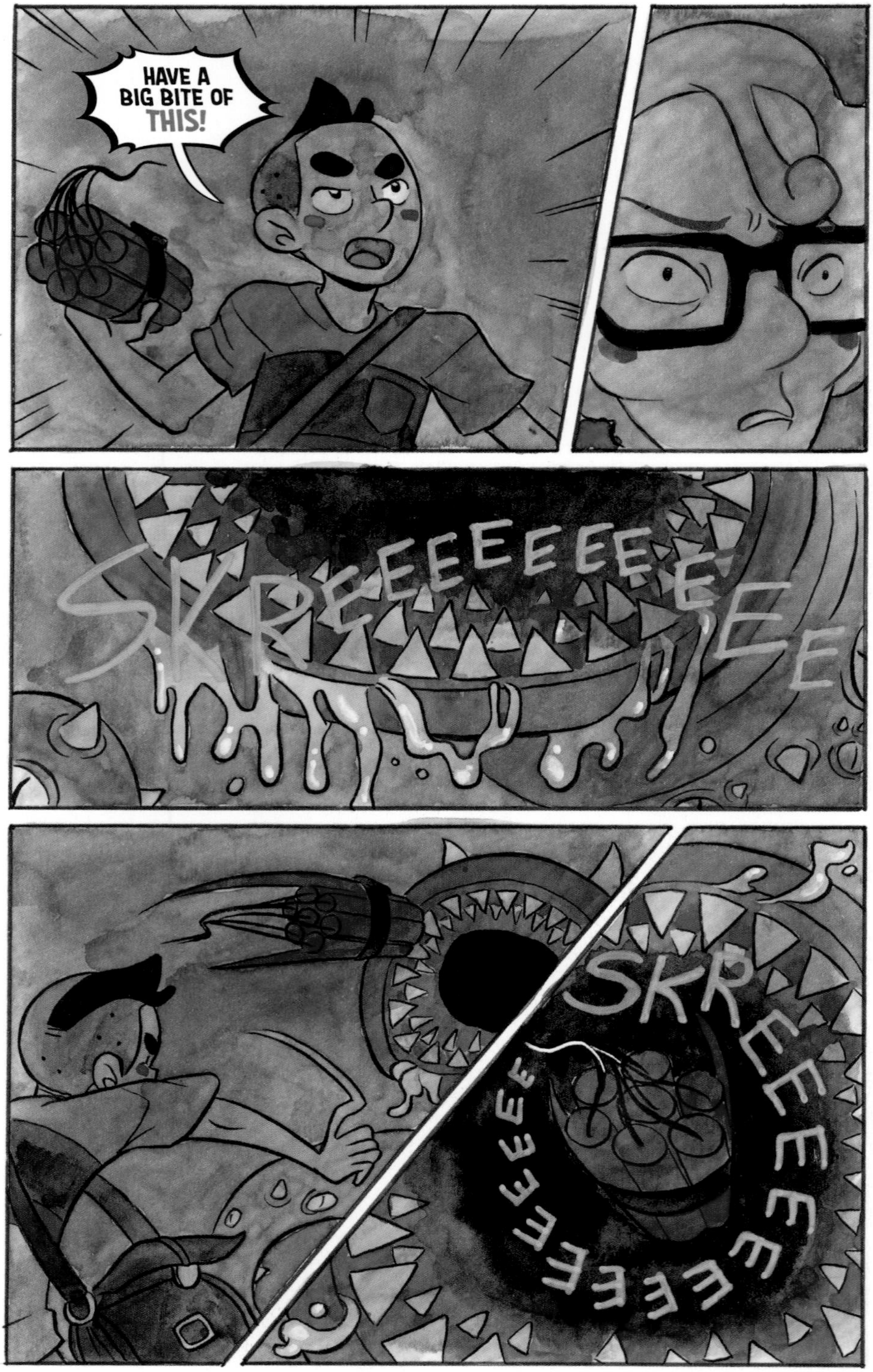
HAVE A BIG BITE OF THIS!
SKREEEEEEEEEEEEEE
SKREEEEEEEEEEEEEE

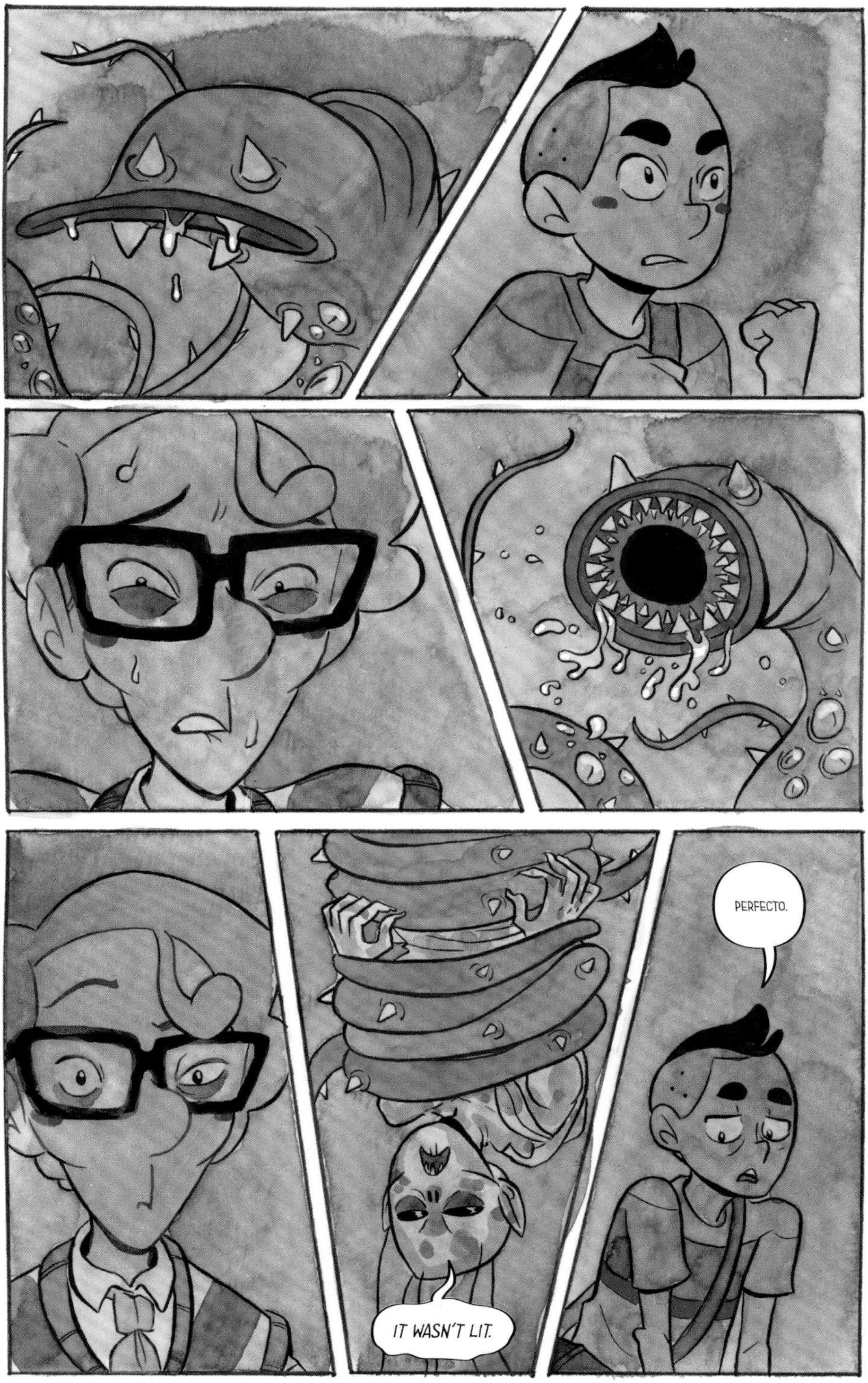
PERFECTO.
IT WASN'T LIT.

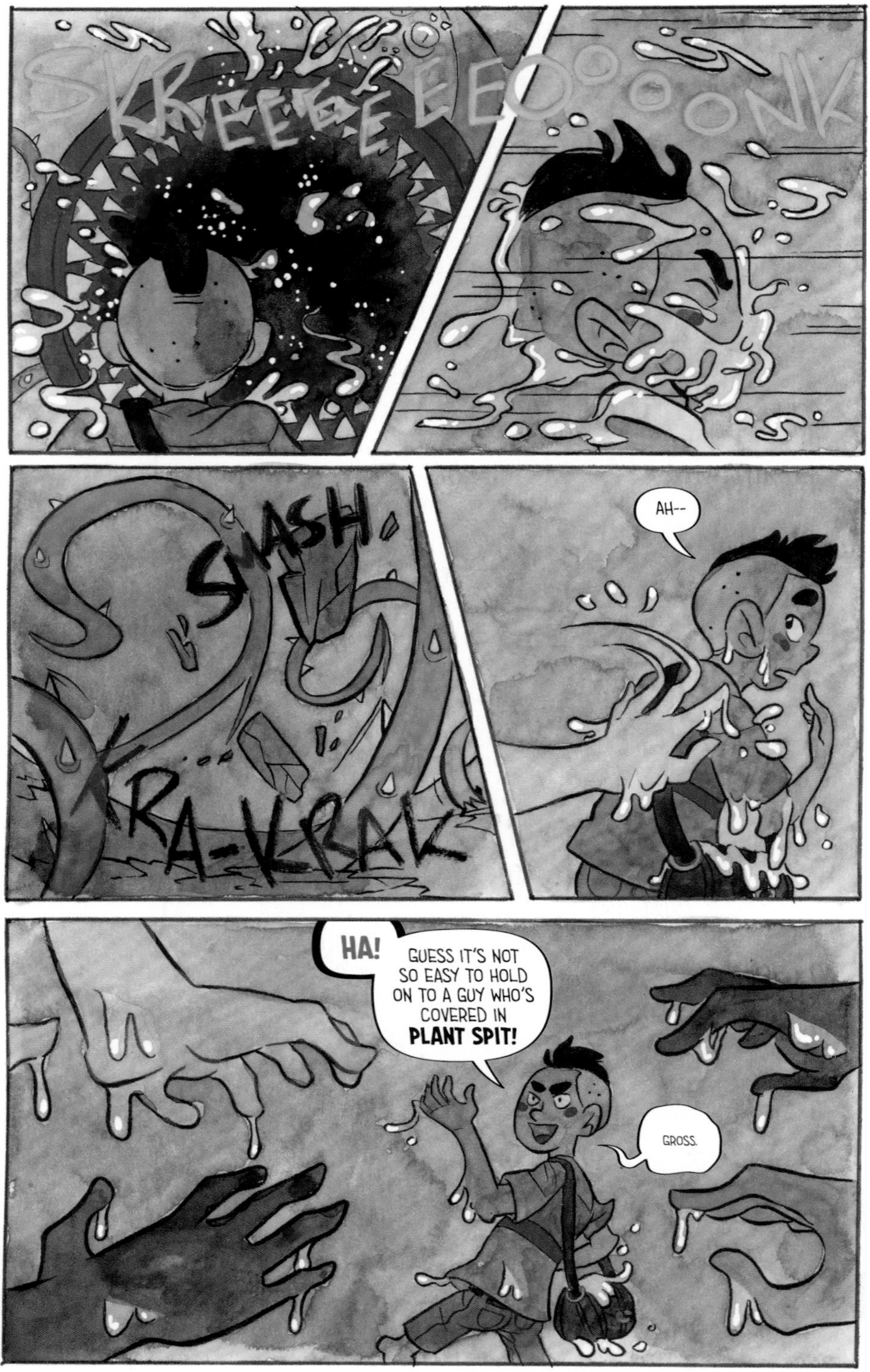
SKREEEEEEOOOOOONK
SMASH
KRA-KRAK
AH--
HA!
GUESS IT'S NOT SO EASY TO HOLD ON TO A GUY WHO'S COVERED IN **PLANT SPIT!**
GROSS.

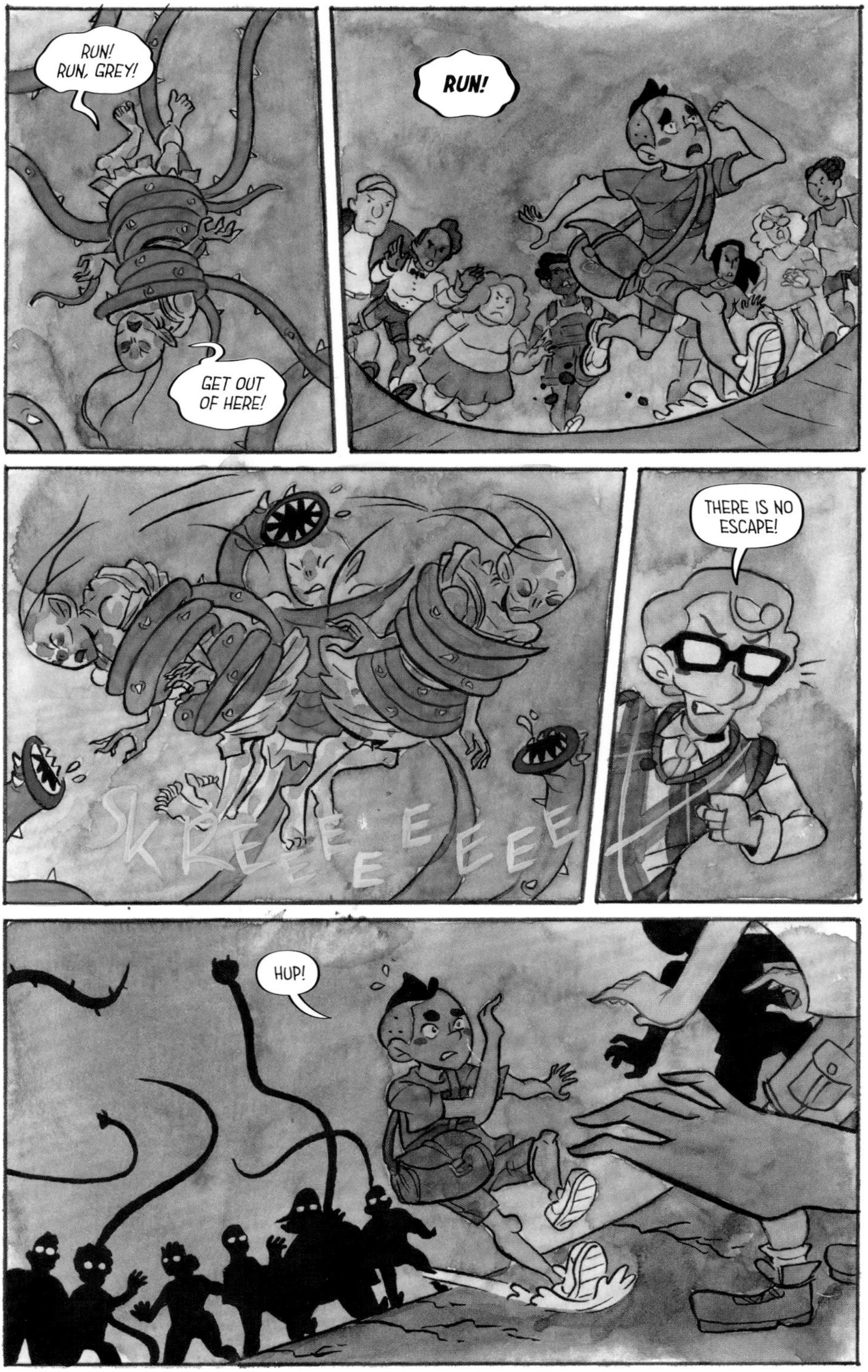
RUN! RUN, GREY!
GET OUT OF HERE!
RUN!
SKREEEEEEEEE
THERE IS NO ESCAPE!
HUP!

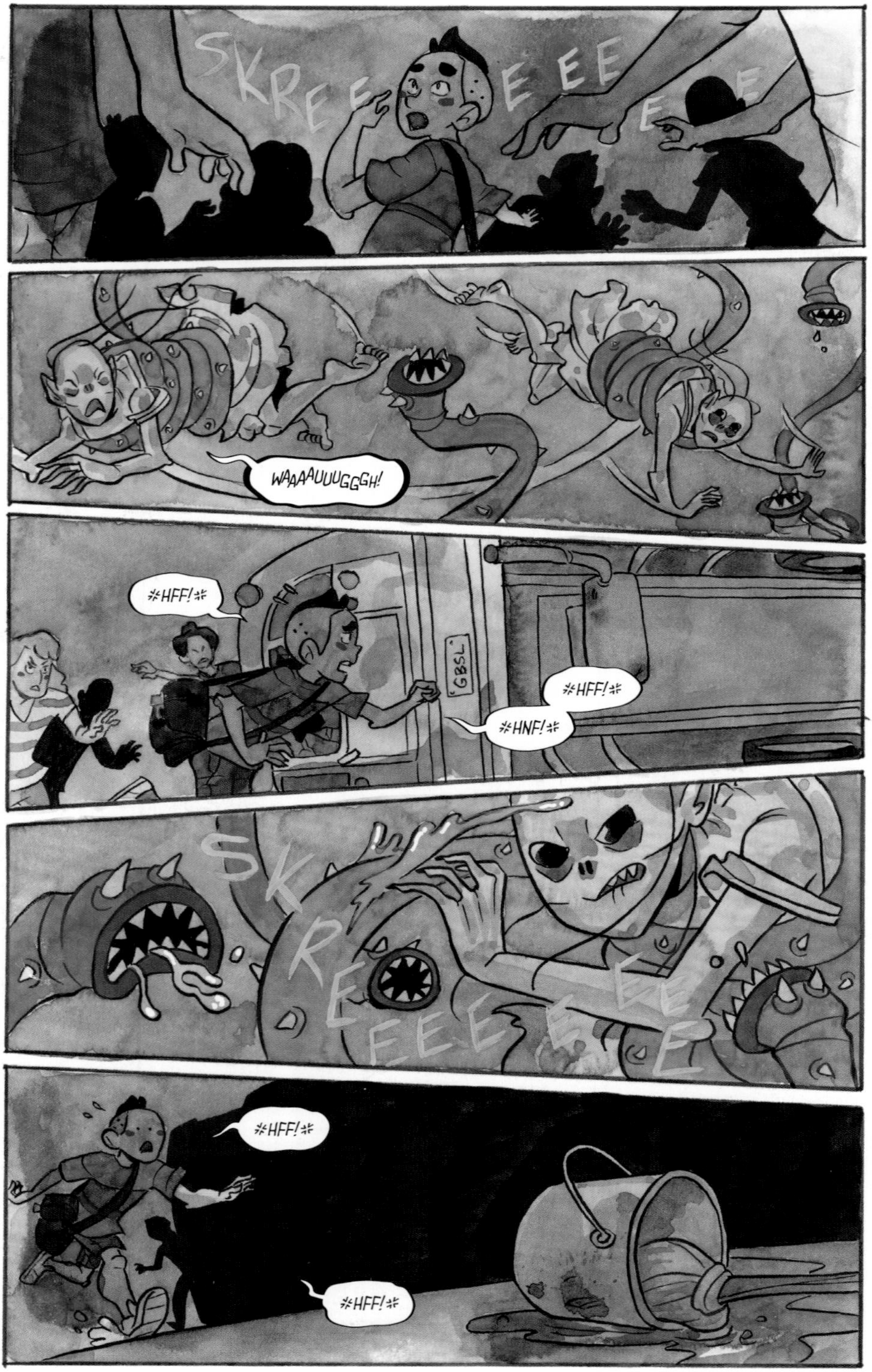
SKREEEEEEEE
WAAAAUUUGGGH!
HFF!
GBSL
HFF!
HNF!
SKREEEEEEEE
HFF!
HFF!

GET BACK!
#HFF!#
DON'T MAKE ME USE THIS...
#HNF!#
...MOP!
SAVE YOURSELF!
GET OUT OF HERE!
DON'T YOU DARE TRY TO SAVE ME LIKE LAST TIME!
UNLESS YOU HAVE, LIKE, A **REALLY GOOD PLAN!**
WHERE AM I SUPPOSED TO GO?
WHACK
UH...SORRY?

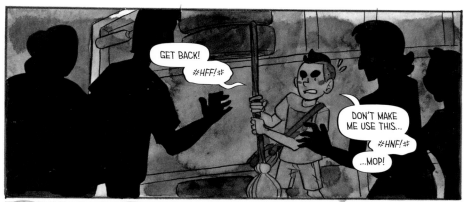

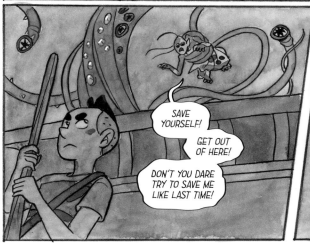

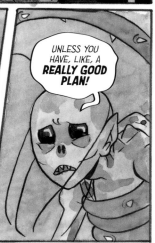

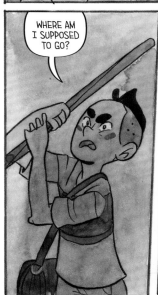

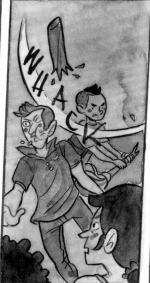

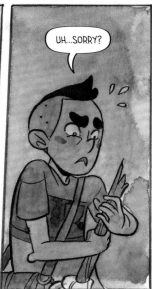

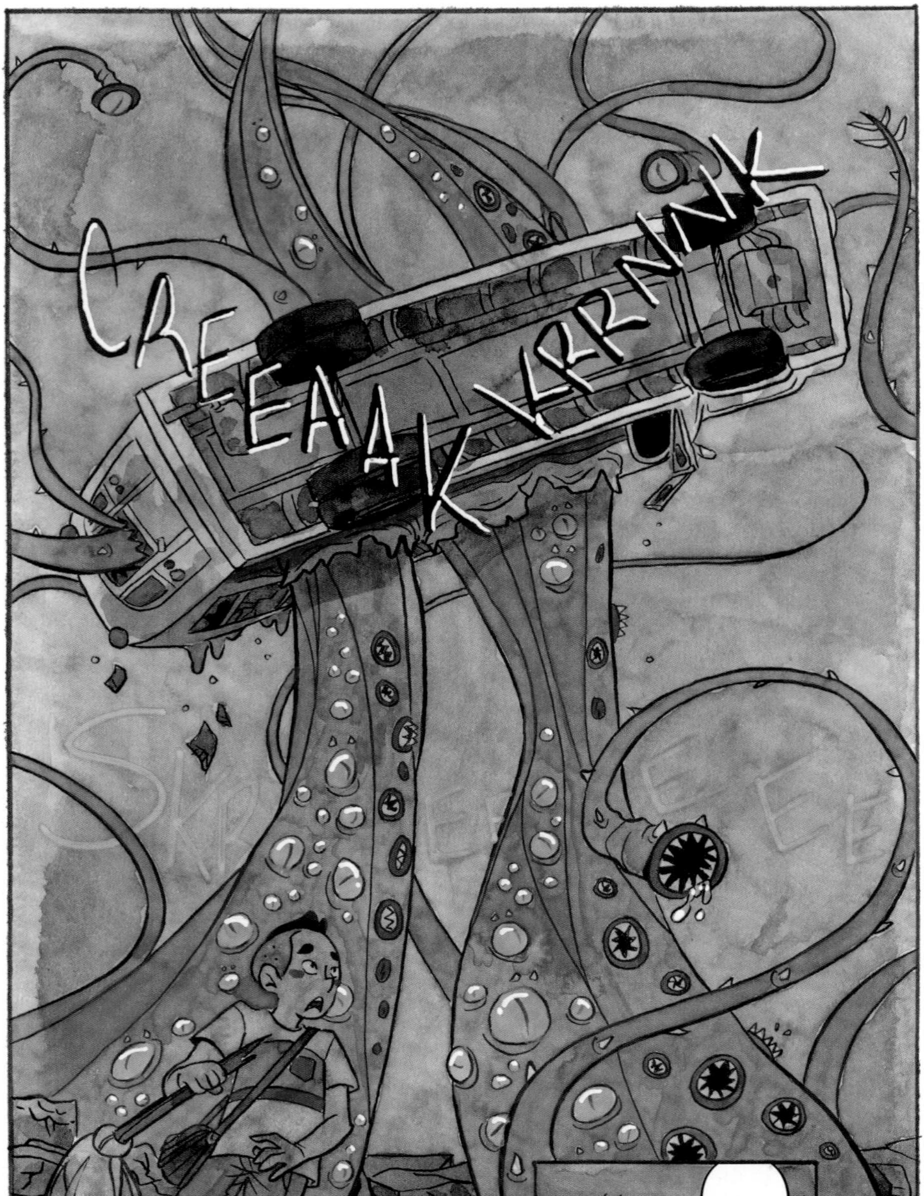
CREEAAK
KRRNNK

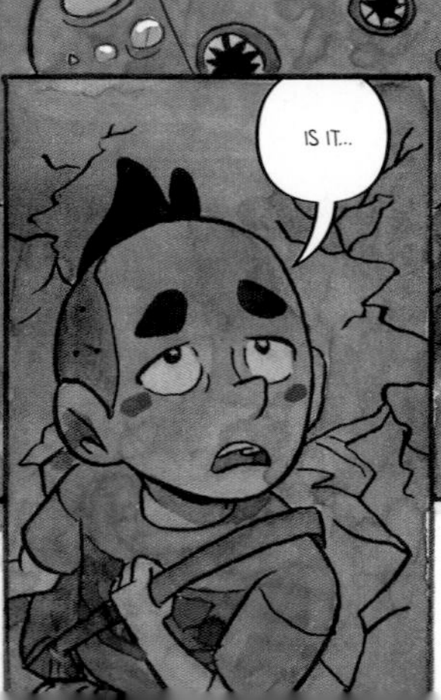
IS IT...

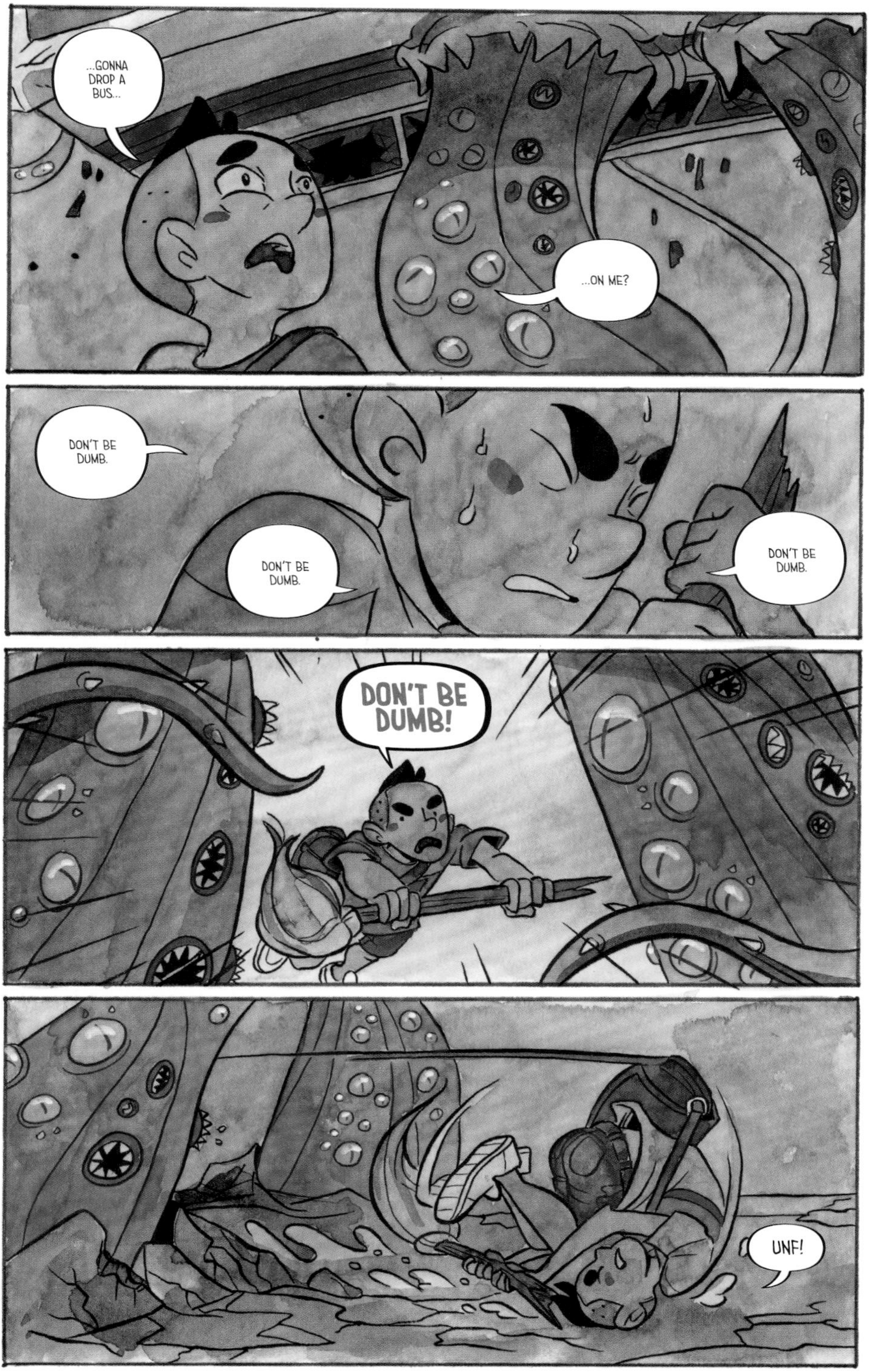
...GONNA DROP A BUS...
...ON ME?
DON'T BE DUMB.
DON'T BE DUMB.
DON'T BE DUMB.
DON'T BE DUMB!
UNF!

YES!
THAT'S IT!
NOW GET THE HECK OUT OF HERE!
YAAAAAH--
LAVINIA!

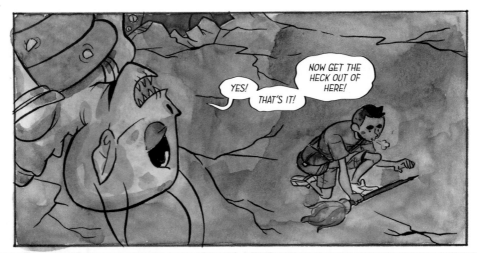

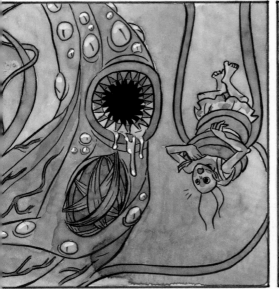

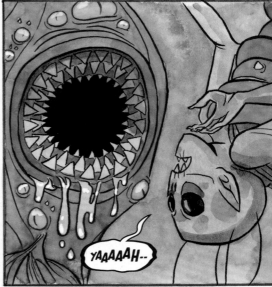

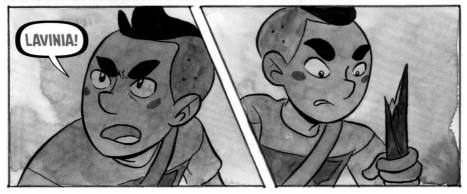

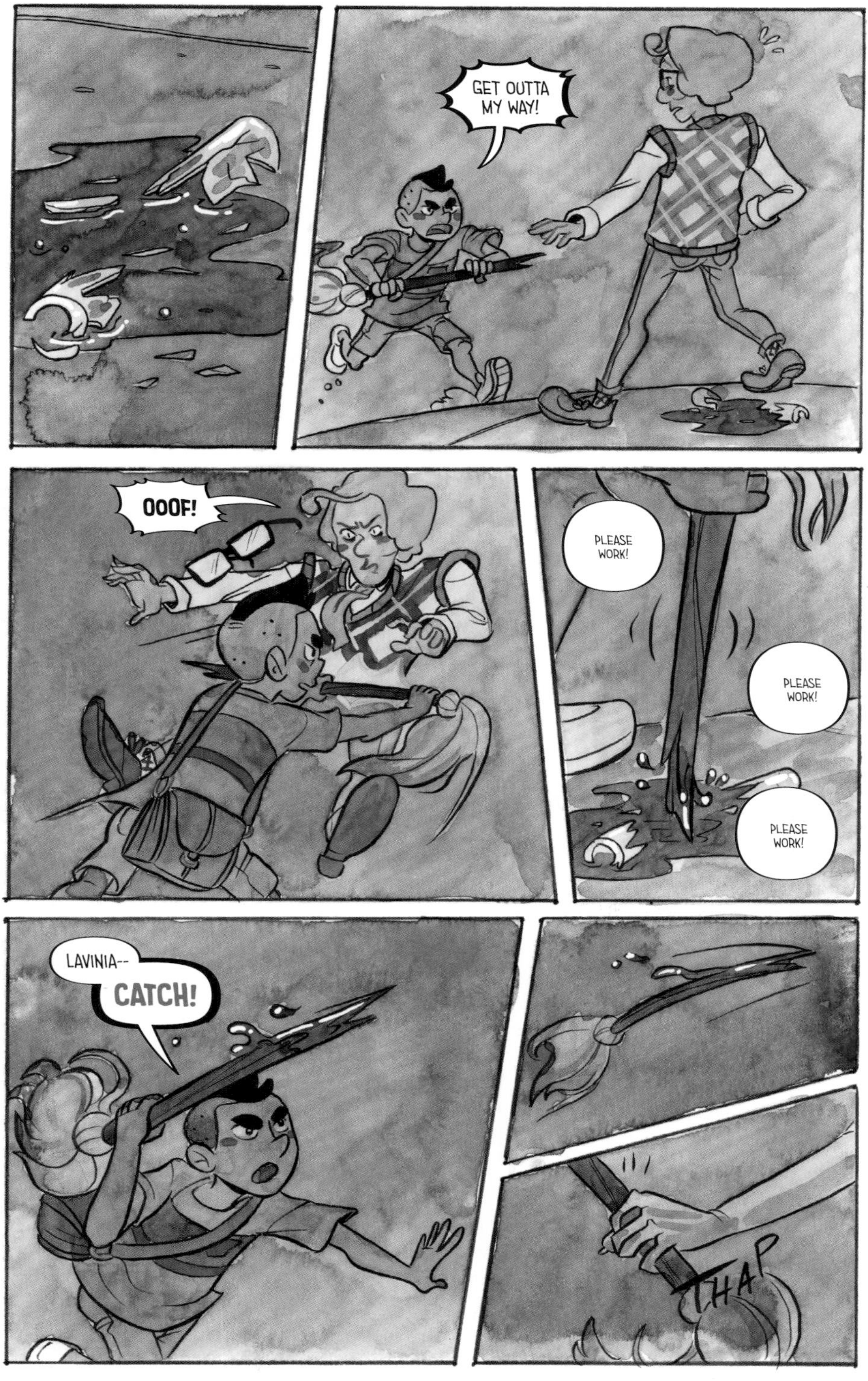
GET OUTTA MY WAY!
OOOF!
PLEASE WORK!
PLEASE WORK!
PLEASE WORK!
LAVINIA--
CATCH!
THAP

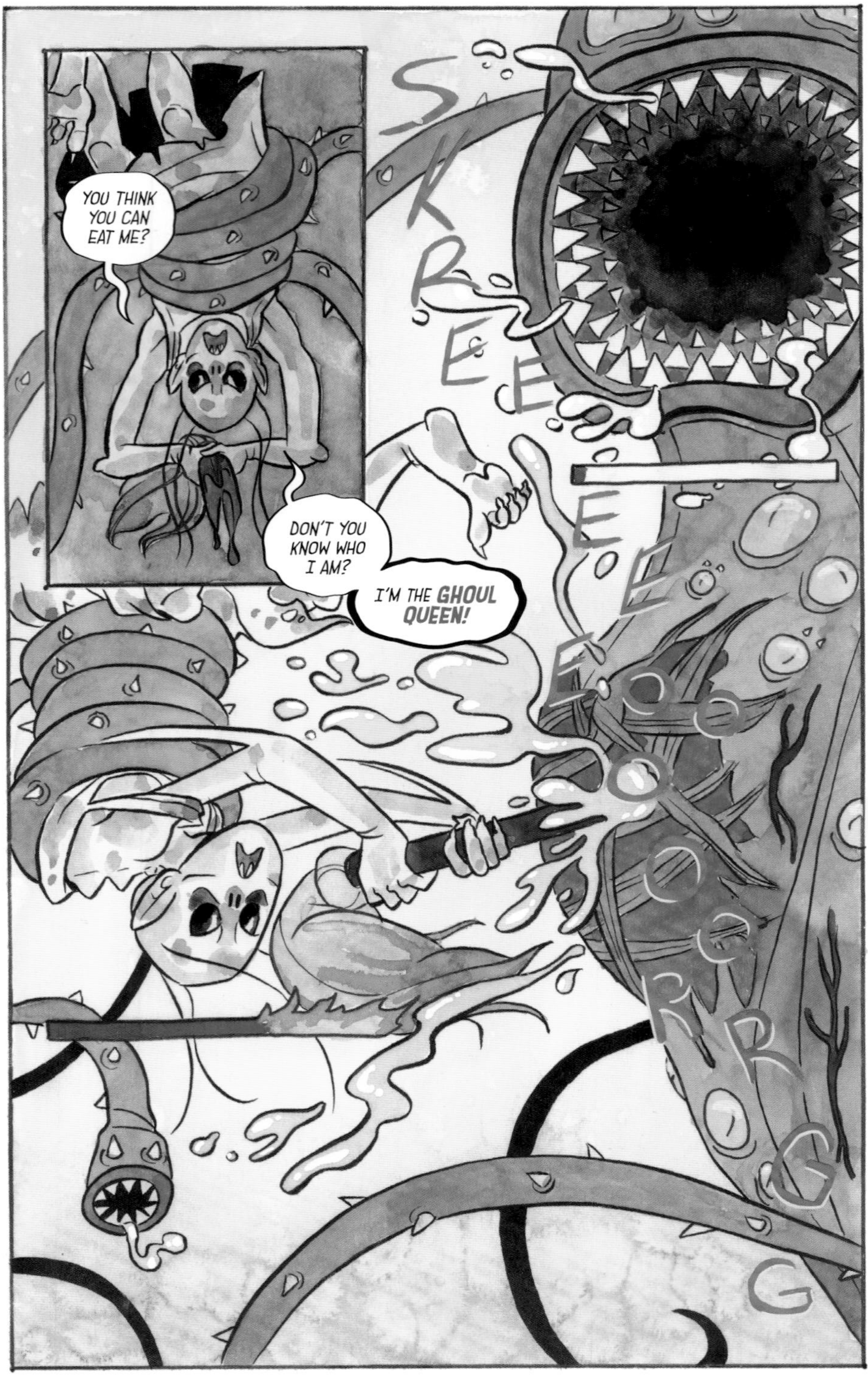
YOU THINK YOU CAN EAT ME?
DON'T YOU KNOW WHO I AM?
I'M THE GHOUL QUEEN!
SKREEEEEEE
OOOOOORRRG
G

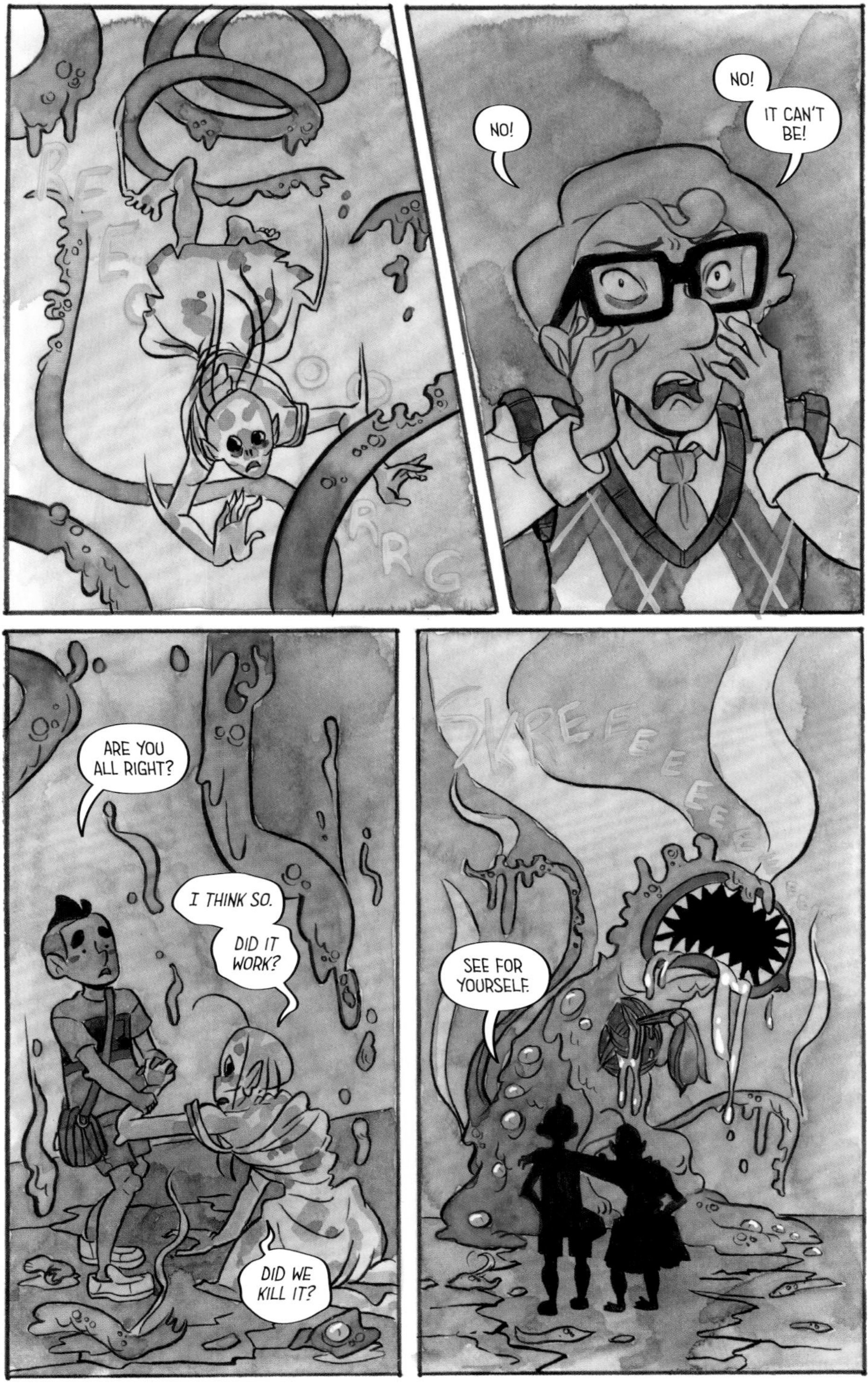
NO!
NO!
IT CAN'T BE!
ARE YOU ALL RIGHT?
I THINK SO.
DID IT WORK?
DID WE KILL IT?
SEE FOR YOURSELF.

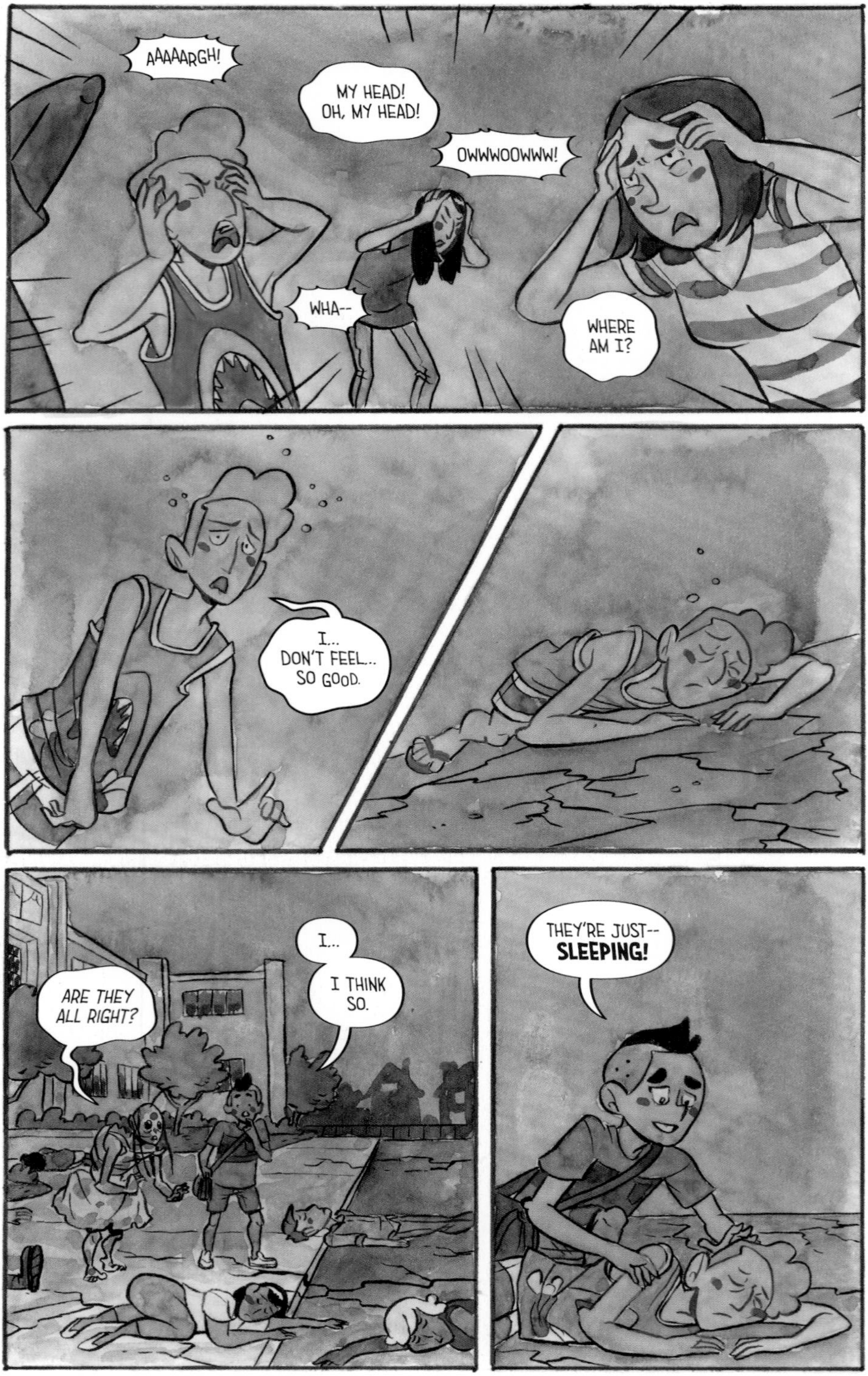
AAAAARGH!
MY HEAD! OH, MY HEAD!
OWWWOOWWW!
WHA--
WHERE AM I?
I... DON'T FEEL... SO GOOD.
ARE THEY ALL RIGHT?
I...
I THINK SO.
THEY'RE JUST-- **SLEEPING!**

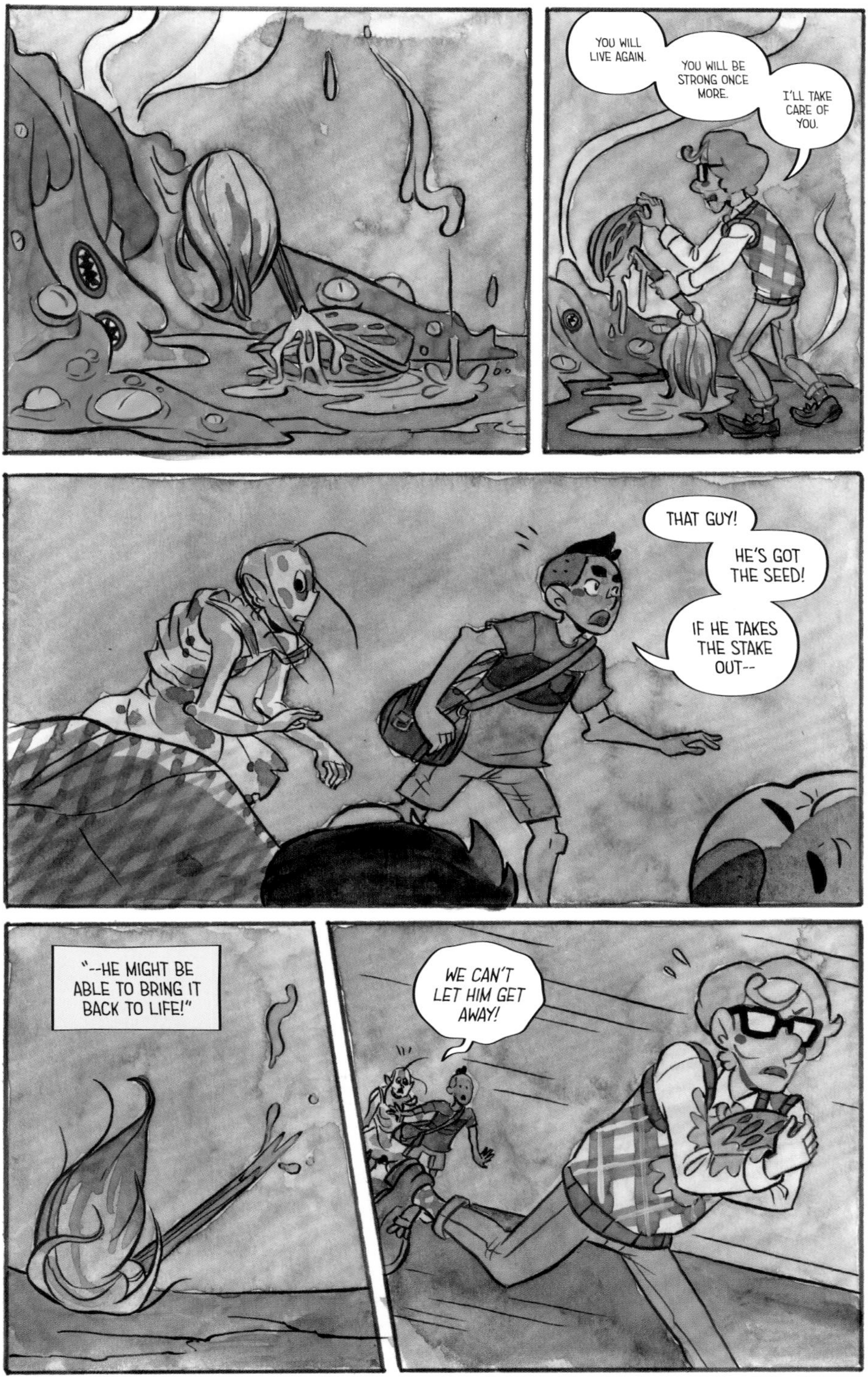
YOU WILL LIVE AGAIN.
YOU WILL BE STRONG ONCE MORE.
I'LL TAKE CARE OF YOU.
THAT GUY!
HE'S GOT THE SEED!
IF HE TAKES THE STAKE OUT--
"--HE MIGHT BE ABLE TO BRING IT BACK TO LIFE!"
WE CAN'T LET HIM GET AWAY!

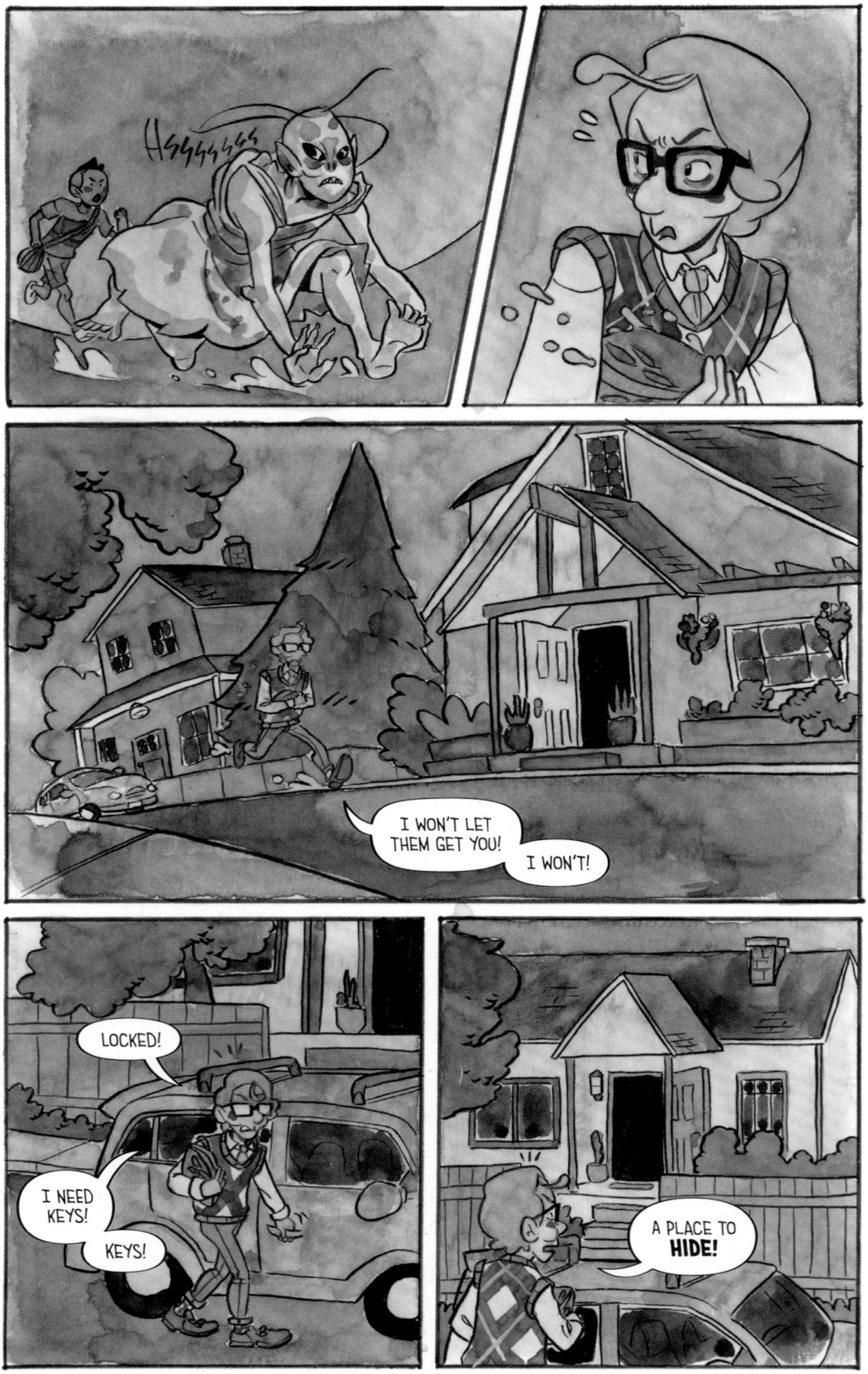
HSSSSSSS
I WON'T LET THEM GET YOU!
I WON'T!
LOCKED!
I NEED KEYS!
KEYS!
A PLACE TO **HIDE!**

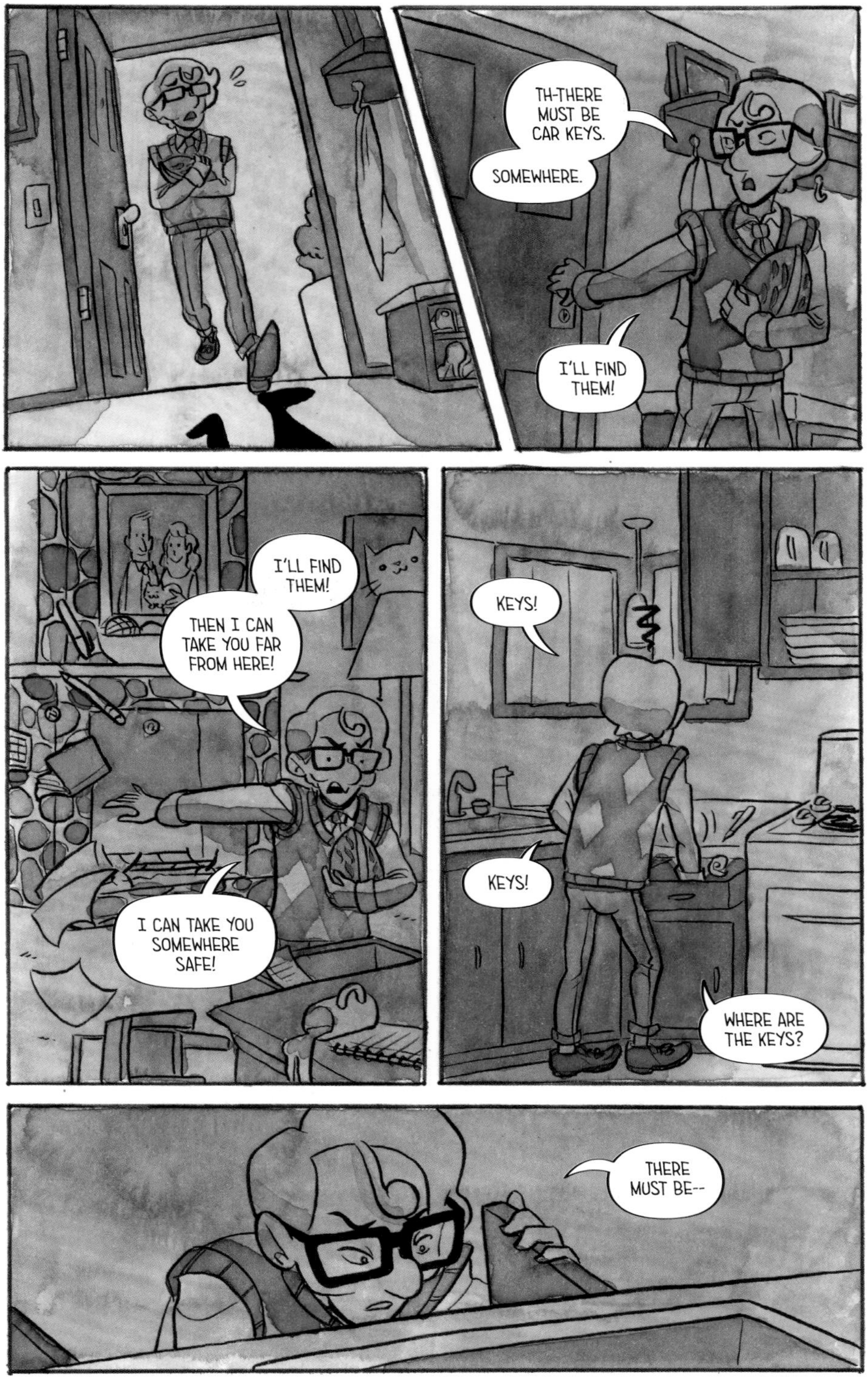
TH-THERE MUST BE CAR KEYS.
SOMEWHERE.
I'LL FIND THEM!
I'LL FIND THEM!
THEN I CAN TAKE YOU FAR FROM HERE!
I CAN TAKE YOU SOMEWHERE SAFE!
KEYS!
KEYS!
WHERE ARE THE KEYS?
THERE MUST BE--

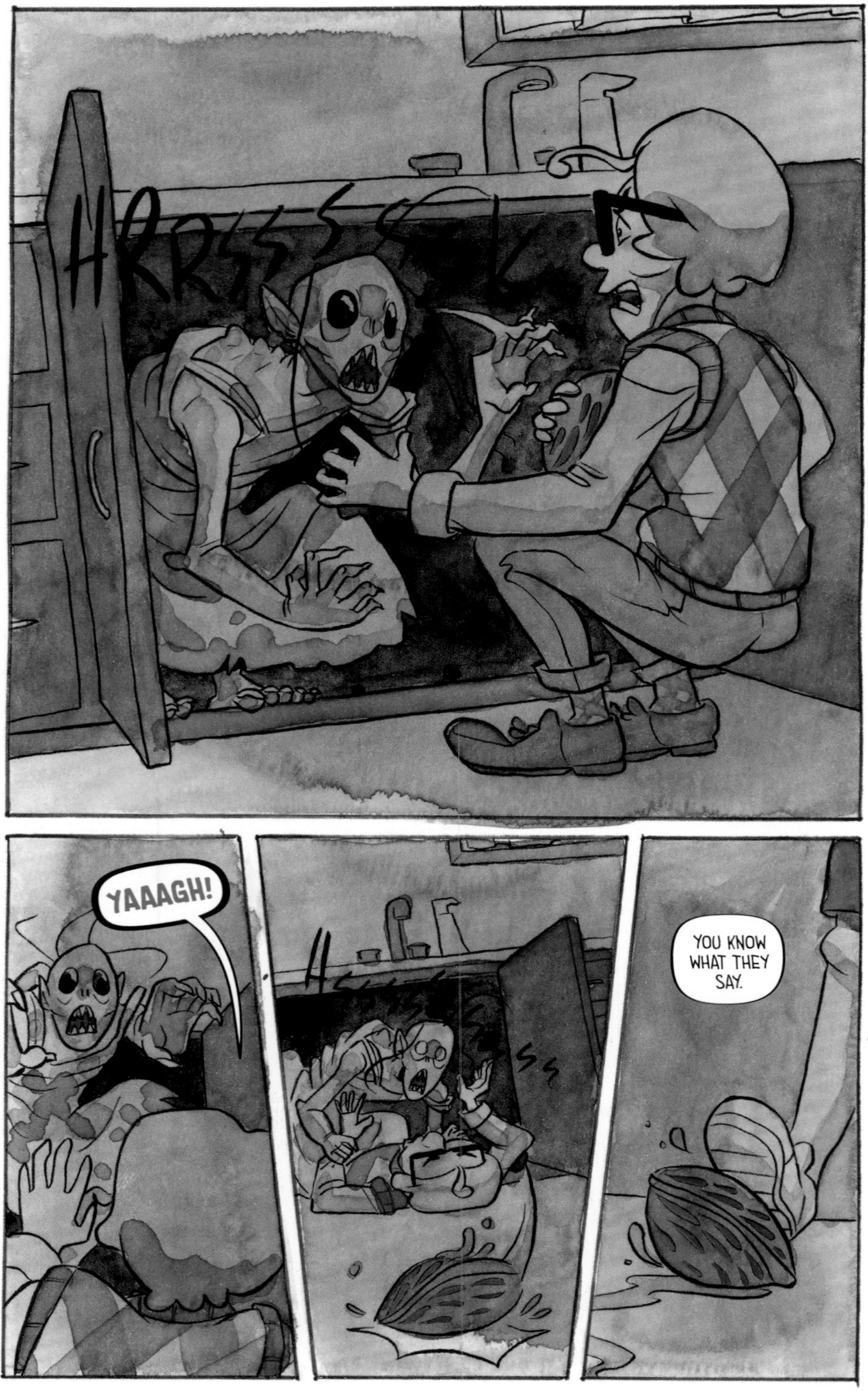
HRRSSSSK
YAAAGH!
YOU KNOW WHAT THEY SAY.

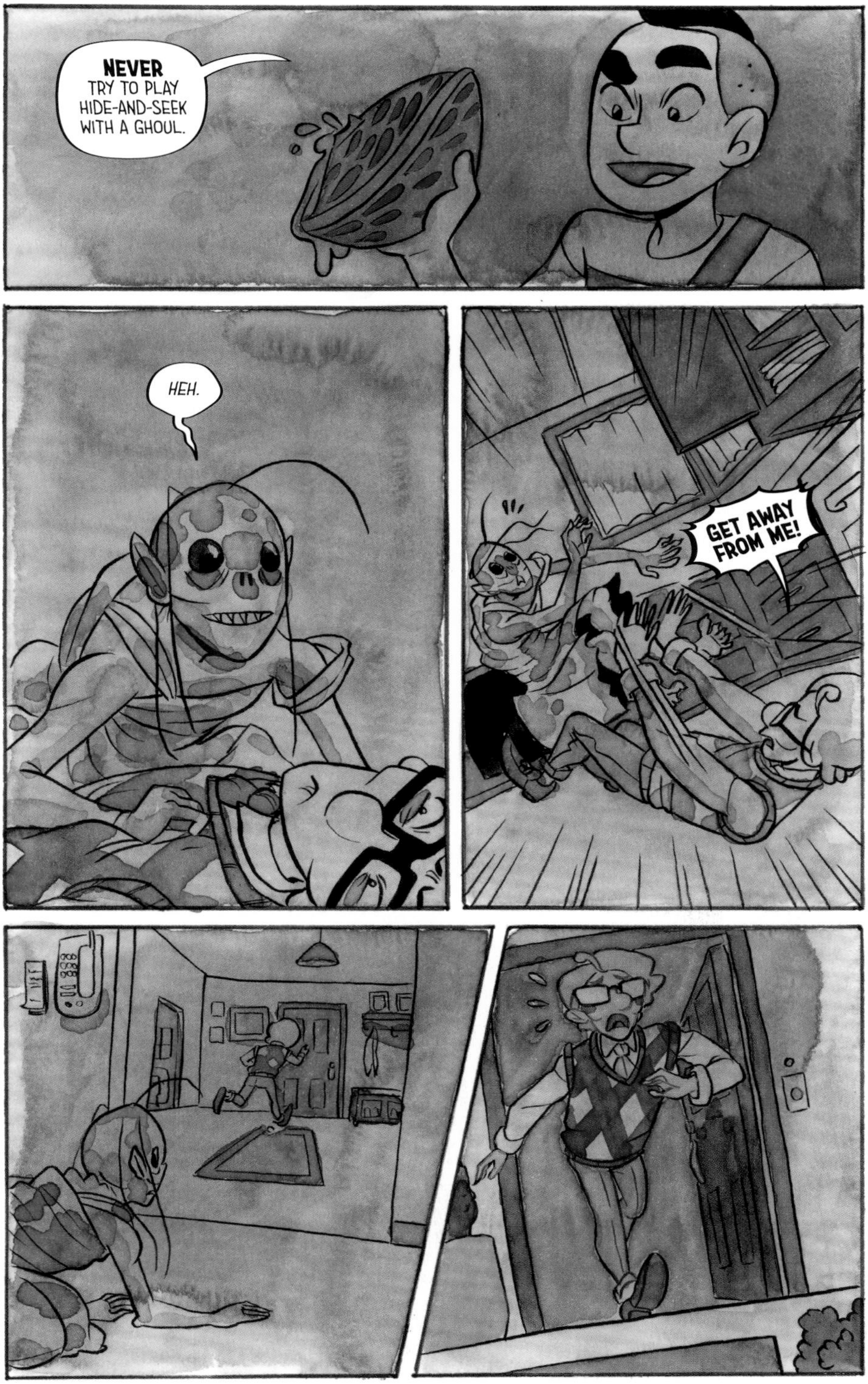
NEVER TRY TO PLAY HIDE-AND-SEEK WITH A GHOUL.
HEH.
GET AWAY FROM ME!

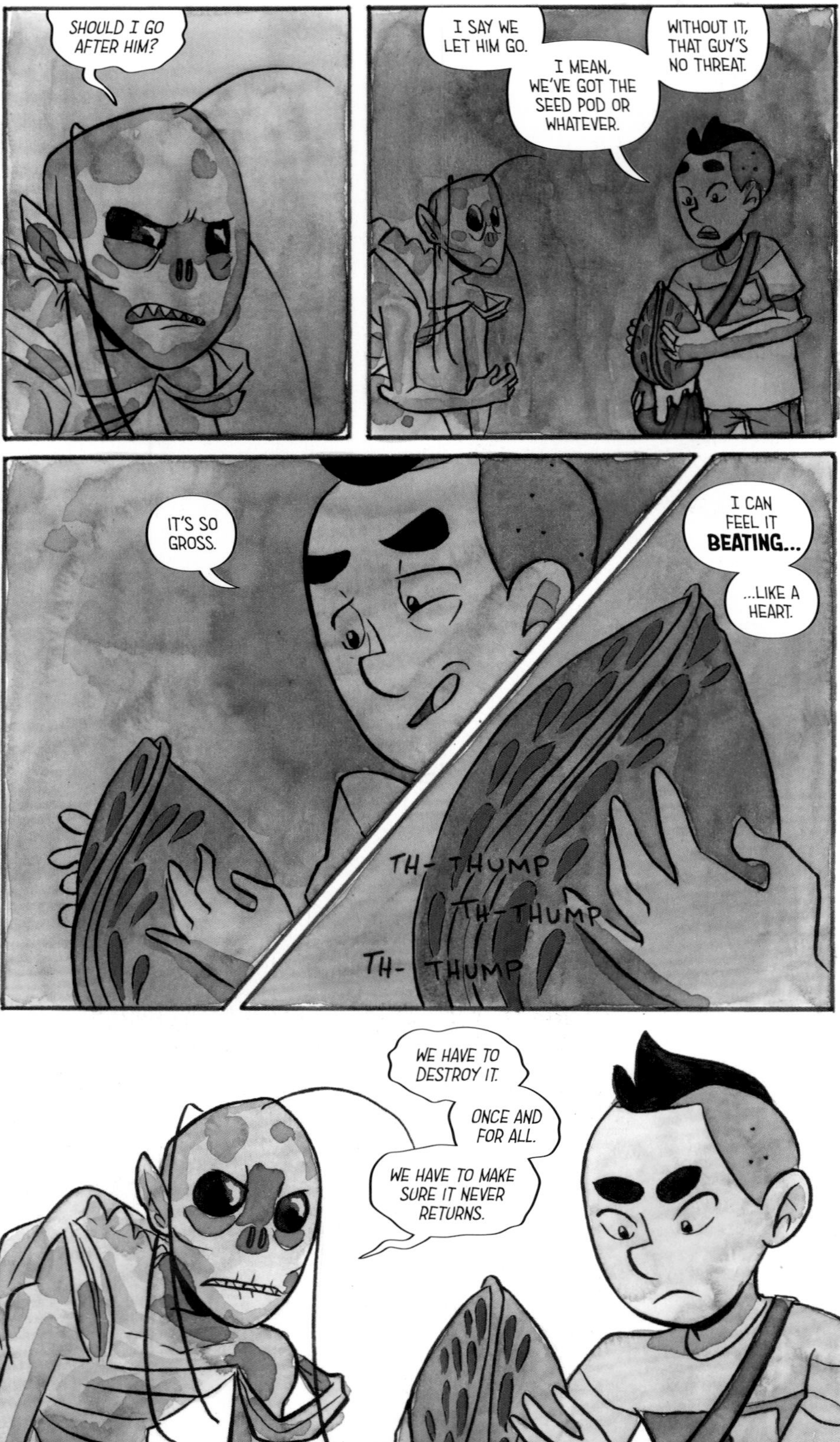
SHOULD I GO AFTER HIM?
I SAY WE LET HIM GO.
I MEAN, WE'VE GOT THE SEED POD OR WHATEVER.
WITHOUT IT, THAT GUY'S NO THREAT.
IT'S SO GROSS.
I CAN FEEL IT **BEATING...**
...LIKE A HEART.
TH-THUMP
TH-THUMP
TH-THUMP
WE HAVE TO DESTROY IT.
ONCE AND FOR ALL.
WE HAVE TO MAKE SURE IT NEVER RETURNS.

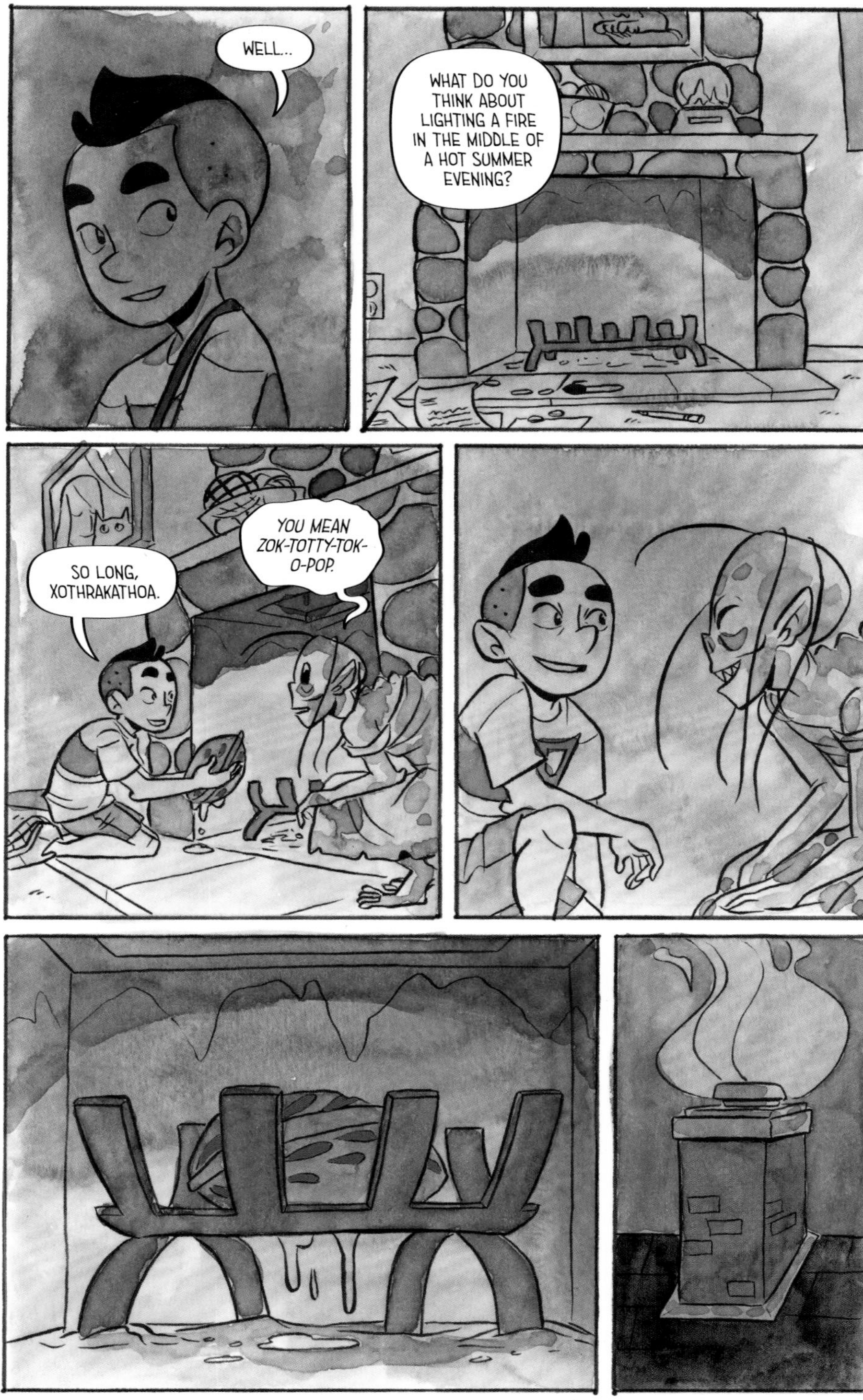
WELL...
WHAT DO YOU THINK ABOUT LIGHTING A FIRE IN THE MIDDLE OF A HOT SUMMER EVENING?
SO LONG, XOTHRAKATHOA.
YOU MEAN ZOK-TOTTY-TOK-O-POP.

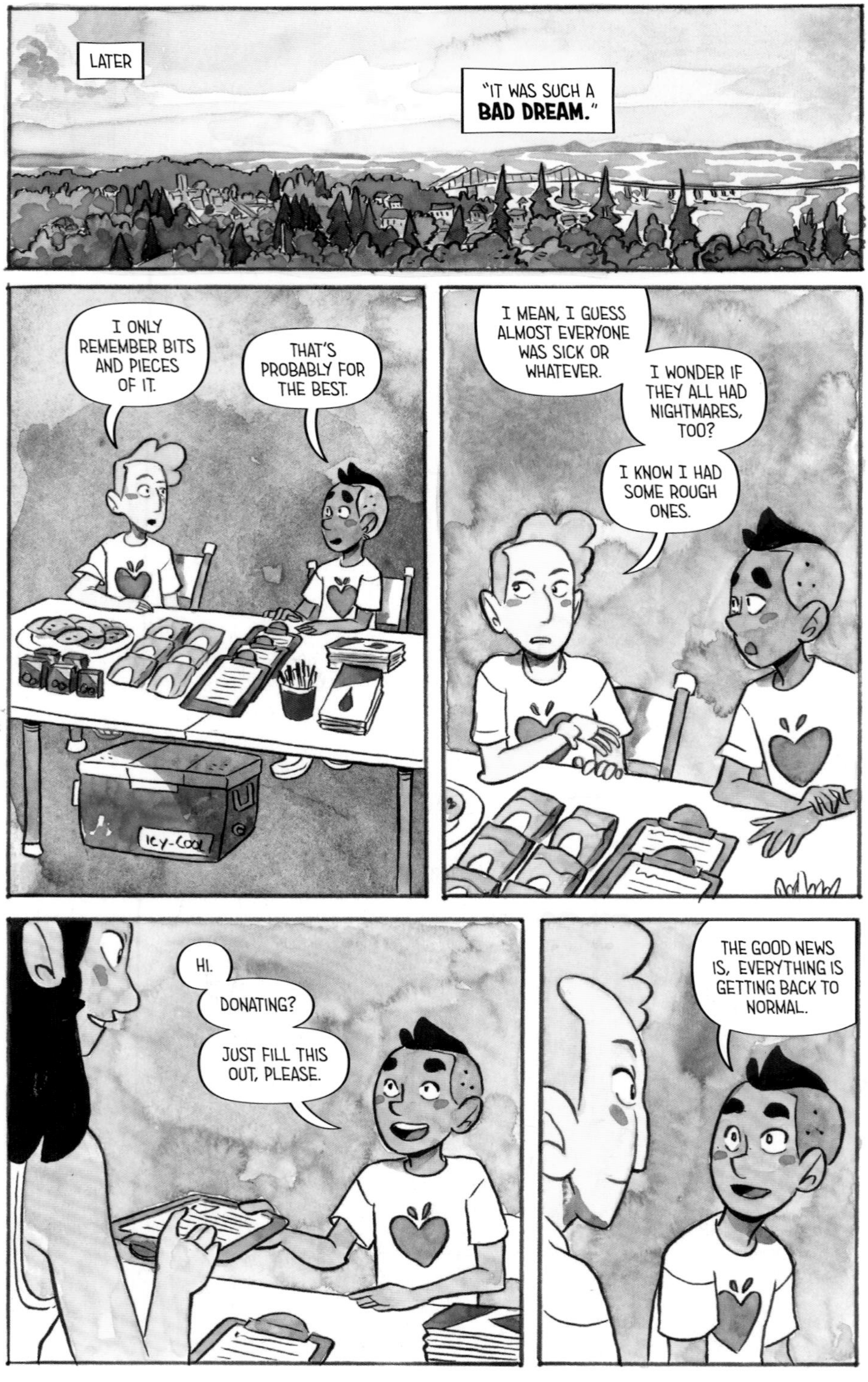
LATER
"IT WAS SUCH A **BAD DREAM.**"
I ONLY REMEMBER BITS AND PIECES OF IT.
THAT'S PROBABLY FOR THE BEST.
ICY-COOL
I MEAN, I GUESS ALMOST EVERYONE WAS SICK OR WHATEVER.
I WONDER IF THEY ALL HAD NIGHTMARES, TOO?
I KNOW I HAD SOME ROUGH ONES.
HI.
DONATING?
JUST FILL THIS OUT, PLEASE.
THE GOOD NEWS IS, EVERYTHING IS GETTING BACK TO NORMAL.

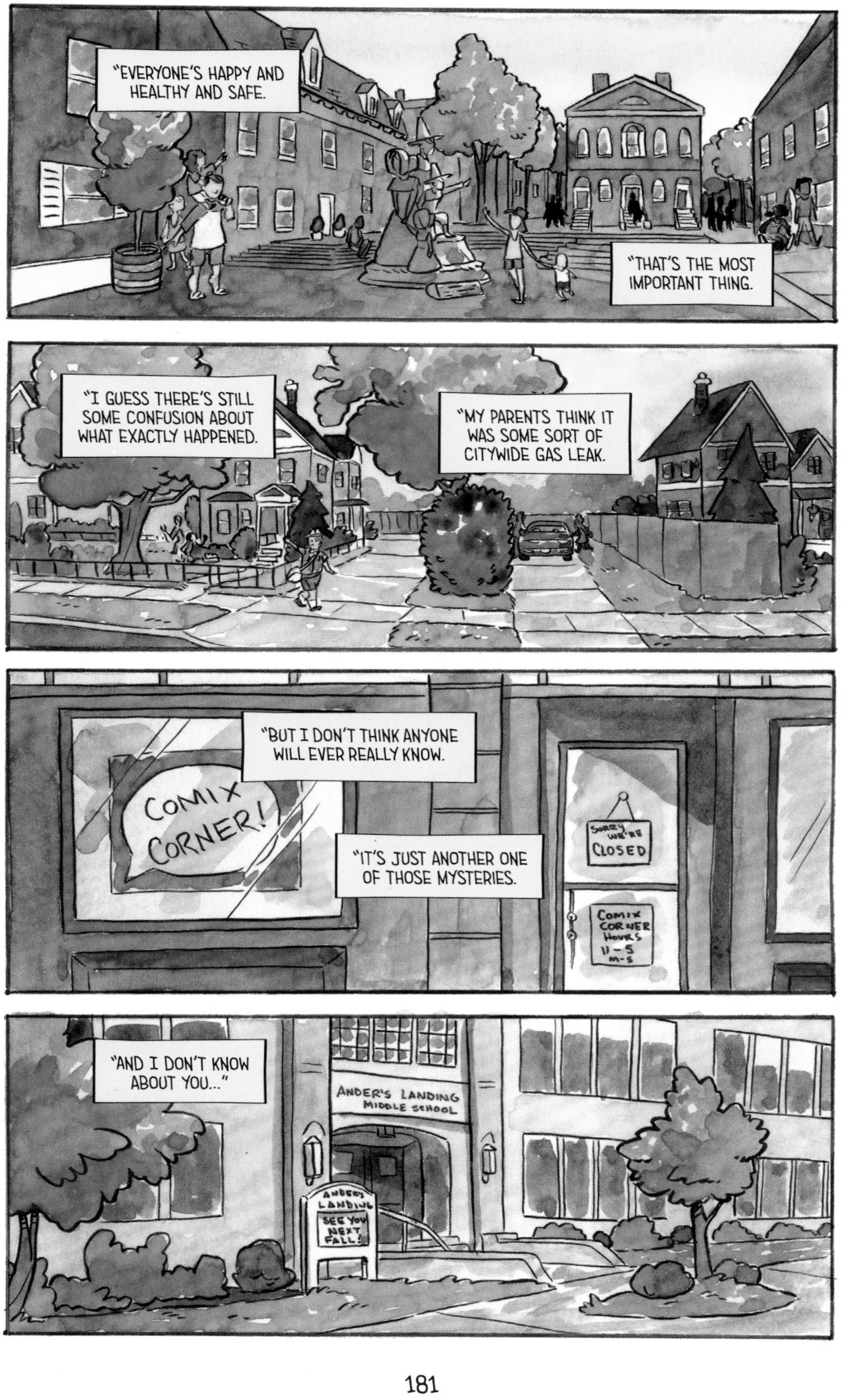
"EVERYONE'S HAPPY AND HEALTHY AND SAFE.
"THAT'S THE MOST IMPORTANT THING.
"I GUESS THERE'S STILL SOME CONFUSION ABOUT WHAT EXACTLY HAPPENED.
"MY PARENTS THINK IT WAS SOME SORT OF CITYWIDE GAS LEAK.
"BUT I DON'T THINK ANYONE WILL EVER REALLY KNOW.
COMIX CORNER!
SORRY WE'RE CLOSED
"IT'S JUST ANOTHER ONE OF THOSE MYSTERIES.
COMIX CORNER HOURS 11–5 M–S
"AND I DON'T KNOW ABOUT YOU..."
ANDER'S LANDING MIDDLE SCHOOL
ANDERS LANDING
SEE YOU NEXT FALL!

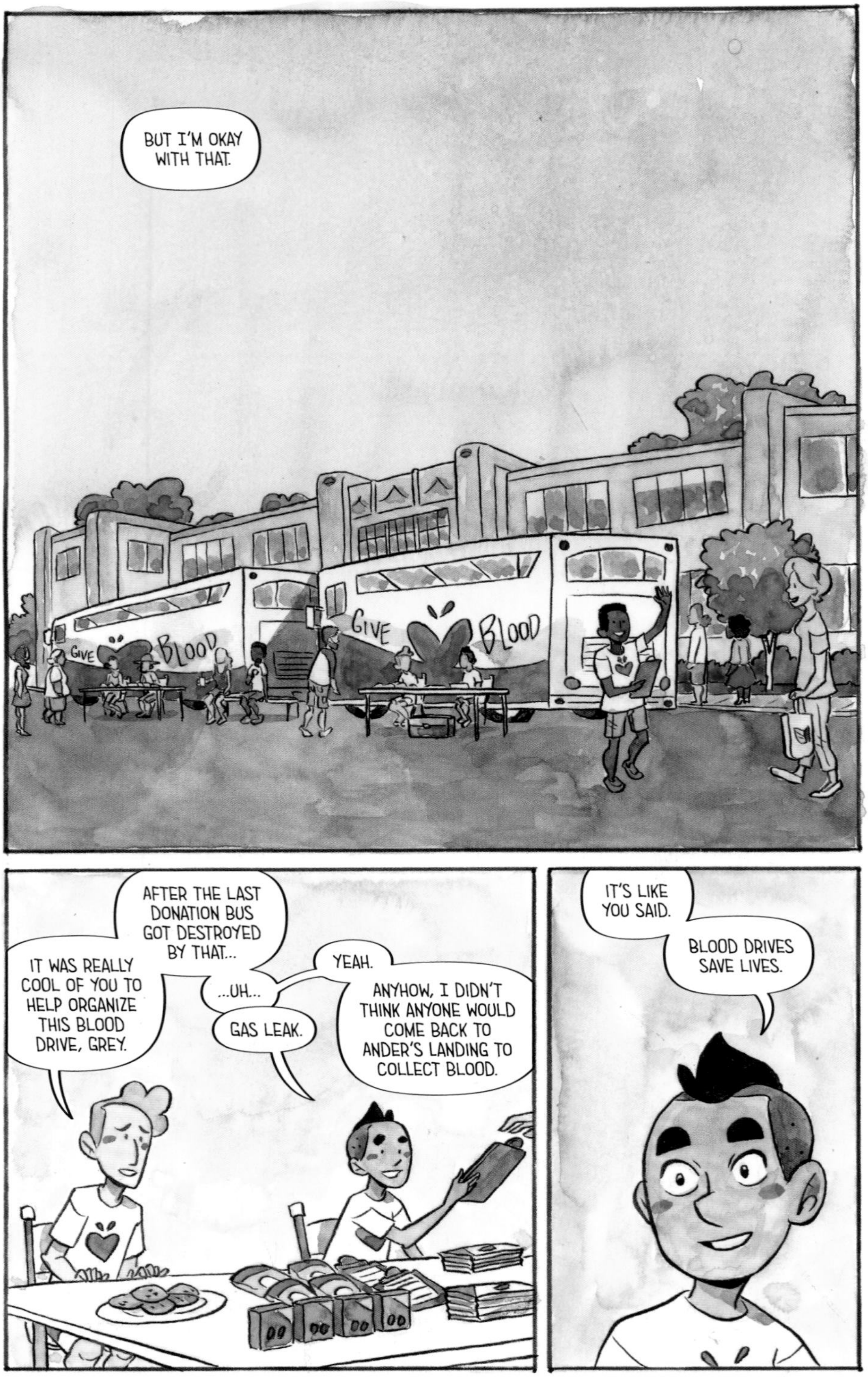
BUT I'M OKAY WITH THAT.
GIVE BLOOD
GIVE BLOOD
IT WAS REALLY COOL OF YOU TO HELP ORGANIZE THIS BLOOD DRIVE, GREY.
AFTER THE LAST DONATION BUS GOT DESTROYED BY THAT...
...UH...
GAS LEAK.
YEAH.
ANYHOW, I DIDN'T THINK ANYONE WOULD COME BACK TO ANDER'S LANDING TO COLLECT BLOOD.
IT'S LIKE YOU SAID.
BLOOD DRIVES SAVE LIVES.

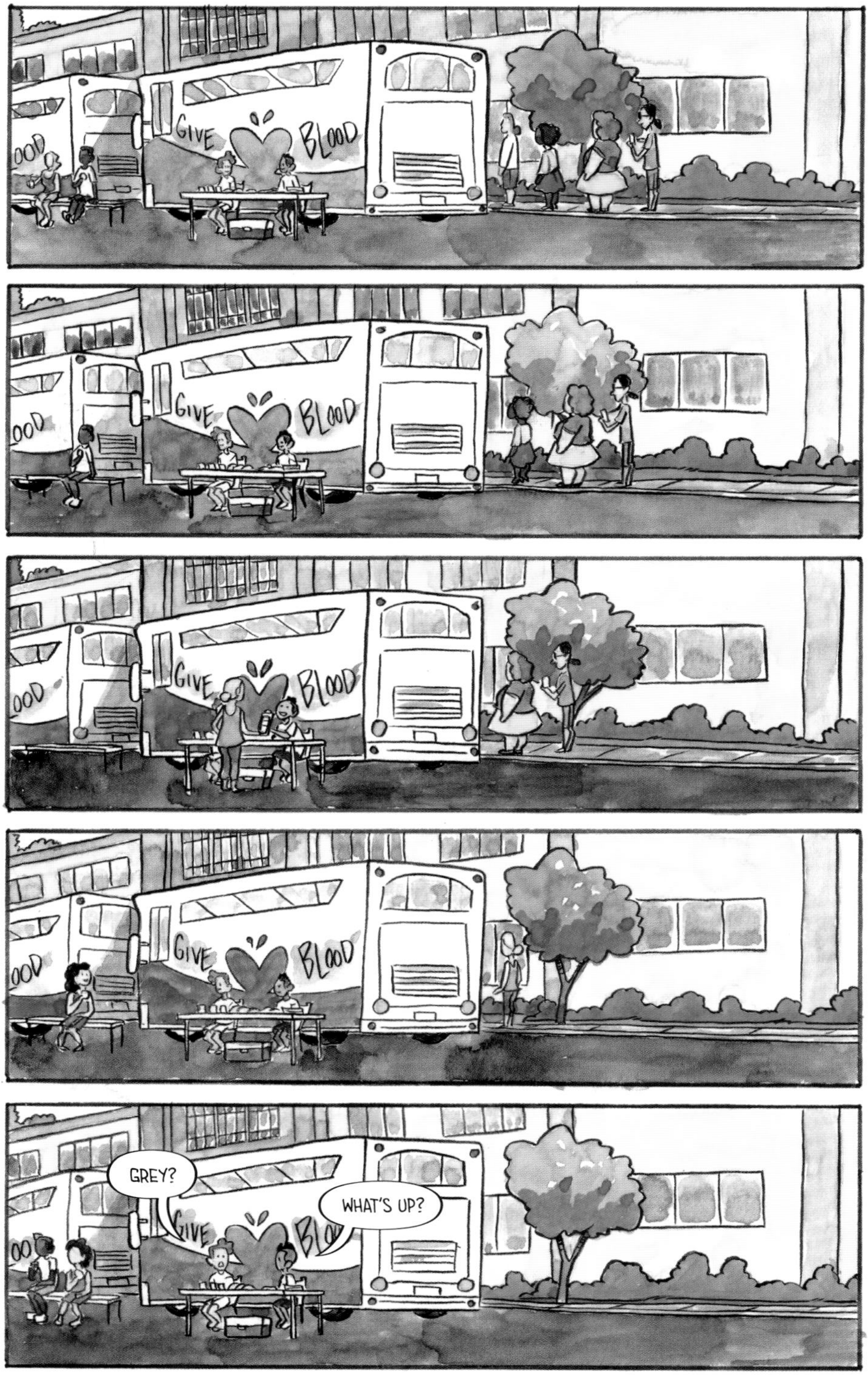
GIVE BLOOD
GIVE BLOOD
GIVE BLOOD
GIVE BLOOD
GREY?
WHAT'S UP?

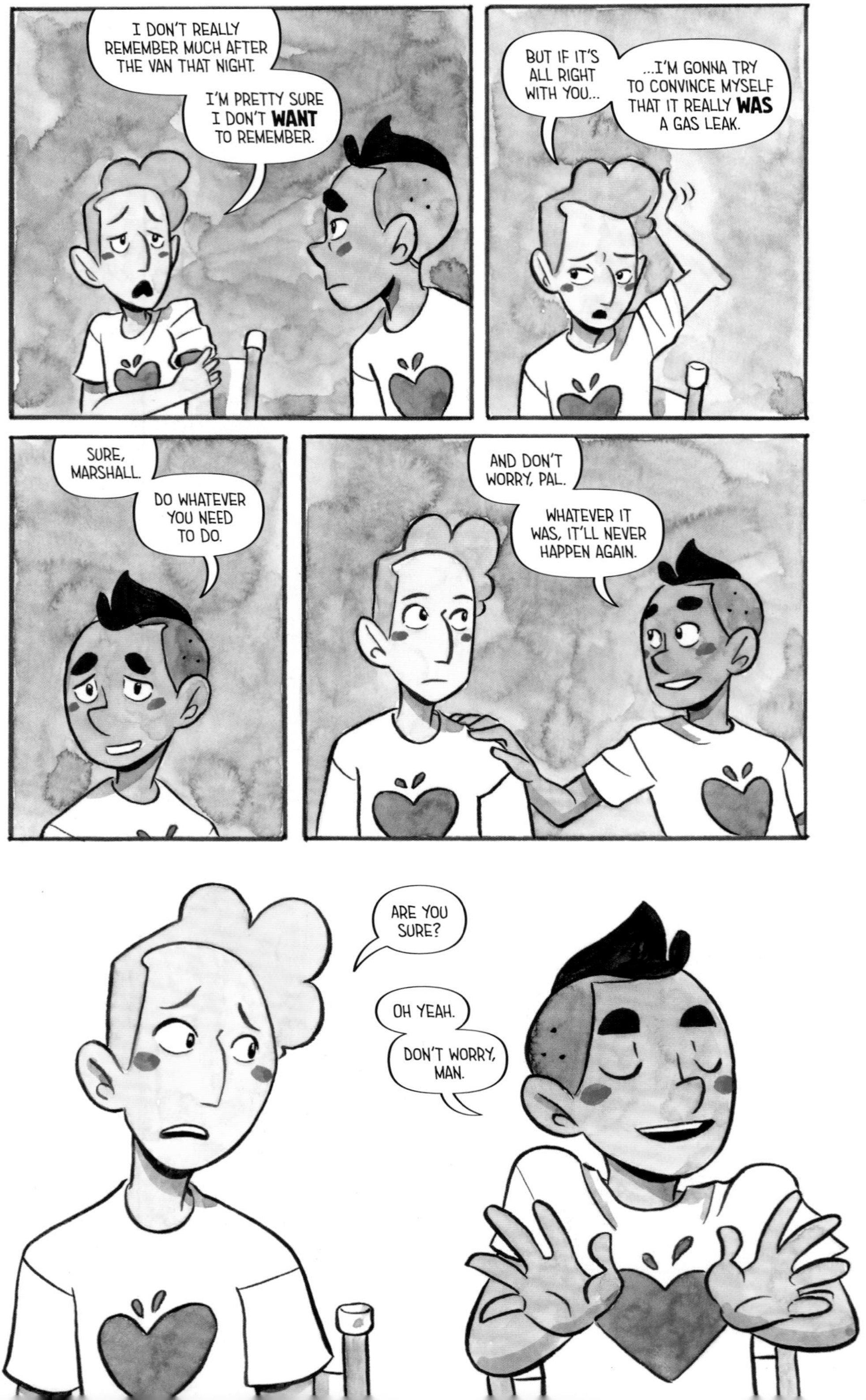
I DON'T REALLY REMEMBER MUCH AFTER THE VAN THAT NIGHT.
I'M PRETTY SURE I DON'T **WANT** TO REMEMBER.
BUT IF IT'S ALL RIGHT WITH YOU...
...I'M GONNA TRY TO CONVINCE MYSELF THAT IT REALLY **WAS** A GAS LEAK.
SURE, MARSHALL.
DO WHATEVER YOU NEED TO DO.
AND DON'T WORRY, PAL.
WHATEVER IT WAS, IT'LL NEVER HAPPEN AGAIN.
ARE YOU SURE?
OH YEAH.
DON'T WORRY, MAN.

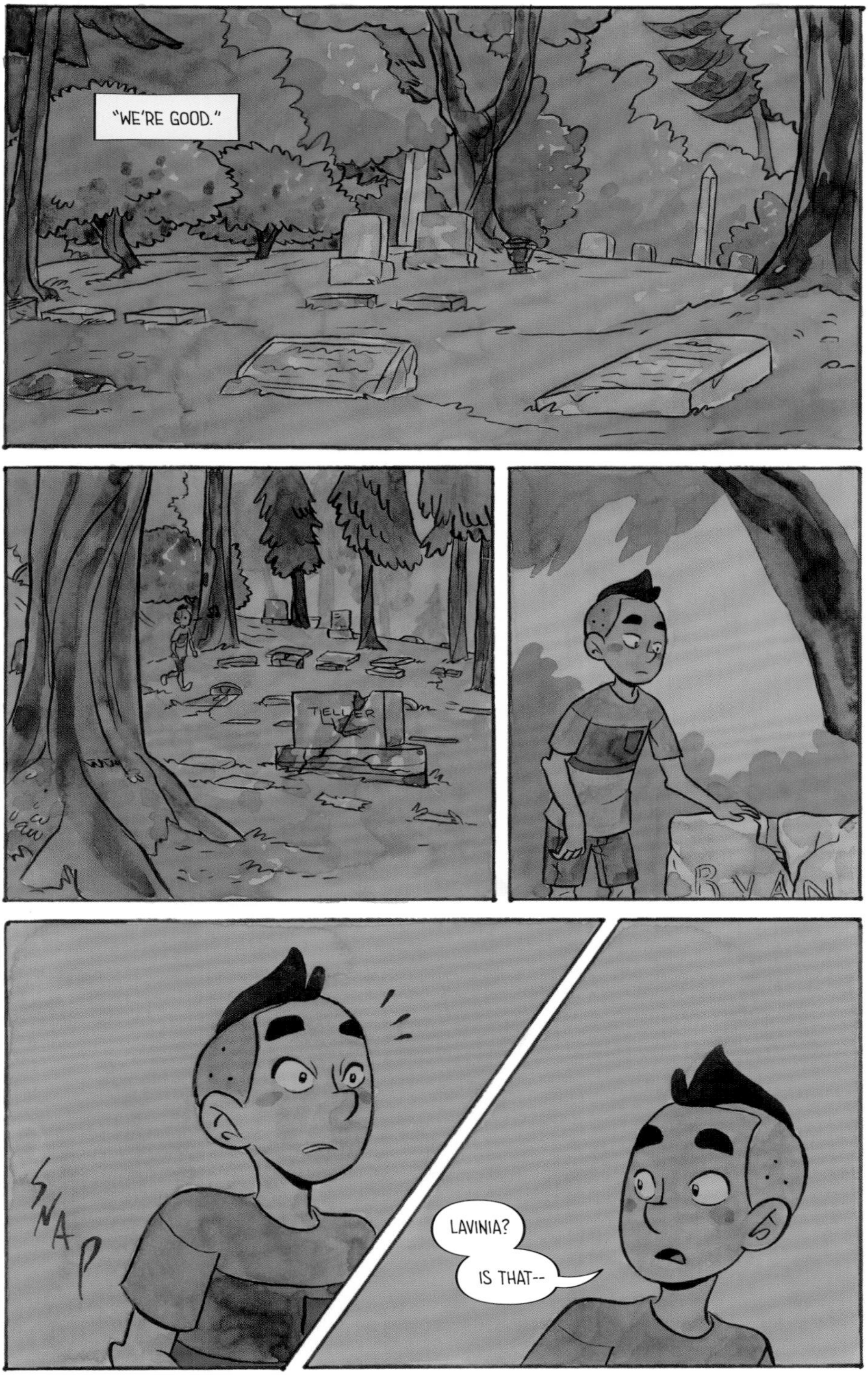
"WE'RE GOOD."
TELLER
RYAN
SNAP
LAVINIA?
IS THAT--

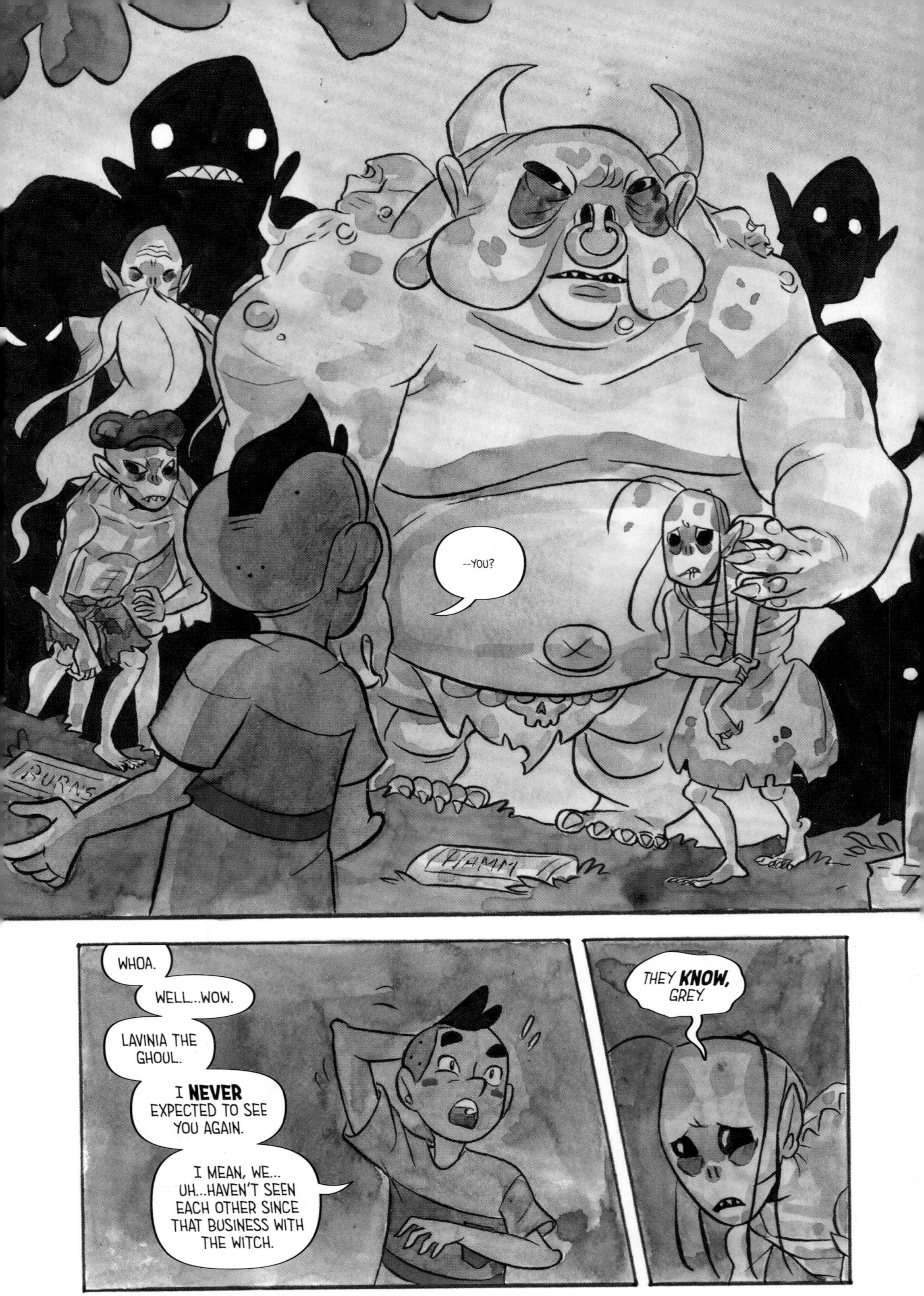
BURNS
HAMM
--YOU?
WHOA.
WELL...WOW.
LAVINIA THE GHOUL.
I **NEVER** EXPECTED TO SEE YOU AGAIN.
I MEAN, WE... UH...HAVEN'T SEEN EACH OTHER SINCE THAT BUSINESS WITH THE WITCH.
THEY **KNOW,** GREY.

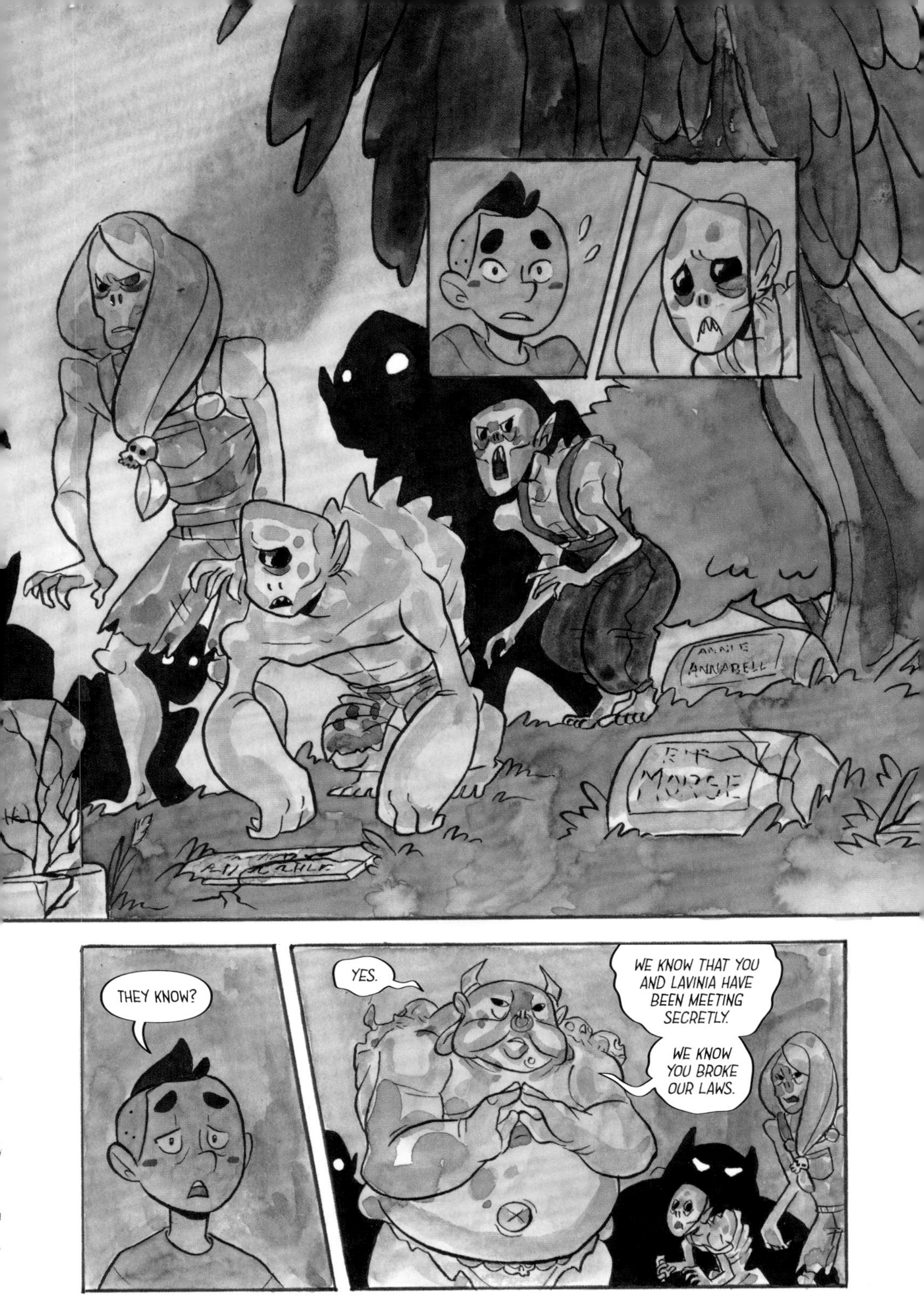
ANNIE
ANNABELL
MORSE
THEY KNOW?
YES.
WE KNOW THAT YOU AND LAVINIA HAVE BEEN MEETING SECRETLY.
WE KNOW YOU BROKE OUR LAWS.

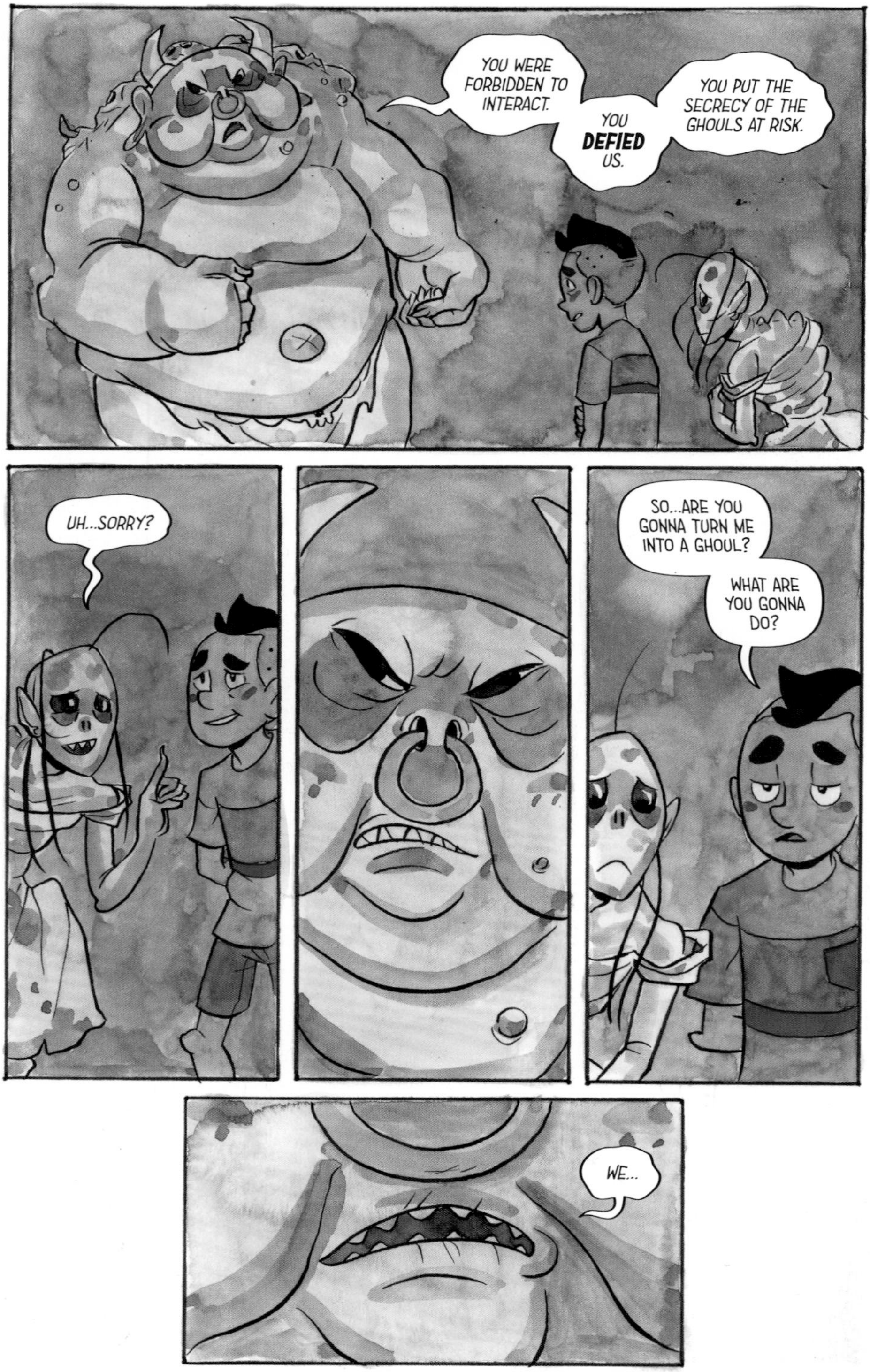
YOU WERE FORBIDDEN TO INTERACT.
YOU DEFIED US.
YOU PUT THE SECRECY OF THE GHOULS AT RISK.
UH...SORRY?
SO...ARE YOU GONNA TURN ME INTO A GHOUL?
WHAT ARE YOU GONNA DO?
WE...

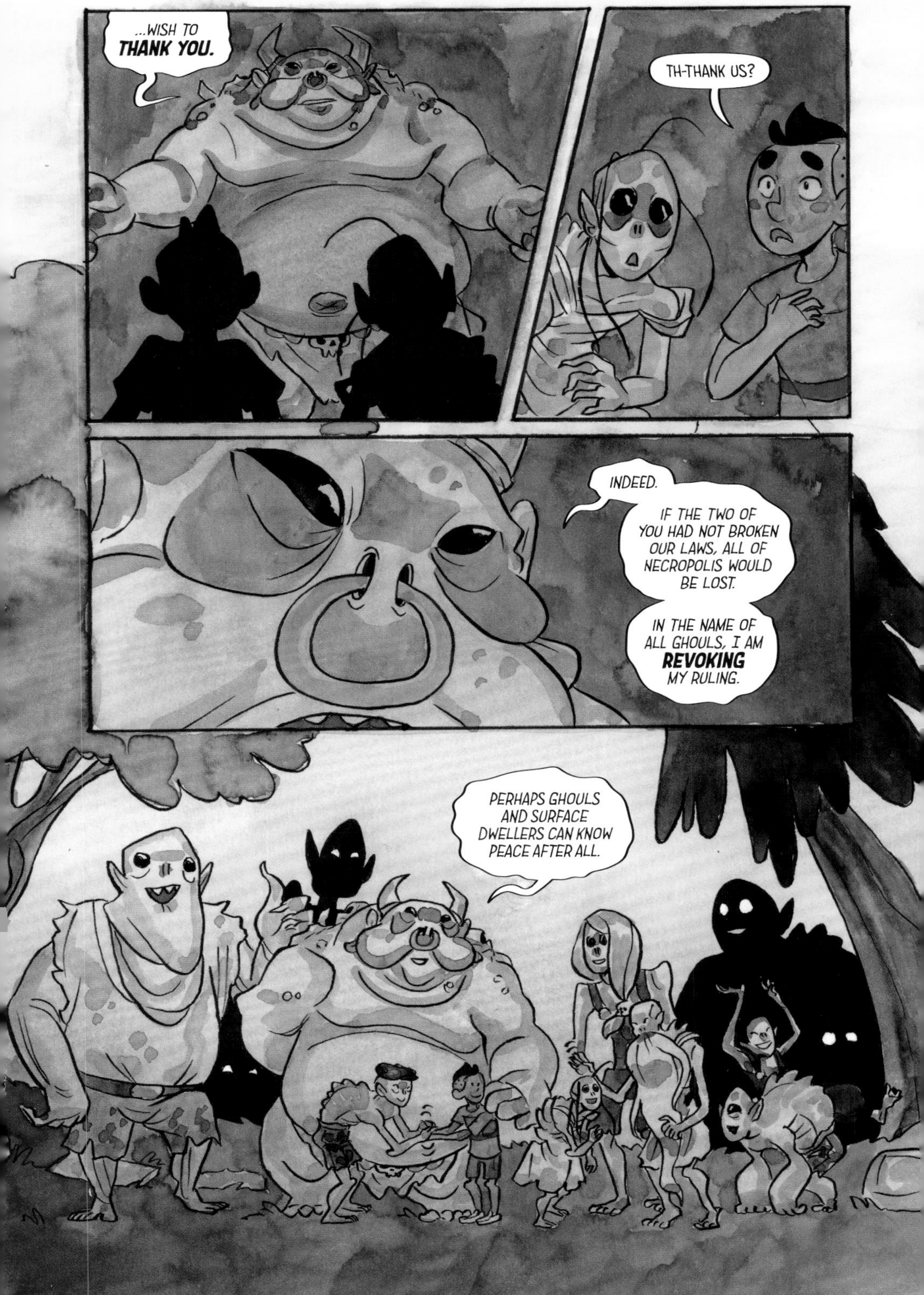
...WISH TO THANK YOU.
TH-THANK US?
INDEED.
IF THE TWO OF YOU HAD NOT BROKEN OUR LAWS, ALL OF NECROPOLIS WOULD BE LOST.
IN THE NAME OF ALL GHOULS, I AM REVOKING MY RULING.
PERHAPS GHOULS AND SURFACE DWELLERS CAN KNOW PEACE AFTER ALL.

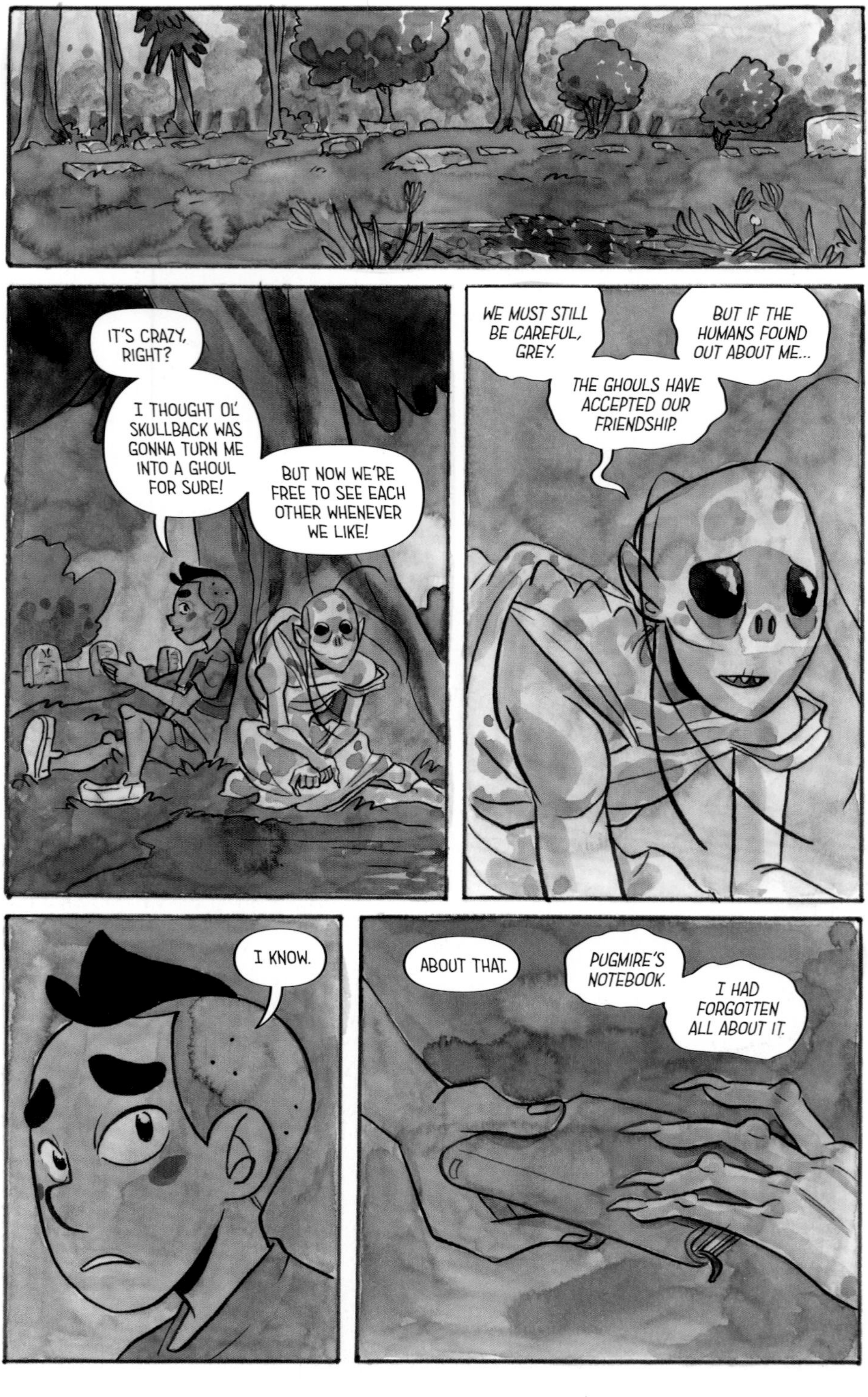
IT'S CRAZY, RIGHT?
I THOUGHT OL' SKULLBACK WAS GONNA TURN ME INTO A GHOUL FOR SURE!
BUT NOW WE'RE FREE TO SEE EACH OTHER WHENEVER WE LIKE!
WE MUST STILL BE CAREFUL, GREY.
THE GHOULS HAVE ACCEPTED OUR FRIENDSHIP.
BUT IF THE HUMANS FOUND OUT ABOUT ME...
I KNOW.
ABOUT THAT.
PUGMIRE'S NOTEBOOK.
I HAD FORGOTTEN ALL ABOUT IT.

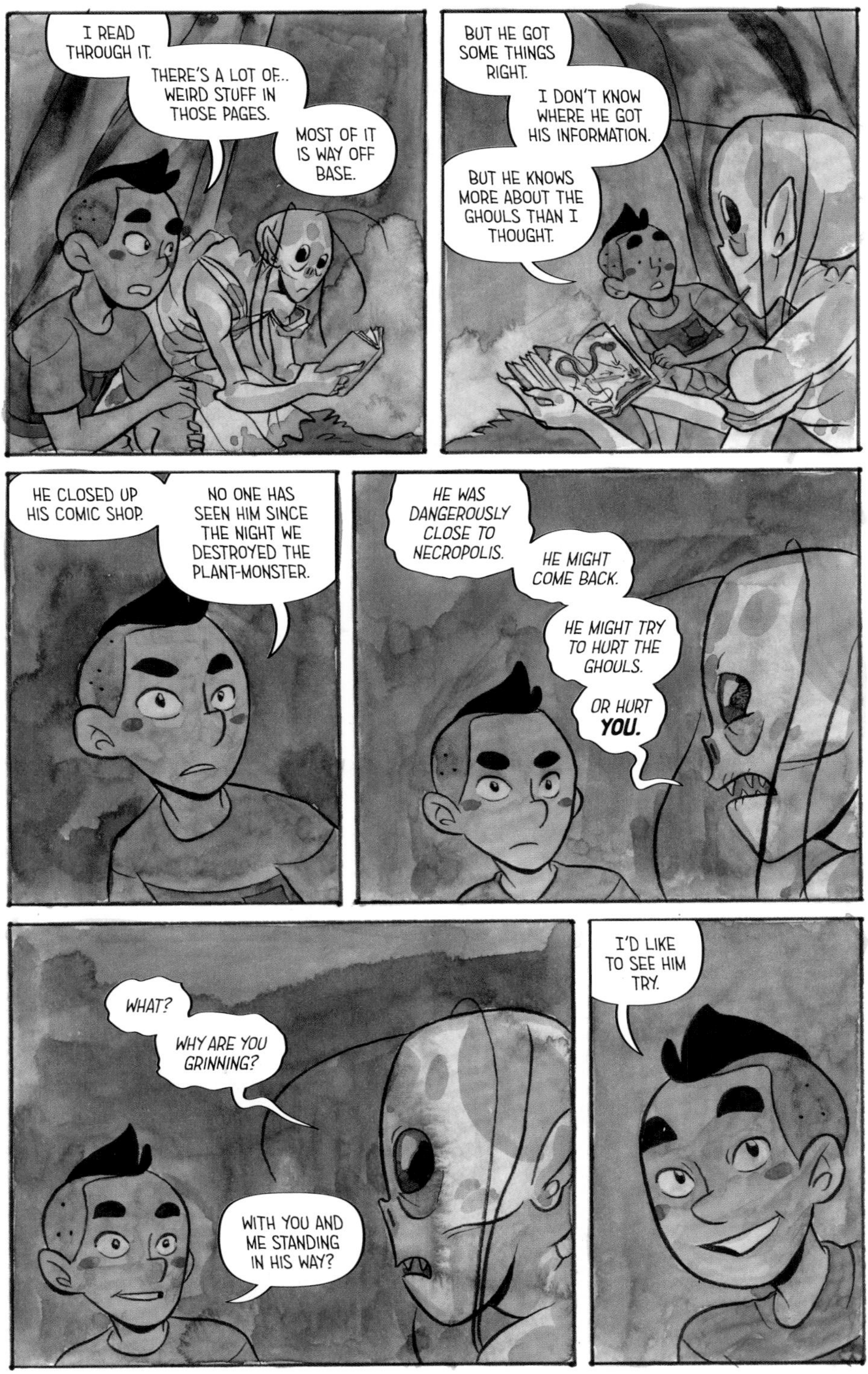
I READ THROUGH IT.
THERE'S A LOT OF... WEIRD STUFF IN THOSE PAGES.
MOST OF IT IS WAY OFF BASE.
BUT HE GOT SOME THINGS RIGHT.
I DON'T KNOW WHERE HE GOT HIS INFORMATION.
BUT HE KNOWS MORE ABOUT THE GHOULS THAN I THOUGHT.
HE CLOSED UP HIS COMIC SHOP.
NO ONE HAS SEEN HIM SINCE THE NIGHT WE DESTROYED THE PLANT-MONSTER.
HE WAS DANGEROUSLY CLOSE TO NECROPOLIS.
HE MIGHT COME BACK.
HE MIGHT TRY TO HURT THE GHOULS.
OR HURT YOU.
WHAT?
WHY ARE YOU GRINNING?
WITH YOU AND ME STANDING IN HIS WAY?
I'D LIKE TO SEE HIM TRY.

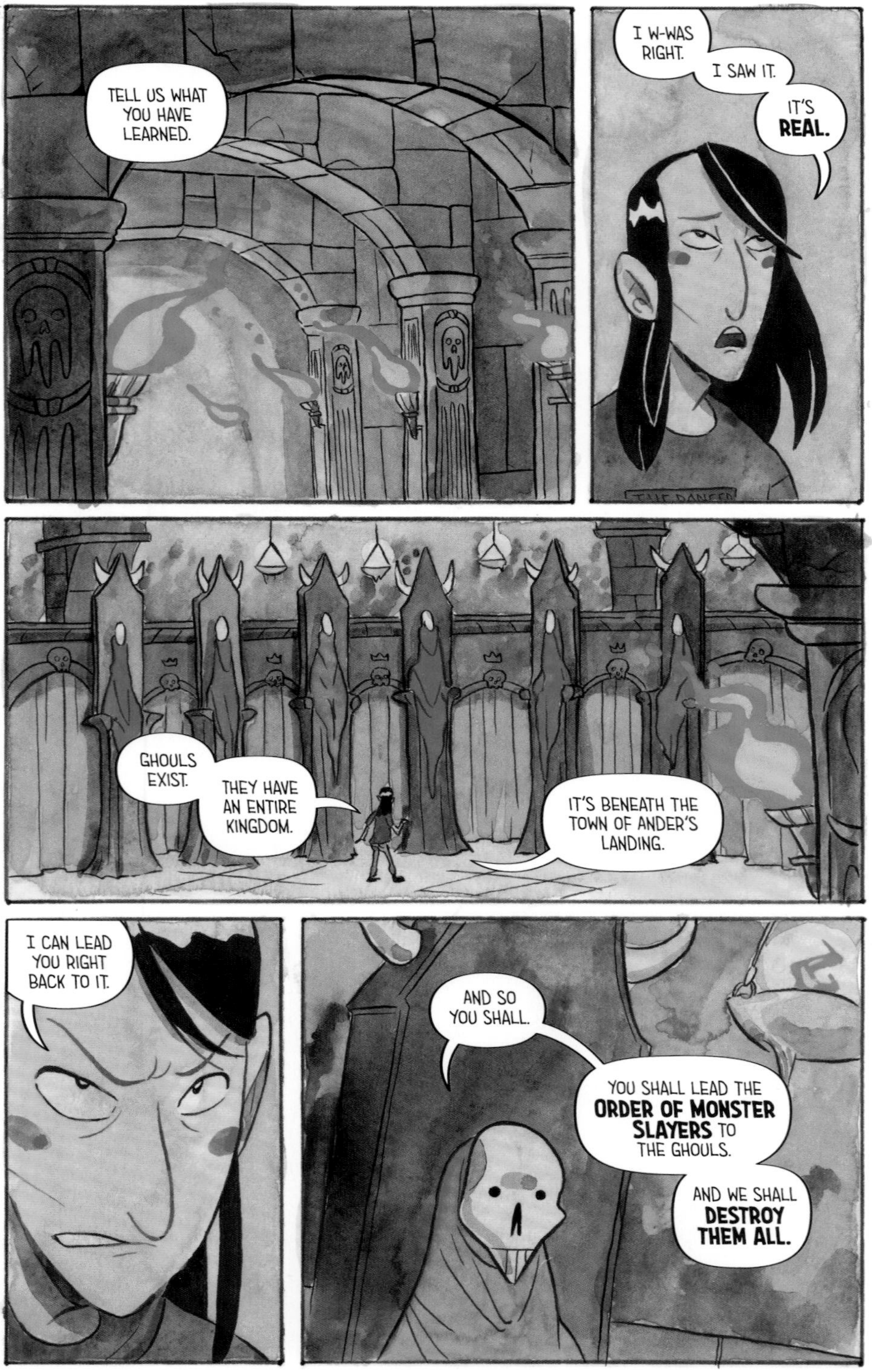
TELL US WHAT YOU HAVE LEARNED.
I W-WAS RIGHT.
I SAW IT.
IT'S **REAL.**
GHOULS EXIST.
THEY HAVE AN ENTIRE KINGDOM.
IT'S BENEATH THE TOWN OF ANDER'S LANDING.
I CAN LEAD YOU RIGHT BACK TO IT.
AND SO YOU SHALL.
YOU SHALL LEAD THE **ORDER OF MONSTER SLAYERS** TO THE GHOULS.
AND WE SHALL **DESTROY THEM ALL.**